Praise for Paula Fox and her novels:

"Paula Fox is so good a novelist that one wants to go out in the street to hustle up a big audience for her. . . . Fox's brilliance has a masochistic aspect: I will do this so well, she seems to say, that you will hardly be able to read it. And so she does, and so do I."
—Peter S. Prescott, *Newsweek*

"Brilliant, . . . Fox is one of the most attractive writers to come our way in a long, long time."
—*The New Yorker*

"As a writer, Fox is all sensitive, staring eyeball. Her images break the flesh. They scratch the retina. . . . Fox's prose hurts."
—Walter Kirn, *New York*

Desperate Characters:

"A towering landmark of postwar realism . . . a sustained work of prose so lucid and fine that it seems less written than carved."
—David Foster Wallace

"Absorbing, elegant. . . . What gives this slice of life its timeless urgency is Fox's spare yet penetrating prose, shifting imperceptibly from present to past, external to internal, revealing the hushed despair, absurdity, and latent violence that lie beneath the most humdrum words and routines."
—*Entertainment Weekly*

"Among the best things we have in contemporary literature—original, enduring, charged with intelligent, articulate life and with the tension of modern survival: brave, witty, alarming, and quite wonderful."
—Shirley Hazzard

"A piercing portrait of a modern couple at bay. . . . Relentlessly honest, brilliantly crafted, passionate."
—John Gabree, *New York Newsday*

"A reserved and beautifully realized novel."
—Lionel Trilling

"*Desperate Characters* takes its place in a major American tradition, the line of the short novel exemplified by *Billy Budd*, *The Great Gatsby*, *Miss Lonelyhearts*, and *Seize the Day*. . . . Grueling and brilliant."
—Irving Howe, *The New Republic*

"A brilliant performance, quite devastating in its mastery of the brutish New York scene."   —Alfred Kazin

Poor George:

"The best first novel I've read in quite a long time. . . . A merciless uncovering of the exurban wastelands of the spirit."   —*New York Review of Books*

"Compared by critics then and now to Chekhov and Melville and Muriel Spark and Nathanael West and Batman and Robin, really, and rightly. She's good, she's good, she's more than good."   —Jonathan Lethem

"Like a sealed bottle of pure mid Sixties. . . . *Poor George* feels fresher after a third of a century than do most novels written yesterday."   —Jonathan Franzen

The Widow's Children:

"Chekhovian. . . . Every line of Fox's story, every gesture of her characters, is alive and surprising."   —Christopher Lehmann-Haupt, *New York Times*

"Demonstrates once again Fox's original unsettling talent. . . . Astounding in its portrayal of the textures of emotional life, moment by agonizing moment. . . . Fox releases conflicts and passions of great intensity, and sets them simmering, combining, and exploding like volatile liquid elements."   —*Saturday Review*

"Compelling. . . . It has in it, especially apparent in the wit, a worldliness which it could not do without, and which is that of someone who has lived long enough to have learned a great deal. . . . Remarkable."   —*New York Review of Books*

The Western Coast

OTHER BOOKS BY PAULA FOX

Poor George

Desperate Characters

The Widow's Children

A Servant's Tale

The God of Nightmares

The
Western Coast

Paula Fox

Introduction by Frederick Busch

W. W. Norton & Company

New York • London

To the Memory of
Amos Elwood Corning,
and for Max Markowitz
and Sara Chermayeff

"... *our existence is at every instant*
and primarily the consciousness of what
is possible to us."

ORTEGA Y GASSET

Contents

The Price You Pay / xv
Introduction by Frederick Busch

PART ONE
The Convention / 1

PART TWO
Meetings / 137

The Price You Pay

Introduction by Frederick Busch

Paula Fox's third novel, *The Western Coast*, is about a place both myth-ic and actual: Hollywood, USA. It is the Sargasso Sea of the soul of the United States and has perhaps been considered the province of male authors. You might think of Tommy Wilhelm in Saul Bellow's *Seize the Day*; to demonstrate that his protagonist is infected by dreaminess and a wish for instant success, Bellow has him forsake college to try to become an actor and, of course, fail. In Nathanael West's *The Day of the Locust,* Tod Hacket is devoured by the dream. Monroe Stahr of F. Scott Fitzgerald's *The Last Tycoon* dreams Fitzgerald's dreams and chokes on his author's rue. Norman Mailer's *The Deer Park* manages to send the memories of Charley Eitel and their repository, Sergius O'Shaugnessy, off towards the "green light" of Fitzgerald's American Dream. These are novels by men about men; even when they are among the supernatural beauty of Hollywood women—say Mailer's Elena, whose glories pre-figure Mailer's obsession with Marilyn Monroe—their stories are male, men's disappointments are expressed through women, and the women fail or betray the men who carry the narrative. But here comes Paula Fox, in 1972, with this large tale about the drift to the west in America. Her protagonist is not a man lured by a woman but a woman who, bruised and educated by the American Dream, expresses in her own way no man's—but this brilliant author's—sense of what Jean-Paul Sartre called *nausée*, a spiritual dismay, an abhorrence of oneself in the world.

Annie Gianfala, seventeen years old and forsaken by her father, is penniless and alone. She goes west, as America did, but she journeys in the years before World War II. She drifts on the currents of the Depression, of enthusiasm for the Communist Party and Russia, and of distaste for the Party and its birthplace. She meets, and is educated by, in the senses as much as in the mind, louts, layabouts, jaded intellectuals, lovers of various stripes—including Walter Vogel, the merchant marine sailor whom she marries—as well as varieties of Party functionaries, black men, gay men, and every kind of failed and failing writer. Annie is both a waif and a woman of power. Men bring her their bodies as if bearing a gift, and she tends to accept them. Sad news for men: their bodies do not matter much. This novel, which so splendidly inhabits the senses, transcends them. And so does Annie. Early on, in fact, a kind of physical revulsion in her is clear; soon enough it becomes spiritual. Then we realize that we are in a territory shared with Paula Fox by James Purdy—in the fauvist, piano-playing boy of the book's beginning and end; in Annie herself, an innocent with whom men beg to entrap themselves—as Ms. Fox writes victims who are pitched up upon demanding, even dangerous, people and learn from them, willy-nilly, life's cruel lessons.

First readers of *The Western Coast* will find a narrative intelligence so strong, an analysis so piercing, that they will be unsurprised to find that a number of intellectuals of the 1970s averted their eyes. They found themselves in this novel—as (among others) the Party Pasionaria, Fern, unshakably, stupidly loyal to her dogma; seeking to skewer others, she skewers herself while condemning "the soft-brained New York swimming-pool Jews with their hysterical, vicious anti-Bolshevik attacks on Comrade Stalin's tactics." A generation of blind political enthusiasts is drowned in that condemnation. But Ms. Fox's eye is not only cruel: it is accurate, it can be gentle, and it is always just—as we find in this description: "Fern's father had been a bookbinder and, once out of work, moved through the little rooms of the house like an exiled prince, remarking acidly on the fine and dependable qualities of leather." That description evokes a lifetime's imprisoned conclusion, and its sorrow is palpable.

Annie, for all that she is an innocent abroad in the United States at one of its great moments of change—the waning days of the Depression, the acceleration into World War II, the accompanying end to so many certainties—is, despite her lack of schooling, no fool. She sees herself, she sees her context, and she learns about one in terms of the other. " 'Everybody teaches me,' she said ironically, 'as if I were the world's village idiot.' " She observes herself with Walter, and what she sees is crucial: that, making love to her, he "invaded her . . ." and that "she fled him even as she lay there so passively." Such moments are essential Paula Fox: the disgust with others, but also with oneself, and the sense—despite a need to merge, physically or psychically, with others—that one does so at a great expense. She writes, of course, about the price one pays for giving oneself, for tempting others to believe that one is accessible to them: the cost of being lonely, needful, generous—human.

Wary as she is, Annie, because she is like us, is available to the dream that flourishes on the West Coast. During a period of her life that would seem familiar to Dostoyevsky's Underground Man, to Bellow's *Dangling Man*, to Ellison's *Invisible Man*, Annie, while waiting for her life's next event to overtake her, lies low and essentially does nothing but go to the movies: "It was the movie music that hypnotized her—those swollen pulsating chords, the pudding texture of beaten pianos and whipped violins as the lovers kissed, as the mist covered the mansion, as the ship's prow rose and sank upon orderly oceans . . . she wept . . . because of that music, a smothering syrup that drowned her brains, yet released in her a flood of melancholy that through some alchemy became a kind of exaltation." This is as good an analysis of sentimentality as we could ask for. It says what one can about the confected dreams of Hollywood. Ms. Fox's dark humor, her sense of the absurd, is richly conveyed in those beaten pianos and whipped violins. Furthermore, this passage accompanies two important sets of events in the story of Annie's becoming a self she might wish to be. First, she becomes a model and, on the fringes of Hollywood's body cult, is openly and commercially adored by men; Hollywood's commodification of sexuality, and actors' and models' commodification of themselves, is confronted. More important, Annie's sexual activity—at the time when her soul is most enmired—increases: "She discovered, or, rather, recognized at last, that men wanted to do this thing to her they wanted to do to anyone. Her body, the object, was of no value to her. Yet somewhere, like a hidden depravity, she felt love for it, pitied it like the lost animals she sometimes saw slinking into the doorways of closed shops late at night." The character's insight into herself, as she grows intellectually, is large and frightening: while an odalisque, she is also an analyst; you covet her body, you look up it to her face, and she is staring into you, understanding both you and herself all too well. The disgust here is ferocious. Young women, beginning to write in 2001, can learn much from this woman who, in 1972, was speaking on their behalf.

Annie's voyage of discovery takes her from New York to California to New York and then to Europe. On her way, she twice experiences something like an unfettered innocence of experience. Each takes place in the American West. Each is a retreat, from society and from cruel consciousness, to the pastoral. Once, in Yosemite, she is with Walter Vogel, the returned husband whom she will divorce. The second time, she is with Myron Eagle, a physician who saved her life and now is her lover. With Eagle, it is the "last real time she spent in California," it is "timeless, mindless pleasure" in an absolutely rustic setting. Such moments of the pastoral are, traditionally, the place away from civilized complications where nature—including human sexuality—may hold sway. But the lovers, taking a walk, come upon "the remains of an old movie set," looking "like a small frontier village." And soon thereafter, Eagle tells Annie that "'You can't ask people not to have a viewpoint—to simply *look*, the way you do. One of these days, you'll have to come to some conclusions . . . like the rest of us.'" For a disengaged innocence is no entitlement, Ms. Fox seems to be alerting her protagonist: even an Edenic landscape may be as artificial as a movie set; we pollute what we inhabit, we are cursed with consciousness, and absolute innocence is not, finally, available to the thinking human animal. We have an obligation to evaluate. We are condemned to do so.

Annie's journey must be into that contention, and it must involve a confrontation with her own disgust. She seems to consider herself, by the end of this disquieting, brilliantly observed novel, more free than fettered. She says, so perfectly, "'I was taken to California. . . . After a while, I escaped.'"

PART ONE

The Convention

Chapter 1

Even on the most bitter afternoons of the winter of 1939, a man wearing neither coat nor hat marched up the rise to the Claremont Inn, paused there for the instant it took him to draw himself upright and salute the old building, then strode on toward Grant's Tomb. Often, the wind blew hard across the Hudson River and lifted the loose grains of snow from a graying crust that shrank and hardened day by day as though it ate the ground it lay upon. In the winter clarity of the air the man, his loose shirt billowing about his waist and meager breastbone, seemed to send forth a livid light of his own.

To most of the students of the International Hostel across the street, the man was an incidental object in that gelid landscape. The older residents rarely took notice of him as they grazed among the periodicals in the reading and visitors' room, the windows of which fronted on Riverside Drive. New students or their guests, having heard about the eccentric, nearly naked marcher, or else catching a glimpse of him as they hurried indoors to the foyer, paused at the windows, speculating on his circumstances, his painful and bizarre appearance.

What could he be saying to himself? His lips never ceased to move in silent speech. At intervals, he held his arms straight out and turned in slow circles, then listed like a slackening top, and at last straightened up and stood facing the dark Palisades across the river.

If anyone laughed at the man, it was usually a Swiss back from his classes in hotel management at Columbia University a few blocks south of the hostel. "Don't laugh!" a Spanish student would say sternly, at once adding an ironic comment of his own about the man's arcane ritual.

The day after Christmas, a Japanese opened the door to the reading room and, noting a chess game in progress between two Chinese in a corner, abruptly withdrew. Someone laughed. Mehta, one of the Indians from New Delhi, who had been standing at the windows observing the man salute the Claremont Inn, turned and explained to the room at large, "It was phosgene gas, without doubt. I have read about your war . . . extensively."

Walter Vogel, an unemployed actor since the Federal Theater Project had ended a few months earlier, hated the Indian, who had once said to him, smiling, "Walter, you are like a snake who eats the tiny eggs of birds," a reference to Walter's girl-hunting in the hostel cafeteria.

"Ah, India . . ." said Walter, opening his *Daily Worker* in Mehta's face. He disliked all Indians, with their borrowed voices and their women who would look, he imagined, the same lying down as they did standing up.

"Phosgene or chlorine," Mehta continued, now speaking to an Indian friend. "They used it at Ypres, the German people. But the *Allies,* as they were called"—the friend smiled—"found the gas mask to be somewhat effective, and, *naturally,* used gas themselves. The French employed gas shells. Interesting, don't you think?"

"The West is very inventive," Mehta's friend said. "In India, of course, we are not so advanced."

"How superior of you," said Hannibal Salazar. "Don't you think India superior, Walter?"

Walter sat down without replying and continued to read his paper. Hannibal looked toward the window where the girl Walter had brought with him stood, still peering out of it. He went to her.

"A thing thrown away," said Hannibal softly. "That man . . ."

"How can he bear it?" the girl asked, her face nearly touching the pane. "The cold . . . it's even cold in this room."

"The wind is always so bad up here," said Hannibal. "But perhaps in his madness he doesn't feel it. I suffer so from this horri-

4

ble weather." He looked down at his own plump, short body. "This climate may account for the number of brutes you have in this country."

"I'm going to California tomorrow," she said. "It's warm there." Then, her intent gaze following the man's stumbling run back toward the Drive, she said, "Oh, he must feel the cold!" In a moment or two, the man was lost to view in the early December dusk. Hannibal touched her arm. "Come away. It's too cold here. What's your name? Walter is very crude not to have told me your name."

"Annie," she answered, still straining to see. "Does he have a place to go? His head looked shaved, completely shaved. Doesn't someone take care of him?"

Walter had joined them, the paper refolded and held under his arm. Hannibal glanced at him, then at the girl. She was young like all of Walter's girls. Her clothes were so shabby. How much he would like to kiss her young neck! But he could only make girls laugh. They liked his jokes, and when they laughed, in the midst of their laughter, he could touch their arms and hands, their hair, and they allowed him that, he supposed, as payment.

"Nobody takes care of anyone," said Walter. "It's part of the sickness of a capitalist society."

"But can't someone give him a coat?" Annie asked.

"Come on, baby. Leave the window. If you think *he's* bad off, you should see the basket cases in the vet hospitals."

"Yes," Hannibal said, rubbing his fat clean hands together. "Let's leave this room and have a coffee in that disgusting cafeteria. I have a phenomenal story, Walter, about Alberto and his two Chinese girls . . ."

Walter said, "No. I want to talk to you about the Spanish Refugee Committee."

"I will not speak of Spanish committees," Hannibal said. "Tomorrow perhaps. Not tonight."

The Indians had gone. The chess players nodded over their board on which only a black king and his pawn and two white bishops and the white king remained.

As Walter made for the door, it opened, and a young boy of sixteen or seventeen entered the room and went to stand next to the grand piano. He averted his eyes as the two men and the girl passed him. Walter gave him a faintly contemptuous glance. When he saw that Annie had stopped to look at the boy, he took hold of

5

her arm in his two hands and shook her. "Stop staring at people!" he said loudly. "Stop dreaming!"

Hannibal touched Annie's hair and sighed. "How can you put up with such a coarse fellow, eh?" he asked, and laughed away the insult.

As the door closed, the boy sat down on the piano bench and began to play the opening chords of *La Cathédrale engloutie*. He touched the keys lightly, bending close over his hands as though afraid to attract the attention of the silent chess players in the corner.

Chapter 2

"How can there be a beginning?" Fern asked. "You're born into someone's life. You're carried along, a nothing, flotsam. My first independent action, my own true beginning, was to join the party."

Max closed the book from which he had been reading aloud and placed it between them on the front seat. Fern's driving, frightening in the city traffic of Los Angeles, was now, on this country road, merely negligible. He had asked her twice to stop riding the brake pedal. Her short-fingered hands in their white gloves rested on the steering wheel with a tentativeness toward machinery he characterized to himself as feminine. Male chauvinism, he supposed. Yet he was touched by the gloves. She was wearing them because of the convention, the way a woman wears gloves to church—hands hidden from the Lord.

"What does he say?" she asked irritably, poking one finger down at the book. "That his birth was the first of his misfortunes? Sentimentality!"

"Because it cost his mother's life," Max said.

"It may have been his first luck," she snapped back.

"Take your foot off the brake."

The stubborn foot slid off reluctantly.

"You break away if you can—if you *can*," she said. "I haven't yet. Last week I was to Redlands. As soon as I walked in, my mother started up about the earthquake. That was eleven years ago. Then about the child that was murdered, her head stuffed into her schoolbag, and that was seven years ago. An earthquake and a murder! That's my harmless little bourgeois mama! Anything to stop me from talking! I just *mentioned* the Spanish refugee camps in France, and she began to tremble. I could *see* her fingers shaking, and my father went out into the yard to play with his damn lemon tree! But God! I fall back into the same old rituals. I clear off the table after dinner as though I were beating the devil to the sink. You think we could sit around the table and have a proper, serious discussion? No! Joan Crawford's divorced again or remarried or something. My stomach is a wreck. I tried to stop my mother from teaching my little niece that ghastly prayer—she's only two—you know that prayer? 'Now I lay me down to sleep, I pray the Lord my soul to keep, if I should die before I wake, I pray—' "

"There's someone up there ahead. See? Sitting up against a tree," Max said. "Fern, stop tormenting yourself about your family. Everyone's got one."

"It's my weakness. I can't stop thinking about them."

"I thought I'd managed to distract you," he said.

She glanced down at the book.

"With him?" she asked scornfully. "All that innate goodness of man? Back to nature?"

"That's a dumb simplification," Max said. "What you're talking about was a point of argument he used in an essay. Try to get things right! He never held society could return to a state of natural innocence. Didn't you even like the little story of the walnut tree?"

"I've never been faintly interested in Rousseau," she said, clearly reproving him. "There's too much for me to read that's important."

Max had a sudden picture of himself with his hands around Fern's neck, just a little squeeze or two. But that was part of his own bourgeois problem, that profound sense of violation he so often suffered at his comrades' boisterous or outraged dismissals of so many of the writers he secretly admired, had nourished himself with through the days of his adolescence. But his comrades were right, of course. There were more important things to think about now, to act on now. Later would be time enough.

8

"It's a girl!" he exclaimed. "What's she doing there? We're hours from a town."

"She was probably taking a walk and has sat down to rest," Fern said, accelerating slightly.

"Slow down," Max demanded. "Come on, Fern. Stop the car." He took hold of her arm, sensing her impulse to drive on, not to get involved. Fern made a face, but she drew up at the side of the road and stopped a few yards from the immobile girl who did seem to be sleeping, her head back against the tree trunk, her eyes closed.

For a moment or two, Fern and Max were silent in the sudden stillness of the warm car. Fern did not look at the girl; her eyes were on the road ahead. Her thoughts, Max knew, reached out to the comrades as they threaded their way among the yellow-slatted camp chairs set up for the convention, thin but tenacious thoughts.

He had been reading paragraphs at random from the first book of Rousseau's *Confessions*. It was not the first time he had ridden with Fern, and he knew how her driving affected him; he had read to take his mind off the possibility of a fatal collision. Once, on some trip, he'd asked to take the wheel. She'd exploded into rage, and the tact with which he'd made his request was laid waste by her accusation that it was his nervousness which made her drive so badly.

"Next time, I'll fix you," he said. "You'll get the rural electrification program in the Ukraine . . . or the woman question."

"Your levity is frowned upon in certain quarters," she said stiffly.

"Oh, Fern!"

The sunlight, its heat intensified by the windshield, lay upon their laps, upon Fern's gloved hands, their knees. Fern remarked that they should have eaten the hard-boiled eggs right away—the smell reminded her unpleasantly of school lunches. A car passed them slowly. Two Chinese were sitting in the front of the dusty black Packard.

"They're going to the convention," said Fern. "I bet."

"Comrade delegates from the Charlie Chan branch."

"That's chauvinistic . . ."

Max opened the door and got out. He stretched and yawned, watching the girl. She didn't stir. He felt a faint prickling of his skin. Her bare legs were crossed, stretched out before her. The

9

thick tweed suit she wore surprised him—it must be the only such suit in Southern California.

"Hello," he said softly.

Her eyes opened. She smiled instantly and pressed closer to the tree, then her hand went up to her face to touch her own smile. She got to her feet as though there weren't enough space to stand straight.

"We thought you might be in—" He hesitated. The word *trouble* had occurred to him, but in the face of her shyness it seemed too personal. "Difficulty," he finished, explaining the *we* by waving back to the car at Fern, whose face could be glimpsed in outline through the dusty windshield. "You're a long distance from anywhere."

"I'm on my way to San Diego," she said. "I'd gotten a ride from Los Angeles. But the man let me off here." She looked back at the tree.

"Here?"

She said nothing. Her face was blank. He wasn't going to get an explanation.

"We'll take you," he said. "We're going to San Diego."

"That's so kind," she said, smiling again, her tone formal. Then she seemed overcome by uncertainty, looking from him to the car.

"Fine," he said, hearing a touch of stridency in his own voice, wondering at it, wondering why the girl was disconcerting.

"I'm meeting a friend there," she said, her voice low.

The man who had dropped her by the road must have tried to do something to her, Max thought. She'd said "gotten a ride," hadn't she? "My friend is in the merchant marine. I had the name of the ship written down, but, I don't know, I must have lost it. It was a simple name. I think it's the Matson Line. Matson?" Now, she was almost whispering.

"There is such a shipping line," he said. A bird trilled very close by. He and the girl both looked off at once into the trees. They listened, but the sound did not come again.

"My name is Max Shore," he said, "and that's Fern Diedrich there in the car."

The girl nodded and brushed at her skirt. Someone had surely given her that suit, it fitted her so poorly. Folds of the thick fabric were bunched beneath the belt she had buckled around her waist. She touched her hair; short wisps stood straight up from the encircling braid. He thought, the braid doesn't suit her at all; she doesn't know what to do with her hair. She was tall, handsome perhaps. Bits of grass and smudges of earth clung to her legs. She couldn't be over eighteen.

She preceded him to the car, looking back suddenly with her hand on the door as though to make sure it was still all right. He waved her in. She stooped, her black handbag, its leather cracked, hanging straight from one wrist.

Fern nodded to her shortly as she sank against the back seat. "Hello. Watch out! Don't sit on the eggs," she said. "I wish you'd eat them. The smell is driving me crazy."

Max sighed. Cars were boring and alarming. There was still a distance to be traveled. The camp chairs were already set up in the hall; the more important people, people like his own wife, Eva, were already there, trying out the microphone. "Comrades . . ."

As Fern wrenched the car into second gear, Max asked, "What's your name?"

"Annie."

She had answered like a servant. Max regarded her questioningly, but she only lowered her head.

"Where are you going?" asked Fern.

"To meet a friend," the girl replied. "He's on a ship coming to San Diego sometime today. Maybe he's already there."

"How about your last name?" he pressed.

"Last night, did you see the planes?" Fern asked, turning for an instant to the back seat, her voice young, even girlish, with interest. The change of tone was so marked in contrast with the indifferent way she'd inquired after Annie's destination that it broke Max's preoccupation with the mystery of the girl's presence on the road.

What kind of man, he wondered, might Fern have stashed away in San Francisco? Or was she another of those young-old girls for whom the party gave a world of reasons to explain all that was meager in their own lives? He was instantly ashamed. What if they were forlorn, discordant? It was their devotion that counted. Who was he to ask for purity? Yet Fern . . . Oh, Fern!

At breakfast that morning she had nearly shouted that she'd never spend a cent on clothes while there was still a single volume to add to her Marxist-Leninist library. And how bitterly she had gone on to denounce those girls who learned their politics in the beds of certain functionaries whose names she preferred not to mention at the moment, although, she managed to imply with a prig's menace, she'd have something to say on the subject in due time. That she might be deficient in more than books seemed not to occur to her. But what an odd answer she'd given him when he'd suddenly asked her if she didn't intend to marry someday.

"I want someone who isn't even alive," she had said in a submissive, confessional voice. Max had been astonished, thinking she'd had a love affair after all. Perhaps someone in the Lincoln Brigade who had left his bones in Spain, or, less romantic, someone else's husband smashed up in a car wreck in Oakland. But a moment later, he'd known his speculations were foolish, and looking at her now as she drove the car without deference to what she was doing (gloved hands lifeless on the wheel, back stiff against the seat, foot riding on the brake pedal), he knew she'd meant exactly what she'd said. She wanted someone who wasn't alive and never would be.

"The Japanese planes," she was saying. "They flew over the city last night. Aren't you from L.A.?"

"I live just outside it," the girl said, "toward Hollywood."

"They were so far up, I've never seen planes in the sky that far up. It'll serve *them* right, selling scrap iron to a militarist regime, after Nanking, as if they didn't know—"

"They? Them?" he asked, only to provoke her.

"American capitalists," she said in a low furious voice.

He turned to look at the girl, and she smiled at once as though she had heard nothing surprising. Her teeth were small, even, neglected. The smile was a painful habit, he thought, like a tic—or a kind of camouflage.

"Annie, what's your last name?" he asked once more.

"Gianfala," she answered.

"The newspapers said that next time they'd bomb L.A.," Fern said. "What a joke!"

"You're Italian?" Max asked, looking at the fair skin and hair.

"One of my grandfathers," she said.

"Are you hungry?"

But he was pressing her. He could see it in the way she pushed back against the car seat, and he felt an answering nervousness. He wished suddenly Fern had had her way, and they had not stopped. He folded his hands on his lap. Paper rustled. She was opening the lunch sack. Why was she so furtive?

"A joke in the sense they damn well might," Fern said. "When

12

an advanced monopoly capitalist society piles up armaments . . . Max, why do you tease me so much?"

In spite of himself, Max turned again. A brief glance showed him the girl looking at the egg in her hand. "Crack it on your elbow," he advised softly.

"Thank God! She's eating the eggs!" exclaimed Fern.

". . . always thanking God."

"Never mind, Max. I inhaled a lot of opium before I left the church," Fern said sharply. "Don't trip me up on little things like that. You'd do better with a little self-criticism."

"With you around, I don't need it," he said wryly.

"Be sure and eat them both," Fern called out to the girl.

"If you're hungry," Max added.

The girl finished both eggs and put the shell fragments back in the sack. Max lit a cigarette, then offered her one. She took it quickly. It was the first vigorous gesture he'd seen her make, reaching out and grabbing the cigarette from his hand. She inhaled deeply. Fern removed one of her gloves and snapped her fingers. "I want one," she said.

Fern had called a few days earlier from San Francisco, asking to be put up for the night and offering, in exchange, a ride down to the convention in San Diego. Although she had a brother who lived in Los Angeles, she couldn't stay with *him,* she'd told Max's wife, Eva, who'd banged the receiver down and said, "That family of hers! I wish she'd keep them out of party matters."

"She was only asking for a room for the night," Max had replied mildly.

"She's a delegate! This isn't a social arrangement. Do you know, I heard her bring up those people of hers at a party meeting one night? She dragged them into a discussion about democratic centralism, for God's sake."

"How?"

"How? I don't know how. She just did, that's all."

Fern arrived several hours after Eva's departure, just as Max was putting out the garbage. Eva had said, "Don't leave the garbage lying around, Max. You'll start reading and forget. Put it out, Max. Put it out."

He had made up a bed in the living room for Fern while his two-year-old son, Thomas, had played with dusty potatoes on the floor. Later, after he'd put Thomas to bed, he and Fern ate the chile Eva had left and sat around talking for a while. The bore-

13

dom he'd experienced had been so intense as to verge on the comic, but it assuaged the uneasiness he had begun to feel this last year in anticipation of any large gathering of party people.

He'd known Fern for years, since their senior year in high school. Eva had been in the same class. Unlike himself, the two girls had come from Depression-soured families; grateful to be in school, away from homes whose atmospheres had grown querulous with incomprehension. Fern's father had been a bookbinder and, once out of work, moved through the little rooms of the house like an exiled prince, remarking acidly on the fine and dependable qualities of leather. Fern's mother took domestic work—she called herself a housekeeper—to feed and clothe the family, and eventually, Mr. Diedrich found a place for himself in a small real-estate office in Redlands, where his withdrawn nature and a certain poise issuing from his long practice of an exacting craft gave clients the impression they were dealing with someone with class.

Eva's father, a master plumber, cried between bouts of sodden drunkenness that if it hadn't been for his damned kids, all female, he could have weathered the bad times like a man instead of taking goddamned Roosevelt handouts.

But Max's family had tracts of timber, theirs for several generations; his father had owned a newspaper in a town in the north of Oregon. They did with one car instead of two, one maid instead of three—it was hardly deprivation, Max had once been fond of saying until Eva told him he was just showing off. One of Max's uncles, in trying to recoup what he'd lost in the stock market, had schemed his way into a madhouse, carrying with him, until a male attendant wrenched it from his hands, a suitcase bulging with an ugly metal invention which, he'd sworn, the government was preventing him from patenting because certain inventor rivals were in highly placed positions. During the year of his father's long dying from cancer of the bladder, Max had been sent to live with an aunt in Los Angeles to finish out his senior high-school year. He received his diploma half an hour after his father had died in a Portland hospital, Mrs. Shore standing by the bed, the wool of an unfinished sweater she'd been knitting trailing from her fingers. Only his aunt had come to Max's graduation. There had been enough money for Max to go to the University at Berkeley. He had married Eva there during his junior year.

His wife and Fern shared one characteristic, as different as they were in all other ways. They both liked to give orders to men. Suspecting something irresolute and captious underlying their bossiness, he put up with it good-humoredly. He was inclined to put up with a good many unpleasant things in people if he sensed they were really uncertain about what they were doing.

Fern had been tired last night, and she looked better when she was tired. The morning's energy, her bursts of excitement at the coming convention gave her a look of craving he found repugnant. Although she and Eva were around the same age, Fern looked older. Fern would age fast, he thought, looking at her profile. She glanced at him with a touch of challenge as though she'd suspected what was in his mind.

She'd been a pretty little girl in a sharp, brunette way, dark and fast-moving, her narrow feet shod in saddle shoes, the tips always carefully whitened, the brown saddle gleaming with polish. She wore no ornaments, only plain blouses or her sweater "set." She wasn't as trim these days as she had once been. Her worn-down heels, the stains on her clothes, the uneven hems of her dresses bespoke neglect. But she still wore gloves. Those gloves!

Eva had not been as pretty, except for a striking small-waisted figure and beautiful narrow ankles. In the darkened rooms where she and Max made love any time they could, he would forget her sharp voice, its complacency fed and fattened by meals of Engels and R. Palme Dutt, by party meetings in dusty boardinghouse rooms in Berkeley, by faction and dissension and discussion. In those days, only a few years ago, that eager, fresh-skinned, heavy-fleshed girl, every feature of her round face imprinted on his neck and shoulder and belly, seemed to have no connection with the young functionary tough, *la commandante,* as he called her. But she was loving with their son—a kind of sexual romanticism excluded the infant from the daylight world of politics and tied him to those darkened rooms of love and its motions.

But, he thought, most of the party women, especially the younger ones like Eva and Fern, suffered a touch of disjunction in their beings. He didn't understand it. Last night, out of his boredom perhaps, out of a deliberate misreading of "Comrade," he had looked at her with a certain tentative sexual inquiry. He hadn't been fully aware of it himself. But she must have sensed something. Abruptly, in the middle of a sentence, she'd arisen and said, "I need my rest." Her voice had been high, thin; she'd avoided his eyes. At first, he wondered if the chile had given her

15

indigestion. He'd observed before that she was one to pick at food and push it away. There was a lot of distaste in Fern.

But later, when the planes had waked them both, and they had gone to the window to look up at the play of searchlights, her excitement at this *event*—it was unprecedented, those tiny planes pinned between earth and the night sky—had illuminated a momentarily unguarded side of her nature. Yet afterward, listening to the radio news bulletins which insistently proclaimed the planes to have been Japanese, she had assumed her usual postures, scolding imperialism, "pointing out" the inherent contradictions of capitalism, the contradictions of her own nature left abandoned by the window where the curtains had fallen back into place.

"Max! Are you deaf? I asked you if it's true that Ethel is sick? I heard she wasn't coming."

"Ethel?" he asked wonderingly. He had forgotten where he was, where he was going. She poked him with that hand so quick to poke. He looked resentfully at her hand, then at her. She nodded briefly toward the back seat. No names, Max realized, that was what she meant. He was a little amused, mostly irritated. Who did she think that poor stray was? An FBI plant? A Trotskyite infiltrator?

"She's had a recurrence of the old trouble," he answered, annoyed at being circumspect, and conscious of the self-importance that tends to swell a voice that brings bad news. The old trouble —eleven knife wounds. Ethel Schaeffer, who in 1911 had taken part in the mass strikes which had organized the needle-trades industry in New York, who, in the twenties, along with other comrades, almost succeeded in taking over the union from Dubinsky, who nearly died, a real heroine. She was the only comrade he'd ever known who could speak of "the bosses" without making him flinch. A very small woman with silver hair and gray eyes, she had a single-mindedness of purpose that invested the most banal political slogan with the exaltation of her own commitment. Her voice was a caress; the students who clustered around her after her classes at the L.A. party school seemed, by contrast, oafish, inauthentic. A clean little mother from Eastern Europe, scarred like a saint, undefiled by secret irresolutions. He loved her for the unity of her being; he envied her for it. And she was a kind of monster—like all saints.

He wasn't a good Communist; he knew that.

16

"I love her," Fern said vehemently. "She's a great woman!"

"She is unique," he said dryly.

"That's the kind of compliment she would detest."

"Could I trouble you for another cigarette?" asked the girl. Max handed her his pack. He glanced at the handbag on the seat next to her. The catch was broken, the bag gaped open. He saw a half-empty pack of Camels. He felt bad at her inept chiseling. Was there any money in the bag? His curiosity to see what was in it was so intense, he had to turn away.

"Is your friend an officer?" he asked, thinking, There is probably nothing in the bag, a comb, a lipstick, a key to a door.

"A.B.," said the girl, then, "Able-bodied seaman." She spoke as though practicing a foreign phrase.

"He's from the West Coast?" Fern asked, a touch of interest in her voice.

"New York."

Fern looked meaningfully at Max. "I heard a vile story about Bull Curran," she said in a low voice. "Vile!"

"Oh, yes," the girl said eagerly. "He's president of the National Maritime Union."

Fern grimaced.

"Let it go," Max said coldly, then to the girl, "It's not a passenger ship then, is it? A freighter?"

"I think so," the girl replied, then bravely, taking a chance, "Yes. It must be a freighter. But there are tankers, too. It could be a tanker."

He couldn't place her accent. It wasn't uneducated, yet it didn't tell him anything about her either. He couldn't account for her at all. Why did he want to account for her? Fern, stupidly wary, was speaking of organizational matters. He caught the drift. She might as well use pig Latin. He was suddenly aware he was squinting and he realized, surprised, that they were already on the coastal road, traveling through the glare of sky and sea.

Fern went on and on . . . the Hollywood comrades preoccupied her, she was saying. They were so unstable, so superficial. And some of the European refugees—those German Jews—who had slipped into the film industry had brought with them the poison of the Social-Democratic party, unsettling the soft-brained New York swimming-pool Jews with their hysterical, vicious anti-Bolshevik attacks on Comrade Stalin's tactics.

Max's mother had said, last August after the Hitler-Stalin pact, "So now you've swallowed Hitler too! What a digestive system my son has!"

He had argued with her, argued against the sardonic stare of those narrow blue eyes, but then, knowing his passionate self-defense to be familial, not political, had given it up. Eva, who had been with him, had gone on shouting, waving her hands while his mother watched her imperturbably. Max knew she thought Eva "common," even worse, dull. But she doted on her grandson. When Thomas was born, Mrs. Shore stopped arguing with Eva; she just listened, waiting for the baby to be brought to her arms. Max had been happy then—he had watched the baby for hours. Yet there had been some reservation in him, a touch of dread as he gazed at his child. This morning, just before he and Fern had left, he'd taken Thomas to the neighbor who often cared for him when he and Eva were away. Making the practical, ordinary arrangements in the neighbor's oilcloth-smelling kitchen, he'd felt a great wrench as though he might never see the child again.

There were many who had not swallowed Hitler, friends he could no longer see. He looked at Fern's thin mouth, opening, closing, opening, closing. . . . He was violently irritated. Beyond Fern's voice, the unsettling malaise of the girl in the back seat, the heated interior of the car, was the glittering Pacific, the white sand of the shingle far below, the cloudless May sky, a string of sea gulls riding the wind. He was sick of women.

"The Nazis are in Belgium today," he interrupted Fern. She opened her mouth. Impulsively he placed his hand over her lips.

"Is this your first trip to San Diego?" he asked the girl.

"Yes," she said, her eyes so wide she looked blind. "I've never seen this part of the coast before."

His hand fell from Fern's mouth. He felt a faint dampness on his fingers as though her words had left a foggy imprint on them. Fern smiled angrily. "I sometimes wonder, Max, just what you're up to."

So did he.

They had reached the outskirts of San Diego, and he suggested to Fern that she drive as close as she could to the waterfront.

"We haven't got time," she said.

Yes, he thought, she is yearning for those camp chairs, the thrilling silence that followed the opening speaker's first word, "Comrades . . ."

18

"We *do* have time," he said.

The girl leaned forward; Max felt the proximity of her face just behind his shoulder.

"I wonder if you know where I can get a room in L.A. or Hollywood?" she asked. "I have a place now, out on Hollywood Boulevard. But there's a man next door who beats his dog all night. I can't sleep, the dog cries so."

Fern glanced quickly at Max; her mouth twitched with incipient laughter.

"That's dreadful," Max said.

"They're so helpless," the girl murmured.

Fern's face seemed to swell, but not with laughter. It was indignation. "There are worse things in the world than crying dogs," she said.

"The man's German, I think," the girl said apologetically.

"I know an actor who's planning to leave for New York next month," Max said. "Although you can't tell about actors. He has a room on Sycamore Street. I'll write down his name and you can call him. I've forgotten the number. He may know of something, even if you can't get his room."

"I pay eight dollars a week now. I can't really pay more than that," the girl said.

"You'd better stick with what you have," Fern said. "You can't get anything for less than that."

"His name is Jake Cranford," Max continued. "You can tell him I gave you his name." He needn't have added that last part, giving the girl a link to him. It was taking on too much; he'd done it only to spite Fern.

Fern pulled up to the curb. "You won't have much of a walk from here," she said.

Max could smell the oily waters of the harbor. It always excited him; the waterfront was the first place he went in any city he visited. He had stood on wharves in San Francisco, in New York, in Boston, in Seattle, staring down at the parrot colors of oil stains moved back and forth by the tides, sighting along a hawser until, with a thrill of delight, he saw the great bulwark of a ship rising above him.

It was the waterfront that had brought him into the party. He had been in his senior year at Berkeley in 1934, just six years ago, when the maritime workers struck. Half dreaming among the leaning stacks of books in the Sather Gate Bookshop, he had been

19

awakened from his languor by a classmate who had snatched away the book he'd been holding in his hands. "My God! A general strike!" the man had cried. "What the hell are you reading Stephen Crane for? Let's go!"

Joseph Conrad, Stephen Crane, blending insensibly into the ranks of the longshoremen in their white caps and blue workshirts, into Harry Bridges, into the silent ships at rest, into the fear and hilarity, the joy at the real conflict that was coming; yes, it had been extraordinary, like the quiet that precedes an earthquake, the air breathless, the earth waiting.

"Thank you," the girl was saying, moving to the door. "I'm so grateful. I don't know how I'd have gotten here without you."

"Someone would have picked you up," Fern said, looking the girl full in the face. The girl flushed as though accused.

She got out of the car, dragging the ugly handbag after her.

"Good-by," she said to Max, smiling.

"Call Jake!" he cried as Fern shifted into gear. The girl had walked a few steps away when she suddenly turned. "Wait!" she called back. "Your name? What is your last name?"

"Shore," he called out from the window. "Max Shore."

She nodded and turned and walked away. He continued to watch her as Fern pulled the car awkwardly out into the street. He was struck suddenly, after all that smiling, those apologies, by a curious conviction that the girl was stubborn, that she had will. Almost at once, he missed her presence and he was bewildered by the force of his feeling.

Fern said, unexpectedly, "Well, Max, you're kind. I'll say that for you."

Max, astonished by Fern's compliment, thought of Rousseau's priest, M. de Pontverre, about whom he had remarked, "a kind man, he certainly was not a good man."

I am not a good man, Max thought, without much regret, only a sense of something lost, lost too long ago for mourning. He sighed and turned his thoughts toward the convention.

Chapter 3

"Cormack Traveler came in this morning. Couldn't be Matson, kiddie," said the man. "That's passenger lines." He waved a curved hook at the docks. "That's the only one's due in today. Nobody come off it yet."

Annie didn't know where to stand and wait. She didn't want to ask any more questions of the hard-faced man with the wide leather strap around his wrist and the menacing hook. A man pushing a loaded dolly passed between them, and Annie moved back to lean against the wall of a dispatcher's shed. After the dolly had gone, she saw the man with the hook swing off to join a group of men in work clothes who were watching the slow descent of cargo from a boom on the deck of a ship called the *Molly Good*. The net fell to the ground, a dozen hooks flashed in the sunlight as the men moved forward. Just beyond the aft section of the *Molly Good,* she saw the *Cormack Traveler,* whose decks appeared deserted. Then a man walked to the rail wearing a dark-blue watch cap. She was too far away to see whether it was Walter Vogel. She took a few steps forward and a young man cried out, "Look out, my beauty!" He was bent beneath the sack he carried on his back but as he went by, grinning, he reached out a large square hand toward her. She went back to the shed. Walter had written that she might have to wait; there was no telling when he'd come ashore.

It had grown very warm, and the tweed suit stolen for her by Johnnie Bliss from the Paramount costume department hugged her body like a rough-skinned animal. The boards of the shed, gray, splintered, salt-worn, glistened with heat; she felt sweat on her neck and face. When she rubbed her cheeks, her fingers came away stained with orange Max Factor make-up. She had hoped to look so dashing! So light! Johnnie had brought her the suit wrapped in newspapers. She had wanted to look new, unapproachable. No! Indifferent! That was it. Good clothes could make you indifferent.

She lit a Camel and smoked it as if she were thinking about something complicated. Men said things to her. She puffed. A new worry assailed her—had Max Shore known she'd had her own cigarettes? He'd looked at her handbag so often. Had he suspected? But he'd been so kind—she could have explained it all, not having any money, really any at all, how you did things that were shameful.

An arm went around her neck. Walter's face sunk into her neck between shoulder and chin, her sweaty neck. "Annie, Annie," he muttered, and with his arm around her waist pulled her away from the shed, back into the hot sunlight. They looked at each other for a moment. Four months after and three thousand miles from where they'd first met, she suspected he was already beginning to laugh at her. He was tanned and plumper. She was dazzled by his presence. He took her hand and they walked away from the docks.

"You all right?"

"Fine," she said.

"Your make-up is running."

"I got a job. And a room. But it's not very wonderful."

"Poor Annie," he said, and put his head against hers. "Not very wonderful," he mimicked. "Why don't you learn to talk straight."

In a waterfront café, he drank rye with a beer chaser, and ate fried eggs and bacon. She had a meat-loaf sandwich and coffee and thought she'd gone mad with hunger, hardly able to chew for the sheer bliss of filling herself up.

"Tell me . . ."

She told him about the first part of the ride, the fat man wearing glasses who handed her a book to look at. "Pretty pictures, he said. At first I thought it was about Greek art, all the faces were like statues, you know? But the drawings were bad, and these statues were all doing things to each other."

22

"Dirty book . . ."

"Yes. Then he said he'd *show* me, and he stopped the car. I got out and ran into the woods. He was too fat to follow me for long. I walked a long way, then came back and sat down on the road . . . didn't really know what to do. I was afraid to thumb another ride. But I was saved. A man and a woman stopped and picked me up. The man was very nice really. But the woman wasn't. She was talking about boring things and trying to make them sound important and acting as if I was not to know what she was talking about. I don't know why I'm so hungry. . . ."

Walter went up to the bar and returned with another shot glass of rye.

"What am I to do with you?" he asked, raising his eyes to the ceiling. "In one fix, then another."

"I couldn't *walk* to San Diego."

"A bus?"

"There's the money."

"How was the trip out west?"

"That crazy woman May Landower—she was drunk all the way. We had a flat tire in Arizona in the middle of the desert. She got out on the road and started to pray, on her knees, in the middle of the road. In Virginia, she said we had to go look at a natural bridge, it was in the cards that morning. There weren't any people there in the park, and she began screaming we were in mortal danger. Once, in a store where we'd stopped to get cigarettes, there was a woman with hair growing all over her face. After that, she talked about nothing but the menopause, said I'd look like that someday, then I'd see what life was. She had a little aspirin box she kept pills in, said they were ground up monkey glands and did her a world of good. The only nice thing was the man we picked up just before we got to the Rockies. He was a tall old man with red hair, a cook at a CCC camp, and his wife was having a baby in some little town on the other side of the mountains. So he drove us. It was night. It was such a narrow road. There was fog sometimes. You could see, way down, the lights of maybe one other car. He drove like the wind. He was so worried about his wife. She was just a girl, he said. And we got to this little town, in the middle of the mountains. There was one hotel, and he left us there and ran down the middle of the street to the hospital. It was three in the morning. They gave us some white bread to eat, we were so hungry. She'd been drinking out of her bottle all the time he was driving, saying, 'My, it's nice to have a man to drive, isn't it, Annie? My, my!' "

He sat absolutely still, his eyes never moving from her face. She began to eat the toast he'd left on his plate.

"And then?" he asked. She felt she'd won a victory of some kind. He wanted to hear more.

"That night, drunk as she was, she consulted the Ouija board. It spelled *tears*. She said sorrow was in store. I said it meant we'd have another flat. Oh, it was terrible, terrible! That's why I had to get out away from her. In Hollywood, she wasn't just crazy; she said I was too, everybody was."

"How did you get my letters after you moved out?"

"There's a man, Johnnie Bliss. Somebody she used to know. He's been bringing them to me."

"Just the letters?"

"He doesn't like women."

"A pansy?"

She didn't answer. "What kind of job?" he asked.

"Stock girl. In a store in Los Angeles. They sell dresses, women's things."

"How much?"

"About fourteen dollars."

"About?"

"Thirteen fifty."

"And the room rent?"

"It's eight dollars."

"How the hell did you manage to pick a woman like that to drive out here with? All right, all right . . ."

His hair looked damp. She did not tell him about the German and his dog. She looked at him as he played with the shot glass, his eyes half shut, and she imagined with what disgust he would look at the room she'd rented. "I'll tell you about my trip," Walter said, placing the shot glass in front of him.

It was hard for her to listen. She was thinking of that room, its ash-colored walls, the screech of the rusty springs when she pulled the bed down from the wall, the two grease-encrusted burners of the stove, the dusty, decayed smell of the apartment house.

"Did you hear me, Annie?"

"What?"

"I can't sign off till Seattle. It'll be another week or so. I've only got a few hours before I have to get back to the ship."

24

She concealed her relief—at least he wouldn't be able to see the room for a few more days. Then she wondered how she would get back to Hollywood. Somehow, she hadn't thought of that. She had imagined returning with Walter.

"Did you notice a bathroom?" she asked timidly.

"In the back, past the bar," he said, grinning suddenly. "Where did you get that suit?" She rose quickly without answering him.

The toilet was dirty. The suit bunched up around her waist. She knocked her head against the naked light bulb. The toilet itself was in an unresolved condition; it neither flushed nor ceased to pour down into the bowl a trickle of water. Walter's grin accompanied her discomforts; she was painfully shy about bathroom functions. What a heaven of unconstraint other people must inhabit! People were always getting up, or leaving rooms, to go to the bathroom; she herself had a weakness for imagining the exalted and great roosting on toilet bowls. What an idiot she was!

On the way back to the table, an old man lurched away from the bar and grasped her arm. He was drunk and smelled of catsup. Croaking like a rusty mechanical bird, he said, "What a life!" She caught a glimpse of Walter watching her. She put her hand over the hand that grasped her arm. "I know," she said. "The hell you do," he muttered.

As they walked away from the café, they argued about the old man. "You sentimentalize everything," he said. "He was a used-up old bum. He only wanted to cadge a drink from you." But he hadn't, she insisted. He only wanted to talk to somebody; he wanted to say *what a life* to someone living, who would respond to him. What else was there?

"Socialism!" Walter said angrily. "A society where old men don't wind up begging for drinks."

"But he didn't!" Walter walked resolutely ahead of her. "Goddamnit!" she cried. "He didn't!"

Walter strode on as though he were alone, and it seemed miles to Annie as she straggled along behind him, exhausted by the day, by unjust accusations, by her utter dependence, at this moment, on Walter. They had left the outskirts of San Diego behind them; they were walking along a cliff above the beach. The California landscape was so wild, so unassailable in its un-human nature; one no sooner left some colony clustered about the milder reaches of its coastline than the noise and busyness of town life seemed empty deception.

Walter suddenly sank to his knees among hummocks of sand and sword grass, then lay down, his arms outstretched, and shut his eyes.

Annie stared out at the Pacific. Her father had said it was the only thing, except the desert, worth looking at for more than five minutes; as she gazed at the vast emptiness through narrowed eyes, it seemed a nebulous waste, a shapeless moving waste. On the beach below, she caught sight of a lone swimmer as he leaped into the surf, arms swinging, knees cranking.

"Lie down, Annie," said Walter sleepily.

She sat and looked at him. He'd come all this way, down one coast, through the Panama Canal, up another coast—for her? His demand was heavy on her, as though it carried all the hours, the days of his journey. She was not worth it—he seemed to know that already. She leaned toward him. He lay there like a stone, a man on his back, his feet pointing straight up in their heavy work boots, smelling of warm skin and clean cotton work shirt. He placed his hand on her back.

"Annie?"

He had written her nine letters, the last one mailed from Colón; his handwriting was like barbed wire strung across the pages. The letters were all about *her;* her ignorance, her exhibitionism—did she remember the night she had paraded around in her underwear in Jersey Lighter's loft?—she was ignorant of the world, of people, of her own class origins, of sex, of money. She knew nothing of the world of struggle, of what it was like to work for a living. She was spoiled; all women of her class were spoiled. Working women, working-class women were different; he described them; he said they met men on real terms; they had real cunts, he wrote, and knew what to use them for. But he was going to change her —he was going to teach her.

The letters thrilled her as much as they repelled her. To be told what one was! Such unforgiving criticism argued honesty, exactitude. He knew her! Yet she destroyed all the letters—she did not like to touch them as she dropped the scraps into the garbage pail. She imagined them to be damp, as though a faint sweat covered them; the letters were about her, but in them was the presence of other women, grown-up women, and she snatched her fingers from the paper as though she might reach right through them to glistening female flesh.

"Let me," he muttered, and pressed her down into the sand and

26

rolled over onto her. She twisted her head away for she remembered he did not like to kiss her mouth. Beneath his chest, pressed against hers, his hands struggled up to clutch her breasts. "It's all right," he whispered. "This way, it's all right."

She heaved him off of her and sat up. One of her braids slowly lifted itself from the anchor of hairpins and drooped down the side of her face.

"I don't like virgins," he said coldly. They stared down at the beach. The swimmer had gone.

He was silent most of the way back to town. He'd put on his watchman's cap and pulled it down over his hair. When he did speak, it was in a milder voice than she'd had any reason to expect. Had he known how she was going to behave all along?

Did she have any money at all? he asked. No? Not even bus fare? She lied. He pressed some bills into her hand. Back at the docks, he put his hand on the back of her head and pulled her toward him, kissing her cheek. Just before she turned away from him, she caught sight of his eyes fixed on her. They were his best feature, his eyes, large, brown, limpid. What a mystery he was! She felt dizzy with a rush of excitement; she could have him— even if she didn't want him; a Communist, a sailor, a woman-knower, he held the world's secrets. Perhaps she'd find out something after all—she would allow him to do that simple thing to her, and in entering her body, perhaps he would free her from some other, more significant ignorance.

At the bus station, she looked at the bills he had thrust at her —thirty dollars. Food, rent, safety for a little while. In her imagination, she embraced him with pure gratitude.

Chapter 4

The first time Annie saw Walter Vogel, he was drunk. A high-school teacher from Summit, New Jersey, had taken her to a party at a Greenwich Village walk-up on Perry Street. It was early December; frost-glazed muck glittered in gutters; a strong wind blew through the nearly empty streets, tumbling lids from garbage cans, rolling them along like hoops.

In a smoke-filled room on the second floor, a Negro guitarist sat on a high stool, a black ship in a gray fog. He played a song, "The Midnight Special." When Annie asked him to play it again, he glared at her from red-veined eyes. "You like that song?" he asked. "It's lovely," she said. "Hunh!" he grunted. "You don't know nothin' about that song. But I'll play it for you 'cause it's *me* that's lovely." He wasn't smiling. He leaned over the guitar and seemed to thrust it into his belly. He flung the words at her, his eyes never leaving her face. The guitar moved under his hands like the piston of a locomotive, thrusting now toward her. A man leaned against her, laughing. She thought it was the high-school teacher, amused at her discomfort—the guitarist seemed to be trying to play her to her knees—but it was a handsome young-ish man in a thick black sweater. "He jus' *loves* you," he'd crooned. She saw the guitarist's eyes flicker—"when the midnight special come to town," he suddenly roared.

The stranger found a corner behind a couch. "I'm Walter Vogel," he said, pulling her down to the floor beside him. The guitar music had grown softer; around and above them, the party cranked on in its noisy way. She couldn't see the high-school teacher; she didn't really care if he was still in the room. She drank a sickening sweet wine from Walter's paper cup; he placed the cup between them on the floor; he held both her hands in his; their knees touched. His rapt attention to her, drunken or not, made her giddy. She knew she was talking too much. But how he laughed! "Who are you, who are you . . . ?" he asked softly. No answer would have been worthy of the mystery, the significance of such a question . . . who was she, indeed? But she tried. The party vanished from her consciousness. He'd pitched a tent for her in the desert—she threw aside her veils. She had never known she could be so *charming;* she'd never seen how *comic* her life had been, was . . . her mad-for-marrying father who had only recently left her alone in a West Seventy-third Street flat with a case of beer and twenty-seven dollars, left her, to marry again, of course, and her former stepmother, Bea, the one who'd taught her solitaire to amuse herself with, and—suddenly, the veils looked like rags. Walter Vogel, winey mouth and glassy eyes, was laughing *at* her with disbelief, or could it be disgust? In anguished self-recognition, she stood straight up, back into the party. He rose unsteadily and clasped her at once in his arms. She struggled; he held on.

"Now, baby, now you stay still. Here . . ." He let go of her for a minute and thrust a crumpled pack of cigarettes in her hand and a pencil. "Now, you write down where you live, right there on that little corner. Write it." And she did, hopelessly.

The high-school teacher had his coat on and was standing by the door. "I won't have time to take you home," he said, "it's so late. I've got a long ride to New Jersey, come on, I'll put you in a taxi."

To Annie's astonishment, Walter Vogel came to her door the very next night.

"Hello," he said. "I've come to take you to a meeting."

He walked into the little apartment, looked at it critically, shook his head. "Hurry up. We're going to be late as it is."

"What meeting?"

"A discussion . . . maybe you'll learn something."

In a small loft building on lower Broadway, a dozen or so people sat in a long narrow room listening to a man speak through a stern bristle of mustache. Several people nodded to Walter as he and Annie sat down.

"I ask you," said the man, frowning, "to consider the strange frivolity—and frivolity is by far too mild a term to describe the notorious behavior I am about to describe—of these so-called comrades who have so quickly abandoned their faith in the country of socialism, the Union of Soviet Socialist Republics, the seat and heart of the triumphant victory of the working class over the tyranny of class repression—the faint hearts of these comrades, the *soft brains* of these comrades"—a man laughed somewhere behind Annie and Walter—"who are unable or, to put it more properly, refuse stubbornly to understand Comrade Stalin's strategy. How many of us have been subjected to cries of 'poor little Finland,' following only by weeks the defection of those weak hearts, these *Mensheviki* I shall call them, with their childish and willful refusal to understand the *necessity* of the delaying tactics involved in Comrade Stalin's pact with the German, Hitler? It is of utmost importance that we distinguish between tactics and strategy, Comrades, utmost . . ."

Walter was standing. "For the benefit of a guest, would you discuss the difference between tactics and strategy?" he asked the speaker quite formally. The speaker looked broodingly at Annie, then nodded briskly. Annie didn't listen; she perceived, vaguely, that she was among people who saw the world she hastened through so nervously, so uncomprehendingly, as having meanings, categories, explanations that made it possible for them to know where their next thought was coming from. That Walter should be one of this group made her feel, for the moment, at rest; the speaker's words didn't matter; that he struggled in a thicket of lost sentences didn't matter. Whatever it was he was talking about, he was convinced!

Later, everybody was so agreeable to her. A middle-aged man and woman, dressed incongruously in rusty evening clothes, held her hands. A young man touched her braided hair. "Well, Walter, where did you find this little dearie?"

Walter took her to a cafeteria. They ate rice pudding and drank several cups of coffee. He took a volume from the pocket of his jacket and pushed it across the table to her. She picked it up. It was called *Man's Fate*. "I want you to read that," he said. They walked up Broadway. Above the spires of a dark church, two brilliant stars appeared to drop downward toward their own impalement.

"He's an old-time functionary," Walter said, referring to the speaker at the meeting. "Self-taught. He never even went to school —his people were immigrants."

She thought he sounded defensive. "Oh, he was fine," she said, her heart lifting with a kind of happiness as she looked up at the little stone church.

"He's dry as sawdust, but he can't help it. The main point is that he's loyal," Walter said.

"I didn't even know he was talking about Russia until he said Stalin," she said.

"You don't know much," he commented. "Where have you lived your life? In a hole in the ground?"

She hadn't thought much about where she'd lived her life, only each day of it. Her father had said he would be back in a few weeks. A few weeks had passed. The case of beer remained in the closet along with a tweed jacket of his. Her mother had died when she was two. Annie lived, had lived, in a world of men. Now she would have a new stepmother, another woman who would behave toward her, she imagined, more or less as Bea had.

"What do you want, Annie?" her father had asked her some months ago. "You *have* to *want* something." The outcome of the question—she had been unable to answer it—had been her father's insistence she attend some kind of school. So she continued to go, even after his disappearance, several days a week to the Art Students League, where she played with clay in a back basement room under the casual eye of a short Russian sculptor. Sometimes she modeled for a muralist or a drawing class.

She was accustomed to having empty pockets; a dollar or two would keep her going from day to day. She carried nearly everything she owned in the pockets of her coat, a camel-hair coat given her by one of her father's woman friends—she'd forgotten which one.

The sculptor once told her she had talent, then he'd laughed and said talent was itself a minor talent.

Her father had paid the rent on the apartment for two months —she'd seen the receipt. The apartment house, which was small and shabby, was owned by a Tunisian homosexual who occasionally gave Annie Arab dinners and told her his troubles in a high,

31

hectoring voice. She often helped to tie or pin him into one of the female dance costumes he liked to wear at his parties. His favorite was a red ruffled rumba skirt, open all the way to his thick waist. Once he had awakened his few tenants at two in the morning, screaming, "Where are my TITS!" Up and down the hall stairs he had stumbled, weeping and cursing the bitch who had stolen his beautiful appurtenances with the molded nipples. Annie had observed him from behind the banister of the top floor—she'd been awake, listening to the *Milkman's Matinee* on the radio—thinking of an obscure but terrible vengeance against something, someone. The Tunisian, Samuel, had staggered up to her—everyone else had locked their doors. He was drunk, his wig on backwards, his make-up streaked.

"You don't know, you silly slut," he moaned, and walking stiffly into her apartment, had slid at once to the braided rug, where he'd slept until morning. She made him coffee then, and he told her how he hated the United States of America and the Jews who ran it, how, if he hadn't run away from home at fourteen, his life would have been sane and he would have had six fat children by now. From now on, he assured her, he was her friend, even if that bastard father of hers didn't pay another cent of rent, and he'd let her stay on for nothing, well, nearly nothing. His promises made her painfully uneasy. From then on, he invited her to his drag parties—she didn't go—and now and then slipped a dollar into her pocket. But he had moments of real-estate passion when he regarded her coldly, and she knew he was figuring on how long she might have the nerve to stay after the rent money ran out.

She received, within one week, two colorful cards from her father, who was in New Mexico. The second one asked, "Do you need a spot of cash?" But since there was no return address, the question was pointless. A young woman in her sculpture class gave her two cheap cotton dresses and told her she ought to try to get a job modeling in a fashion agency. People frequently admired Annie's looks, but although she heard their compliments they did not penetrate an incomprehension of her own person that was central to her nature.

Dutifully, she went to a model agency on Park Avenue. The waiting room was crowded with girls, large black portfolios resting against their thin legs. They were so pretty! Eventually Annie was ushered in to the office of the head of the agency. He looked at her legs, the cotton dress, her braids. He told her to let her hair fall free and bend over, then back. Did she have any clothes? Any professional photographs? No, no, she didn't. He said he'd send her out on a catalog job the next day. She left, flushed with excitement. She'd heard of the incredible money models made—five dollars an hour, sometimes even more.

The next day, wearing the other cotton dress and the camel-hair coat, she went to an address in the East Fifties. Through an iron grille, she looked at a pretty, marble-fronted little house. Inside the open door, she saw cameras mounted on tripods, clothes strewn over delicate-legged furniture, and several well-dressed young girls talking to two young men. She left, without pushing the iron gates open.

She saw a good deal of Walter after that meeting; he was waiting to ship out, he said. There was no acting work to be had. He frequently tried to make love to her but desisted at the slightest sign of resistance. She always resisted. He didn't take her to any more meetings but brought a copy of the *Daily Worker* for her to read. Once he took her to the Stanley Theater to see a Russian movie, *Potemkin*. He spoke to several people in the lobby after the end of the film. She was silent, desperately silent; the movie had terrified her, but she took comfort from the terror; her troubles were nothing . . . there was a whole world of trouble.

Two weeks before Christmas, her father wrote he had decided to stay in Taos for a while. It was wonderful painting country. He enclosed a money order for fifty dollars but still no return address. Feeling rich, she went to the League cafeteria on the top floor and ran into the Summit high-school teacher, whom she'd not seen since the party where she'd met Walter Vogel. The teacher had been taking classes with Kuniyoshi. He greeted her laconically. While she told him about the modeling job she hadn't taken, thinking to amuse him, he drew a picture of her in his notebook. "Let's have dinner together tonight," he said, pushing the drawing across the table to her. The girl he had sketched wore an insipid smile but she held her head in a lofty way.

He had bought her good dinners in the past and besides, although he was not a very attractive man—his eyes were muddy and he tended to speak out of the side of his mouth—he was kind to her in an impersonal way. He took her to a nightclub where a reddish-skinned obese Negro woman sang off-color songs, accompanying herself at a small studio piano in the middle of the dance floor. "From the old days in Paris, she was famous then . . . ."

said the teacher who had already told her he'd never been to Europe. "But you wouldn't know about those days," he added.

He took her to her apartment. "You have allure," he said and kissed her. His saliva was abundant and sour. She fought him off, thinking she might have to scream for Samuel. But abruptly the teacher let go of her. "You're a poor wild thing," he said in his dry flat voice. "You're not serious."

A nearly irresistible impulse made her clamp her mouth shut. His disappointment shamed her; she was ready to say "I love you" to this sandy old stranger, even now tidily arranging his shirt, which had escaped his belt during their struggle.

"Why aren't you in school? Why don't you live in a real home?" he asked, as though these elementary considerations had only just now occurred to him.

She hastened to explain. She hadn't always lived this way, alone. It was true that her father was a wanderer and his arrangements for her welfare were erratic and tended to break down, but she had been to school, even high school. It had just petered out, and she guessed her father thought she was old enough to be on her own now.

"How does he expect you to eat unless you're fed by men?" he asked her shrewdly. The question was like a blow; she had no answer.

"You need a mother," said the teacher. Then he told her he wouldn't be seeing her again. He shook her hand formally. He had certain needs, he explained. Someday, she would understand.

A few days later, in sculpture class, a middle-aged woman confided to Annie in a loud whisper that she was going to California. "Thomas Wolfe said you can't go home again, but I can. I'm sick of this insane climate and all these rotten people. I've been watching you. You're not rotten, that's why I'm telling you what I'm telling you." She invited Annie to tea that afternoon.

Her name was May Landower, and she lived in a cluttered, birdseed-smelling basement apartment on the East Side. Two canaries clung to a narrow perch in a cage set near a dirty window which looked out onto an interior court piled high with trash. In the middle of the room, on a round table, sat a Ouija board. A grand piano lurked in the shadows like a dark, stunned animal. May poured them each a shot of whiskey.

"No tea," she said. "Not when I'm planning. Tea is for permanence." She spoke grandly, waving her hands about slowly, as though her thoughts were too lofty for mere words. When she walked about the room, objects fell off tables; she picked them up, grunting, swaying, her full skirt gathering dust from the floor in its folds. She was drunk, Annie saw. In an earlier time of her life she might have been good-looking, in a pinched midwestern way, with her narrow nose and hairpin lips, the large faded blue eyes, a curling-iron frizz of henna-colored hair above her broad low forehead.

She picked up a pack of cards, holding them daintily in her thin hands. A small diamond ring on one finger glittered in the light from a rickety lamp. "What isn't foolish?" she asked rhetorically. "A dear friend of mine chose a camp for his son by tossing a dart at the New York *Times* camp list page. It turned out for the very best. I tell my fortune every morning with the cards. Every evening I consult the Ouija board. Does it make any difference? Fate is fate. I have a few dollars saved, enough to purchase a second-hand automobile. There are children in Hollywood, California, waiting to learn their scales." She gestured toward the piano. "I have even found an elderly woman to take my dear little birdies. My husband left me at the height of the Depression—of course, it was all height. No matter. I've made my way. He died two months ago, a lonely death. California is clear for me now, now that he is no longer there."

"Are you interested in sculpture?" asked Annie as one of the canaries ran through a limp repertory of disheartened trills.

"Something to get through the day," replied May. "Like you, my dear, so what are we waiting for?"

"My father, I'm expecting him back at some time. He's just remarried—"

"No, no . . . if he's not back yet, he won't come back."

"But you don't know anything about it!" protested Annie.

"You're an orphan," said May positively. "Like me. Your aura is sickly. All orphans have sickly auras. They have to generate their own energies. It's hard, hard . . . drink up! I need a traveling companion. If you can get fifty or sixty bucks together, I'll take care of the rest. I was not meant to have children, only loyal friends."

She dropped the cards on a table and went purposefully to the piano, where, still standing, she ran her fingers over the keys. "I knew Gershwin," she shouted above the elaborate cadenza. The canaries hopped to the bottom of the cage.

May returned to the cards and looked intently at Annie.

"It'll take me a little time. The modeling at the League hardly pays. But my father might send me another check. Well, I'll try to get the money."

May made a cage of her fingers through which she peered at Annie. "I'll take you to see Swami Besharandi. I'll regret leaving him, almost as much as my two birdies. He'll give you the repose you need to raise the money."

That evening, Annie met Samuel coming down the stairs from her apartment. He looked ashen. As soon as their eyes met, he began to sob dryly. "I think I'm going to be arrested," he cried. She clutched the bottle of milk and the loaf of bread she had bought to her chest and started to pass him.

"Wait!" he begged. He followed her into the apartment and fell into a chair.

"Danny's threatening to turn me in."

"Danny?" she asked.

"Danny!" he shouted. "You know goddamn well who Danny is! He's been living with me for five days!"

"I never saw him," she said.

"The little bitch! Seventeen and as evil as an old hustler . . ."

"Do you want some beer?" she asked, hoping to mollify him.

"I had tea. I suppose you know what tea is? A little broad like you? The kind of tea that isn't tea? And he wanted to try it. It made him sick. *Everybody* knows it makes you sick the first time! Now he's screaming I've poisoned him and he's going to call the cops. It's blackmail! Just because I own a little real estate, he thinks. . . . For God's sake, I've lived off my own fat since '35. And that stupid little twat who's got a mother and an estate and goes to some shitty famous prep school, who never washes his armpits, *he's* going to turn me in because he stuck a reefer in his ugly face!"

"Samuel. I don't know what you're talking about."

"Marijuana. My Christ! Don't you know anything?" If anyone ever asked her that question again, she would kill him. That's all, just kill him. Samuel sighed. "You think he's serious?" he asked.

"No," she said shortly.

"You're smart," he said. "I always knew that. Will you talk to him? I'll take you to dinner after. Will you?"

Annie didn't turn down meals. Since the departure of the teacher, she hadn't had a really good dinner, only bits of food here and there. The faint gnawing in her belly was persistent, like something imprisoned trying to get out. If only, she had often thought, she'd known where her next meal was coming from, the night fears and the day fears might be softened into bearable alarm.

They went downstairs together, into Samuel's large apartment with its red velvet drapes and soft pillows, its smell of incense. She knew the room well. A thin boy rose from a corner of the large couch. Samuel turned on a light.

"Talk to him," he begged Annie.

The boy's eyes rolled upward. "Christ!" he shrieked, and fell back into the couch, covering his face with his hands. Annie sat down, close beside him. A pungent smell of sweat made its way through his thick tweed jacket. She took one of his hands from his face. Although he shuddered, he allowed her to hold it. "What's the matter?" she asked softly.

"Oh, God!" he moaned. Samuel began to cry.

"I can read palms," Annie said.

"Jesus! *She* can read palms," cried the boy.

"You have a beautiful hand, like a little fish," she said.

"Do you know what *he* did to me?" asked the boy. "That one with his dirty opium?"

"It's not opium," sobbed Samuel.

"He tried to kill me. I've had nightmares, falling, falling, falling . . ."

"Do you play the piano?" Annie asked, gently, insistently.

Danny let his other hand fall from his face. He looked intently at Annie, so close to him. Samuel was snuffling, bent over in his chair.

"Well, yes . . . I do. I'm musical."

"I can tell," said Annie.

"I haven't been home for *days!* My mother would die if she knew what I'd been through." He closed his eyes; his head sank back against the curve of the couch. His Adam's apple was like a little tent of flesh staked out on his thin boy's neck. He looked, Annie thought, even younger than seventeen. Such long black lashes. For an instant, Annie imagined him dead, a little corpse, someone weeping.

"But you're all right now," Annie said, patting his hand.

"I'll *never* be all right," the boy said, sighing. He turned toward her languorously and smiled. "Last year I was only home on Christmas Day. I told them I'd never do it again."

Startled, Annie looked to Samuel as though for confirmation. The store windows, the tinsel—she'd been walking through Christmas for a month and not even known it.

"Christmas," echoed Samuel in a melancholy voice. "Yes."

"And soon, I'll be going back to school in Massachusetts," Danny said, his eyes on Samuel, "where I have two roommates. One is an oaf. But not the other." He smiled winsomely and lowered his beautiful lashes. When he opened them, he looked indifferently around the room. "I'm so bored," he said quietly, "I wish I were dead."

"So do I, sometimes," Annie said quickly. Samuel hugged himself and stared silently at the boy. She supposed he'd forgotten about dinner. She stood up. Samuel looked at her.

"Wash your face. I told you, didn't I? That I was going to take you out? Haven't you got another coat? Look at your legs! They're all red from the cold. My God! Don't you wear stockings or anything? I'll give you a pair of socks. Wait . . ."

He disappeared into the bedroom, where, Annie knew, he would pause a moment to draw his hand across the black velvet bedcover. Danny said coldly, "Where did he pick *you* up?" On a sudden impulse, Annie hit him in the arm with her fist. He laughed almost affectionately.

Samuel returned, a pair of socks in his hands. "Here. They're not the right color for that gorgeous coat of yours but at least your feet won't freeze. My God! You could get gangrene!"

"Good-by, Danny," Annie said.

The boy had sunk back into himself. He waved a finger at her. "Oh . . . Merry Christmas," he said derisively to the world at large.

"Come back in twenty minutes," Samuel said at the door, already turning back into the room.

He took Annie to a French restaurant a few blocks away. "Now get a good meal," he ordered. There was a trace of powder on one of his cheeks. He ate lightly and looked thoughtful, unlike his usual self. He asked the waitress for tea and shook his head when Annie requested a second cup of coffee. "You don't take care of yourself," he observed. "You insult your body. Too much coffee —you smoke too much. Who ever taught you anything?"

"Everybody teaches me," she said ironically, "as if I were the world's village idiot."

"Never mind," he said. "You ask for it."

Spoiled boys drove him mad, he said, those boys with their handmade shoes and mothers who gave marketing lists to servants. They knew nothing of the wrench of life, the truth he had dimly sensed so many years ago, standing on the shores of Chott el Djerid, the great salt lake of Tunisia, beyond it the desert.

"Nothingness," he said. "That is the name of the truth." Then he smiled. "Money, money covers nothingness."

After they had eaten, he took her to a movie, looking indifferently at the marquees that lined that section of Broadway, saying captiously—"Oh, this one. What's the difference?" It was a French movie, the first Annie had ever seen, *Grande Illusion*. Later, walking back to Seventy-third Street, Samuel said, "I always wanted to meet someone like that aristocrat, the thin one, not the German. But you and me, we don't have that kind of luck." They passed two young men idling in front of shopwindows. Samuel giggled faintly, saying the blond member of the couple was wearing a toupee, having lost all his hair at an early age, "all over his body—oh, it's too much!"

Annie didn't want to listen to his sex gossip. She was in a mood of melancholy movie exaltation—if the workers of the world, as Walter had told her, had more in common with each other than with their own countrymen, so did the aristocrats. How noble the doomed French officer in the film had been, washing his white gloves, death in attendance. Noble! Where had she picked up that word? From her father, probably—noble gestures, noble causes, noble because they were doomed.

Samuel fiddled restlessly with his keys. She suspected he would leave for the street as soon as she went upstairs, *cruising,* he called it.

"Samuel, I want to leave New York."

"You're paid up to next month," he said impatiently. "That bastard father of yours took care of that, at least. I was thinking of how you could stay on—you know, clean my apartment once a week, something like that. I simply couldn't let you stay here for nothing. You understand . . ."

"I want to borrow fifty dollars from you, Samuel," she said, bracing herself for his outburst. He said nothing. "There's a woman at the League who's driving to California. She'll take me with her."

Samuel heaved a great sigh, the keys hanging from his fingers.

"I earned my way," he said. "From ship to ship, from Sfax to

Piraeus, from Naples to Barcelona. Oh—you should have seen me then—like a ripe little fig!"

"I'm sorry," Annie said humbly. "I'm really sorry. I just thought I'd ask. I'll try to make it modeling."

"Why don't you wire that old devil? He's out there drinking up his new wife's money, if I know him. You could take him to court for nonsupport. Did you know that?"

"I don't even know his address."

"Well, I do!"

She was mortified and he saw that at once. "Listen, I told him if I was going to be your mama, he had to give me someplace I could reach him. He's in Taos—"

"I know that much—"

"—and don't think he's living in any teepee either, not that one!"

"I can't ask him for money," she said desperately. "I can't." Her father had said, "Annie, you're without greed . . ." To ask him for money, to ask him for anything, was to destroy the only connection she felt she had with him. She couldn't now even ask Samuel to give her the Taos address. Maintain silence, smile when questioned, ask nothing. That was the law. She wished to break it; she wished she were without will, in a lunatic asylum where everything that restraint served to keep back would tumble out of her like broken china.

Samuel was staring down at his small feet in their cordovan shoes.

"Oh, come here," he said harshly. She followed him into his apartment. It smelled musty, unused. Samuel went to the bedroom and returned carrying a cigar box. When he opened it, she saw that it was full of money in change and bills. There were also two very large diamond rings. "They're fakes," Samuel said. He handed her five new ten-dollar bills.

"Get a man, some big strong man. Stay away from Jews. Have babies. For God's sake, don't be a bum. You don't know it yet, but time passes." Then, with palpable effort, he added, "And forget about the money. I'll take it out of that son of a bitch's hide someday. Merry Christmas, dear. Now, go to bed."

"Your socks . . ."

"Oh, keep them . . ."

On the last day of the League classes before Christmas, May Landower told Annie that December twenty-seventh was a propitious day to leave, and on Christmas Day at noon, Walter Vogel came to her door wearing a seaman's cap and a pea jacket over his blue jeans and work shirt. He had brought her his play to read, what he had written of it, thirty-seven pages. He seemed distraught, restless, but she suspected he was playing at something.

"Read it now," he ordered, turning a chair around so his back was to her. "I haven't eaten breakfast," she said. "Eat something, then . . ."

She drank yesterday's quart of milk and ate a piece of bread.

The play consisted, so far, of three scenes. In the first, an actor arrives home to tell his wife the Federal Theater is no more. She is expecting a child. They have no money. Her parents are—"What's a kulak?" asked Annie.

"A rich peasant, and exploiter," he replied in a tone of contempt, whether for the kulak or her own ignorance, Annie didn't know.

The couple embrace, cursing the bosses and imperialists. While the actor's wife sleeps on the cot, the actor cleans an old Winchester gun. In the second scene, the next morning, the wife wakes and screams when she sees the gun. There is no food in the icebox. A neighbor storms in to say that the husband has impregnated her daughter. The wife faints. In the third scene, the actor speaks directly to the audience. He had known months earlier that funds were to be withdrawn from the Federal Theater. He'd gotten drunk, knowing that miseries under capitalism had no end. On his way upstairs to tell his wife she would have to have an abortion, he had seduced the neighbor's daughter. But because, *precisely because* of his brief stop-off at the neighbor's apartment, his baby's life had been saved!

"Who is he going to shoot?" Annie asked.

"Nobody. It just shows his powerlessness."

"Oh."

"It's a little crude . . ."

"No, no . . ."

"Agit-prop . . ."

"What?"

"It's to teach, a kind of teaching play, for workers' study groups."

"Oh."

She wanted to fall down on the floor with embarrassment. Yet she was touched. Her father had said there was no purpose to life,

41

a stirring of worms, mindless energy. Yet Walter was trying to do something with his awful play. She changed her mind about telling him how she had felt about the film, *Grande Illusion*. He was trying to do something for her, wasn't he? Bring some order to her life? She remembered how kind people had been to her at the meeting he had taken her to. She remembered him saying there was nothing wrong with her except that she was a victim of middle-class values. That, at least, was better than being *somebody's* victim.

"It's very good," she said at last. It wasn't the worst lie she'd ever told. He nodded grimly.

She told him that a muralist at the League had invited her to drop by that afternoon for some drinks and food. The muralist, who was from Louisiana, had often shared his lunch with her. She'd modeled for him. She was sure Walter would like him. Walter agreed to go, still looking rather grim. She handed him his manuscript. He rolled it up and stuck it in his pocket.

On the way downstairs, she said, "You know, I really am going to California."

"I know," he said. "You can't help yourself."

"The day after tomorrow," she said, ignoring his comment. He suddenly gripped her in a ferocious and painful embrace. One of her feet dangled over the next step. She was afraid one of the tenants would come out into the hall, or, worse, Samuel. Walter muttered something and kissed her neck. "Don't!" she pleaded. He pressed more strongly against her as though forcing a jammed door. He would never kiss her lips—he said that was movie horsing around. She'd asked him if people didn't kiss in the Union of Soviet Socialist Republics. He'd told her not to be so goddamned arrogant.

"Walter!" she cried. He let go of her abruptly and raced down the steps ahead of her. There was a light snowfall. The few cars parked along the curb looked like deserted hovels. Annie and Walter walked quickly, silently, toward Columbus Circle near which Leonard Poole lived in a small flat with his wife and two children.

The door was open. A stifling odor of old radiator pipes did not quite overpower the delicious smells of corn bread and fried chicken which Annie tracked down to a card-table buffet set up near a Christmas tree already withered in the tenement heat.

Nearby was another little table on which reposed a large mixing bowl, a ladle hanging from its rim.

Walter seemed almost instantly drunk, one of his arms around a young painter Annie knew slightly, the other circling the plump shoulders of Leonard Poole's fat sleek Georgia wife, an abstracted smile on her baby's Tartar face. Annie ate steadily. She had been in many rooms filled with people. Outside of the food—which no one seemed about to take away from her—only the two small Poole children caught her interest. The girl was around ten, plump, her face benign, dressed in a long white cotton nightgown, a gold cross hanging from a chain around her neck. The boy was about five. And as Annie, holding a chicken wing in one hand, a piece of corn bread in the other, observed them, the boy put his small hands on his sister's thighs and rested his head on her lap. His fingernails looked like little red candies—he must have gotten into his mother's nail polish. The girl looked down dreamily at his nestling head, then up at the adults circling around them, talking and shouting. She smiled faintly as her glance came to rest on the scrawny tree with its dusty chains of popcorn.

Annie choked back a kind of wail of protest. Where had it come from? She hadn't had anything to drink—she liked alcohol but was afraid of it because it made her talk too much. She pushed her way down to a little hall and opened a door to a small bathroom. She was coughing violently; she covered her face with her greasy fingers. A magazine reproduction of the *Mona Lisa* had been pasted over the mirror above the sink.

"Are you all right, honey?" asked a liquid voice outside the door. With a mighty effort, Annie cleared her throat . . . "Fine," she said, "just caught a piece of chicken in a tooth."

The door opened, and Mrs. Poole, her barbaric loop earrings swinging, looked at her tenderly. "You sure?"

Lord, she was pretty! Imagine looking like that!

"Ah, now," said Mrs. Poole. "Christmas makes us all miserable." She took a firm grip on Annie's hand and led her back to the party room. Walter was standing in the middle of the room, shouting that the oppressed colonial peoples of the world would one day join with the downtrodden Negroes of the American South and rise up, and—"Blah! Blah! Blah!" screamed Leonard Poole and fell, laughing, against Walter's back. No one paid them any attention.

"I have to put the children to bed," said Mrs. Poole softly. "You come along with me."

Annie followed her and the children to a tiny hot room. Two unmade narrow cots stood against opposite walls. The children murmured sleepily, holding their mother's arms, the little girl sliding Mrs. Poole's bracelets up and down her fine skin. A new doll sat on one pillow. The boy asked for his truck and his mother said no, it might hurt him if he rolled over on it in his sleep. Kisses. The slow drawing up of the blankets.

Mrs. Poole led Annie to a larger bedroom and sat her down on a bench in front of an elaborate dressing table. "It's the only thing I brought with me from New Orleans," Mrs. Poole explained. "Leonard had a fit, said I was no painter's wife. I told him I was *his* wife . . . I had to have a little token of past glory." A slender volume, *The Prophet,* lay next to an empty perfume bottle. From its sepia-colored jacket, a frail face gazed out with an expression of mild lunacy. Annie picked it up. "One of his students gave it to Len. We haven't read it, but my little girl says the man on the cover is God . . . Now, look here. Your hair's all wrong like that, braided up so tight."

She took Annie's hair down, throwing the rubber bands into a basket. "They'll ruin your hair, break the ends," she said. She brushed and combed the long mane. Annie watched her drowsily in the mirror as she made a thick chignon and pinned it in place. She felt an extraordinary peacefulness. Mrs. Poole suddenly laughed. "My little girl just hates to have her hair brushed. Now, here. I'm giving you this lipstick. It makes me look like a gypsy. I've only used it once or twice. How old are you anyhow? Seventeen, I bet. Leonard says you're a wonderful model, so quiet."

"I like to model," Annie said. "It makes everything stop."

"What stops?"

"Oh, I don't know . . . the noise of things."

"That man you came with is very good-looking," said Mrs. Poole. "He's too old for you, isn't he? And what's he carrying on about like that? Just drinking, I guess. When men start drinking, I sit and wait till it's over. I told Leonard he made that punch too strong."

"I think Walter was a little drunk before we came."

"Oh, well, then . . ."

At the threshold of the living room, Mrs. Poole paused and

sighed softly. "We're going back to New Orleans in the spring. I'll be glad. This is not my real life, mooching around these nasty rooms, keeping the children occupied."

Party voices slammed into Annie's consciousness, shattering the peace she had felt in the bedroom. A tall, thin girl, well made up, elegantly dressed, was gesturing excitedly at Walter.

"I can't *stand* people who talk about Shakespeare and Russian movies the way you do!" she cried. "When I hear people talking that way, I feel *crazy!* I can't *abide* your self-importance. That look on your face . . . all greasy with self-importance! God! It makes me want to *belch!* What do you *mean,* you laughed at *The Cherry Orchard* and shocked the people sitting around you? Why, you were just trying to show how original you are! We're all a bunch of obscene monkeys parading around as if we were *real!* I laugh so hard I can hardly get to sleep at night. . . ."

"I can believe that," murmured Mrs. Poole. Walter grinned provocatively. The girl suddenly burst into laughter. "You, a radical!" she exclaimed, rocking slightly on her long thin legs. "I never knew one yet who wasn't in it for personal reasons. . . ."

"Well, you damned well know everything," Walter replied. How remarkable it would be, Annie thought longingly, to be able to talk to Walter like that—to tease him!

Later, as they walked toward the Columbus Circle subway station, Walter talked about the girl. "Terrific!" he said. "Did you see the way she was dressed? She knows exactly what she looks like and just what to do with her looks."

"I haven't got money to look like that."

"It isn't just money. It's style."

"You're always saying it's money."

Now, he said, as they went down the subway stairs, he was going to take her to meet some of his friends who lived in the Village. Elmira, the wife of the couple they were to visit, had formerly been married to his best friend, Kenneth, a great mad Irishman. "He brought me into the party." Once, he told her, Kenneth had taken him to a wake; they'd broken the corpse's legs and arms so he could sit up and join in the drinking. Elmira was married now to a dim fellow, but he didn't blame her. No one could have stayed married to Kenneth. He was larger than marriage. Walter sang to himself on the train. He was very drunk.

The Lighters lived in a loft. Annie and Walter found the door ajar. There were smells of glue and straw. Jersey Lighter was sitting on a stool, looking thoughtfully at a wire figurine he was holding.

"Merry, Merry Christmas!" shouted Walter.

Jersey looked up. "Hello, Walter. There's some wine over there on the shelf. Elmira will be back soon."

"Here's Annie, my little Annie!" cried Walter, pushing her forward toward the man.

Jersey removed his eyeglasses. He had a small quiet face; his smile, only a slight widening of his narrow mouth. "Hello, Annie," he said. "See this object? It's going to be draped in silk in the display window of a swanky department store. Walter, we've hit. Elmira's gotten orders from most of the big stores. I'm going to have to hire people."

"Capitalist!"

"I hope so," said Jersey mildly.

"Where's Elmira?" Walter's voice had become subdued; he was watching Jersey's thin fingers manipulate the figurine. It was cold in the loft—there was an atmosphere of sobriety.

"There's a party down the block to raise money for the Spanish refugees," Jersey replied. "Elmira is the chief exhibit. I painted a roulette board on her belly. People put quarters on the numbers. If the baby kicks their quarter off, they win a copy of *The Underground Stream*."

He looked up at Walter. "What did you mean? Calling me a capitalist with that Vogel sneer? Listen, Vogel, we're naming the baby Franklin Delano, boy or girl."

"When's it due?"

"Next month. We're going to have to do something about the climate in this place. It's too cold for a baby. Or maybe we'll call it Popular Front—Poppy for short."

"You sound bitter, Comrade," said Walter.

"I'm tired," Jersey replied. "There's going to be a terrible war. I don't understand it . . . I don't understand the party. I just want to be let alone."

Annie wandered around the big room. On long wooden tables rested gluepots and paints, scraps of cloth, armatures, tools, excelsior. She felt that Walter's changed mood—the men were talking quietly in the corner—had released her to herself. She stood half dreaming over a drawing table. It was like the best of times, when

46

her father had been really working. Work had a smell of its own; sharp, clean, vigorous.

Elmira soon returned and heated up a pot of spaghetti for them. She was a small, energetic woman, ducklike in her pregnancy. She spoke with a barely restrained lisp in a shrill animated voice. But with all her animation, in the midst of her chatter with Walter, she kept an eye on Annie with a certain calculation. Annie thought, she's acting. Jersey beckoned to her. Annie walked over to him, leaving Elmira and Walter at the table. She was queasy after so much food.

"I don't usually eat so much," she confided to him shyly.

"It's too bad we can't store up food like camels, for the lean days," he said. "You want some bicarb?"

"It's not that bad."

"Jersey!" cried Elmira. "Do you remember those marvelous theater sets Kenneth did when we were all in Washington, you know, sort of Breughel-like? Walter, listen! Now he's living in the woods and won't see anybody! Just painting trees."

Jersey said, in a low voice to Annie, "She didn't leave Kenneth for me. She just left him. I think she married me because I was the only one of their friends who didn't worship him."

"Jersey! Tell Walter what Kenneth wrote you last month . . . that note. Tell him. Listen to this, Walter!"

"I *hated* him," Jersey whispered, putting the figurine in Annie's lap and standing up. "He wrote, 'Don't let that Queen Bee breed off you. You know what happens to drones.' "

Elmira shrieked some incomprehensible word, then rested her head on Walter's shoulder. "Can you imagine?" she asked. "Our old Kenneth? So *reactionary!*"

Annie's father was a bit like that, always talking about women, how they destroyed men's energies, demon brides, bent on begetting, materialists pretending to be romantics. What was the meaning of that word *reactionary?* Jersey might tell her. She turned to ask him but he was dragging an old mattress into a small room she hadn't noticed earlier. Elmira nodded and smiled when Walter said the baby inside was sleepy too.

"Who won the book?" asked Jersey, holding an armful of blankets. "You're staying, aren't you, Walter?"

"Oh, I didn't pay any attention," said Elmira. She was sitting on the double bed, taking off her shoes. "Now, you can't work any more tonight, Jersey," she said petulantly. "The light will keep us all awake."

The mattress Annie and Walter were to use had been pushed beneath a little window. Walter walked around the room naked, his expression malicious. Annie undressed down to her pants and brassière, looking uneasily at the open doorway to the main room. The lights went out.

They struggled for a few minutes, she and Walter; flesh struck flesh. Walter's hand gripped her between her legs. "Oh, stop!" she whispered. "They'll hear us!" "What do you think they think we're doing?" he whispered back angrily. But he fell asleep at last, his back against hers.

She heard sleepers' breathing from the next room. Walter snored delicately. Annie lay inert, feeble with exhaustion. Watcher's fatigue, she told herself. If only she wouldn't watch people so much! The least change of their expressions, the slightest shift of their bodies, threads on their clothes, holes in their shoes, stains on their fingers, their dangerous and unpredictable glances, nose pickers, tooth suckers, cheek scratchers, aroused in her a macabre and anguished response! But to what? To what!

Suddenly she heard the sound of singing. Raising herself carefully on one elbow so as not to awaken Walter, she looked down. Four people stood beneath a street lamp singing "Silent Night" to the darkened windows of MacDougal Street.

They had coffee with the Lighters in the morning. Walter was sullen, and Elmira, apparently piqued by his lack of response, began to question him belligerently about when he was going to work again. "I'm shipping out," he answered her snappishly.

Just before they left, Jersey handed her a piece of paper. "It's something I copied down a long time ago. It's a description of a painting of Giotto's, the *Annunciation,* I think."

She must have looked startled. "I don't know," he said, looking quickly back to Elmira and Walter, who were speaking in low voices near the drawing table. "I thought you might like it—a kind of Christmas present." He smiled suddenly. "You're nice," he said. "Too nice for Vogel."

She put the scrap of paper in her handbag, her eyes on Jersey's face. "Thank you," she whispered. It had been a secret transaction.

She arranged with Walter to meet him later in the afternoon at a restaurant on Twelfth Street and Sixth Avenue, then she hurried off, uptown. On the subway, she took out the scrap of paper. It read: "An angel has entered by the door and knelt. In the silence between the andirons and the sideboard, the destiny of the world is to be decided."

She read it several times. How beautiful! How mysterious! Why had Jersey given it to her?

But she began to worry about money—the destiny of the world had little enough to do with her.

Back at the apartment, she opened the top drawer of a maple chest. Wrapped up inside a suitcase were her mother's bracelets, two of them, thick gold bangles, one set with three small star-shaped diamonds. Her mother's only brother, Uncle Greg, had given them to Annie, counseling her somewhat circumspectly not to mention them to her father. She recalled how Bea, her father's second wife, had once said to her, "Anyone married to your father, my girl, makes a fast acquaintance with hock shops. . . ."

Annie found a loan-company office a few blocks from the League. Cringing, she pushed the two bracelets across the counter toward the unforgiving scrutiny of a yellow-skinned man. He gave her thirty-five dollars and a ticket. "But—" she began to protest. "Gold's a drug on the market," he said.

"The diamonds?"

"Diamonds! They're nothing but chips."

She went directly to May Landower's where she found the older woman standing amid a welter of straw suitcases, blowing dust from a handful of books. The birds and the piano were gone. May was a shade drunk.

"I was right about Thursday," she said, speaking with her usual weighty emphasis. "I've looked it up in my horoscope. But we must make every effort to arrive in California on a Tuesday. Any Tuesday will do. I'm a Tuesday person. You can't guess how much I've accomplished! I've sold my piano, the car is ready. I've broken entirely with my life here. I feel . . . I feel out in space, my dear, and have a drink to celebrate, will you? No? Thank God Christmas is over! How I remember the past! But—one must look to the future. In truth, there isn't any. I had a nosebleed this morning. A good sign!"

"I have over one hundred dollars," Annie offered.

"Oh," said May, with a wave of her hands, "those things take care of themselves. I really can't be bothered with money. Fate decides."

"I've never had so much," Annie said, "all at one time."

"I used to live like a queen!" May cried, dropping the books on the floor. "I had thirty-two pairs of shoes, Balmain dresses. How unimportant it all is! All I need is a piano, a little fragment of nature, a bird, a plant . . . we must rid ourselves of the passion for material things. Freedom! I shall never cease to regret that you did not meet the swami . . . heavenly man . . ."

"We are leaving in the morning?"

"I have worked it out on the chart. Ten o'clock is auspicious. You will forgive me for not coming to pick you up? But I must leave from *here*."

Annie agreed to be at May's by 9:30 for coffee—"so we won't have to stop for a few hours until we escape the aura of this city. It extends farther than most people suspect!"

She went back to Seventy-third Street, where she met Samuel on his way out. He was morose and cranky, pressing her for information as to the exact minute she planned to leave, and when she protested, he cried, "Listen, I'm not running this business for your *beaux yeux!* I've got to make a living. Nobody is going to take care of *me* when I'm an old lady!"

Annie washed out her few undergarments and packed up her clothes in an old leather suitcase of her father's. Its edges were worn and scuffed. But it was a handsome bag. Hefting it, she felt a jolt of excitement. She was actually going to California! She noticed her father's tweed jacket hanging in the closet. She shut the closet door with a bang. Let the next tenant have it.

The book Walter had given her to read, *Man's Fate,* poked out from under the bed. Perhaps she would be able to finish it on the way west. She had read a few pages for Walter's sake.

She thought, as she hung her underwear over the bathtub rim to dry, of the loan-company man, how he had never looked at her once—if he had just glanced at her, she would have been less ashamed at pawning those last reminders of her mother's existence. Then she remembered Uncle Greg.

Oh, she ought to go and see him before she left! The bus to Nyack was only an hour, then a walk of a couple of miles up to the old house on the hill behind the cemetery. No. It was too late. But at least she would phone him.

She could see, as though her hand touched it, the bronze statue of lion and mouse that shared the table with the phone, which so seldom rang at this time of year—Uncle Greg's slack season.

After church, they would drive home in the Ford, the thick Sunday newspaper resting on the back seat, hiding among its folds the red and yellow pie-stealing Katzenjammer Kids and Maggie and Jiggs and Snuffy Smith and the hideous, chinless Gump family, and later, lying on her back after having consumed the "funnies" in a gulp, she would stare up at the lion, one paw outstretched toward but never touching the mouse. Near that table stood the radio, a big box with rodent features, two knobs for eyes and a dial for a mouth. After supper, she and Uncle Greg listened to *Amos 'n' Andy,* and before bedtime, she could look at the latest *National Geographic* on the bottom shelf of the bookcase. Above the bookcase was a framed picture of Edwin Markham which, as evening came on, faded into the dark pussy-willow-patterned wallpaper her grandmother had loved so. Bedtime! A church bell rang. In memory, she went slowly upstairs, reluctant to leave the day—pausing to press her face against the stained-glass panes of a narrow window which, during the morning, bathed the oak stairs in a reddish glow, then up to the top, past the pier glass in the hall, down a passageway that smelled of the dried flower petals Uncle Greg stored in jars, to her own room. It had been her mother's room too.

She dropped the book into her suitcase; how awful everything was! Walter and Samuel and May and that stupid little Elmira! Grimacing and gabbing, caught like flies on flypaper in their own opinions about the world, about her, about fate.

Yet those days with Uncle Greg had been shadowed with sadness—she could feel it now, rainy summer twilights coming across the cemetery like a slow tide, rising to the windows of the old house her grandfather had built, subduing the souls of the small girl and middle-aged man as they sat over their supper of canned salmon and boiled potatoes.

Poor Uncle Gregory! After all that education—he'd actually gone to the University of Heidelberg—he'd ended up a gardener. He was often silent. Yet every gesture, every word had been informed by a quality of kindness, of long patience. And he had fits, always unexpected, of pure playfulness; they played hide-and-seek together sometimes, the old house livened up with racing footsteps and bursts of laughter. She'd spent many years with him. She'd gone to school in a red brick schoolhouse down the road; in the summers, in spring and fall, she'd gone the rounds with Uncle Greg, who worked on some of the estates down by the river where the rich people lived.

"Uncle Sugared-Tomato" Annie's father had called him because of the old man's fondness for putting sugar on nearly everything, and Annie had laughed, if reluctantly, susceptible always to her father's sense of the ridiculous even while she sensed its danger.

She went out to a drugstore on Seventy-second Street and piled up change. The Nyack number rang a long time. He could be anywhere in the house, going through old trunks in the attic, reading in an upstairs room, then moving slowly, without much interest, to the phone. It might be work, he would think, although not likely at this time of year, and he needed the money. The little income left him by his father barely sufficed to repair the roof, pay the taxes. At last she heard his tentative light voice.

"It's Annie, Uncle Greg."

"Annie dear! I was only just thinking about you this morning! I was doing a little dusting and I came to the lion and the mouse. You remember? Is everything all right? Are you with your father?"

"He's married again. He's gone to live in New Mexico."

"You're alone, then? Are you alone?"

"Well, in a way. But I'm going to California with a lady. She's driving out there. We're leaving tomorrow."

"I've never been to the western coast," he said. "It's new, you know, geologically speaking. Well . . . but does your father know where you're going, Annie?"

She hesitated. "I guess—he will know."

Uncle Greg coughed lightly. "Would you like to come here, Annie? I don't like the thought of your being alone."

"I'm really not, Uncle Greg. But I wanted to call, to see how you are . . . I'll write. I know I haven't. But I will." And she meant to, she made a resolution to write to him, no matter what.

"I'm all right, Annie. You know. I go along. This is the quiet season for me. I've gotten very interested in George Washington. Have you ever read much about him? Well . . . I found some books I didn't even know were in the house. I guess Father must have been interested in him too. Oh—I'm fine, really."

"I'm glad."

"The Hudson Valley is full of American history. I always said the Hudson was the most beautiful river, the noblest. You know,

I've been on the Rhine and the Danube. But— Oh! such a terrible time in Germany! That awful common fellow. I hear him on the radio sometimes, those speeches. His is the voice of the cave, Annie. But—well, I have plans . . . a little history trip to Lake George in the spring, if I can manage it."

He had friends; she remembered them all, the ladies from the church who made him birthday cakes, old Mrs. Gerow who'd left him her mahogany sleigh bed in her will, all the people who used to give them Sunday dinners.

"Uncle Greg, when I come back from California, I'll come and stay awhile."

"I'll be glad of that," he said. "I just don't like to think of you so alone."

"I'll be fine."

"I'm very consoled by George Washington," he said. "You find something too, Annie, something that consoles you."

"I have a strange question to ask you. Do I have a middle name?"

"That's not so strange," he replied. "Let me see. I have your birth certificate somewhere. I can go fetch it. It may have been Elizabeth, after your mother, you know. My mother loved the old names. My middle name is Luke. She was very fond of the Apostles."

They said good-by, each exercising a restraint for which the other was grateful. Annie walked down Broadway, thinking of her new name, a dark, fragrant name. The nearly empty shops gave the street an idle, post-Christmas dispirited look. Haunted by thoughts of Uncle Greg, worried about things she undoubtedly had forgotten to do in preparation for the next day, she turned into a movie house that was showing *Wuthering Heights*. Uncle Greg had given her the book years ago. Movies were like a faint thumbprint pressed on recollection; as handsome and intense as he was, the actor playing Heathcliff violated some private notion of her own.

Afterward, she took a subway downtown to the restaurant on Twelfth Street. Walter was late. Annie sat in a corner, averting her gaze from the hopeful glances of men standing at the bar. Then Walter appeared in the door. She was startled at the pleasure she felt upon seeing him.

As he held his hands around the candle on their table, she observed a small flat mole on one of his fingers. She touched it delicately—he stopped in the middle of something he was saying —and there was a yearning look on his face that seemed to have no connection with their gasping bodily struggles in hallways and on beds.

For a while, he spoke of himself, of his father who lived in Sacramento and whom he hadn't seen in eight years. He was a terrible man, Walter said. Once, when he'd taken some friends home from Berkeley—yes, he'd gone to college for a year—the old man had gotten into a rage because there'd been a ring of dirt in the bathtub, and he'd said Walter's friends weren't fit to be in houses. So Walter had told him what a petty bourgeois bastard he was with his nasty little real-estate business. He walked right out of that house and there'd not been a word between them all these years.

A girl came in and went to the bar. Walter stared at her intently. Then, turned to Annie, he said, grinning, "I thought I recognized her back."

Annie shrank back into her chair. Walter grabbed her hands. "Take it easy," he said. "You're so easy to tease, baby!"

"You always laugh at me . . ."

"Come on. Let's get out of here. I'm taking you uptown to meet a Spanish friend of mine."

"Another meeting?"

"No. He lives in an international youth hostel up on the Drive where foreign students can stay while they go to school. There're damn few youths among them. It's worth the trip just to watch the Chinese students ignore the Japanese, and the Texans ducking behind furniture every time a Negro walks into the lobby."

"Couldn't we just stay here? I am going away tomorrow . . ."

"No," he said amiably. "Anyhow, I'll be seeing you sooner than you think. I went down to the NMU hiring hall today and I'll probably get a Panama run to the West Coast."

Chapter 5

The room Annie had rented, about which she had told Walter as little as possible that morning in San Diego, was on the second floor of a small stucco apartment house midway between Hollywood and Los Angeles. The area itself was desolate, and it throbbed day and night with sickly pulsation, as though Hollywood was continually flushing its rejects down the abject streets with their clumps of runt palmettos. Here were bit actors who'd never been successful enough to fail, dim luminaries from the silent movies who talked to themselves in rooms where they feared they would die, and old folk from all over the country who'd come to California, ending up in this backwash, with their mouse savings, hoping to stretch the money just a little further. Country boys and girls, escaping the deathly boredom of towns that had begun to die in the twenties, stayed a few days in sour rooms, never even unpacking their suitcases.

Annie's room held a few pieces of rickety furniture, a washbasin, a stove of sorts, a toilet in a closet, and the wall bed. She often wondered how the old people got their beds down at night, and she visualized grotesque scenes of struggle and defeat, the aged bodies hanging helplessly from the pull bar like dead fruit from a bough.

The gray walls were smudged and thin; every sound carried

from room to room. Perhaps the man next door would stay out all night as he occasionally did. But no sooner had she dropped her pocketbook on the three-legged maple table than she heard his voice, rumbling, thick and heated, filling her own room with foreign intonation. She stood motionless, waiting for the sound of the first blow, the dog's yelp, the man's rising cries, the tumble of movement as the dog ran about the room, trying, she guessed, to hide itself beneath and behind furniture, and the man's heavy tread on the floor. The dog's scream gained something of human anguish even as the man's shout dropped into animal growls— there were thumps as things fell, crashes of objects thrown against the wall, then a small whimper but whether from the man or the dog, she couldn't tell. Then it began all over again. Annie flung herself against the wall, beating it with her fists, crying, "Stop! Stop! Oh, God! Stop!"

Total silence.

Then the sound of a heavy object dragged across the floor. A trunk? Then another frenzied yelp, a thud, the sound of a man sobbing grievously.

Annie ran out into the corridor and banged against the man's door, her fists sore, her heart beating violently in her throat. Movement within the room ceased. In her mind, she struck the man's head until it burst open.

Now he had begun to sing; it was something in German.

"Liebe . . . liebe," he crooned over and over. She heard footsteps behind her and turned to see a woman observing her from a half-opened door a few yards away. The woman took a few steps toward Annie, one arm reaching back as though to protect the vulnerability of her own half-glimpsed room.

"Mind your own business, you crooked fool!" she snarled. "Go to your room this instant, I say!"

"He's torturing a dog!" Annie cried.

"There isn't any dog," the woman spat out scornfully. "He *makes* both voices. Like a ventriloquist. He's a dog ventriloquist specialist."

"You're lying to me!" Annie said furiously. "I can hear the dog!"

"He's working up a little turn," the woman said in a flat voice. "For stage, screen, and radio. There never was a dog." She shook a thin finger at Annie. "Stop persecuting us!" she cried. Annie fled to her room. There wasn't any noise from next door, only a radio playing somewhere, a car shifting gears out on the street. She ate an orange she found in the cupboard near the sink. It was huge, tasteless, nearly dry.

She would have to find another room—she couldn't endure this place! Her job started in two days. Except for the League modeling, she'd never worked; she couldn't imagine how it would be. She almost wished it were possible to slip unseen back into May Landower's little house on Beechwood Avenue in Hollywood. She and May—the whole arrangement had come to a grotesque ending, Annie running through the living room with her suitcase as May banged out hideous dissonant chords on the piano and Johnnie Bliss danced like a moth-eaten bear on the street outside. That night, with no place to go, he'd let her sleep in the back of his old Model T; she nested among scraps of fabric Johnnie had stolen from the property department at the studio where he was, he said, "a seamstress." There had been other things beside fabric—rope, tools, cases of sewing needles, spools of thread, and the canned food he carried around in case he got locked out of his own room.

"You're better off," he'd told Annie that night. "The old bitch is off her rocker. I should know. I've known her for several hundred years." He'd first met May in the brilliant gone days when he himself had been a leading lover of the silent screen. May's husband had been an actor too. "He preferred me to that cow!" Johnnie told Annie, up in the Hollywood Hills where they'd parked for the night. "Oh, she was a cow even then. You can spot them when they're ten. Princess Cows. That's how they raise them in the U.S.A."

"Am I a cow?" she asked drowsily from the back seat.

"You!" he cried, and twisted his ill-fitting toupee to make her laugh. He'd been locked out of his own room that night because one of his young men had cut a wrist and run bleeding through the landlady's parlor, dripping blood over her Turkey carpet, Johnnie weeping and wringing his hands, stumbling after him. But the landlady would get over it, he told Annie, she always did. That's why he'd stopped by to see May, nothing else to do, and he could always get a drink out of her. Annie might not have nerved herself up to leave May's place if he hadn't been there.

The two of them had been sitting in the living room, Johnnie belching softly after one of May's Mexican dinners. She'd gone out with her recently acquired Pekingese. Johnnie was retelling Annie about the grand old times when his hair was rich and curly

57

and black and his teeth hadn't gone bad and he had had his pick of the most beautiful boys the world had ever seen. . . . Now, he just drove around in his sinful old car and picked up what he could in the way of sewing jobs and young men. When she said she was sorry, he'd shown her his brown stubs of teeth and said, "My life has been a dumb thing, but don't you cry for me, Susannah."

He was not at all like Samuel. He worried wholeheartedly about Annie, and comforted her from his small store of mercy. And unlike Samuel, he was miserably poor. They paid him so little for his work at the studio. "It's worse than being a nigger," he said. And then added softly, "There's a beautiful colored boy who does errands out at the studio. He moves inside a cloud."

May had come back from walking the dog, actually she had staggered back, her hair in disarray, her dress pulled down on one fat freckled shoulder. The Peke was yapping. Johnnie had risen to his feet, walked toward her in a crouch, an arm flung across his forehead like a tragic hero.

"Don't you make fun of me, you rotten pansy!" May cried, and burst into sobs. "What is it? What is it!" Annie begged, as May lifted her mascara-streaked face from her hands.

"Two blocks south of here," she began in a kind of chant, "in the dark . . . a man bit me" . . . her voice rose to a scream . . . "on the breast!"

"Bit on the tit!" Johnnie sang, banging at the piano.

"Out!" howled May.

"Why, you made that up!" Johnnie cried. "You lovesick old cat! Don't you just wish—"

Annie ran out of the room to her own small cubicle and packed up her bag. It was enough! Every night, May came back with a new tale of assault. She was drunk in the morning, sick until midafternoon, then, attired in a kind of monk's robe, she cleaned the house, flinging furniture about and complaining bitterly about Annie's idleness—Why the hell had she ever taken on such a helpless infant? Not even the goddamned Ouija board could be trusted!

She hadn't spoken to May since that night. Johnnie, bringing her Walter's letters, said she could forget about her. "She blames you for anything that goes wrong, and believe me, everything does! I told her she should go and kneel at the little white feet of Aimee S. McPherson. Oh, don't look so *scared!* She'll forget all about you soon enough."

But Annie worried about it; she owed May something. Although she knew May had long since removed herself from the sound of human voices, living in a spectral world of Ouija-board spirits and the chance fall of cards, she wanted to explain herself to the old madwoman.

It seemed to her that every time she left a place, she trailed a wake of debris: broken promises, disappointed expectations, expectations she had aroused without intention. Was there something exceptional about her? Something beyond those special circumstances of her own history, which by comic inversion she made into an entertainment just for the sake of making a claim on someone's, anyone's attention? But that was the misery of it! The story merely announced the presence of the storyteller; that was the hell of it!

Was that why she was so moved by transient meetings? As though only in such fleeting episodes someone might catch sight of her, inadvertently? She thought of Mrs. Poole who had brushed her hair, the slim boy in the bulky suit who had stood by the piano in the hostel on Riverside Drive, Jersey Lighter handing her the scrap of paper, the old man in the bar this morning in San Diego.

Next door the man was weeping; he must be standing next to the wall for his wretchedness seemed to sweat its way right through the thin partition. Annie got her purse and left the room. She wouldn't be able to reach Johnnie; his landlady refused to call him to the phone in her living room, and he hadn't had a telephone of his own in a decade. Johnnie just appeared at odd times of the day and night; sometimes he brought her sacks of groceries when he'd made a dollar or two.

She stood on the street irresolutely; perhaps she just ought to go back to the room, stuff her ears with toilet tissue and try to sleep. Then she remembered that years ago her father had spoken of an old friend of his, a screenwriter who'd come to Hollywood in the late twenties. James St. Vincent, that was his name! She went into a public telephone booth and got the number from information. Without giving herself time to think, she called. "St. Vincent residence," said a man's voice. "Mr. St. Vincent? This is Annie Gianfala, Anthony Gianfala's daughter." "Just a minute," said the voice. A minute later, a slurred shout came through the receiver.

"Annie? Annie, is it? My God! I've not seen you since you

59

were a babe in arms . . . you're here, then? In Hollywood? Come out here instantly!"

She knew the sound of liquor. "I'm closer to Los Angeles than Hollywood," she said.

"Take a taxi. I'll pay for it. Come right away. It's important . . ."

His intensity made her uncomfortable, yet the hectic command was thrilling. He gave her his address, a place called Arizona Canyon.

She found a taxi on Hollywood Boulevard. It was a long ride down the whole length of the Boulevard, through the Sunset Strip where the driver said, the only time he spoke, "That's the Trocadero where *they* go. I'm available for tours, tell you where the stars live and all . . ."

They turned up a narrow road that wound among hills. Through trees and thick plantings of bushes, above sloping lawns, lights shone from mansions of such multiform character that they were more like exhibits than homes. It was as though the owners had feared they might miss even one architectural style, and so had crammed together in one structure turrets, Greek columns, Spanish balconies, and colonial façades.

When the taxi stopped, Annie heard the sound of a running brook. A Saint Bernard dog was throwing itself against the taxi door, wagging its tail violently. Then the dog was heaved aside by a man in a dark jacket who paid the driver and led Annie up a driveway toward open doors. She was suddenly conscious, as brightness poured from a brilliantly lit hall, of how bedraggled she must look. She stepped inside uneasily. A voice from another room called out, "Come in, lass. Come in!" Annie followed instructions and entered a large dining room.

Motionless, grim-faced, two women and a young boy sat at the long table, all three heads bent slightly forward over serving plates. At the head of the table sat a man with a linen napkin completely covering his head. As he spoke, the napkin quivered where his mouth must have been.

"You look like neither of them," said the napkin. "What do you think, my dears?"

The woman who sat next to him kept her head stubbornly bent, but the other woman looked briefly at Annie and said in a tired voice, "I've not seen either of them in years. How would I know?"

"How would I know?" mimicked the man ironically. "It's an

endearing way you have of speaking. What was it made out of, that sentence? Hand-hewn stone? Sit down, poor girl, and tell me about your old man."

But Annie remained on her feet, staring at the napkin. There was a muffled laugh. He said, "I can't bear to look at these darlings of mine. I'm hiding out."

The boy gave Annie a covert glance. A colored woman came through a swinging door at that moment carrying an elaborately iced cake. It had fallen in on one side as though someone had pressed a hand down on it.

"You want coffee, mister?" asked the woman listlessly, hardly bothering to wait for an answer as she went back toward the kitchen. The Saint Bernard, Annie observed, was creeping forward from the hall on his belly, moving with great artfulness as he silently advanced one heavy paw after another.

"Beat it, Byron!" said one of the women sharply. It was only when the dog rose, his head hanging in dog apology, and left the dining room that Annie realized the woman had been addressing him.

"I'm surrounded by hostile women and a child unduly influenced by them. Now, I'm presented with this boring cake, sugared to death. Let's get out of here," said the man, and twitched the napkin from his head. "No coffee!" he shouted at the closed kitchen door.

James St. Vincent's head was long, his face narrow. Gray hair, streaked with black, purled over his skull. His was a faintly simian face; the long narrow eyes moved restlessly. The face conveyed impatience and yet uncertainty, as though a child's bewilderment at the strangeness of life had remained unmodified, unanswered, by all the data accumulated by those clever eyes.

The woman next to him said, "But I want coffee, and Grace wants coffee, and—who knows? Andrew may want coffee!" The boy shook his head mutely and continued to stuff pieces of cake into his mouth with little pointed fingers. He looked fourteen or fifteen but seemed even younger.

James St. Vincent rose, dropping the napkin on the table, and walked over to Annie to take her arm. "Upstairs!" he whispered.

He led her to a bedroom where intimations of feminine fussing remained like a faint echo among the disordered papers on the floor and table, pencils on window sills, a typewriter lopsided on the silk-upholstered seat of an armchair, a man's raincoat in a

61

heap in a corner. There was a telephone on a pillow, its black wire curling over the beige satin cover.

"Well, pal! What the hell are you doing out here?" He sat down, then reclined fully on one of the two beds. His gray sweater was full of small holes. She noticed his hands were like the boy's, pointed, catlike, vaguely repellent. The dog appeared in the doorway. "Poor Byron. Come in, lad," St. Vincent said to the dog, who at once jumped up on the unoccupied bed and groaned himself into a mound of white and brown fur. Annie moved the typewriter to the floor and sat down.

"A lady was driving out from New York. I came along," she replied, knowing that it was no answer.

"Why aren't you in school?"

An equally unanswerable question. "Well, I don't really know," she said. "I guess I move around too much," she added smiling, searching around in her mind for something to distract him from herself. "My father says you used to write plays . . ."

Jim held up his hands as though she'd held a pistol to him.

"I did that," he said unhappily. "Yes, I did that. But no luck *there*. And I have not just Andrew, the poor fellow downstairs eating his cake, but two more sons and a girl, a year or two older than you, perhaps. I came out here in '28 because of the sound of money, not the money itself, you get me? It flows through this house like a flash flood every few months, then leaves us dry in a matter of days. . . . No, it was the sound of it, the *idea* of it, thousands of dollars for a screenplay I used to be able to knock off in hours, not always, but there was a time when, in twenty-four hours, with the help of a little Benzedrine, I've done a script and gotten ten grand for it! Then we have a party for a while—I pay the girl's tuition and buy a thing or two."

Annie wondered about the two women in the dining room. She didn't brood on his lapse in not introducing her to them. Why should he have? He probably had his reasons. She liked being here alone with him. The presence of other women would have destroyed her pleasure. Other women made certain assumptions about her, the nature of which she only vaguely understood. St. Vincent was staring at her pensively.

"The ladies downstairs . . . Hope who despairs, and Grace who is a lout . . . are sisters. My wife died, you see, a few years ago. I've known Hope for years . . . my wife was ill for a long time . . . well, never mind that. And so she moved in with ghastly

62

Grace. Ghastly Grace says, 'I don't see why you eat that *stuff,* I don't see why you have that huge dog, I don't see why you go off to that boring Victorville, that boring *sand.*' She maddens me with all that, yet I always feel impelled to try and *explain,* when I know that all those questions are just little curses of rage. She follows me from room to room, making observations about the way I light a cigarette, how long I pause before a window. . . . But old Ghastly—the magic words, *I am at work,* and she is my slave, not from respect, pal, but financial expectation. Then she tends to my needs like a priestess when all I'm doing, for Christ's sake, is turning out a *movie!* She's easier on me than Hope, though. Poor Hope! She's just given up! Ah well . . . I've done it myself, wrecked the women, pulled down the walls."

He sat up and rubbed his hands together vigorously. "We had good times together, your old man and I, before the harpies got us. He was awful with women, you know, fawned on them disgracefully. You see that stack of paper? It's a play, it may be my getaway. If it's any good, pal, I'll be back on the East Coast in a flash of your eyes. Now, take the first ten pages, read them aloud to me, there's a good kind girl!"

Annie read, holding the manuscript tightly in her hands. It was a commonplace conversation between a married couple. At one point, St. Vincent exclaimed, "Ah!" as though struck by a valuable thought. Walter's "play" had moved Annie simply because he'd written it. But this!

"You see?" he asked her when she'd finished the ten pages. "You see what their problem is?"

"Is it because they're married, Mr. St. Vincent?"

He laughed. "Call me Jim. Yes, that is the problem exactly. But they no longer love each other and they wish to, again. What once was true, isn't. They have begun to manufacture it. They are trying to *recapture* love. Did you see that? Truthfully?"

Why was he asking *her* about recaptured love? How was it captured in the first place? Angered, perhaps, by his dumbness in expecting her to know anything about such matters, and in this way making her feel a fool, she said aloud, "Are you supposed to capture love in the first place?"

He looked apologetic at once. "It was unfair of me," he said, smiling sweetly at her. "It was mean. You know, your being here, it's a little as if you were your father. Oh, God! I've got to phone Brazzi. He's waiting for me at the gym. Hold the fort, pal!" He grabbed the phone from the pillow and gave a number to the operator.

Annie went over and stroked the dog. He placed his big head in her hand and looked up at her with saintly eyes. She felt a pang of hunger. She wished someone had offered her a piece of cake. She hadn't eaten anything since that stale orange.

Jim's voice had undergone a curious transformation. Now its timbre was rough, his speech like a movie gangster's. He finished his conversation and turned back to look at her. She grew restive under his silent investigation. "You have," he said finally, "a very good face. Although I don't know what's behind it. . . . Brazzi is a prize fighter and might have been a good one if he hadn't given himself over to women. It's worse than drink. I've put a lot of money into his sad career. Ah, well . . . now I propose we get clear of this house and have an evening."

The jacket he took from a closet looked much like that one of her father's she'd left in the Seventy-third Street apartment.

Interrupting her wary recall of those rooms, Jim said, "Beatrice is out here, did you know that? I've seen her twice but she won't speak to me, holding me responsible for the break with your father, no doubt. Women do that. . . ."

When she didn't reply, he came over and stood in front of her. "Beatrice?" he repeated with a touch of irony.

"Oh! That Beatrice. I always called her Bea."

"But you lived with them, didn't you?"

"Years ago, for a little while."

He touched her cheek with his fingers for an instant. "Well, the old man wasn't much good in the father department, was he? But it's just as well. Beatrice is a very rough girl. Your old man thought she was the spirit of Italy, but for all her temperament, I knew her for the Mediterranean haggler she is. Low-class vamps specialize in temperament. I'll tell you some fine funny stories about her . . . if you like." He took her hand and she stood up. "We must tiptoe," he warned. "We mustn't let the Gorgon ladies know what we're up to. Byron, lad, don't give us away!"

The house felt deserted. They met no one on the stairs. It was only when they came to the front doors that the servant who had paid Annie's taxi fare glided up from under somewhere, the rug, perhaps, and silently opened the doors. Jim said, as they walked out into the fragrant eucalyptus-smelling night air, "He's in my gang. When the play is produced, he'll go east with me. He's very good about the play, got me out of second-act troubles with a touch of genius. Brazzi is crazy about him."

She made no comment—the people, the connections, the things of his life were utterly strange to her. She sensed he was glad to have her company, and that was enough. He took her around the house to a garage. The sound of the brook was louder here. "Is there a stream?" she asked. "Artificial," he said. "Oh, Christ, look at the way they've parked the car! The hell with it. Let's take a taxi." She looked at the big Buick, at an angle half in, half out of the garage. "Come on," he urged. "They'll see us from a window."

They walked down the road, Jim holding her arm tightly. "Garland's house," he said, gesturing vaguely up the hill. A car passed them slowly, the driver's face lit by the dashboard. He looked familiar to Annie. A movie star? "The Brandleys' cook," said Jim. "Given to opium, I've heard. I've played golf with him . . . very elegant fellow with a terrible slice. He won't talk about anything except golf; he calls it the green mistress."

At a crossroad, they saw a taxicab parked in front of a driveway which led up to a large Tudor-style house. Jim went over and spoke to the driver while Annie stood a few steps behind him. "I'll pay double his fare," Jim promised. "And a good deal more than that before the night is over."

"I'm sposed to wait," said the driver.

"He'll never come out, pal," insisted Jim, almost singing his words. "I know who lives in that house. You'll be here until the morning, and I'll give you odds your fare beats it out the back way."

"Well . . ."

"Yes," Jim said decisively. "You know I'm right. We'll have a grand time." He held the door open for Annie, and as she settled back he turned to look at her directly. "Where is the old man?" he asked with such somber accent that she felt a quiver of apprehension as though her outrage about her not knowing her own father's whereabouts might have led her to *think* him into extinction. She answered Jim hastily. "He's somewhere near Santa Fe, in a place called Taos—I don't know where in Taos, or even what Taos *is* —and he's married again, I never saw his new wife."

The news did not appear to surprise Jim. "Your mother was a nice girl," he said reflectively. "But not up to it. Not up to living. And so for his next wife, there was Beatrice. Your father played with illusions—sometimes she was an Italian peasant, sometimes an aristocrat, depending on the bastard's mood. She was so tough, he thought, she'd live on her own, leave him to his work. But they never do . . . women."

By the time the exhausted taxi driver had pulled up to her apartment house, its stucco softened by the first rosiness of dawn, and Jim, gray-faced, slumped against the seat, his catlike hands folded into each other on his lap, Annie knew she'd been in an unearthly region where money was not counted, where the impulse of the moment had the authority of law.

They first had stopped at a miniature golf course where Jim had led her through the doll-sized puzzlements with a kind of pedantic protectiveness that made her instantly happy. On the tiny putting green, she began to whistle, and he broke into loud laughter, saying he wished it was as easy to please other women. They stopped in a number of small bars where Jim, without visible consequence, tossed down drink after drink. In a place called the Melody Garden, he broke into a conversation between two sailors and a thin tanned blonde girl whose honey-colored hair coiled at the back of her head in a heavy braid. She said she was Viennese. The sailors said they were hillbillies, goddamn all! And took to calling St. James "Pappy."

The five of them crowded into the taxi. The driver, enjoying himself now, caught up in that expectation of the great adventure Jim managed to imply was waiting for them at the very next stop, drove at reckless speed to Santa Monica. There, Jim directed him south until they came to an amusement pier where an orange glow licked up a portion of the moonless sky.

"I love Venice Park," the driver said. Jim ran off and returned shortly with two hot dogs, which he thrust in the driver's hand, then he gave him a fistful of change. "Enjoy yourself, lad. . . ."

They walked down the long stretch of the pier lined with shooting galleries and funhouses, Ferris wheel, chute-the-chutes, snap the whip, what Jim called "contrived delight." Here and there they stopped to toss darts at balloons, or to shoot at wheels of circling ducks, until they came to the pier's end where the narrow tracks of a roller coaster, supported by spidery black struts, rose directly from the water, rose to hidden heights, the inclines lit here and there by naked bulbs feebly lighting the way to certain annihilation.

"You must!" Jim insisted to Annie, as the sailors and the girl, Karin, stepped into a waiting car. "You must do it, because it frightens you. That's the reason, nothing else." Wordlessly, she shook her head.

"Yes," he said. "What one is afraid of becomes one's only real life. You cannot let it be a thing like this. You will be riding this beast forever—if you don't do it now."

"Come on, Pappy!" shouted one of the sailors. Karin sat primly between them but they pushed up against her, their arms entwined about her rigid shoulders.

With an impatience that made him seem suddenly commonplace —it was a fleeting thought, she was too frightened to pursue it— St. Vincent grabbed Annie's arm and pulled her into the front seat, which the sailors had left empty, perhaps out of deference to St. Vincent as the king of this night's pleasures.

Machinery rattled, the little car moved and swayed violently as it turned the first corner. Annie looked down at the black water. She saw the pilings which held up the pier, the stilts of the roller coaster walking the flat sea. "Oh, God . . ." she moaned. Jim put his arm around her. "It will be over soon . . ."

It was never over. The car clanked up the swaying inclines, paused viciously at summits, lunged forward into a hellish drop, an abandoned fall that drove her lungs against her spine, emptied her of air, her screams, drowned like those in nightmares, her mouth open, larger than her whole face. In a valley, she said shrilly, "Make it stop . . . I'll kill you! I'll kill you!" But Jim was leaning over the side of the car, vomiting. The sailors shouted joyfully. Only the Viennese girl was silent. When Annie glanced back to see if the worst torment was over, she caught sight of Karin sitting up straight, her face utterly composed. Annie turned back and gripped the iron safety bar with wet hands. Suddenly, it was over; the car rattled back to its place. The sailors leaped out; Karin straightened her skirt and refused the help of hands extended toward her. Jim, a handkerchief held against his mouth, took Annie's arm and pulled her free of the car. "Very good, pal," he murmured through the handkerchief.

Trembling, she yanked her hand away. "Ah, well, I don't blame you. I'd be sore too," he said.

In the taxi, she held the stuffed bear Karin had won at a dart booth. She was silent all the long way to Malibu Beach, listening without interest to the talk among the others, Jim with his poking comic questions, his speeches about women and money and work, his sudden shift of accent when he lapsed into the jargon of prize fighters. The sailors asked about the secrets of the movie stars, and punched each other with delight at his sardonic replies. But Karin didn't laugh; she watched him stolidly, her eyes never leaving his face. Jim said, "You want to be a moom pitcher star, do you, lass?"

"Yes."

"And what for?" he asked with somewhat menacing gentleness. The driver cried, "And why not! For God's sake, looka the money they make! Looka the things they do! I could tell you—"

"No, lad," Jim said with that same unpleasant softness, "you could not tell me anything."

"How did you know there'd be a party?" Annie asked as Jim told the driver to park the car right there, in back of that house.

"There's always a party," he said. "Have you forgiven me now? Am I to take it you've forgiven me?"

This time, the driver stayed with them. Once, during the hours that followed, Annie saw him sitting on a woman's lap, counting the pearls in her long necklace. The party house was shaped like the midsection of a small steamer. There were portholes for windows and a ship's ladder instead of stairs. The women, most of them, wore gaily colored beach pajamas; the men's white linen trousers set off their bare tanned feet. The atmosphere was charged with a peculiar intimacy which instantly absorbed the newcomers. Yet the easy familiarity had a thinness to it, as of a light mist through which one passed briefly to emerge with a slight dampness of the spirit. Perhaps, Annie thought, it only seemed that way because of the vast amounts of liquor being consumed by all these handsome men and beautiful women whose voices rose like the cries of tropical birds as they caressed each other with glances and hands.

But as they questioned her, eagerly, hopefully—what did they want of her?—they began to look different. Their delicious tans covered but did not conceal shoulders thick with fat; the men's bellies strained against gold and silver buckles; teeth so white and gleaming at a distance looked, close up, like matched sets of cheap china. She saw the traces of lines where eyebrows had been plucked away and raised to pencilled heights of hauteur. A woman with a great angel's halo of ash-blonde hair kicked off her shoes, revealing a large mushroom-colored bunion on one narrow foot. They touched her a great deal, they kissed her, they said she was a darling. Whose girl was she, though? Wouldn't she tell? Not that old hack, St. Vincent's, surely? And my God! Why was she wearing that depressing tweed suit?

She escaped up the ladder stairs. At the top was a "Captain's Bridge," a small square bedroom, as Annie discovered when she opened the door. On the bed, which took up nearly all the space inside, a naked man straddled a woman whose head was half hidden by a pillow, her hands drawn into fists. Annie brought the door to, but the picture remained, snapped up by her mind—the man's thighs, hairy and gleaming with sweat, gripping the woman whose long legs shot out from beneath him, her feet upright at the end of the bed, the soles soiled and the heels orange-hued.

She went back downstairs to find Jim reading aloud to a group gathered around him, silently miming attention. Karin watched him from a corner; her eyes glittered. The sailors were lying on the floor like sailor dolls while the woman with the bunion danced in exaggerated abandon around them—or was it exaggerated? Did she imagine herself at that moment to be superb?

Jim glanced up from the book and, seeing Annie, pushed it into the hand of a man standing next to him. She saw the name, Rupert Brooke, on the cover. "Let's go for a walk," he said. They went out the door and on to the beach. No one seemed to notice their leaving; the people to whom St. Vincent had been reading stood together apathetically, as though no one had told them the entertainment was over.

Lights from other beach houses faintly illuminated the wide stretch of sand. The beach dropped off suddenly into darkness where the slow somber fall of waves followed one another like an unknown word repeated over and over. A line of whiteness gleamed against the dark horizon. "Reef," said Jim softly. They walked by the water's edge, which was made visible by a line of silver luminescence.

Jim stooped suddenly and picked up a handful of tiny silver fish, held them up for her to see, then flung them into the waves.

"They come to the sand to breed, and die, thousands, millions of them. It drives me mad. It's why I won't get a place out here." Then, in a paroxysm of stooping and straightening up, he flung handfuls of the little fish into the sea. As she watched his hectic efforts, she was overcome by hilarity. He could command cars and women and dogs and sailors, he could produce parties and amusement parks, yet was helplessly, furiously opposing himself to the dumb fate of these bits of tide-driven creatures.

He shook her by the shoulders. "Don't laugh," he shouted. But she only laughed louder and shook herself free of his grip. Then, leaning toward him, she caught a glimpse of his contorted face. He is sick from drinking, she thought, sick of all the awful fun, and her laughter died.

They walked in silence to the last house. A few yards beyond it they found a sloping bank of sand upon which they sat. Then, snapping his fingers and rubbing his hands, as though words alone were not enough to convey his feeling, he talked about a getaway.

"The play . . . the play. I've had fearful luck, and the theater has changed so much since the twenties, I don't know. But Gaskin called from New York last week and he's interested, more than mere interest, although he's not wild for the third act. He may be right, but I can't abide this moving around of ideas like so much furniture to appeal to an idiot audience. Oh, your old man and I, we were as young as you once. When we first met, we hated each other, circled each other like warring cats, then we became the dearest of friends until I came out here and, well, really, it was before that, when the marrying started. He was sore at me for coming to the Coast, said I was on the road to ruin. It only goes on and on and on. . . . But if this play works, I'll take the whole tribe back east, away from here where we live like mad gypsies—"

"But why do you stay anyway? If you hate it so?"

He laughed shortly. "I'll be damned! And why the hell shouldn't I? I suppose it won't cut any ice with you, but I've got that pack of children to take care of. . . . Why, I hate the silly brutal place. I'm only happy when it rains. . . . Nobody brings you to work, you know, you bring yourself to work. Let me tell you, your old man was the bigger fool! Bea demanded the soul out of his body—she ran him ragged so he turned out *art* layouts for the Macfadden magazines, for those beautiful stories about girls named Tanya from Cornflakes, Nebraska, who get knocked up by gray-haired cads—*filthy* stories! Yes! He did that to keep Bea in twenty-five-dollar shoes and it was life's blood to her, his life's blood, but you know her, lass, you know her . . ."

"But what about you?"

"Never mind about me!" he cried. "I pay my damned dues."

"I don't really remember her," Annie said, placatingly. "Just her eyes . . ."

"Her eyes," he echoed. "Extraordinary, like a wild animal's."

"She didn't like anyone to be sick," Annie said absently.

"No. She hated that," he agreed. "She hated all helplessness."

"I just remembered a time when I told Tony—"

"You call him Tony?"

"Yes. Tony. I told him I had a toothache. She was there, pacing around the room with a drink in her hand. She said she'd take care of my toothache. Well, she lifted me up—I must of been six or so—and dropped me into a rumble seat of some car they had at the time. She drove up the Storm King Highway along the Hudson River, I could see her through the back window, bent over the wheel like a demon. I thought the seat would close over me."

"They lock into place."

"I didn't know that!" Annie exclaimed. "How could I have known that? When we got back she asked me, 'Well, is the toothache gone?' "

"And was it?"

"Yes."

"My mother was a lush, an Irish lush, the worst of the worst," Jim said, clasping his knees. Annie lit a cigarette and he took it from her companionably. "And the dear old man, St. Vincent himself, left us and beat it back to Donegal or County Clare—I never inquired—and there we were, the seven of us, in Boston, with her falling down, urinating in her clothes. Well, we all had to go to work, except the littlest girl, and she died anyhow. We had to beg the money for a box for her. I can tell you all of it in a few minutes, fourteen years of it. The truth may not be important in the way of real lives, anyhow. By the way, would you like to see Bea?"

She could make out his grin even in the dark.

"La Siciliana," he said when she remained silent, then in a melancholy voice, "Your father never writes me, never calls. He's afraid of me, you see. It's too bad about you, but he always was the slave of grown-up women—and how they hated him for it! When your mother died, he was fair game. He would have left her in the long run, I fear. She didn't beat him sufficiently. She was a pale thing, from a nice Irish Protestant gang, not the ghastly mad Catholic sort at all."

"You knew her well? I didn't know you'd known Tony so long."

"Oh, hardly. She was not knowable, being so modest and still and nearly dying at the sight of a human face."

"I might have liked her."

71

"Like?" he cried. "Oh, no! I like my old sweaters and my golf clubs. But not my children. Nor they me. Nor my dead mother and my brothers. Like is no word for such things. It's all passions . . ."

"The water's coming up," she said, one of her feet slipping forward in the wet. He rose silently and stood behind her. There was a tinge of gray in the black sky. "I suppose you don't have a watch?" he asked. "Well, no matter. We'll get that gang and take you home."

They went back to the shiphouse, passing other houses, dark, silent, facing the sea. As they mounted the steps of the deck, they saw through the windows that the room was almost empty. A man slept on the floor, his mouth open; a woman lay curled up on a wicker couch, near her shoe protruded the head of a dachshund, resting on his paws. But upright and awake in a corner chair, a half-filled glass in one hand, sat Karin.

Through the window, her eyes met theirs.

"She won't make it here," Jim muttered. "She can't dissemble her greed, and she has no style at all. She's just a little whore."

The girl was strangely still as though listening to an absorbing account. A whore?

Jim opened the door into a silence broken only by a low crackling sound which, Annie saw as she moved toward the back door, came from eggs frying on a stove. Looking down at them, a fork in one hand, was a thickset man in white tennis shorts. Annie recognized the man from the bedroom. Evidently he was hungry; there were four eggs in the pan.

"So long, Jack," said Jim over his shoulder. The man waved the fork, his unwavering glance fixed upon his food.

The driver was asleep in the back of his taxi. Jim shook him gently. The dark, runty little face lit up with a smile of expectancy. Jim laughed softly. "The party's over. . . ."

They drove south toward a great expanse of pale-gray sky which gradually turned into the penetrating blue of a California morning. The driver smoked a bent cigarette and said he'd had a fine time of it, seeing how the other half lived.

Karin lived in a bungalow off Melrose which, she said, she shared with two other girls. She asked Annie for her address. Just before she slipped out of the taxi, she looked back at Jim. "Well, *Herr* Jim, I suppose I must thank you for this Hollywood, California, evening. And you, Annie, I will hope to see again." She walked sedately up the cement walk to her door.

"A bad girl," Jim said. "But smart. She knew I'd not help her! Oh, I don't feel good!" he said, sighing, and fell back against the seat. He looked suddenly old. Then he opened his eyes. "It's all right, I've not really left you . . ."

Annie saw the familiar Model T parked near her apartment house. It was, unexpectedly, a welcome sight. Just before she got out, Jim reached into his pocket and took out some bills which he pushed into her hand, opening her closed fingers one by one with a last flicker of energy. "I'd give you more," he said, smiling, "but our friend up front gets my fortune for tonight." His eyes closed, his jaw went slack. The driver assured her, "I'll get him home. I'm used to them. . . ." Next to him, on the front seat, sat the stuffed bear from Venice Park.

The air was sweet with the first freshness of the new day. Annie peered in through the window of the Model T. Johnnie Bliss was lying on the back seat on his rat's nest of things, his stocking feet sticking up over the front seat. He was snoring softly. She leaned against the car, looking around at the palmettos, the silent houses, the shaded windows of her apartment house, the wide heavens. It had been a long long day. She'd been to the sea in the morning and then at night, to that same coastline along which Walter's ship was even now making its way. She thought of Max Shore and the woman with the white gloves. Their meeting, or whatever it was they had been going to, must be long over.

"My God!" Johnnie's cross voice broke into the stillness. "I thought you'd *never* come back! I suppose you've been out catting around, you sly thing! Oh, oh! My back is broken in three places."

When they reached Annie's room, they counted the money Jim had given her, thirty-five dollars. All was silent in Germany next door. She told Johnnie little fragments of the evening, but he showed no special interest. He'd been to all those parties, he commented, and better ones than she'd ever see. Then she pulled down the wall bed while he yawned and scratched his backside, complaining about the spools of thread that he'd been sleeping on.

They both lay down, fully dressed, too tired to take off anything except shoes and jackets, he with his head at the foot of the bed, she with her head on a pillow. He was asleep at once. In the light that filtered through the gray window shade, she looked at the

73

heavy, elderly man. A faint rancid smell of perspiration and cigarette smoke emanated from his clothes. She tried to visualize him as a young film star, a lover with a profile to cherish. She thought she heard a scrabble of dog claws against the wall from the next room. But then, comforted by Johnnie's presence, she too fell into a deep sleep.

Chapter 6

"The dog may *like* it," Johnnie Bliss said irritably. "You could do a lot worse than this place." He looked with disgust at the shoe in his hand. "Look at that! I'll be walking around in newspapers yet. I'm too mortified to even take these things in to a shoemaker." He pulled the shoe over his foot, groaning with the effort of leaning over.

"Coming back here at night, it's like being punished," she said. She dried her face and hands and went to the window. A breeze rustled the window shade.

"You're a boob, Annie. Some absolute stranger tells you to call another stranger, and you think you've got a swank suite to move into. What if the rent is five times what it is here? What are you doing with your suitcase open? You haven't even called the man yet!"

"It's not only the dog—it's the German grunting and crying all night. And these crazy old people who live here."

"Listen, my dear, with the money we have, that's our crowd you're being so hoity-toity about." He giggled.

Annie split open a brown paper sack and emptied her handbag over it. Shreds of tobacco and a dozen or so pennies fell on the paper along with a New Jersey bus timetable and a square piece of cardboard to which had been stapled a dozen small vials of the world's greatest perfumes Annie had bought in the five-and-ten. She sniffed at the card.

"I'm going out to call that actor. Where's Sycamore Street?" she asked.

"Up by Grauman's," Johnnie answered, snatching the perfume samples from her hand. He uncorked one of the miniature bottles and rubbed the entire contents over his chin. "What do you intend to pay the rent with? Faith?" he asked.

He looked grimy and unlovely sitting there on the mussed bed. She understood that he liked the way things were; he didn't want her to move.

She was wearing an old white shirt of Walter's and a pair of Levi's he'd bought for her at a seamen's supply shop in New York. She sat down next to Johnnie to put on her sneakers.

"Bring back something to eat, will you?" he asked.

"I have to find another room before Walter comes," she said.

"Walter! Some sailor whistles and you fall down all in a heap!"

"He's not some sailor. He's an actor and a playwright."

"I know actors. You'd be better off with a sailor."

They wrangled while she made the bed and Johnnie shaved over the sink with the razor he carried in the pocket of his jacket.

She went off to the drugstore to call Jake Cranford. A woman with a speech defect answered the phone; it seemed to have affected her hearing also, for Annie had to repeat Cranford's name several times. All at once a bell clanged loudly, drowning out the woman's voice. There was a momentary silence, then a man said, "Yeah? Jake Cranford here."

"Mr. Cranford, I met Max Shore yesterday. He said you were giving up your room. He said I might be able to rent it."

"Not for two weeks I'm not, I don't think. Who are you?"

"Annie Gianfala," she said. "Well, do you think I could come and look at it anyhow?"

"Right! Any time."

"Today?"

There was a deep groan, a whispered "Just a minute." Had he hung up?

"Mr. Cranford?"

"I let my prescription run out," his voice came back strongly. "I'm all right now. I've got colitis."

"I'm sorry to call when you're sick."

"Never mind. I'm *always* sick. Yes, come today, after five, all right? The room isn't bad."

"I'll be there then."

He gave her the house number. "There's one thing though," he added. "The place is full of cats. That's a drawback. It can smell pretty bad."

"As long as nobody beats them . . ."

"What?"

"I hope you feel better soon."

"Never!" he said gaily.

She bought a pack of cigarettes, some oranges and a loaf of bread at a grocer's. After they had eaten, Johnnie said he had some sewing to pick up from the wardrobe department. She drove out to Paramount Studios with him and waited in the car while he went to fetch it. Outside the gates, on a triangular patch of wiry grass, sat a canvas tepee. In front of the tent flap, spread out on a wooden camp chair, socks and a man's undershorts were drying in the sunlight. As Annie looked at the tepee wonderingly, the tent flap was pushed aside and a young man emerged wearing cowboy boots, tight jeans and a plaid shirt. With a flourish, he placed a ten-gallon hat on his big head. He felt the underwear, shook his head, then did some fast kneebends. Not one of the people passing back and forth through the studio gates gave him so much as a glance. Johnnie returned after a few minutes clasping a box tied with a string.

"Thank God for old lovers," he said, flinging the box into the back seat. As they drove away, she asked him if he had noticed the cowboy. "Oh, he's been there for months," he said. "He thinks he'll break them down someday. But movie people are funny. He's trying too hard and they're used to freaks. They only get interested if you ignore them. Then they feel insulted and have to give you something to do just to save face."

"But how does he live?"

"Oh, Annie, how do I live? Maybe he's a hustler. Maybe he saved up a little money before he pitched that tent. Maybe he eats babies. What's that address on Sycamore? Listen, could you buy a little gas for this poor old biddy? Now that you're so rich!"

She opened a little cloth change purse and gave him a five-dollar bill. "My God! You're keeping me!" he said.

"If you drop me off now, I'll be too early."

"Well, dear, you'll just have to be too early."

He's up to something, she thought. He glanced at her quickly as though aware of her suspicion. He pursed up his lips. She braced herself for one of his fits of obscene reminiscence. But he merely smiled.

"I'm hungry. Let's go eat something at the Greek's."

He said, "I won't be able to keep my mind on food with all those young caddies bending over the ski-ball game."

He parked near the Greyhound station on Cahuenga and they went into a small restaurant owned by a hugely fat, bald Greek. The place was deserted at this time of the afternoon and no one was bending over the ski-ball game near the bar. The Greek brought them minute steaks, and they ate with passionate absorption. Annie thought if she could just have three meals a day, she'd be willing to sleep on the sidewalk.

Just as they were leaving, a prosperous-looking, middle-aged man with a shaggy mop of red hair walked in. The Greek laughed and clapped his hands over his ears. The man gave him a sly wink and went to the jukebox and made his selection. Annie peered curiously over his shoulder and saw he had pressed the button for a record called *Finlandia*. As it began to play, the red-headed man hid his face in his hands and swayed back and forth as though grief-stricken. The Greek shouted, "Why you play that goddamn thing alla time. I'm going to throw that record out. Whyn't you go back to Finland, for crissake?" He winked at Annie and shrugged his shoulders.

Johnnie dropped her off in front of a ramshackle shingled house bulging with oriel windows. Several cats lay on the steps leading to the wide porch like merchandise on shelves, asleep in the late-afternoon sunlight.

"Listen, darling," Johnnie said. "Don't give in to impulse. Don't just take the room because it's available. I know you and men! I think you'd lay down on a third rail even if it was me asking you to. Don't be so available yourself!"

Annie walked up the steps, over the cats, through the open front door into a dim hallway that smelled of dust and cat urine and age-soured wood. She heard the noisy flush of a toilet somewhere up the stairs. An elderly woman limped toward her from a room leading off the hall and stood silently, looking at her.

"You wanted something?" she asked at last, her voice shaped

into a squeak by a mouth so small it looked as though it been stitched solidly at either end.

"Mr. Cranford."

"Mr. Cranford," repeated the woman, and shook her head as though she'd hoped for better news. "Go on up, then. He's on the third floor, first door as you pass the clock."

A cat padded down the stairs. Except for the black-painted doors, everything in the house, wallpaper, furniture, ceilings, was faded brown or gray. Cats came out of corners, from beneath tables, ignoring Annie's presence, in search of patches of warmth beneath the dusty windows.

She passed a grandfather clock, its pendulum stilled, and knocked on the door to its right. She heard the sound of bedsprings, then footsteps. Next to the door she read a hand-lettered sign: "I won't ring the bell more than once for your phone calls, tenants."

The door opened, and she gazed into the hazel eyes of a very young man. His light-brown hair, wavy, as insubstantial-looking as loose feathers, was combed back from a wide, unlined forehead.

"Mr. Cranford?"

"Yes. You Max's friend?"

She nodded; she'd explain that later if she had to. He stood aside to let her pass. The room, compared with her own, was spacious. Three large windows looked out on an old house that was the twin of the one she was in. Across the bed—a real bed with two pillows stacked up on one side—was a bright afghan throw. There were two wicker armchairs, several small worn rugs on the floor, and a table with a colored glass lampshade.

"It's a nice room," she said, staring at the afghan.

"My mother sent me that blanket," he said. "I'd have to take that with me but everything else stays. It's pretty quiet here except when things start popping at old Ivan's." He pointed toward a shadeless window in the house across the way. Annie looked straight into the other room. Piles of manuscript lay heaped up on the floor, and a number of chairs were arranged in a circle as though for a meeting.

"When you can't sleep," Jake Cranford was saying, "it's as good as a movie, watching those crazy people over there." He waved her to a chair. "I'd offer you a cigarette but I'm broke at the moment."

Annie gave him her pack. He took a small frying pan from a shelf over a hot plate and placed it on the floor in front of her. "An ashtray," he said.

She puzzled over what kind of acting parts he could possibly get. He looked so frail; his expression was obliging and bland. But when she looked at his hands, she saw they were worn and hard as though he'd done physical labor with them.

"Where are you living now?"

"Out on Hollywood Boulevard, near Los Angeles," she answered. "The room is bad but that's not the trouble. It's the man who beats his dog. He's right next to me, and the walls are so thin."

He made no comment, only continued to look at her with calm eyes. "This place is six bucks a week," he said. "You're not supposed to have cooking privileges but you can, because of Mrs. Corrigan's cats. I mean, since the tenants have to put up with her cats, we get to cheat a little. It's a kind of bargain."

Her spirits lifted. The room was two dollars less than she was paying now. Walter would be pleased with her.

"I'd love to have it," she said.

"Why not? But you know, it'll be three weeks or so."

"I thought you said two—"

"Since I talked to you, my agent called. He's got something for me in some musical about New Orleans. That's the way it goes. You never know."

Annie was silent. Perhaps she could sleep in Johnnie's car for the week. Then when Walter came, maybe he would do something about the man and the dog.

"I don't have my own agent, really," Cranford said, smiling. "That sounded important, didn't it? It's only an agency I'm registered with. They always stick me in the boys' chorus lines, in the back, because I'm tall."

"Mr. Shore said you were going to New York. Is that where you're from?"

"Oh, no . . . my home is just outside of Phoenix. My folks have a little ranch. Well, it's a farm really. We just call it a ranch. I thought of going east, thought I might do better in the theater. Only if there's a war, I suppose I'll go into the army. Actually, I don't have much hope about the theater. Any job will do, now. I don't want to be in Arizona or Ohio. I only like coasts."

"You like the ocean?"

80

"No, no. I just don't like being *inside* the country, you know? I want to be on the very edge! How old are you?"

"Eighteen."

"You trying to break into pictures?"

"No."

"Oh, come on . . ."

"No, really."

"Then, are you from California?"

"I'm from New York."

"I don't know what you're doing here. It's the you know what of the world."

"Everybody I've met hates it," she said. "But still, they stay."

"Actually, I don't know why I bother to stay myself. It's just another two-step job in the chorus line."

He was funny, trying so hard to be accurate about what he really meant.

"How old are you?"

"Twenty-three."

They put out their cigarettes at the same time.

"It's this money thing," he said in a puzzled way, bending forward and clasping his hands together. "It drives me crazy. I lie here thinking up ways to make money. I've got a buddy who's worse than me. When we get together—you can't imagine all the crazy schemes we think up! Sometimes I think he'll end up in jail! My nature isn't especially criminal though."

"I wonder a lot what it's like to have money. Last night I was at a movie writer's house. It had an artificial brook in the garden and a dining table longer than this room. He must have given the cabdriver a hundred dollars for taking us around all night."

"What's his name?"

"James St. Vincent."

"Yeah, I heard of him." He was silent a moment. Then, "You know, I just thought of asking you to introduce me to him, but then, right away, I thought how they treat writers out here. Nobody pays them any attention at all."

"But they pay them so much! He told me he gets ten thousand dollars for writing a picture."

Jake repeated after her, "Ten thousand dollars!"

She handed him another cigarette. "I shouldn't smoke," he said, lighting it. "It makes my gut hurt."

"It would take care of me for life," she said.

81

"I don't think so," he said thoughtfully.

"But there's nothing but poor people in this country—"

"—plotting to make fortunes." He laughed. "I'm poor. Out here, they say broke. It has more class."

"You aren't poor. You've got a family with a ranch. I meant, really poor people."

"There always will be the poor. It's the natural way. Rich and poor. Max Shore rags me about my attitude. Did you know he was a Communist? I'd never met one before. He tried to organize the extras once, you know, into a cell or whatever they call it. After months of work, he got about twelve people together, and two of them were a hundred years old and only came in case there was free coffee and a little something to eat. He's too nice a guy to be mixed up with that bunch. They ought to go back to Russia." He looked at her and smiled. "Not that I would mind going there myself. I'd like to go everywhere before I die. How did you come to meet Max?"

She told him, leaving out her only reason for having gone to San Diego which, without reflecting upon it, she did not want to tell him. But he didn't pursue the subject further, only remarked she was lucky not to have met Max's wife who was, he said, like a sergeant. Hadn't she ought to go and speak to Mrs. Corrigan and make sure she'd get the room? Annie wondered about that. He assured her she wouldn't have any trouble. Mrs. Corrigan only paid attention to cats and rents.

"Have you got any money?"

"A little," she said.

"I've been hoarding a few dollars. You want to have supper and go to a movie? I love the movies!"

"Yes," she answered without hesitation, aware she was doing exactly what Johnnie had warned her against, acting on impulse, making herself available. But Jake Cranford was such a nice peaceful boy. She felt easy with him; what questions he had asked lacked the pointed belligerence she was accustomed to from people who were either her own age or close to it. She didn't like the company of very young people—they forced her back into the singularity of her own life, imprisoned her in her own strangeness.

"You don't mind paying your own way?" he asked her.

"Oh, no . . ."

"I worry all the time I'm going to blow my fare to New York. I knew a guy did that. He gave himself a big party before he left here and when he woke up a day later, he'd spent his ticket. Listen, you know you could report that man to the police, the one that beats the dog."

"I'd be afraid to do that," she said. She put her cigarettes back in her purse, and catching sight of the card of perfume vials, felt a brief flicker of concern for Johnnie. But maybe he'd be able to go back to his own place tonight—she couldn't always be available to Johnnie either, could she?

"Well, why did you come out here?" Jake was asking her.

"There was a woman I met driving out. I was just hanging around in New York. She offered me a ride and I came along."

"I've never been east," he said. He opened the door of a small closet and took out a shiny jacket like a basketball player's. She thought of her own clothes hanging in that space. They wouldn't take up much room. And Walter's! She turned away toward the window, suddenly apprehensive, as though she'd glimpsed Walter himself looking out at her unforgivingly from the closet.

Across the way, she saw a heavy-set man wearing a thick brown sweater moving about hurriedly as he rearranged several chairs. As she watched, he suddenly threw up his hands and began to conduct as though an orchestra sat before him. A minute later, she heard the faint strains of music.

"He does that all night," observed Jake, standing next to her. "And he plays the same records over and over, classical stuff."

She glanced briefly at his jacket. It looked too big for him. "My brother's," he said.

"Do you know the man over there?"

"Oh, yeah. I spend the evening there once in a while. It's a real show. I'll take you there sometime. They let in anybody. I think they like people to watch them."

Just before they left the house, Annie spoke to Mrs. Corrigan, the limping woman who had directed her to Jake's room. "You can have the room, I guess," Mrs. Corrigan said. "Why not? They come and they go. There are nothing but wanderers in this town. . . ." She appeared to have sewn another stitch in her mouth. Annie could hardly hear her.

She suggested they go to the Greek's. The food was cheap and good. Over their coffee, she admitted to him that she was not quite eighteen. He laughed and called her San Quentin quail, and when she asked what that meant, explained it had something to do with taking underage girls across state lines.

"Carson Brody, that buddy of mine with the criminal mind, he comes from Boston, your part of the country. You'll have to meet him. He knows so much—I never knew anybody had so much information. You know why the movies are out here? Carson told me. It's because of the Mexican border being so close. Movies really started in New York, before the World War. The biggest outfits got special patents. But a lot of little companies couldn't afford them and made movies anyhow. So those little companies came out here and kept on making pictures, figuring they could get away to Mexico before they could be stopped with injunctions. Carson's always reading law books."

"He wants to be a lawyer?"

"Carson? He doesn't want to be anything. He's just waiting for a chance . . . he says you have to know everything, then people won't do you in. I don't see it quite the same way. You want to see a Jimmy Stewart movie? There's one a few blocks from here."

"I don't like him much, that lower lip of his . . ."

Jake laughed. "Listen, he's made a fortune out of that lower lip. Well, I'll take you to Ivan's. That place is as good as any picture. Since you told me your real age, I'll tell you that my name's really Jack. Carson told me to change it to Jake. He said I'd do better because people would think I was Jewish and there's so many Jews in the picture industry."

He put down his coffee cup with extreme care, then bent toward the table, his hands flying toward his belly. Alarmed, she reached out to him with her hand. He shook his head, his eyes closed, his mouth gripped with pain. "It's okay," he gasped. "All the cigarettes and coffee. I shouldn't go near coffee."

He straightened up, gave her a weak smile, and took a medicine bottle from his pocket; there was hardly anything in it. He poured out the few remaining drops of green liquid, swallowed it quickly, then sank back into the chair. "I'm supposed to eat baby food and take phenobarbital. But that chewed-up stuff makes me gag and the phenos make me blue."

"But what is it?"

"I've had it for years. Colitis . . . my colon goes into spasm. It hurts, but it passes. See, it's going away already. You know, they looked at my gut once through a fluoroscope. I digest five times faster than a normal person. If it showed, I could go on tour. Come on, it'll help me to walk. A man on a bus told me the trick was to walk, brings the blood to where— Oh, hell! I don't know."

Annie was looking at his roughened hands, one of which still grasped the medicine bottle. He caught her thought. "I know I look as if I were going to keel over any minute, but I was a good hand." He stuck the bottle in his pocket. "I worked for my father on the farm all the time I was going to high school. I was up at 5:00 A.M., you bet, working like a fool."

"I'm going to work tomorrow," she said. "I got my first job."

"Yeah?"

"In L.A. It's a dress shop. I'm called a stock girl."

"What's the pay?"

She hesitated. But, she realized, she didn't have to lie to him. "Eleven dollars a week," she said.

"That's pretty skinny pay," he said, shaking his head. "That's one thing I'll give Max. It's a crime the way people get paid. I mean, you get eleven dollars a week, and St. Vincent gets ten thousand bucks for a script—"

"But I don't really know how to do anything," she said.

"Listen, you could make a lot more, waiting on tables or in a drive-in. The picture people give big tips. Or you could model—if you have any clothes. Have you? I guess not. Well, that's not such a hot idea. These model agencies, some of them are no better than —" he paused, leaving the sentence unfinished.

He hadn't wanted to offend her, and she thought of Samuel and Johnnie, of Walter and her own father, who did not spare her. Jake was really innocent.

"You mean, they get girls for men?" she asked softly.

"Yes. And for women too." They looked at each other seriously. Suddenly, he flushed. "Let's go now and see what Ivan's up to." In the end, he'd paid for both their suppers, saying it didn't matter, he'd manage the fare east, and anybody who was working for eleven bucks a week shouldn't be made to pay their own way . . . think what Max Shore would say if he, Jake, exploited the working classes. "The pro-le-tar-iat!" he intoned.

They walked back to Sycamore Street. It was almost as if they were walking home together from school, she thought, recalling her brief sojourn in the Nyack high-school sophomore class where she had successfully conjugated Latin verbs and flunked math.

At Ivan's, they were at once plunged into the particularities of mad existences. Only a few minutes after Ivan had waved them to a wooden bench, his roommate, the Sheriff, arrived, carrying a large burlap sack which he emptied on the floor in front of them.

85

Out of it fell alarm clocks, trusses, capsules, lipsticks, blue bottles of Milk of Magnesia, cigars, a hot-water bottle, an enema bag, bars of candy, bottles of castor oil, tins of Ex-Lax, and a Mickey Mouse doll.

"Get the Beast down," commanded Ivan. "This will interest him."

The Sheriff flung off his cowboy hat. "It's sickening!" he cried in an outraged tenor voice.

"You see!" Ivan exclaimed. "He has no respect for his work. How the hell did you get out of the place with that sack, Sheriff? You're branching out, I see. God! You'll be showing up with the contents of the whole Owl drugstore next week, then the entire chain of them, then Los Angeles, then California itself, goddamnit! Now everybody shut up! I'm going to play Number 39 in E Flat. You like Mozart, girl? What's your name?"

Annie nodded silently, watching Ivan's tic. It was a kind of folding of the upper cheek against the bottom lid of his eye and it seemed to be having a separate conversation with her. "Annie," she said almost inaudibly.

The Sheriff opened a can of beets with a pocket knife and began to spear them, chewing them morosely, one by one.

"I said," Ivan cried irritably, "to go and get the Beast. He'll want to pick over the night's haul, and I enjoy that. You shock him silly."

"Nothing shocks him," replied the Sheriff, his mouth bleeding with beet juice. "That's just another of your fairy tales."

Ivan shrugged. He picked up the record carefully, wiping it with a shirttail. " 'In the country of the blind, the one-eyed man is King,' " he chanted ponderously. "Annie, you're just a sweet young girl. You can't imagine what a sordid hole this place is. The landlady is an old sot, gin bottles under her bed, with all the English airs she puts on to make me feel low-class."

"She *is* English," observed the Sheriff.

"He," Ivan said, pointing an accusing finger at the Sheriff, "torments her. He told her there'd been a landslide in Iceland—her son is stationed there, in the army—and that the entire population had been wiped out. Sadist!" He roared with laughter, his tic accelerating so it seemed about to consume his eye. Abruptly, the wild shouts ceased. Ivan glared at the Sheriff. "She was so drunk today, she couldn't have taken a phone message. God! What if someone had called me? You

86

may well be responsible for my having lost a stupendous assignment, you bastard!" He turned his attention to Annie. "This is a house of freaks," he said. "There's a giant who lives in the next room. He has a seven-foot-long bed. Once a week, he brings home several Filipinos, and the ensuing racket drives me mad!"

"Don't discuss that," said the Sheriff angrily. He kicked away the empty beet can and lay down on a narrow cot. "It's very nasty."

"And this maniac lying there works in the Owl drugstore and steals them blind once a week and leaves this trash around for me to take care of. He doesn't even fence it. How the hell *could* you fence Ex-Lax? Why don't you steal something useful, you insane creature!"

The Sheriff closed his eyes.

"Now we will listen," Ivan said quietly. He wound up the phonograph but no sooner had the music begun than he pulled up the arm, staring at it with an expression of hopeless rage. "Why don't you swipe some new needles for me, you fool!" he shouted in the Sheriff's direction. "It's the only pleasure of my life! Look at that novel!" He waved at the pages of manuscript piled up around the corners of the room. "It's over two thousand pages long—for sheer length, I should be given an award. By now, the first pages have already turned yellow. I might as well be dead and buried. Annie, are you in pictures?"

"No."

"That's a good girl. I'll tell you a story. You tell her, Sheriff, about Cusimano."

"Why is he called Sheriff?" Annie whispered to Jake. "I never found out," he whispered back.

The Sheriff began to speak tonelessly, his eyes closed.

"Cusimano had a clean little barbershop in Chicago. One day he read in a magazine that Sam Wood was making the life of Rudolph Valentino. He sold his shop, gave most of the proceeds to his wife, bought himself a pin-striped suit, and came west to Hollywood. By a miserable stroke of bad luck, he ended up in this very house. He was fat and fifty. Ivan found out soon enough that this idiot had it in his mind to play the leading role, Valentino himself. Ivan suggested to him that in Hollywood you don't merely arrive and announce your intention—no, you have to do something splendid, extraordinary, to attract notice. The poor dumb sonuvabitch listened to Ivan like it was Moses talking. Ivan said Cusimano would have to get a horse, dress up like a sheik, and ride out to the studio at five o'clock in the morning—"

An enormous man wearing nothing but shiny black trousers and felt slippers marched into the room, kissed Ivan on the cheek and, groaning with the effort, lowered himself to the floor. "Ah, God! It's been a black day!" he said.

"Shut up!" exclaimed Ivan.

"Pinochle?" asked the man plaintively.

"So Ivan," the Sheriff resumed, "undertook to provide Cusimano with horse and costume. On the morning agreed upon, Ivan arrived here with a horse he had stolen from a milkman. Ivan knows nothing about horses, fears them in fact, but he was so intent on destroying Cusimano that he was able to undo the animal's traces and lead it by its reins—"

"Oh, Christ!" exploded the fat man. "I've heard that goddamned story a thousand times. Who's that girl?"

"Almost up the stairs and into the room," continued the Sheriff imperturbably. "Ivan had already stolen a few dollars from the landlady's cookie box while she was out cold on the kitchen floor, and with it he had purchased several lengths of white cloth and a yard or so of green braid. Ivan, aided by myself, dressed Cusimano and escorted him to his steed, which was trying to lie down on the sidewalk."

"That horse wasn't in such bad shape," observed Ivan mildly.

"The horse looked abnormal, like a camel with an inverted hump. That horse was abnormal like Ivan and the Beast—"

"Don't call me abnormal, you *gonif!*" shouted the Beast, scratching the black curling hair of his chest.

"But Cusimano was so unhinged by the thought of the glory that lay ahead, he didn't notice the animal's condition. At the very last minute, after he was astride the horse, I saw that he was wearing Al Capone shoes, black, so we removed them—"

"Wait!" cried Ivan, darting to a closet from which he took, handing them to Annie, a pair of tiny black pointed shoes.

"We gave the horse a kick or two. We were only an hour over schedule. It was six in the morning."

"I may get a six-week go at Warner's," said the Beast. "They've been kicking around an Ambrose Bierce story for months, and Larry Green said he might give me a crack at it."

Ivan looked at him scornfully.

"I'm not making this up," said the Beast. "Seventy-five dollars a week."

"I'll believe you when I see the money," Ivan said.

"What happened to Cusimano?" Annie asked. Jake was laughing under his breath.

"How the hell do I know?" asked Ivan in an offended tone. "He never came back here."

"The loony bin," said the Sheriff grimly. "What else was there?"

"That's a terrible story," Annie said distinctly to the room at large.

"Annie darling!" Ivan protested. "It's just what he deserved. That dumb wop! Why should he have gotten away with his delusions—any more than the rest of us do?" He handed the Beast a ratty pack of cards, and sitting down on the floor with him, said, "Deal, stupid!" The Sheriff appeared to have lapsed into a coma.

"I'd better go," Annie said to Jake. "I haven't got an alarm clock and it'll be luck if I wake up on time."

The Sheriff suddenly rose and, leaning over his loot, picked out a large plain-faced clock, handing it to her, a look of irritation on his face. "Don't thank me," he said hastily. "It's stolen. Bad luck."

Annie stood up. "Don't go, darling girl," said Ivan, looking intently at his cards. "Your presence improves the atmosphere."

"Good night, Ivan," said Jake. "Thanks."

"Sorry not to have been able to offer you anything," Ivan said, without looking up from the game. "But we're broke right now. Next week the Beast will bring us delicious things to eat and drink, won't you, you lying bastard?"

"Gimme three cards," said the Beast.

"But what are they?" Annie asked later as she and Jake stood on Hollywood Boulevard waiting for the streetcar which would take her home.

"Writers," said Jake.

"Writers!" She thought of James St. Vincent. "For what?"

"Ivan says he used to work for MGM. The Beast too. But I think the Sheriff is from the moon."

"They're so rough with each other," she said.

"Let's walk a ways," he said. "I don't see anything coming."

They set off, passing Grauman's Chinese Theater, empty shops, a few dimly lit bars. A dull thud accompanied their steps. "Damn!" exclaimed Jake, hopping on one foot. The sole on the other shoe hung from the heel like a cow's tongue. "I had it fixed just a few weeks ago." He started to laugh. "Look at that big ugly clock you're carrying. We are a pair! Here. Let me wind it. Guess what time it is?"

They were just passing in front of a jewelry store. Inside, a wall clock was striking midnight. The sound of the chime came delicately through the glass.

"At least, it doesn't snow here," he said. "It must be awful to have nothing in a cold climate."

"It's awful to have nothing anywhere," she said.

They both heard the rumble and clank of an approaching streetcar. He said, "Let's have supper tomorrow?"

"Okay."

"At the Greek's, around seven?"

She waved at him from the car window. There was only one other passenger sitting in the rear. She took a seat in the middle of the car. A minute or so later, she heard movement behind her. The man had moved up to take the seat directly back of hers. She kept her head stiffly forward until just before her stop when she glanced out the window.

Beyond the sidewalk, she saw the dark apartment house. A flicker of white was reflected for an instant in the trolley window. She heard the rustle of a newspaper, and, caught between reluctance and curiosity, she darted a look at the other passenger. He was old; his eyes were half closed; in one hand he held up a furled newspaper revealing for her his naked genitals resting on his lap like a newborn cluster of hairless animals.

Johnnie Bliss was not waiting for her tonight. She was relieved. She'd had enough talk for the day. The bed dropped down with its hideous squawk. She listened tensely for a moment, her head against the wall, but there was no groan, no whimper from the room next door.

The people she'd met the last forty-eight hours were like beads from a broken string, rolling senselessly all over Southern California. Except for Walter, whom did she know who *had* purpose? She shuddered at the thought that she too might roll away into some corner and die, grow crazed like Ivan, grow old in a room like this, become a witch like the crone down the corridor and frighten some young girl not yet even born.

She had liked Jim St. Vincent and Jake, and especially Max Shore, even Ivan. But Walter might save her. She did not, she whispered to herself, like Walter much.

Chapter 7

Whatever notion Annie might have had about becoming a regular wage earner, she was by the end of her first day in the dress shop so disheartened that she wondered where she had gotten the idea that working for a living would give her a sense of legitimacy, the appearance, at least, of being like everyone else. She had wanted to break out of that precarious and anarchic life in which only chance ruled.

Still, to live, one had to eat.

By late afternoon, it struck her that anyone with an ounce of sense would never have agreed to confinement in a basement for nearly nine hours each day in order to collect eleven dollars at the end of a week.

The stock she was supposed to organize rose in pyramids of flimsy boxes. Beyond the few feet lit by a weak bulb, the vast basement was dark. Water dripped constantly in the farther reaches of the darkness. She heard rats. Once stepping outside the circle of sickly yellow light, she ran into a cardboard herd of monstrous deer propped up against a wall. Around their necks hung pine wreaths which disintegrated at her touch.

At midday, a voice shouted to her from above that she should go and get her lunch. She went to a lunchroom a block or so away and ate an egg-salad sandwich, blinking a little in the white dusty light that all but obscured the sky. People looked whey-faced. She passed through a Japanese section on the way back to the store. The toys and cups and fabrics in the display windows emitted a special cheap brightness; in the depths of these shops, small figures moved like silhouettes. In the morning, she had overheard the store manager say to a clerk, "They ought to send all those Japs back to Tokyo." Walter had once described to her how Japanese soldiers were trained in the use of bayonets—they kept them away from women for months, "to harden them," he'd said, and they used live Chinese prisoners for spearing. He'd shown her a photograph—soldiers bundled up like children about to go out and play in the snow, plunging their bayonets in bound prisoners at the bottom of a ditch. A bleaching substance appeared to have affected the sunlight; the color of things ran together, turning the streets gray. All of Los Angeles was a basement.

In the last hour of the day, the manager summoned her upstairs. "Go help Miss Gluck," he said. Miss Gluck, a middle-aged woman wearing an enormous pompadour of jet-black hair, twitched and shook and mumbled as she snatched dresses from the long metal bars on which they hung and pushed them brutally into the hands of old Negro women or Mexican girls or very fat white women looking for odd-size dresses.

"They don't wash," Miss Gluck whispered harshly to Annie as she stuffed dresses into paper bags. "They sweat like pigs—they can't speak God's language. One day, they'll rise up and destroy us . . . there'll be nothing left in God's world. Close your pocketbook! Close it! Don't ever leave it lying about like that! They're so dumb. Imagine buying this *shit*. I wouldn't buy this *shit* if I had to go stark naked up the Angel Flight Stairs. Here comes Aunt Jemima with an evil look in her eye! She's a thief. That old nigger lady'd steal your teeth. Watch her!"

Miss Gluck's own odor was suffocating, stale apricots and ammonia with an overlay of musky perfume.

The day ended; the clerks rushed out into the dusk. Tomorrow it would begin again.

Annie arrived at the Greek's a few minutes before Jake. The restaurant was full. A number of men leaned on the bar watching a girl in high heels play the ski-ball machine. The Greek moved lightly about the room, a soiled white cloth tied around his enormous belly. Two waitresses with ferret faces and dyed yellow hair carried plates ranged along their arms and slammed them down before their customers.

Jake looked eager and happy as though he'd had good news. He slid into the chair across from her. "How's the working girl?" he asked and grabbed her hand and pressed it. He was very sweet, fresh as clover, yet his question angered her. She couldn't bring herself to answer him. Instead, she read the food-spotted menu. "Hey?" he asked.

"It was terrible," she said. "I spent the whole day, nearly, in a cellar that must run under the whole town. These poor people buy dresses for a dollar ninety-nine. If you washed them, they'd melt. The store has going-out-of-business sales, but they're never going to go out of business, not from what I saw in the basement. I took twenty-five minutes for lunch and you're only supposed to have fifteen. When I came back the manager asked me if I thought I was doing them a favor, 'lending your presence to our little emporium,' he said, and didn't I know the Depression wasn't over, and how many places would hire someone he doubted even knew the name of the capital of the state. I'm supposed to have the stock organized in a week. After that, I expect, they'll kill me. The last stock girl, somebody told me, stole four dresses and wore them all out of the store. She must have been in a bad way—to steal that stuff."

"Well, stay there a few weeks. You can get another job, you know."

She hadn't even thought of that.

"It's always easier to get a job when you have one, I don't know why."

"I don't know why I think I can never get out of things," she said, defeatedly. "There's something so dumb about it. You're right. I'll find another job." Her spirits rose. The Greek's seemed a cheerful place to be.

"Well, I got that job," he said. "You must bring me luck. It's nothing much, but it's something. Maybe some big director will spot me behind all the midgets. Listen, why don't you get that writer friend of yours to help you get a screen test?"

"Not me."

"Okay," said one of the waitresses impatiently. "Let's have it. You want the special, shrimp cocktail and steak?"

"Could I have a sandwich?" Annie asked, smiling placatingly up at the girl.

"Looka the menu," she said.

"Have a real dinner," Jake offered. "I've got money."

"No, I'll just have a ham sandwich and coffee." She felt nervously along the bottom of her pocketbook. There were a number of coins among the tobacco shreds. She wouldn't be paid for two weeks, the manager had told her. Probationary period.

"Look!" she exclaimed. "There's a red-headed man I saw here before. I think he just comes here to play a special record. He looks rich, doesn't he? I wonder why he comes to a place like this? He's drunk, don't you think?"

The red-headed man was peering into the jukebox. He shoved in a nickel, then looked truculently around the room. Quite suddenly, as though she'd called him, he made straight for Annie. He swayed above her, ignoring Jake.

"You like Sibelius?" he asked in a husky, slightly accented voice. Before she could answer, he hit the table with his fist. "Greatest damn living composer!" The Greek was there in an instant. He led the man to the counter and placed a cup of coffee in front of him. The man pushed it away and rested his head on his arms. The Greek smiled triumphantly at Annie.

She laughed at the expression on Jake's face. "That's always happening to me," she said. "If there's a drunk within a mile, or a crazy person, they head straight for me."

"I saw Max last night. He asked me if you'd called. It's funny how people meet, isn't it?"

"Max?"

Then she remembered. She grew ill at ease. Had they talked about her?

"He asked about the man and the dog."

"The man and the dog!" she cried. "I forgot to tell you. When I got home tonight, before I came to meet you, the police were there. The man started howling in the middle of the afternoon, and I guess the other people got scared. They took him away."

"And the dog?"

The waitress placed their orders on the table. Jake took out his medicine bottle and swallowed a few drops.

"The dog . . . I don't know about it. Maybe the old woman was right and there wasn't a dog. . . . That's not true. I heard it whimpering. People can bark but they can't make that hurt sound. I hate to think about the dog."

"Did you see the man?"

"No, no . . . I closed my door. I didn't want to look at him."

"Listen. Do you have any dresses? You look like you're dying in that suit."

"I've got a dress," she said.

He looked so sorry for her, she laughed. "Maybe I'll get a discount on some of those numbers in the store," she said.

They stayed a long time at the Greek's, long after the diners had left, after the red-headed man had been led to the door by one of the waitresses, until there was only a solitary drinker at the bar talking quietly with the Greek, who was picking his teeth thoughtfully, one huge hand grasping a glass of beer.

Jake was telling her about himself. At first she listened without much interest, content to observe him as though he were a pleasing landscape, noting the small shifts of his body, the expressions which gave unexpected life to his face. Then, as she nodded sympathetically at the somewhat halting narrative, she realized its ordinariness, full of a triviality of event inconsonant with the intensity of his voice.

She felt a thrill of anticipation, of fear too, at the thought of what he'd say if she told him a few things about herself. He probably imagined she came from some Sears, Roebuck life like his. There'd be disbelief, indignation perhaps. He might even dare to pity her! At the very idea of such a thing, she glared at him scornfully!

But how could he have noticed when there were tears in his eyes? He was speaking about a girl named Wendy.

Wendy! From some half-remembered conversation among forgotten adults, Annie dredged up the memory of a voice, her father's?—someone's—saying that certain names were a dead giveaway of low-class origins—names like Wendy, April, Dawn.

And Jake was crying! Over a *Wendy*. Annie's sense of possessing a personal saga of dramatic superiority collapsed.

The girl had married his best friend a month after high-school graduation. She'd met him down near the spring where the cows drank, given him back his high-school ring. That's really why he'd left and come to California, and he'd been out here for years, but, "I'm still not over it. I still think about her and how she could ever have done that to me."

She felt her heart would stop with envy. She coveted that girl's life, wanted to be that girl, already a mother with two children, living in a small town with a husband who had his own second-hand car, and a little house, and Sunday dinners with—

"Hey, what's the matter with you?"

"What?"

"You're scowling so!"

"No, no. I'm fine, just listening to you—" Why, her life had been shameful! She might as well tell Jake the story of the man on the streetcar who had exposed himself!

"Would you like to go see Ivan?" he asked in a subdued voice. He looked at her worriedly.

"No, not now," she said. And then, her voice cracking with dismay, she cried, "I'm a freak myself!" He turned pale and looked hurriedly around the restaurant. She took his hand instantly. "It's all right," she said. "It's only the job, the dog, everything . . ."

The Greek was standing next to their table.

"Come on, kids. I gotta close up now."

Later, as they walked up Cahuenga, she asked him why he wanted to be an actor.

"Oh, the money, I guess . . . I always liked movies. I'm a good dancer, you know. And I didn't want to be stuck in a small town all my life."

She glanced at his face. He wouldn't make it. She didn't know why she knew, but she did. His *being* was too plain; it was his virtue, his limitation. They stopped in front of a shoe store.

"Look at those red shoes," she said. "Aren't they pretty!"

He put his arm around her and his soft hair fell against her cheek as he ducked to kiss her. "I'll get them for you," he murmured. She pulled away from him violently. "What's the matter?" She looked at the few people walking down the street. He saw the direction of her glance. "They're not thinking about us," he said. Then, "Come back with me, to my place."

She was silent.

"Come back," he repeated softly.

She looked at the red shoes. "But what did it *feel* like to be you?" she burst out. "Oh, I've looked in windows, I have seen people sitting around a table together, but what's really going on? You've told me about basketball games and cows and Sunday dinners and cold winters. Cows! And a graduation ring! And you just decided to be an actor, just decided to come to Hollywood! How does that happen? How do you decide? What does it mean? And you got drunk with your brother and drove the truck into a ditch. What did you feel about it? And your mother made you that blanket and you had a teacher you liked. What it's *like* to be you!"

He retreated into the recessed entrance of the shoe store from where he stared out at her in astonishment as though she were about to assault him. A man passed them and looked questioningly at her.

"Oh, I'm sorry," she said humbly. "Come back, come out of there . . ."

He took a few cautious steps. She smiled. He laughed nervously. "You didn't do anything to be sorry about," he said.

They walked on. "You must have felt I'd left out something," he said finally. "I did. I stole a car and spent six months in jail. I don't know why I did it. I was just eighteen. There it was, parked in front of the movie house. Sometimes I worked there at night, changing the posters, you know, behind the display glass, and ushering. The key was in the car. I drove it out of town past the Burma-Shave signs, and when I got to the last one, a state trooper was waiting for me. I knew him, we all did, the kids always do in a small town like that. They went easy on me. I could have got a lot more time. My father cried. I won't be in the army, even if there's a war, because of the record, a criminal record." He was silent for a while. "It wasn't criminal though. It was an impulse. I didn't *want* the car. It was just there! And I felt like breaking out . . ."

He gripped her arm. "You were so smart to know I'd been hiding that." She said nothing. She didn't know how to explain that what she'd wanted from him was not his secret. Could no one ever tell her what it was like to be himself?

She held his hand on the way back to the room on Sycamore Street. He didn't turn on the light. For a while, they smoked and watched Ivan's window.

The Beast, wearing a dark suit, was drinking from a jug of wine, and Ivan was fiddling with his phonograph. A murmur of sound crossed the few yards separating the two windows. It was a quiet night in the freak house. Jake held her arms and hands when they weren't smoking. It seemed uncanny to sit there and watch that room.

Finally, Jake stood up and led her to his bed. He placed the afghan carefully in a chair, then undressed himself. She took off the hateful suit and removed her underwear. She was frightened because there could be no backing out. From that moment when he'd emerged so uncertainly from the shoe-store entrance, she had marked herself for this.

It hurt her in a way she had not expected; it was such personal secret pain. And she was dazed at the suddenness with which it happened and then was over. Jake was brief and light and nearly silent—she listened to his heavy breathing thinking of Walter's mad howls that had always filled her with embarrassment even though things had never gone this far between them.

The silence was total; the man lying next to her, so slender, so silken-skinned, seemed now a manifestation of the darkness, something she'd imagined. Then he spoke, his mouth against her ear. "You were new," he said, whispering. "I didn't know that." There was a touch of pride in his voice. She suddenly felt angry, angry in the same way she had been with Walter when he'd said he hated virgins. Jake was making some claim on her. She wouldn't allow it.

"I should have used something, I guess," he said. She couldn't worry about that—how could they have made a baby when she lay there like the dead.

He went all the way home with her. The light was beginning to break over the hills, a light the color of water in a tin pail. "I'll come and get you from work tomorrow," he said. He kissed her before she went in. She liked that, his light boy's kiss.

Underneath a door was a telegram from Walter that announced his arrival for the following Sunday. She looked at the Sheriff's alarm clock, two hours left for sleep.

Lying awake in her bed, knowing she wouldn't sleep at all, she thought of Walter. She thought of her father, laughing and on his hands and knees in front of a fat woman in some Village bar he'd taken her to once. She thought of the high-school teacher from Summit, his awful kisses. She thought of Jake.

Her job was terrible; she'd never get Jake's room now. But she'd done one thing for Walter. She'd removed the condition he'd objected to. Then, wanting to cry out with shame, she said aloud, "Jake did it. I got him to do it. . . ."

Chapter 8

On the second day of her job, Annie asked the manager for a stronger bulb for the basement. He said, she could see the boxes, couldn't she? Well, then, enough is a sufficiency; there hadn't been any complaints before—maybe her eyes were at fault.

She imagined that after a few weeks in that basement, you would lose the heart to complain. The day was no better except that Miss Gluck, with rather insidious smiles, seemed to suggest they were allies against the poor women who searched so dejectedly through the racks of sleazy dresses.

Beneath the weak yellow light, she made lists of stock, tossed away into the darkness damp boxes covered with mold, and whenever the manager shouted down to her, carried up the articles he demanded, emerging into the store with a pile of boxes in her hands, half blinded by the bright lights. Like a mole, she began to prefer to be underground. She suspected that the manager and his salesladies were afraid to descend the long flight of stairs leading into her dungeon. She felt malicious and triumphant and made a point of telling Miss Gluck about the rats, concealing a mean smile when she saw the woman's thick throat pulsate with disgust. She went back downstairs, thinking the basement was the only fit place for a nature as cruel as her own.

All day she'd been troubled by a vague physical discomfort;

perhaps she was about to menstruate. Uncle Greg had taken her off to a doctor when she was thirteen. He'd shown her a drawing of a naked woman pasted on a piece of thick cardboard. She would see that woman forever—she'd had no face. Numbered arrows pointed to various parts of the woman's body. The doctor, looking at her sternly, had read aloud the explanatory legends which had matched the numbers. But she'd known all *that* for years. One of the girls in school had carried around a sanitary napkin in a business envelope with her father's address printed on the back. Her classmates had all touched it in the girls' lavatory, giggling and shuddering. She remembered how she'd angered them, saying, "It's all boring. . . ." But she hadn't meant to be superior—she didn't know what she'd meant. When she was very small, her father and Bea had taken her with them to a movie. It had been *The Squaw Man*. She wondered to this day what there had been in the movie that had made her ask Bea, as they walked out of the movie house, "How are babies made?" Bea had answered in a voice of glacial rage, "Sexual intercourse!" What had James St. Vincent said about Bea? She hated helplessness. Sex made people helpless.

The store was closing for the day; Miss Gluck was gathering up her parcels, her cardigan sweater, her purse; the salesladies went home; the manager smoked a cigarette. Annie saw Jake across the street, waiting for her.

She waved at him timidly. His arms went up in a gesture of welcome. If he knew how she'd used him! She moved nervously out of range as she approached him, fearing he would embrace her. "Wait . . ." she said. He took her arm and led her into the entrance of an office building. There, he kissed her cheeks, pulled at her braids, and draped his thin arms around her shoulders. "I'll burn down that place for you," he said.

Tonight, the Greek recognized them and took them to a table himself. After dinner, they went directly to Jake's room. He'd bought a flower for her, a gardenia, lying in a wrinkle of white tissue paper. Its aroma filled the room.

"I've told my buddy, Carson, about you, and he wants to meet you. He's decided to be a stunt man—they make lots of money— and he wants us to get a place together, maybe rent a little house. I'm going to stay. Did you hear me, Annie? I mean, things are looking up, aren't they? Do you want me to stay, Annie? If Carson and I get a little house, it would be nicer for us than this

100

room, wouldn't it? I had another idea for you, The May Company. It's the biggest department store out here. They'll give you decent wages."

Annie saw the future—herself returning to the "little house" where Carson, the stunt man, and Jake, the dancer, waited. Like the Sheriff, she would return with a burlap bag full of stolen objects. Soon, they would both begin to call her the Sheriff, too. She looked down at her shabby shoes, the heels so worn on the outside that it was a strain to stand upright.

"My father told me there were hotel rooms that cost five hundred dollars a week," she said.

Jake frowned. "What?"

"Just that."

"Saturday, we can go to the beach."

"Every Saturday? You and me and Carson?"

"I mean, this Saturday." The frown gave way to bewilderment. "What's the matter?"

"Sorry," she said coolly, smiling. Uncertainly, he smiled back. "How's your colitis?"

"Okay," he said, subdued.

"When does your picture start?"

"My picture?" He walked to the window. "It's only a few days' work."

"Are those little houses you were talking about furnished?"

"I don't know."

She pitied him as she might have pitied an animal being baited, a little less, perhaps. He could stop her if he only knew it. She looked at the waxy petals of the gardenia. What was that? A celebration of *sexual intercourse?* That loss of grace, that sprawl of limbs, that revelation that only the outside of life was dry and imperishable but that the inside was all wetness and blood and the perishable and perilous beat of pulses?

Frightened by the tumult of anger that raged within her, she began to pace about the room.

There was a noisy thud, her ankles were gripped and she fell to the hard floor. Jake had tackled her; he lay on the floor at the end of her own length, his hands still holding her ankles. They were both gasping, the wind knocked out of them. Jake began to climb her as if she'd been a rope, hand over hand, keeping her immobilized, until his face was only a few inches from hers.

"Annie, Annie . . ." he said.

101

She clenched a fist.

"You're crying."

"I'm not," she cried.

He helped her up and led her to the gardenia. "Now smell that," he said, and pushed it in her face. "Smell it good!"

Later, he showed her a contraceptive. "That's the ugliest thing I ever saw," she said. "It looks like something old dwarfs make in a cellar."

He wanted her to stay the night and go to work in the morning from Sycamore Street. But she couldn't, she said. He took her home on the streetcar. From its windows, she spotted Johnnie's parked car. Hurriedly, she began to tell Jake about him. He listened without comment. "He's helped me so much, shared his food with me. When I haven't had anyone to talk to . . ."

"Where does he sleep when he stays over?" Jake asked.

"On the floor . . . he gets into trouble and can't go back to his room."

"Those people are always in trouble," he said.

"So is everybody!" she cried. "It's not the same," he said as he followed her over to the car. Johnnie was sitting up in the front seat, squinting at a newspaper in the light of a street lamp. He looked up as they approached, his eyes on Jake.

She introduced them quickly, then grabbed Jake's arm and led him away toward the streetcar stop, aware that Johnnie was watching them intently. She felt everything was about to be revealed, all her secrets, all her lies. She wished Jake gone forever.

"I'd better go back," she said pleadingly. "I haven't seen him for a while and I owe it to him. He's probably just going to stay an hour or so."

"I want you to come back with me," Jake said.

"Oh! I can't, Jake!" She was exasperated. "I'm too tired!"

He gave in with a shrug, then kissed her cheek. She turned away, frantic to be in her room, not caring what Jake thought. "Tomorrow?" he asked almost timidly. "Yes, yes . . ." she promised.

She looked back once. Jake stood there, looking down at the tracks, a tall lank figure, his head drooping.

"So that's what you've been up to," Johnnie said. "You bad thing . . . you certainly fooled old Johnnie."

"Oh, hush!" she said.

He continued hectoring her even as he took his accustomed

place on the bed. She hated the sour smell he gave off when he shifted from side to side. But she suffered from her own ingratitude. She sensed that she hadn't wanted Johnnie to see her with Jake; she didn't want to be painted with Johnnie's brush—sexual intercourse. For God's sake, how could she explain to him that she didn't see what all the noise was about? That what she loved was lying there with Jake, talking softly in the dark, their legs tangled, their faces close together, their hands clasped. It was such a comfort! What did Johnnie's awful stories about thin little men with enormous sex organs have to do with that?

The next evening, she met Carson Brody. He had an ugly hard-looking skull and narrow gray eyes. In his presence, Jake grew excited and expansive. Carson, at first, was silent, watchful. She felt the iron quality of his suspicion. He refused to speak to her directly, but his words seemed meant for her, sentences that uncoiled like snakes, about bitches and bastards, about stunt men who drove motorcycles off cliffs and bashed in their brains, about a certain bar where they kept a record of those men who'd survived three assignments without breaking a limb. But mostly he spoke of the bitches who "snowed" men, who took them for a ride, who wanted to "get laid," who betrayed men as naturally as they breathed. Jake was a baby, he said once, a rube who didn't know his ass from his elbow, but he, Carson, was there to see to his interests; Carson would never let him down. Jake glowed. Carson said he couldn't see how a nice American Arizona boy like Jake could get mixed up with a goddamned Communist like Max Shore.

"He's all right, Carson," Jake said. "You just take it easy there."

But Carson grew more venomous, like a spider that poisons itself; his outbursts grew louder; he flung out observations, warnings, threats like bottles, and they shattered haphazardly against the surface of a world he judged to be without hope of redemption. Now, it was Hollywood.

"All the pansies in the U.S. of A. come here and get themselves little nests and drag these boys off the street and corrupt them . . . they wanta be actors so they can show their asses to the world under the hot lights, rubbing up against women like they like it when all the time they got their eyes glued to some poor little hick who's running errands for the director . . . you notice how their eyes look when they're supposed to be mooning over some actress? I've studied them, studied them. They're thinking of all these lost little boys that come out here for fortune and fame, and not asses, like they do. And the women, they're all crazy because there's no men out here, just pansies and gypsies and fortunetellers and Communists . . ."

"Carson, cut it out," interrupted Jake amiably. "You're talking too rough."

Carson lifted his lip in what might have been a smile.

"We ought to get in that war," he said. "Purify the whole country, get them all in uniform, yes sir! No sir! Get their asses in those uniforms, they'd stop waggling them for sure."

His flat blunt fingers played with the brown fabric of his trousers where it tightened over his knees. His bullet head was aimed at her but his eyes rested on Jake. He sucked down half a bottle of beer.

"Were you born out here?" she asked.

"Boston," he said curtly.

"Why did you come to California?"

He didn't answer her at all. "Jake, what's doing with that movie. I bet there'll be some beautiful gash walking around half naked." He shot her a sudden glance.

Annie stood up. "I'd better go," she said to Jake. Brody's fury was swallowing all the oxygen in the room. She could hardly breathe.

"I thought we'd go out and get some coffee at the Greek's," Jake said uneasily.

"No. I've got some things to do," she said. She went to the door, seeing Carson out of the corner of her eye, slumped over the bed, fiddling with the afghan. Jake joined her at the door. "I'll go down with you," he said.

On the stairs, she said, "Oh, Jake, he's—"

"No, wait!" He put a finger on her lips. "He really worries about me. He's had the saddest life I ever heard about. His father died and left his mother and nine children. She had to put six of them in a foundling home."

They went out to the porch. A cat leaped from the shadows and ran into the house. "Listen," Jake said. "There was nothing to eat. I mean *nothing*. His mother had some withering disease, it just ate her up, day after day. He was one of the three kids that stayed with her, so he had to watch it happen. Her relatives were as bad off, and he saw how the priests didn't help her, and they would have starved to death if she hadn't got a job scrubbing floors in an insane asylum outside Boston, taking home garbage the patients wouldn't even eat. He ran away when he was just a little kid. He was always so big no one knew he was weak—because of that build. He got jobs, and for two years, he told me, he just ate, day and night. Then he worked for the CCC and wanted to send the thirty dollars a month back to his mother. But they couldn't find her."

"Boston's where St. Vincent comes from," Annie said. Jake continued, as though he hadn't heard her.

"She'd just gone up in smoke," he said. "He's never been able to track down a single member of his family, he's never had the money to really concentrate on it. I think it drives him crazy, all those people just disappearing, like a boat sinking, and you're the only survivor."

"But why was he so angry with me?"

They started down Sycamore Street.

Jake spoke seriously, as though he were really trying to think about it.

"It's not you. It's me. I'm the only real friend he's got. I met him back home. He was working in a place near the farm. My family was pretty nice to him. He thinks women are two kinds, bad and worse. The bad ones are old and can't do much to you. He knows all about the worse ones. He thinks I'm a pushover, you see, and that I'll get taken advantage of."

"Did you tell him about me?" she asked, a tremor in her voice.

"I tell him everything," Jake said. "It makes him feel good, like I trust him. It comforts him."

She was struck by the idea that Jake's confidences could provide that starved gray dog with comfort. For a moment she was silent. They were nearing the boulevard.

"Why does he talk so much about *pansies?*"

"He was nervous, he always is in front of strangers. I know he's hard to understand. But he can be really funny! He's got the damnedest schemes for making money. He can talk all night about money, how it can fix everything. Listen, don't go. I know you're only going because of Carson. Look, you go to the Greek's and wait for me. I'll go back and explain—"

"Explain what?"

"I'll tell him something. He'll get the idea. Please. Tomorrow is Sunday. Tonight, you could stay all night, couldn't you?"

105

Sunday.

Her life was blowing up. She didn't know whether to get on the streetcar that was even now lurching toward them, go to the Greek's, go back to her room and wait for the hour of Walter's arrival, go to May Landower's and beg for mercy, get out of California at once, hitchhike her way back east, or just stay with Jake. Yes, they'd get a little house together; Carson could drink beer in the living room and break glasses on the wall while she and Jake huddled in the bedroom. . . . She didn't know what she was doing with coins in her hand, where she was going.

"No!" she cried out.

"No, what?"

"Jake, I've *got* to go!"

But he held on to her and the streetcar passed. She looked at it hopelessly. "Annie, what is it?"

They walked back up Sycamore. "Are you sick? Is that it?"

She told him. She spoke quickly, her eyes on his feet; his footsteps began to drag; she observed, remotely, that he'd had his shoe resoled. Then she stopped talking. She looked up at him. His face ashen, his eyes rimmed in red. "Wait—" she begged.

"You've been waiting for *him* all this week, then," he said in a lifeless voice. "You've just used me."

Her legs were weak. Did he know *how* she'd used him?

"I didn't mean to," she said. She wanted to explain to him that she was caught. But she didn't understand that herself, the *how* of it. Most of all, she wanted to do something, say something that would change his expression.

"My life's been a mess," she said, her eyes on his face, willing him to listen. "Not like Carson's. Just a mess. I don't know anything. I don't even know how to wash my teeth the right way. It's as if, every day, I start all over again, like an ignorant baby. This man, Walter, well, he's a little like Max Shore. I mean, he can teach me." Jake turned his head away, looked up at the houses, the trees, the empty street. What was it some man had said to her once? "I'd like to take you in hand," he'd said, grinning.

"I need to be taken in hand," she said wretchedly.

"You're afraid of that man," Jake said. She began to deny it. Out of Ivan's house, a giant suddenly appeared carrying a stuffed pillowcase. She and Jake went back a few steps. The giant had a chin like a ledge.

"Santa Claus," Jake whispered. Annie laughed weakly. "Maybe

106

he's gone into business with the Sheriff," she said. Jake placed a hand on her arm.

"You don't mean it. Stay with me. You looked sick when you were talking about Vogel. My God! He's twelve years older than you!"

For a long time, they argued back and forth passionately. Then she saw him glance up uneasily at the windows of the house, worrying about Carson Brody, she knew.

"He's a real son of a bitch, your old buddy," she exclaimed. "Where do you get off, telling me what to do? What's good for me? You sat there all evening with a silly grin on your face while he vomited on everything."

"He's loyal!" Jake cried. "You wouldn't know about that!"

"I'm going."

"Go!"

"Jake?"

"He was right. Carson was right!" he shouted and suddenly bolted, leaping up the steps to the porch, coughing and sobbing. She saw him flying toward the stairs. She listened for several minutes as if to catch the last echo of his weeping. The grief was about *her*. What was the matter with her that she should stand there listening, hoping to hear more! Stand there, touched by joy as though she were increased, made substantial by the grief she'd caused. Yet something neutral in her stood aside; neither she nor Jake had felt as much as they'd pretended. She ran past the freak house, down to Hollywood Boulevard.

On Saturday night, the small bars were full. People promenaded, stopping now and then to gaze into shopwindows. From the streetcar window, Annie caught glimpses of the clothes displayed, all so new, so unobtainable. With her job, there was no possibility of saving up enough to buy anything; there wasn't really enough to eat on. Her underwear was ragged, her shoes nearly gone.

At her stop, she looked for Johnnie's car. But it wasn't there. She dreaded being alone.

On impulse she telephoned James St. Vincent before she went up to her room. The woman who answered—Annie assumed it was one of the two who'd been at the dining table that evening— said curtly that Mr. St. Vincent was in Palm Springs for an indefinite stay.

Just after midnight, as Annie was trying to concentrate on

107

Man's Fate, Johnnie showed up, drunk and twirling his toupee. He was carrying a paper bag from which he first took six grapefruit, then a glass orange-juice squeezer. She watched him listlessly, grateful that he was there but too desolate to talk to him.

"Here I worry about you so! You've just deserted your poor old Johnnie." He hacked away at the grapefruit with a pocketknife until he'd managed to cut them into ragged sections. Then, grunting with effort, his toupee askew, he squeezed. He grabbed a glass and presented her with the results of his efforts, kicking away a rind near his foot.

"California!" she exclaimed.

"Shut up, Annie-Fannie. Drink it."

She drank it, then she told him about Carson Brody whose hatred had pursued her to this room and hour.

"There are thousands of boys like that—rough boys out to make a million, plotting how to do everybody in." Johnnie's voice was slurred only slightly; as he spoke he picked up the grapefruit rinds and dropped them back in the paper bag.

"It's something about the way we're all brought up—the way we grow up." He sighed and dropped the bag on a table and sank heavily into the chair. "Everybody wants to make a million. He'll marry some poor Mary, and get six children off her. He'll drink too much and consort with whores. My mother said we all go to God, and every Sunday for twelve years she shoved me into the family pew. Christ! The only joke she ever made in her life—that I heard—was when my daddy died of heart trouble in Chicago —he had a little meat-packing plant and after he left Mama, he married a woman half his age—well, my mother said, after she'd read the telegram, 'He got away scot-free!' My uncles were deacons in the church. The church was everything in our lives. But all the time I was holding the little Jesus-cards in my hand in Sunday school, I was thinking—get out! You got a cigarette?"

She handed him one. He lit it, saying, "Wait! Wait!" as he puffed. And she waited, seeing all those fathers running away.

"I had a French boy once," he was saying. "Claude. He came here to make it in pictures. But he was too beautiful. It made you sick, just to look at him. Well, he said to me, 'You're all so boring wiz your unhappy-happy. . . . Your pricks grow but your leetle minds stay in muzzer's lap. . . .' " Johnnie laughed and coughed. "You too, Annie? Thinking about your millions?"

"No, no . . ."

108

"What then? What are you after?"

"I don't know."

"Whatever it is, this is the place for it." He took off his jacket and untied his shoes. "I drank too much," he said, belching heavily. He lay down on his side of the bed. "Our last night, Queenie. I hate to think what's going to happen here in this bed tomorrow!" He made his Pola Negri love face and buried his head in the blanket.

In the morning, he was cold, distant, sarcastic. Perversely, she wanted to go with him when he left.

Walter arrived in the late afternoon, and Annie, nervous and pale—she'd not gone out for anything, eating a couple of oranges and a box of crackers—looked at him with a frozen face as he dropped his sea bag on the floor, the *thump* she'd been anticipating all week.

"Hello, baby," he said. She huddled against him, feeling the metal buttons of his work shirt pressing against her. His presence made the room shrink; he smelled of soap and machine oil.

"Is there anything to eat?" he asked, unbuttoning the shirt, pushing her away.

"I didn't go out. I was afraid you'd come."

"Later . . ."

Without his clothes, he seemed less massive. There was a thick lurid scar on his right thigh. Jake's thin bones had pressed against her under cover of darkness like the bones of an invalid child; she'd imagined his flesh to be faintly blue. Walter's chest and back were the color of light amber. As he lay down next to her, she wondered what he would feel upon discovering that that crucial, yet ridiculous, obstruction was gone. He might accuse her of having held out on him. She began to invent a story to herself, then gave it up and put her arms around him. He muttered into her neck that she would have to do something about a contraceptive.

His hands, his mouth, at last his sexual organ, invaded her; she could not control the stiffening of her limbs; she fled him even as she lay there so passively.

He was subdued as he had never been when he'd tried to make love to her before. She thought, as the sweat of his exertion covered her belly and thighs, that it would be possible to love him even for this, though that female response he'd had so much experience of, with which he'd taunted her so mercilessly, might be forever beyond her, she might learn to love the helpless animal hidden behind clothes and speech—if it was this humble and sightless and mute. But it wasn't mute! That wordless cry against her breast had tossed into life every human being, the old witch in the corridor, the mad German, the multitudes. As she felt him slide out and away from her, she wondered at the silence of the helpless animal in herself. Had she been born without it?

"You've been thinking," he whispered, "all the time." She looked at his reddened eyes. "Annie . . . sometimes you're a little homely."

She gasped with pain and turned away. He said nothing more. It grew late. She went down to the boulevard and walked until she found an open grocery store. When she returned, he was in his Levi's, shirtless, clean, handsome. He emptied the grocery bag. "Oh, Annie. Christ!"

She had bought little hot dogs in pastry.

"This isn't food!"

"I got what they had . . ."

"You should have gotten stuff like canned macaroni—" She burst into tears. She danced around the room, sobbing. She threw herself across the bed; she rolled to the floor. Wrapped in her grief, she heard remote sounds, footsteps, a strange little whistle.

She coughed. Her sobs stopped and she looked through her tangled hair at Walter. He was buttoning on his work shirt with intent concentration. Their glances met. He smiled.

She got up and went to the toilet where she blew her nose on the rough gray toilet paper. When she came out, Walter was making the bed.

"We'll eat now," he said.

Chapter 9

Annie emerged from the basement at the end of each day to the bright lights of the store, then out to the streetcar, which, rattling and shaking, bore her home to the apartment house. Walter was often waiting for her. Sometimes he was out and did not return until she was asleep. Although the job demanded little physical effort from her, the intense boredom, the isolation, exhausted her.

She met some of his friends, most of them from the Federal Theater days. Their living arrangements measured the degree of success they'd attained in movieland. One couple shared a huge shadowy house with a director and his wife out in the valley. What valley, Annie didn't know. The actor husband came to pick them up in a Chrysler touring car that had seen better days. It smelled pleasantly of leather and mint. Mitchel Lowe, the actor, said his wife had been growing mint and selling it to little markets around town. He drove the old car with great verve; he was happy, he'd just gotten his first substantial part in a movie. He teased Walter about his "shipping out." "Next, you'll be in a factory, Walt. A worker! A worker!"

Lowe was the oddest-looking man Annie had ever seen. He had a jester's face, a huge bony nose, eyebrows like small hedges that rose and fell as he talked. His eyes seemed amused by everything he said, as if they were the audience of his mobile face.

Walter was smiling, somewhat angrily, she thought. "Anyone who changes his name for the movies is hardly in a position to sneer at the revolutionary efforts of a man who's trying to rid himself of middle-class attitudes. For God's sake! Mitchel Lowe! The ultimate Gentile nothing name!"

Lowe grabbed Walter's knee and squeezed it. "Envy!" he shouted. "Wished it was you, don't you, Walt!"

They began to talk about movies, Walter saying that most of the new ones were ruined by Jewish sentimentality. Annie shrank back against the seat. But Lowe seemed indifferent, even amused. "You anti-Semite . . ." he said without rancor.

They rode up a driveway to a house similar in size and architectural hysteria to the ones Annie had seen in Arizona Canyon. Inside the vast living room, a middle-aged woman knitted by the light of a small lamp. A small, elegantly dressed man leaned on a grand piano while another paced up and down, fingering his chin thoughtfully. The room seemed to have very few lamps for its size.

Everyone greeted Walter familiarly. As Lowe was introducing Annie to the knitting woman, a girl walked heavily into the room and went up to Lowe.

"Murray—"

"Mitchel!" shouted the actor. "Lottie, please!"

"Whatever your name is—did you pick up the bread?"

"Forgot . . ." said Lowe, smiling warmly at Annie.

"We were speaking of Chaliapin," remarked the small man at the piano. "Play the 'Death and Farewell' again, will you, Natasha?"

The woman put down her knitting and went to a record player. The pacing man had halted in front of Annie and was staring down at her. He was tall, heavily built, with white hair and black eyebrows. In the dim light of the room, Annie could see how silken his skin was, how rosy his cheeks. "Who's this, Walter?" he asked with a trace of an accent.

"This is my Annie," said Walter.

Natasha glided back to her chair and picked up her knitting needles. "What a young one, Walter," she said.

"Please," said the Chaliapin lover. "No one talk. I want to hear this."

"I'm Gunther Wildener," said the white-haired man, extending his hand to Annie. She shook it briefly. Lottie was looking gravely

112

at Walter. Her eyes widened slightly. "Hello, Walt," she said. They put their arms around each other and stood silently together. When they drew apart, Walter said, "Are you all right? Murray says he has a big job coming up."

"Mitchel!" said the actor. "What are you, my enemies?"

Lottie looked coolly at Annie. "How are you?" she asked formally and turned away at once to her husband. "We won't have any bread for breakfast."

Annie felt a little stab of fear. Lottie was beautiful; Walter treated her so respectfully. But she was so cold!

They were all talking together now—they'd drawn away from her, and she was surprised when a hand took hers. It was Gunther's. He drew her over to the long heavy drapes that hid the windows.

"What are you doing in this insane place? I assume you come from somewhere else? Everyone out here does."

For a second she thought he meant that room they were standing in, and she looked over her shoulder at Walter who was talking animatedly to the knitter.

"Hollywood," said Wildener. "Hollywood, I mean."

"I'm not interested in the movies," Annie said hastily.

"Good for you!" Wildener said, laughing. "Then what are you doing with Walter Vogel? He spends people like pennies, especially people your age."

"We're together."

"You're together?" The conversation on the other side of the room began to drown out Chaliapin.

"Don't bother to try and hear what they're saying. They're talking about Trotskyites. Trotskyites and Russian culture. *Kulturni*. Very grand subjects. But Lottie is thinking about the bread her husband forgot. Lottie pays no attention. Look at that!" He pointed to a painting hanging on the wall between the windows. "A Landseer! Imagine a Landseer in this dwelling. The former tenant had English inclinations, perhaps. Or animal." He walked over to the painting and drew a finger across its surface. Annie had followed him, not quite knowing what else to do. "It's a copy. I must get glasses."

"What a pretty dog," said Annie.

"Yes. Pretty. . . . Were you born in California? Is such a thing possible? Have you seen the avenue of fortunetellers? The swamis? It's the biggest gypsy encampment in the world, Hollywood. These people"—he waved at the others—"they think you can be *good* out here. Some of them have never seen lawns before. They think a lawn is the substance of Paradise! Every day is invented here as if there'd been no day before it. But wait. When we are at war, how things will change! Pretty girls will wear uniforms and march down the boulevards singing patriotic songs—"

"It's an imperialist war," said a voice at Annie's shoulder. It was the man who'd been standing at the piano. He'd apparently given up Chaliapin for the moment.

"This is Israel Kuyper," said Wildener. "He intends to become a famous director, don't you, Israel? What is your last name, Annie? Walter doesn't think women should have last names."

"Gianfala," she said.

Kuyper nodded at her wearily. "We will not be in this war," he said to Gunther.

"Oh, but we will. Before it is over, we will!" Gunther said. "You forget. I've been in Germany as late as last year. I have seen what I have seen."

"We must mobilize the people against imperialist war," Kuyper said insistently. "Tell me, Gunther, how are your students reacting to events?"

"My students," Wildener said, "are either passive or stupid or both. But they are all rich. I have had to teach a little course in the Depression. I told them there is no more bitter sight than men without work. But they think that is the ideal condition of life."

"Would you like to hear Chaliapin again?" asked Kuyper.

"I loathe opera!" roared Gunther. "Especially Russian opera!" Kuyper shrugged.

"So you're a foreigner, like me," said Gunther to Annie. Regretfully, she shook her head; it was pleasant to be included in a group, even a group of two.

Israel Kuyper looked at her impersonally. "Are you in the industry?" he asked.

Wildener barked with laughter. "The industry! Oh, Israel, you've sold out and not even been bought yet! No, she's not in the industry. She's with Walter." He looked across the room at Walter. "He wasn't a good actor, you know. Too much self-drama. He got into hideously knotted relationships with people in authority. Israel, do you remember the time he lost his voice because he hated the director so much? He's a pretty fellow. Oh, this country . . . it takes boobs and stirs them all up with poetic fancies. Then

114

they're worth nothing, nothing!" Wildener seemed really angry for a moment. Israel drifted back to the piano. He was standing over the keyboard, his fingers resting lightly on them. "He wants someone to ask him to play," whispered Wildener. "But no one will."

"What do you teach?" she asked him.

"For the moment, I'm supposed to be teaching German. They'll probably ban it from the universities pretty soon. I have no qualifications for anything else. Actually, I teach more than that. Those students—they can't learn German anyhow, so we talk about the Depression and French literature and even the movies—anything to keep them from going to sleep."

"But weren't you an actor?"

"No, no. Never. I wrote a play and it was produced and then I met these types here. Then Lowe—who used to be Murray Gold —wrote and told me to come out. He's a kind fellow. For an actor, extraordinarily kind. He knew I was without a cent and he mailed me a money order with the fare. For all his narcissism, he thinks well of other professions. Especially writing. I find that endearing in an actor. Once here, I got a teaching position. Now I'm hoping nothing happens, no war, no earthquakes, let the stupid sunlight bathe me. . . . It is the first time in many years I have had money coming in regularly, a place to put my books, my records, a basin in which to wash my socks, and socks to wash. My dearest friend back east has lost his senses as a result of having had no steady work for a dozen years. He's now writing continuity for comic books and has had the horrible idea of writing *Hamlet* in modern-day slang. Poor Fishbein! But, of course, there will be a war. And an earthquake too, probably."

Israel Kuyper had begun to play softly. Annie lifted aside the drapes. She saw the glimmer of a swimming pool near a grove of trees. The branches of the trees were swaying. There must be a wind blowing. She had a momentary sense of being in her own dream.

"You know that joke," Wildener was saying, "about a Communist get-together. 'You bring the gin, I'll bring the Negro.' "

"I heard that same joke in New York," Annie said in surprise. Wildener laughed heartily. But Natasha had heard him.

"That's a very bad joke, Gunther," she said severely. "I do not like chauvinism. It is very serious. It is an attack on the Communist party, on Negroes, and it is nasty bourgeois sneering of the lowest order!"

115

Gunther bowed. "You lack humor, Nat," he said. "But I suppose no revolutionary can afford it."

Lowe and Lottie called everyone into a large kitchen where they all sat around a marble table and were served coffee and black bread and cheese. "I'm sorry there isn't more bread," Lottie apologized. "But Murray forgot . . ."

Kuyper commented that he hadn't thought Hollywood was civilized enough to have such amenities as black bread, and Gunther remarked, "The trouble with Jews is they are so hopelessly parochial."

"That makes two anti-Semites among us," Lowe said. "We are a little microcosm, aren't we, Annie?" He smiled at her with his whole face. Kuyper told a long story about the machinations of some Trotskyist screenwriter who was keeping Communist writers from getting assignments. "What abominations they are!" he said.

"What is a narcissism?" she asked Walter when they'd gotten back to their room.

He looked at her gravely, then sat her down on the bed.

"Narcissus was a boy," he whispered. "And he wouldn't love anyone. So the gods punished him by making him fall in love with his own reflection in a pool of water. But whenever he reached out to embrace his image, it disappeared, and so he began to die of this awful love."

She looked at him, then impulsively flung her arms around his neck and kissed him. "And a Trotskyite?"

"Same thing," he murmured.

"Come on."

"That's too long to tell. We'll talk about it later."

"Lottie didn't like me. But she likes you."

"The only person she cares about is Murray. Anyhow," he added brutally, "she wouldn't be interested in someone like you."

Stung, Annie got up. "You were phony with her," she said. "All that significant silent hugging. And she's phony too, that grim beauty and talking about bread . . . everyone there was putting on an act."

"Everyone everywhere puts on an act."

"I don't!" she cried. "I'm natural."

"That's *your* act," he said, grinning and pulling off his shirt.

"It isn't an act."

"Yes, it is, the biggest act of all." He grabbed her and hugged her. "My Annie is the biggest phony of them all!"

116

Over his shoulder she caught sight of Walter's square black seaman's wallet on the bed, its link chain hidden in a fold of sheet. She'd looked through it that morning while he'd been closeted in the toilet, and found a faded brown picture of a young girl in a bathing suit leaning against a tree trunk, a vapid smile on her face. Another penny of Walter's?

The following evening, she came home to find him drunk, crouched in the chair, his legs drawn up, a bottle of whiskey on the floor. She felt an inexpressible resentment, and dread, too. Walter, drunk, played cruel games with her. Her job had taken an unexpected turn. The store manager, a man of dark moods, apparently caused by his firm expectation of insubordinate behavior from his salesladies, had taken special measures with Annie, calling her out of the quiet, dead dark of the basement to set her on a new task, taking her from it before it was completed, setting her something else to do, interrupting that in turn, and so on until Annie was ready to scream with frustration. Every time she looked up, the manager's face was turned toward her, swollen, lipless, and implacably stupid. She had to get some suitable clothes; the Los Angeles streets shimmered in the heat, the air was dense with dust. She sweltered in the tweed suit, the crape dress was wrinkled and stained with perspiration. The women in the store looked at her disapprovingly and one had said, "You ought to buy yourself some little blouses and skirts—you don't want to look worse than our customers."

And here was Walter, drunk, but clean and fresh and mean. "Annie, I've got a funny story."

She let her pocketbook drop to the floor.

"I want to wash up," she said coldly.

He gave her a quizzical look, which, for some reason, made her feel a little better.

As she walked to the basin, she saw a letter addressed to Walter lying on the three-legged table. He came to stand behind her. She rinsed the soap from her face. "You've got soap in your hair," he said.

She shrugged. He smiled. "I like you when you're stern and soapy." She went and sat on the bed. Walter lifted a bottle of whiskey to his lips, then held it out to her. She shook her head.

"I went to see Paul Lavan today and I was there all day."

"Where?"

"He's a film cutter. At a studio. Listen, have a drink . . ."

117

She took a swallow. It was warm, unpleasant, medicinal. She didn't want to hear the story. It was bound to be something nasty, she could tell by his expression. She wanted him gone; she wanted to be by herself; she wanted to look out the window at the miserable boring street and turn around and find the room empty and the bed up against the wall.

"Well, what about the story?"

"They had a strip of film of a Brazilian dancer doing a samba, one of those South American things, for a movie. She wasn't wearing pants."

She looked at him questioningly. His face darkened and he stood up. "She wasn't wearing underwear," he said, enunciating his words carefully. "The camera was shooting from below. That's all. They've made thousands of prints of this particular strip of film, and the dancer has taken off for Brazil."

"I don't see what the story is."

"All right. There isn't a story, then."

"You spent the whole day looking at the picture?"

"Hardly the whole day. It doesn't take long to look at something like that. What the hell's eating you?"

"And does she look different from other women? Was it wonderful, all of you staring at *that?*"

"Yes. It was wonderful!" he shouted. He took another drink, then stared at her. He looked, she thought, confused, and for the first time since he'd arrived, she felt she'd won a small victory. He was watching her intently.

"Who's the letter from?" she asked.

"A friend in New York," he replied. "Come to bed."

"Now?"

"Now."

"I can't."

"Can't?"

"I'm tired and I'm hungry."

"I bought some things to eat," he said. "We can't go to a restaurant every night." She walked very slowly over to the counter where he'd left groceries. He said nothing. She wondered how far she could push him.

There were oranges, canned luncheon meat, bread, a small piece of butter wrapped in wax paper, a bottle of milk. She prepared supper. After they'd eaten it in total silence, he asked her if

118

she wanted to go to a movie. She was too tired, she said. Later, he went out to buy cigarettes. Annie read the letter.

Most of it referred to people she didn't know, events in which she took no interest, but the last few sentences were about her. "Oh, Walter," she read, "for God's sake, what have you gotten yourself into with that little blonde filly? Cradle snatching! You're not *serious,* are you? Come back here before somebody eats you up alive!" It was signed "Lily."

She didn't mention the letter until they were in bed, the room in darkness except for the light filtering in beneath the window shade. "Who is Lily?" she whispered. There was no answer, only Walter's even breathing. "Lily!" she cried. Walter sat up, turned on a light and reached for a cigarette.

"You read the letter."

"Yes."

"Lily, and a friend of hers, Beth, helped me when I was out of work. They're nice girls. They were nice to me."

"I'm the blonde filly?"

He smiled. "Yes, Annie."

"What did you write them about me?"

"Not much."

"But it makes me feel terrible!" she burst out.

"Terrible!" he mocked.

"Did that man give you one of the pictures of that Brazilian dancer?"

"Maybe," he said. Then he jumped out of bed and went to his sea bag, taking out a small oilskin pouch and bringing it back to her. "Open it," he said. She drew two rings from the pouch.

"I'd pawned them," he said. "Years ago. But I kept up the interest. They belonged to my mother. We'll get married, Annie."

The gold band didn't fit, but the one with the three sapphires slid over her small finger.

"She was little?"

"Normal-sized," he said. "Not a giant like you." He lay down on top of her. "A giant dummy," he said.

She slid out from under him and pushed him away.

"Married?" Was that what he'd had in mind all along? Because of these days they had lived together? Had it been a kind of test? But married? She could not think why. In movies, young people held hands and dreamed of the house furnishings that

119

would someday be theirs. Brides wore white gowns, in order, her father had said, to celebrate their deflowering. What she needed was a pair of new shoes.

"We'd better," he said, as though speaking of medicine.

He had some other surprises in store for her that week. She came home to find him dangling a car key from one of her bobby pins. He took her down to the street, to a 1937 Chevrolet convertible. The leather was cracked, the fenders dented.

"You drive," he commanded.

She did. "Who taught you?" he asked.

"My father."

"I'm going to reteach you. Don't ride the clutch to start with." They went for several miles. He said her father must drive like a fool.

When they got back in the room, he told her he'd been to the shipping-line office that day. They'd only paid him enough to buy the car, a hundred and twenty-five dollars. Then he started to laugh.

"You should see your expression!" he cried. "Oh! There's no point in teasing you." And reaching into his pants pocket, he took out handfuls of money and tossed the bills at her. Money rustled down her skirt, settled on her lap and thighs. "Buy some clothes, for God's sake," he said.

She held handfuls of money, in a voluptuous trance that made her limbs soften. "There's so much," she murmured.

"Not much," he contradicted.

She got off early the next day from work, telling the manager she was sick, about to faint, about to throw up . . . The manager glared, but let her go. She went to meet Walter in a department store on Hollywood Boulevard.

She bought three cotton dresses, some blouses, something called a broom-skirt, which, the salesgirl told her, would keep its pleats if she wrapped it around a broomstick after she'd washed it. She bought two pairs of shoes and a pair of sneakers. Walter took a trench raincoat from a rack in another part of the store, plucked a brown felt hat from a display dummy. "Wear the coat and the hat," he said. He took her to a bar. She looked at her reflection in the long mirror behind the line of bottles. He was grinning.

She was conscious of a kind of thrilling arrogance. Her new clothes made her complete. People looked at her. She didn't smile.

"Annie! You've got a car, clothes . . . you've come up in the world!"

"Anything would have been up," she said distantly. She stared at her reflection as though it were daring to presume on short acquaintanceship.

"Look. You've got to get permission from your father for us to get married because you're underage."

"I don't know his address, just that he's in New Mexico."

"You've got to do it right away, today. Now drink this."

He pushed a shot glass of whiskey and a large glass of beer toward her. "That's a boilermaker."

"I don't want it."

"Go on. Be tough!"

She swallowed the whiskey quickly and followed it with the beer. It had an instant and delicious effect. It added to her new sense of immunity. The hat was beautiful. "I'll have another," she said grandly.

He hugged himself and laughed. She wished to preserve her disdain—a laugh would destroy it. But he looked so funny, huddled on the bar stool, egging her on. Reluctantly, she smiled.

How could she get her father's address unless she telephoned Samuel in New York? But the expense made that out of the question. To imagine Samuel's hectoring voice was to be touched with the point of a knife. Then she remembered that James St. Vincent had said Bea was working in Hollywood. Bea would have the address. She knew her father was still paying Bea alimony. How he'd cursed her!

It was hard for Annie to ask St. Vincent for information. She felt the fragility of her connection with him. Asking for information was almost as bad as asking for money. But Walter pressed her relentlessly. Finally she called. St. Vincent was still away. It was the same woman she'd spoken to before. She asked her timidly if she knew where Bea Gianfala lived. The woman— mistress or mistress's sister?—laughed harshly.

"We always know where Bea lives! She sets up such a ruckus! She works for MGM. You can get her through them. Ask for the story department. And when you talk to her, tell her I'll call the cops if she ever tries to stick her face in my house again!"

Annie called the story department and after swearing she was Bea's stepdaughter—the news that Bea had one seemed to astonish the woman she spoke to—managed to get a home phone number.

Even after so many years, she quailed upon hearing that rough voice.

"This is Annie, Bea."

"Annie? Annie who, for crissake?"

"Gianfala."

"Oh! You!"

"I'm sorry to bother you."

"Then why bother me?"

"I need to get hold of my father. I thought you might know . . ."

"What for?"

"Well—"

"You used to be such a foul little liar. Don't start up with me!"

"Please. Give it to me?"

"He owes me alimony. I could put him in jail."

Restraining a flood of rage, Annie took a deep breath. "You could sell all those paintings of his you took."

"Ha! Sell them! Are you crazy? I couldn't sell them to a junk-man."

"Please, Bea."

There was a pause. Annie heard the clink of glass against glass. Bea was drinking—noisily. She coughed. "He's a painter so he can live like a bum," she said sullenly. "He's too cheap to make money anyhow. He'd only have to spend it. I suppose he informed you he married again?" There was another loud gulp. "He has himself a lush this time," she said with satisfaction.

It was as if no time had passed. Bea had always spoken to her in this same way.

"You remember, Annie, how I taught you patience?" Bea was asking insinuatingly. "You liked that. I showed you eight different kinds of solitaire. Remember?"

"I remember."

"I wasn't so bad, was I?" the voice wheedled.

"No."

Then, hard and combative, she asked, "What do you want with him?"

"I'm going to get married. I have to have his permission because I'm not eighteen yet."

Annie heard a shriek of laughter, the phone dropped with a crash, then Bea came back on.

"How did you track me down?"

"I called the St. Vincents."

"He wouldn't tell you. I bet it was that stinker, Hope. How is that stinker?"

"They gave me your number at MGM."

"Getting married! My God! I should think you'd be cured of that before you even begin!"

"The address, Bea?"

"Maybe I will. Maybe I won't," Bea replied.

"Bea!"

"If he were a real artist, he wouldn't spend all his time marrying. He wouldn't have had you, my girl! He's a senseless man. Senseless! All right. Let me go get the address, and luck to you. Why don't you just shack up with your hero?"

"It was hard, but I got it," Annie reported to Walter.

"Then wire him right now."

"Why are you in such a hurry?"

"Don't be stubborn with me, Annie."

"I thought Communists were all for free love . . ."

He looked prim. "That's capitalist propaganda," he said.

She laughed.

Chapter 10

An answer came the next evening in answer to Annie's telegram.

"I think you're crazy," it read. "I give you my permission to marry as no one can be dissuaded from craziness. Love." It was signed "Papa."

"Papa!" she exclaimed. "I've never called him that in my life. 'Tony,' that's how he always signed his letters."

"He's smarter than you are, baby. 'Tony' can't give you permission to get married."

The details of this endeavor had been so cumbersome, obscurely threatening and clearly irrevocable—the call to Bea, the wording of the telegram to her father, the nervous wait in a narrow shop where an aged hollow-eyed jeweler had fumbled among a tray of wedding bands while Walter watched her try on rings with amused condescension, as if it were all some lunatic scheme of her own, the earlier visit to a doctor whom she'd found not far from the apartment house, alone in his office, patientless and morose, who fitted her roughly with a hard-rimmed rubber contraceptive. And now Walter was telling her that the final act was to take place tomorrow in Los Angeles, he'd made all the arrangements. Each stone was fitting into place across the cave entrance. They were to marry each other. Why did she feel that it was *she* who was being walled in?

"During my fifteen-minute lunch break?" she asked with conscious irony.

He stared at her patiently.

"If I tell them I'm sick, they'll fire me."

"That would be a good thing," Walter said quietly. "It's the worst job I ever heard of. Only you could have found it."

"It is a job. And I can't do anything anyhow."

"There are other jobs where you don't have to know anything, but they pay better."

The morning began with a disagreeable conversation with the store manager. It was clear he didn't believe her. She had an impulse to tell him she was in an advanced state of leprosy. But instead, she apologized immoderately, oppressing both the manager and herself. She said she would be in the following day no matter what. Then, when she returned from the drugstore where she'd made the call, she saw Johnnie Bliss heading into the apartment house. Oh, she should have kept him away, written him a note, said she was leaving town for good! Walter would detest him. He would hold her responsible for his very existence!

It didn't turn out as she had anticipated. Walter was excessively hospitable to Johnnie, pressing him to smoke up the cigarettes, offering him a drink—"At this time in the morning?" Johnnie purred demurely—and when Johnnie left shortly after, clasping his hand warmly. Annie walked down the hall with him. "Are you all right?" she asked him.

"Of course I'm all right!" Without warning he grabbed her hand and pinched her wrist hard. "You'd better worry about yourself," he said spitefully. She gasped with pain. "Why did you—"

But he walked away quickly and waddled out of sight down the stairs. "Johnnie?" What *had* she done?

"Put on your new coat . . . we're due at the courthouse at eleven o'clock."

They went to the Los Angeles Courthouse, where Walter led her through an empty courtroom that smelled of institutional polish. A man in overalls was sweeping the floor. Later, along with a young clerk, he served as one of their two witnesses. The ceremony lasted only a few minutes. The judge had distinguished hair and an overly sweetened voice. Annie fought down a powerful wave of laughter that threatened to engulf her, wash her into the street. The witnesses, smiling at her, left. A ray of sunlight streaming through the large window directed its principal blessing

125

toward the judge's hair. She looked at the dust motes. Her throat still rippled faintly with laughter. Then she realized Walter and the judge were having a heated argument, something about Murmansk . . . the Murmansk run.

"But how can you leave your young wife so soon?" the judge was asking indignantly. Walter answered him with a constrained patience that implied the judge was mentally deficient. The Murmansk run was so perilous that an extra bonus was given; it amounted to a considerable amount of money. As for his young wife, said Walter, she could damn well take care of herself as women did all over the world. The judge patted Annie's hand and gave her a pitying glance.

Afterward, as she and Walter walked along the street, she said, "What is Murmansk?"

"Nothing . . . we're married! What do you think of that?" She was fiddling with the ring on her finger; it was neither heavy nor tight, but it made her breathless, as if two fingers pressed against her throat.

"Annie Vogel!" Walter said.

No! she cried silently. And then, all at once, she felt a vast ease, unexpected and overwhelming. Walter had stopped to look at the pictures behind the display case of a movie house. He'd slipped his hands into the back pockets of his trousers, and he bent forward to look more closely at the pictures. He looked surprisingly young. She drifted over to him, catching sight as she did so of a man across the street. She was sure it was the one who'd given her the ride to San Diego, Max Shore. She turned away quickly, afraid he might remember her, might feel constrained to come and speak to her. She had often thought of Max Shore, of the way he'd looked at her, his comic irritation with that woman who drove the car. He had seemed so sad to her.

"Let's go to the movies!" said Walter. She laughed at the perversity of such an act on their wedding day, and said yes.

They sat in the nearly empty movie house watching Ida Lupino with her tough, pretty, small-dog's face. Annie was hardly conscious of the story. Walter's hand was on her knee. The ring continued to disturb her and, furtively, she slid it back and forth along her finger.

Walter bought them lamb chops and a bottle of wine and two large potatoes.

They had an early supper; she cooked while Walter read a

126

newspaper he'd picked up before they'd come home. She looked down greedily at the frying chops. There were two for each of them, unprecedented luxury . . .

"God!" exclaimed Walter.

"What?"

"This girl. A girl on the society page. She's *marvelous* looking!"

Annie went to the bed where Walter was lying, the paper held up over his head. She reached for it. He snatched it away. She jumped up on the bed and grabbed it, then looked rapidly through the pages. There was no society girl, only a small photograph of Merle Oberon on the movie page. He was laughing insinuatingly.

"Why did you say there was a girl?"

"Hunh?"

"Walter?"

"You're such an easy mark, Annie. It's so easy to get a rise out of you."

She sat in the chair and looked at him wordlessly. Whatever he was thinking, his expression didn't, immediately, change. It held the mocking interest of someone watching the predictable but comic antics of a fool.

"I am not a fool," she said as lightly as she could.

"No," he agreed. "But you are foolish."

She wanted to cry out that she was young! In the same way, she had once defended herself against her father's charge that she was "pleasure mad" because she'd wanted to go to see two movies in one afternoon. "I'm only a child!" she had said to Tony. Recalling that now, she smiled ruefully. It was as though youth was a form of epilepsy which one was obligated to explain, even in the throes of its convulsions.

Why had Walter married her? What did he really want with her? An uncanny question presented itself to her: *Who* was it that Walter had married?

He didn't look mocking now. He looked reflective and gloomy. He sighed suddenly. He looked so melancholy that his face seemed softer. She would have liked to ask him about his thought, but she was afraid. . . .

He drank a good deal that evening, talking fitfully about his acting days. He seemed to be speaking to someone who was not there. He fell asleep in his clothes. She took off his shoes without waking him. As she placed his shoes side by side beneath the bed,

127

she felt concern for the unguarded, sleeping man, a rush of intense sympathy. As she made herself a place next to him, the strain of not waking him giving her a singular pleasure, she thought suddenly of Max Shore. What would it be like if Max Shore were here in this bed? Her half-closed eyes flew open.

Miss Gluck spotted the ring as soon as Annie began to straighten out blouses in a display case.

"No! I'm psychic! I said to myself yesterday that I just bet you weren't sick. I knew you were up to something. And look what you've been up to! And whom did you manage to snare in your little web? Unless you're just wearing that ring because you're living with someone . . . are you? Look out! Here come the natives. I'll speak to you later."

Although Annie tried to avoid close proximity to Miss Gluck, the older woman's eager eyes sought her all day. She caught up with her just before closing time.

"Is it true? Are you really married?"

"Yes."

"Who? I declare! You're just a baby! I hope he's got some money."

And, after Annie had told her the shortest possible story, "A sailor! My goodness!" Miss Gluck dissolved into strange, intense laughter. Annie saw her speaking to the scowling manager. He marched over to Annie. "I can't say I appreciate your lying to me. You might have told me. You could have had the day off— instead of stealing it."

Walter was waiting for her outside the store. She dragged him away, fearful of what Miss Gluck might say to him. She sensed Miss Gluck, once having seen them together on the street, might construct for herself more intimate pictures of them. The thought horrified her, as though Miss Gluck were handling her body.

"It's nice of you to come and get me," Annie said. Walter smiled remotely, then put his arm around her shoulders. He took her to a diner. Something incomprehensible happened at once. Next to Annie at the counter sat two mannish, angular-looking women. They were not young. They both looked quickly at Annie. She instantly removed her wedding ring. Looking up, she saw Walter had observed her do it. His grin was wolfish. She put the ring back on. She had lost her appetite.

"Why'd you do that?" whispered Walter.

Her humiliation was complete. She looked down at the Swiss

steak bathed in greasy gravy. It was one thing to accept Walter's "taking her in hand." But what she had done with the ring made her vulnerable to him in an excruciating way. Oh, if she could only take back the moment, the impulse. Yet Walter seemed merely amused in his usual bullying fashion. What had she been up to with those two disagreeable-looking women?

Later, she hardly noticed where they were walking.

"Annie, we're here," Walter said.

"Here?" she echoed miserably. Then she looked up to see the Los Angeles bus station. He went directly to a wall of lockers, Annie trailing behind him. There, he took a key from his pocket, unlocked a metal door, and dragged out his sea bag. He turned to face her. People milled around them; some hurried to loading platforms.

"I filled up the gas tank of the car," he said. "It's parked right in front of the apartment house."

"But where are you going?"

"New York." He took her hand. "I've got to go. We're almost out of money. I have to go back and get another trip."

"Trip? Where?"

"Maybe the Murmansk run, this time."

"But you didn't say anything!" she burst out.

"No," he acknowledged without emphasis. "But one or two more runs and I'll have enough for a stake. The car, you know, and your clothes, big outlays of cash. After, I'll be back and get a job out here. Won't that be good, Annie? You must have known I'd have to leave soon. You've got to find a better job—that's what you have to do. And keep in touch with the people you met. Paul Lavan is going to get you into some kind of political activity. I want you to get involved with the party—you need that, Annie . . ."

"You didn't tell me," she said again, forcing her voice to be quiet, as though only in quietness could she convince herself of the enormity of it.

"I didn't decide until yesterday. When I worked out the money situation."

"But we were married yesterday!"

"And I knew I had to go."

"Why can't you get a job now?"

"I want some choice. I'd have to take anything now. This way, I'll come back with enough money to look around. Come on,

129

baby, calm down." He shook her gently. They went to the platform where the New York bus was loading up with baggage and passengers. She felt ill and leaned against him.

"Listen, you take care of things. You're a good girl. You'll do that."

"When will you be back?" Her voice trembled. She was trembling.

"Six weeks, two months maybe. It depends on the run. If I take the Panama run, it may be shorter. But I'll write, Annie, and you'll be awfully good, won't you?" He kissed her neck and was gone.

As the bus pulled out, Annie stood there, looking up at Walter's face. He pressed his nose against the glass, made faces, grinned at her comically. She left before the bus backed out of its slot. She ran into people inside the station and looked mutely into their indignant faces. She was surrounded by emptiness. What she had so passionately wished for only a few days ago had happened. She was alone.

She took the streetcar home, but once there, could not bear to go up to the room. She found the car parked where Walter had said it would be. She drove out toward Beverly Hills. At the turning into Arizona Canyon, she felt hesitation, but the emptiness around her was a force that drove her on. The worst St. Vincent could do was to tell her to leave.

The Saint Bernard loped up to her as she shut the car door and went up the walk. But it was Andrew, St. Vincent's son, who answered the door, not Jim's butler and literary adviser. She sensed behind the boy an empty house. Andrew blinked at her, then smiled uncertainly. His eyes were set closely together; he had Jim's narrow head.

"Oh, I thought Mr. St. Vincent—"

"Partying," interrupted Andrew. "Out partying with the girls . . ." He laughed shrilly.

"Well, then—"

"Don't you want to see me? Come in and see me, it's boring when I'm here alone. Even the servants are off somewhere." He snapped his fingers in a parody of St. Vincent's restless habit, as though evoking his father's presence by imitating him. "Daddy talks to me except when he's working. I don't like being alone."

He saw her hesitation. "I have some cake," he offered hopefully.

130

"All right," she said.

She followed him directly to the kitchen where he took a plate from a cupboard, holding the remains of a chocolate cake. Like the one she'd noticed that first night at the St. Vincents' dining-room table, this one was also caved in. Maybe after making it, the cook, in a fit of rage, smashed her hand down on the cake. Andrew cut them each a large piece, got two princely goblets from a cabinet and filled them with milk. On the wall was a box with numbers printed on buttons. She knew its function from all those movies about the lives of the rich. One summoned the maid for breakfast by ringing a bell that buzzed here in the kitchen.

"We'll pretend the milk is Scotch," said Andrew. He raised the goblet. "Here's to itself!" he cried, and swallowed a great gulp. The milk trickled down his chin. He laughed and she joined his laughter. "I look foul, don't I?" he said. He jumped up, a gnome-like figure out of a fairy tale. He snatched a linen towel from a rack and wiped his entire face, peering out at her. The cake was rich and delicious. "We can eat all of it," he said.

He wiped up the icing on the plate with his little fingers. "I only like cake," he said gravely. Then, in the same tone of voice, "I know your father. I remember him. He's a frightful drunk," this last observation in a voice not quite his own, a stolen adult judgment.

Oh, she remembered her father too. She was always remembering him. Life had gone along quietly at Uncle Greg's for several years, then one night when she was around eleven, there had been a flash of light as her bedroom door had opened and closed.

Tony, smelling of liquor and tobacco, had come to sit on her bed. She'd sat straight up from sleep to full waking. He held her hand. He told her things were going to be different. Soon, he would be coming to take her away with him. Would she like to live in the Canary Islands? He'd heard of a fine boarding school in Switzerland. They would have splendid parties in Paris. Everything was possible. He'd kissed her good-by. The door had opened, then it was dark again. In the morning, he was gone. Uncle Greg was agitated all day. No, no, he didn't know when Tony was coming back; it had been an unexpected visit after all that time. She wandered around the old house all day, unable to eat, dizzy with hunger. The Canary Islands . . .

"He's not a frightful drunk," Annie said. "He just drinks."

"My father, known as Jimmy by some people, was his best

131

friend," Andrew said gently, as though he understood he'd wounded her. "They often got drunk together."

"I got married yesterday," Annie said impulsively. "And just before I came here, I saw my—husband—off to New York."

"You got to play the cards the way they falls," Andrew said. "That's what my father says."

He cut them two more slices of cake. "There's one good thing. When they all go away, I can eat what I want."

"Where do you go to school?"

"I have tutors," he said. "You know, my mind isn't quite right. Oh, it's not that I'm crazy. Nothing like that! Just that my equipment is a little different. That's what my father says. Like arithmetic. I can't do it at all. But my father says arithmetic is all made up anyhow. It all depends on what you're good at making up. I'd like you to see my armies. They're the best in the world. My father sends to England for the soldiers."

"Nobody's mind is quite right," she said. "I think . . ."

"You didn't have to say that to me," Andrew said kindly. "I don't require it. I know what I know. I'm useful when we run out of cash. I'm a good driver, superb, my father says. When we move out of here, I get a job driving laundry trucks, just like that!" He snapped his fingers.

"How old are you?" she asked.

"Nearly seventeen," he said. It was shocking—he was so small and bent.

"When you move out of here? Why?"

"When he's on a movie, we stay. Everybody out here lives on credit, you know. After he gets the money for the movie, he pays up everything, and then we go on credit. But sometimes, when it's a long stretch between movies, we run out of credit too. Then we move out to a shack on Old Veteran's Road, and I get a job. No more tutors, no dancing master for my sister."

Dancing master! Annie visualized a slender Frenchman in evening dress tangoing through a salon. "Does he come here?"

"He used to, before my sister went away to boarding school. Let's go see my soldiers."

He took her to a study off the living room. A billiard table took up most of the space. On one wall hung a dartboard. Near the windows was a broad table on which hundreds of toy soldiers were deployed in some kind of order.

"My extras!" said Andrew proudly. Annie was listening to the babble of the artificial brook. "Look!" cried Andrew.

He picked up several of the toy warriors, examined them raptly, then set each one back in exactly the same place. Evidently there was a vast plan located in the depths of Andrew's not quite right mind.

"I'm going to change the situation here," he said. "Now watch carefully!" Rapidly, he moved a number of the little soldiers. In a minute or so, the overall design of the armies had changed drastically. "I have confronted them with new problems," he said. "Did you notice the civilians? You see the woman and her children? I have a crate full of farmers and animals. Von Clausewitz said total war means everything—citizens and property—should be attacked. Have you read *On War*? My father reads me parts of it when he feels up to it. You'd be astonished at how much I understand." He picked up a foot soldier between two fingers, held it toward Annie, then shouted, "Bang!"

"You have to kill so many," she murmured.

"It's not real death."

"Last winter in New York, I saw a man walking almost naked out in the cold. Someone said he'd been gassed during the World War. There must be terrible suffering when you're like that."

Andrew stooped over the board, making some new arrangement. When he looked at her again, there was a stubborn expression on his face.

"But I said—it's not real. Anyhow, man is a killer by nature. It's only that he won't admit it."

"Show me your house," she asked quickly. The little gnome looked very fierce.

"It's boring," he said stiffly. "Just a boring house with furniture. The other place, where we go when we're broke, is better. It's a shack."

He was being contrary. What could he know about shacks? She looked at his beautifully polished shoes. She brooded on what lay ahead for her. For the moment, she doubted Walter's existence; he had simply disappeared, leaving her the inexplicable burden of his name. He'd disappeared, stealing *her* name.

"I'm not a killer," Andrew said pleadingly.

She started as though she'd been asleep. "Oh, I know that!" she assured him. He smiled and replaced on the board a riderless horse that was rearing up from his fingers, its eyes starting from its head, its stirrups flying.

She stayed awhile longer. They sat at the piano together and Andrew showed her how to play "Chopsticks." The intolerable sense of emptiness was returning. She wanted to move on.

"I'd better go," she said.

"Not yet, please . . ."

"Yes. I have to get to work very early."

He looked solemn at once. "Yes. Then you should go. I know all about work."

They shook hands formally at the door but Andrew looked desolate as he turned away into the empty house.

Annie ran to the car. She sat for a long time in the quiet, expensive twilight of the tree-lined street. Then, afraid but eager, she set out for Venice Park. She was tracking herself down, going to all the places she'd been. Perhaps at the end of the trail, she would find something substantial, a token to carry through the days ahead.

The long drive was not oppressive; she was used to being alone, she'd forgotten that. But her thoughts were uneasy, not quite distinct enough for her to say, "Here. This is what I'm thinking about." She concentrated on Bea. She remembered how Bea had roamed at night, a cup of cold coffee in one hand, her black hair disarrayed. Sometimes there were violent fights in the middle of the night, but Bea had a strange bumbling quality and was no match for Annie's father when his expression chilled with distaste, when he called Bea "the primitive" to her enraged face.

During the brief time Annie had lived with them, they'd moved so often that she had made few friends, a French boy jeered at by his schoolmates for his thick accent and small stature, an ugly little girl whose glasses revealed the borrowed eyes of an old woman, a girl named Brooks who fell on the classroom floor and turned blue in the face when she dropped a spot of paste or ink on a piece of paper but who, except for these strange seizures, was more reasonable than any other child Annie had ever known. These "friends" were all transients like herself. Through some convention of childhood they never spoke of their troubles to each other. They played their own games, travesties of the games the acceptable children played, the ones to whose houses Annie was never invited, the ones upon whose heads teachers rested hands that gave blessings. These games almost always ended in wild laughter, outsiders' games, parodies, full of savage disappointment.

She'd forgotten to ask Walter about the scar on his thigh. It bothered her that she'd not asked him. He might never come back. She could see it plainly now in her mind's eye, the scar tissue glowing in his brown skin. And then, just ahead, she saw the lurid lights of Venice Park. But this time, the sky was not so black, and moonlight laid a white tongue along the surface of the water.

Annie walked down the pier. She remembered the shooting gallery where Karin had won the bear. As she neared the end of the pier where the roller coaster rose in menacing humps, she saw a building called the House of Freaks. She did not recall having seen it that first time with St. Vincent. She drew nearer. The lurid posters, painted in colors that looked as if they'd been scraped from living things, promised shocks that would make strong men faint. Two men looked up at the drawing of a tattooed lady. An elderly woman wrapped from head to ankles in a thick black shawl stared longingly toward the entrance, where a man in a booth played with a roll of tickets.

St. Vincent had warned her—what you're afraid of becomes your only real life. She bought a ticket and passed through canvas flaps into a dark passage. From somewhere ahead she heard a low murmur, as of people conversing softly. The passage led into a round room with a high tent ceiling. Just to her right was a small stage on which sat a huge obese man, a black ribbon tied into a bow around his neck. As she quickly averted her eyes, one of his hands slipped indolently from a thigh like a torso. Ringed around the circular wall were other such stages, set off from each other by black curtains. In each one, on a straight-backed chair, sat a motionless creature deformed or hideously marked; all were as silent as stones.

She was suddenly aware of a powerful smell, a combination of rotted fruit, urine, straw, sweat, and the unsettling odor of animals. The murmuring she'd heard had apparently come from a small group of people who were leaning on a corral fence looking at the prize exhibit. A sign clamped to chicken wire announced: HUMAN MOTHER OF MONKEYS.

In the middle of this ring, behind the chicken wire which rose to the ceiling, sat a monumental Negro woman on a small stool. Straw was scattered over the floor, a few wisps of it clung to her hair, a patch here and there on the brown tuniclike garment which

135

left one of her brown shoulders bare. Around her, darting, grimacing, defecating, poking, pinching, and screeching, was a horde of small monkeys. They climbed to her lap, her shoulders; they plucked at her hair that was like a thicket of black heather. Sometimes they sat and held their tails like ladies holding fans. Their little flecked yellow eyes moved like the eyes of thieves and they bared their teeth in batlike grins.

The woman's head was bowed. Then, as Annie started to turn away, the mother of monkeys looked up. One of the animals leaped to her lap and tugged at the cloth of the tunic, then fell to the straw where it instantly mounted another monkey that had paused at the woman's feet. There was a shout of laughter from the watchers at the fence. The woman turned her head slowly, her glance coming to rest on Annie. Her expression was grave, remote. Annie flushed with shame and pity. The woman smiled, holding Annie's unwilling gaze. The smile widened. It was as though the two of them were alone. Annie smiled back uncertainly. The woman nodded her head very slightly. Perhaps Annie imagined it. Then the woman's head drooped; she hid her hands in the folds of her costume.

Driving home, Annie relived that flash of light between herself and the Negro woman. What had it meant? Why had the woman's smile lifted her heart so? What moment's comprehension had brought them together?

When she got back to the apartment house, she found two letters that had been slipped under her door. One was from Paul Lavan, the other from Max Shore.

PART TWO

Meetings

Chapter 11

On an evening during the long rainy spell that summer, Jake Cranford went to see Max Shore. Jake's shoes sloshed, his basketball player's jacket clung wetly to his shirt, and water dripped down his face from his plastered hair. From the doorway, he looked uneasily at Eva, who was painting her nails by the light of a small table lamp, her lips tightened with concentration.

"Jake, it's been a while. Come in."

Max dropped the typescript pages he'd been editing and stretched. The pamphlet was impossible! Before it could be translated into Spanish, it had to be translated into English. The dense airless language, clogged with party jargon, was supposed to reveal to the Mexican community of Los Angeles that its treatment by the police was a matter of brotherly concern to the Communist party. Why had there been that long tangent about the chauvinistic implications of the phrase "fine Italian hand"? The pamphlet was stuffed with such irrelevant asides. But knowing the ex-missionary who'd been assigned the job, Max was not surprised. Calvin Schmitter would suffocate his flock, any flock, with every piece of information he could marshal whether it made sense or not.

Calvin Schmitter was implacable, his washed-out pale little Swede face forever contemplating some judgment day when all the truths he had gathered would be confirmed by the appearance of the Lord. The pamphlets he wrote were usually given to Max to put into some semblance of order, and no matter how aware the committee in charge was of Calvin's deadly turgid prose, they continued to assign such work to him. There was always a fight afterward as Calvin, rigid with insult, tried to put back each irrelevancy Max had excised. He'd accused Shore of being a "literary deviate," of succumbing to fancy standards meant for bourgeois consumption. Why didn't Max respect the plain language needed by oppressed minds? It was clear to Calvin that Max must purge himself of incorrect attitudes.

"Could I speak with you?"

Eva said, "Sit down, Jake, but not in the blue chair. My God, don't you have an umbrella? Do you want wine or coffee?" Eva flexed her fingers under the light.

"Nothing," said Jake, looking warily at her. He could hardly dissemble his desire for her to leave the room. Eva smiled faintly.

Max, feeling dusty, watched the two of them with some appreciation, part of it gratitude to be free of the onerous job he'd only half completed. Eva had a certain shrewdness about the weight of her own presence; she always seemed to know when people would like her to leave. She teased, staying on until it was her pleasure to leave. She knew Jake was shy.

"I don't have *nothing,*" she said. "How about a cup of tea? Or Ovaltine? Or cocoa?"

Jake writhed, water scattering in drops to the floor.

"Oh, for God's sake, take off your jacket," Eva said. "I'll make some coffee."

She moved slowly out of the room, looking at Max to make sure he was up on her game.

Falling over his own feet, Jake ripped off his lank jacket and handed it helplessly to Max. Then he sank into the couch. His bones were prominent, and his hair stuck to his skull. Max saw what he'd look like when he was an old man. He'd known boys like Jake when he was growing up. They'd been his friends. His family's wealth, its position in the community, had not troubled him in those days, not until just before he'd gone off to college.

Lanky, indolent boys who fumbled their way through adolescence, given to secret hero-worshipping sometimes of one another, bouts of heavy drinking, small impulses of criminality that often climaxed those early years and resulted in short jail sentences or probation, from which they emerged abashed and confused; noth-

140

ing in their own understanding could account for what they'd done. He'd asked Jake often enough why he'd stolen that car and Jake simply looked puzzled and repeated the sequence of events as though they might account for the theft. As for hero-worshipping, he'd been the hero to that small group in the town up north with whom he'd run for a few years. He'd come to think they admired him simply because he was rich in options they'd never have; they sensed the larger life his family's good fortune made possible for him. He supposed they'd envied him too. Now, if they knew what had happened to him, they'd get their own back.

"Jake, what's up?"

"I am, I guess," said Jake. "Everything's happened. My old buddy, Carson, and I have split up, and I got done in by a girl, that one you had call me up. And I can't get work. It's the damnedest thing. But I can't get it. You know I've always been able to pick up a thing or two to keep me going. I'd saved some money for going east, and now I've blown that too."

He looked miserable. But Max's sympathy died the moment Jake mentioned the girl. "A girl—Annie," he said, and saw her vividly as he'd first glimpsed her on the road, her back against the tree trunk.

"Yeah, Annie," Jake replied, and began a rambling tale of his betrayal, interspersed with philosophical admonitions to himself that combined Brody's nastiness with a kind of homespun sad wisdom of defeat. "You're well rid of Brody," Max interrupted at one point. "He really is no good." But Jake rushed to defend him: Max had only seen him once, didn't Max know what an awful life Brody had had? What a loyal friend he'd been? How right he'd been when he'd said the best buddies were always getting into trouble over a girl? Well, Brody had been right about this one, and he, Jake, would just have to lump it, chalk it up to experience, cut his losses.

"Stop!" Max said.

Jake paused. Eva came in with a tray of coffee cups and a pot.

"What happened to her?"

Jake looked at him dully, then at Eva.

"I don't know," he said.

Max felt a storm of impatience with both of them, Jake speaking his adolescent drivel, Eva looking so self-satisfied with her fresh nails gleaming over the coffee cups.

"Why don't you spare some of your self-pity for her?" Max

141

asked Jake. "She seems to have been in more trouble than your pal, Brody."

"She lied."

"She omitted to tell you certain things."

"Hunh!"

"Only a kid," muttered Max.

"She lied."

"So what!" retorted Max angrily. "You've never lied?"

"Not about something like that," Jake said.

"You've never been in a position where you felt you had to. You're so foolish with your truth-telling categories! You think the world is as easy for everyone?"

"It's not been easy for me either!" cried Jake.

Eva said, "I don't know what this is all about, Max, but lying is lying."

"No. That's just it. And you don't know what it's about."

"You're on her side," Jake said indignantly.

"Oh, for Christ's sake," Max cried. "I just want you to think about it. You haven't said a thing that would convince me you cared about her at all! Your vanity is wounded!"

"I don't understand what you're talking about," said Jake plaintively.

"I can see that."

Jake got to his feet. Max, as a sudden and inexplicable panic possessed him, grabbed Jake's arm. "Take it easy," he said. "I know you feel bad, I was just trying to understand. But what happened to her?"

"Who?" demanded Eva.

"A girl," Max said shortly. "Fern and I picked her up on the road to the convention."

"You never told me."

"It wasn't important," he said, by which he meant she wouldn't have been interested. She heard the unspoken truth. She said she *would* have been interested, as though he had in fact spoken aloud. Yes, she was shrewd; Max would give her that.

Before Jake left that evening, Max had, upon learning that he wanted to enlist in the army, given him the name of a lawyer who might be able to straighten out his record. Eva had been wild at Max's abetting Jake's joining an imperialist army. For one second, he thought he'd heard her say she'd report him to the party, but then told himself she couldn't have said it. It must have been his

142

own inner voice. No, Eva had grown silent, as though at last he'd really shocked her. She was given to political shock.

But somehow, in the conversation about law and enlistment and lawyers, he'd managed to get from Jake Annie's last address.

He hardly glanced at Jake when he left, looking instead at the wet outline of Jake's body on the couch. Eva came up behind him and put her arms around his waist. She leaned against him. He had the fancy that he was carrying her on his back.

"Max?" she questioned in a low voice.

"I'm out of cigarettes," he said shortly. "I'll go out and see if the drugstore is open."

"You know it isn't," she said, breaking away from him.

He shrugged and gave her a strained smile. They went to bed and lay sleepless, listening to the rain beating against the windows.

A week later, when Max and Eva were in Los Angeles, he'd seen Annie standing in front of a movie house. She'd looked toward him once, then quickly away. He didn't know whether she'd seen him or not. Eva had hurried him on. They were due at a committee meeting about the pamphlet. Max had glanced over his shoulder in time to see Annie enter the movie house with a man.

Then a few days later he'd written her a note.

The instant he mailed it, he was ashamed. The short paragraph had held nothing but gross patronage, offering help for troubles he could not guess at. He thought about nothing else the rest of the day; he realized that his shame came from the deception he was trying to practice.

The real reason he wanted to get in touch with her was curiosity, a wish to *interfere* with her, to get her in front of him, to look at her as long as he wished, to question her as much as he wanted. Max's response to Jake's story, the boy's feeble, pathetic protestation of betrayed love, revealed to Max, the more he had brooded upon it, the extent to which the girl had taken hold of his imagination. To write the letter, he had told himself that he was acting in the best tradition of social responsibility, a political priest concerned about the erring stray outside the saved flock. And upon that thought came the question, Was it because she was a stray that he was so interested in her?

The strays that interested the party were not road wanderers and seamen's girls with unidentifiable accents. A Negro shipscaler, or a member of a reactionary union, a textile worker from the South, a union official, class workers such as printers, anyone

143

working on the waterfront, but not a girl like that. He wasn't desirable himself, a man whose face stiffened when Balzac was referred to as railroad-owning bourgeois or who quibbled about Rousseau, whose income came from "timber barons," who, in fact, need not ever work if he chose not to. Eva gave him, he thought, his only legitimacy. She was real; she was correct, even her impulses were undeviating as though charged by an instinct entirely political. She never said the wrong thing; she never thought the wrong thing.

Several months passed but Annie did not answer his note.

It might have ended. Then Calvin Schmitter brought up Theda Rothstein at a closed meeting at the State School. Theda had been neglecting her weekly column in the party paper, he said. It was clear to anyone who kept a careful eye on these matters that Theda was drifting. He had heard she was writing a book. A book about herself and Simon Concannon. She should have gotten over Simon's death, by now, Calvin said. It was getting to be six years since the painter had been killed in Spain. Furthermore, he'd only been an ambulance driver. She was behaving in an obstinate, improper way. Theda was morbid. Her grief increased with time instead of decreasing—in the correct way. She had walked out of an editorial meeting in a rude manner. Although he felt nothing personal about it, he'd heard she'd referred to him as "that missionary." As a functionary, he represented the party. If Theda was offensive to him, she was being offensive to the party.

Listening to Calvin raging, Max had wondered if, after the revolution, the world wouldn't be largely composed of Calvins. Unless one were permitted to shoot both forward and backward at the barricades.

Unhappily, Calvin had designated Max to go and see Theda and talk matters over in a comradely way. Find out. Report back.

So he'd gone to see her. The door to her apartment was open. Directly across from the door, the leaves of a eucalyptus tree flickered against the window. A table was drawn up against the sill. On it stood a candle in a wine bottle covered with melted wax. There were several newspapers on the table and a mug. Theda was sitting on a bench looking at her fingers. She looked up as Max walked in, then motioned him to silence. "Sixty-three, sixty-four," she said aloud, counting out the numbers on her fingers.

He smiled at her. She looked at him distractedly. Then, without taking her eyes from his face, she pushed a stack of books to the edge of the table, and watched them topple to the floor.

"Mr. Irving Blond was eighty-four when he died," she said. "A French Jew, you think? But he was only sixty when the picture was taken."

When he stood next to her at the table, he saw she was looking down at the obituary page in a Los Angeles newspaper. There was a picture of Mr. Blond taken in 1926.

"Did you know him?"

"No. I don't know any of them." She waved toward the page. "I'm interested in life spans."

He remembered, then, how Theda always asked the names of pet animals in houses, how once, at a meeting in someone's apartment, she had enraged Calvin by interrupting in a loud voice his dissertation on Menshevism to ask the age of the mongrel sitting beneath the table, then figuring out its life possibilities as though Calvin had simply been snatched away by magic. It was Theda's habit to calculate such possibilities. The death of a child whose passing she had noted in a newspaper or whom she had heard about seemed to stun her. "Seven years old," she would say again and again, disbelief and shock in her voice.

"I'd forgotten," he said.

"I haven't seen you in a while, Max, but I'm glad you're here. I'll get you coffee. Or do you want a drink?"

He shook his head.

She went across the room to the stove and brought back a coffeepot. Interrupting his vision of the window, her long arm interposed itself. It was slender, brown, faintly freckled. The coffee poured, she sat down and placed her elbows on the newspapers.

"Have you come to offer counsel, Comrade?" she asked with light irony.

"Are you writing a book?"

She scowled. "Oh, hell. Who said so? I've started a diary, a kind of backward diary. You know, I have all these paintings of Simon's." She waved toward the wall. "I don't know what I had in mind. A memorial, I guess."

"Calvin is concerned about your column."

"Don't speak to me in that unreal voice, Max."

He bowed his head. Her narrow fingers tapped the paper. She drank, put the cup back. He looked up at her.

"Calvin is a dirty little rat," she said pensively. "A knothead, a fool, a tiny monster of voracious vanity, a louse, a loon, a false man."

He began to laugh. Then he was struck by a sudden languor, as though he'd been given a drug. He realized how tense he'd been as he walked up the hill to Theda's apartment. From the floor below, he heard the familiar opening bars of *Showboat*. He looked at the floor.

"They start the day with it," she said. "It's not the only record they have, but it's the only one they play. I wonder what happened to them with that music? You'd think it was their marriage they were listening to, or a Kern version of it. They've got a life-sized picture of Helen Morgan on the wall. Funny."

"Are you all right, Theda?"

"I'm all right."

"How's the reading?"

"Warner's keeps me busy," she said, looking at the books on the floor. "I'm getting damned good, you know. I can read a seven-hundred-page Chilean novel on transparent paper in three hours."

She looked worn. She was older than Max by at least a decade; he didn't know how old, really. She was a tall, thin woman with a face that was plain in repose. But when she spoke, when her interest was aroused, her hands flew about and her shoulders moved, and the plain face with the dark narrow eyes and narrow features radiated a kind of passionate energy. She was never beautiful, in any sense that Max could think of, but she could make beauty seem insignificant. Now, assigned to tell her she was derelict in her duties, he realized how wearisome and grating a task it was. If she was "drifting," as Calvin had said, she would indeed drift.

"Calvin said you were drifting," he said.

"He's right, that flea," she said with a touch of a tall woman's contempt for a little man.

"Do you want to tell me about it?"

"No," she said. "Not yet. I'll tell you this. I'm not going to write the column any more. You can tell them I haven't the time, too much work. Don't say anything about Simon's book."

"Theda. It's been six years since Simon died. And they know you're writing something."

A nerve jumped along her jaw. Her skin turned a shade lighter.

146

She got up and went to a peg where she took down a sun hat and placed it on her head. Then she came back and sat down. She took the hat off, put it on. For a moment he thought she'd gone crazy.

"I'm not crazy," she said. "The sun's in my eyes. I like sitting near the tree, but the sun is beastly at this window. I know how long he's been dead."

He tried to say what he knew he ought to say to her, but uncertainty kept him quiet.

"Oh, I know," she said. "Why am I brooding about him? Well, I never stopped. It simply surfaced. Why did it surface this last year? Because I'm getting old, and all the dead things are floating up. The dead things in my mind. I've been throwing them out one by one. When I came to Simon, I began to grieve all over again as if I'd never grieved before. And I hadn't. What monsters . . . I am a monster, I mean. His death made me into something special for myself, you see. It was exciting. I was excited by his death."

He remembered Simon. His paintings, three lines, beach, sea, sky, always the same, empty as though he'd seen and been hypnotized by a stopped world. Max looked at the ones Theda had hung on the wall. Always the beach, sea, sky, swept clean of all that was animate. He'd met him only once, at the party that had been given him before he left for France, as a "tourist," from where he intended to make his way to Spain. Simon had been silent, stiff with drunkenness in this very room, slumped into the canvas wing chair while Theda, her sallow cheeks flushed, attended him, managing to keep the space around him empty as though she'd known he could not bear the press of people. He hadn't been a party member, just an Ohio country boy who'd traveled to Cleveland once a month to spend his time in the library there, poring through volumes of drawings. In the end, he hadn't drawn anything.

"When I took him to the ocean that first time, it was as if his heart fell out of his body," said Theda. "He gasped. I remember that."

He'd been a womanizer in a glazed, implacable way, even while he was living with Theda. Max remembered at the party the way Simon would focus his vision on a girl, looking at her with a grim sexual desperation.

There was a faded photograph of him in a gold frame on a bureau. He seemed smaller than Max remembered but the delicate

147

blank face was the same, the arrowy nose, and Irish secrecy about the eyes, the thick curly hair. They had surely been an odd couple, Theda and Concannon. She was watching him reflectively.

"What are you thinking?"

"About—attachments."

She snorted faintly.

"Why don't you tell them you're not going to do the column," he said with unexpected resentment. Silly damn long drink of water, picking over a dead man's life . . .

She smiled and took his hand and held it until he began to feel embarrassed, wanting to pull his hand away. She dropped it.

The room felt too warm.

"Max, I'm on my way out."

"Wait—"

"No. you don't want to hear it, even though you know it. I don't have enough sense to have reasons. I know there *are* good reasons, but I don't even want them. I was never good at this, this view of life. I laughed at things I shouldn't have. There are people who would as soon die as leave the party, I know that. It's the content of their lives. Not mine. I don't feel pain about it. I don't want people to be angry at me. But that doesn't weigh as much as what I want to do. I can tell what I'm going to do."

"What are you going to do?"

"You sound scared. . . . I'm going to get a job at Warner's in the story department. I can see it's coming. I'm going to buy a little car and go to the studio every morning. Maybe there'll be someone who would like to marry me someday. Maybe there's someone who will. I'm going to write my diary."

"What was it? The war? The Hitler-Stalin pact? What was it?"

"It should have been. But no. I want a common life. I want to read Jane Austen and make a little money."

"You can read Jane Austen."

"No. Not now. Later." She laughed. "What do you think of my ambitions? And you? Listen, even I know there's going to be a war, we'll be in it, everyone. The party line will change. I don't even mind that. All lines change. But I don't want to be tangled in any lines. They're killing Jews in Germany. They'll kill them in Poland, everywhere. Maybe everyone will die."

"Theda!"

"What about you, Max?" She grinned. "Tell me. I won't tell."

He was silent a long time. The sunlight was touching his hand.

He looked at the glistening leaves of the eucalyptus. Then he told her about the girl, Annie.

"What is it you have in mind?" she asked softly. "You want to shack up with her? You want to leave your little family?"

"No, no, no . . ."

"But why, then?"

He looked at her desperately. "I don't know. She caught my interest. But so do other people. It was more drastic. I can't get her out of my mind. It's as though I *had* to see her again."

"You'd better then."

He felt sanctioned, as though he'd gotten permission. He began to pace about the room.

"I went from college to the party and marriage," he said. "It's as if I had never been outside."

"Yes."

"I've always had something to do. I have a persistent wish to do nothing. To sit. To not think."

"To think," she amended.

"I mean, in the way I have thought."

"You've drifted too, Max. Calvin will have us up on charges, both of us."

"He's always had me up on charges," Max said. "In his head, he's shot me a hundred times."

"Don't be romantic about it."

"I'm not, I'm not," he protested.

She sighed. "You'd better find that girl."

He left her looking back at the obituary page, turning now and again to the window, her face hidden by the straw hat.

He went directly to the apartment house to which he'd mailed his letter and eventually roused up an aged man who gave him the forwarding address Annie had left. Then he drove up Cheremoya Avenue until he came to a plain ugly stucco house sitting on a plot of rusty grass, a hose flung across the cement walk.

A thin middle-aged woman opened the door to his ring. When he asked her for Miss Gianfala, she looked blank. "Annie," he said, afraid he'd come to a dead end.

"Oh, Annie. You mean Annie Vogel," said the woman feverishly. She kept looking uneasily behind her, as though concealing someone in back of the door. "She's in the basement apartment, down there. Go around to the back." A small child with long braids came and stuck her head under the woman's arm. "Who's that, Mom?" The woman pushed the child's head back and abruptly closed the door.

Max followed the cement path around to the back of the house. Several steps down was a door. He knocked. There was no answer at first. He was prepared to sit down in that damp corner until she came home. The door opened suddenly.

They looked at each other for several seconds, neither of them speaking.

"You're the man who gave me the ride," she said at last. Behind her the room was dark. She looked pale and thin, as though she'd lived for too long in that darkness. He didn't reply, being speechless, frightened, wishing he had never come.

"You wrote me too. It was nice of you to write me. I'm sorry I didn't answer."

Then she stood aside; he walked in as though she'd asked him to. Instantly, he stumbled into a table.

"Wait!" she said. "I'll put on some lights."

The room was a square of fourteen or so feet. A sofa bed, unmade, was in a corner. Across one wall ran a line of utilities, a small refrigerator, a stove, a white laundry sink. A huge shapeless chair sat in the middle of the room, a chenille throw covering it. He righted the table he'd bumped into.

"Please, sit down," she said.

He had not yet said a word. She looked ill but the smile was as he had remembered it. How had she landed up in this cave with its musty smell, its promise of damp corners and insects and mold? She'd changed her hair style. The braids were gone. Her hair hung down, bedraggled, limp. She was wearing a man's shirt and blue jeans, and her feet were bare. As she sat down on the bed, she tried to hide her feet beneath the blanket which drooped to the floor.

She waited.

When he finally spoke, his own voice was unfamiliar to him.

"I wondered what had happened to you," he said.

"Nothing," she said. "Nothing at all. I'm fine."

"I saw Jake Cranford and that's why I wrote."

She didn't answer. Jake's name evoked no response. She looked broodingly at the floor, then up at Max. Her eyes were strained, enormous. It struck him she was possessed of some immense idea that was taking up her entire concentration, her being. She really didn't see him.

150

"I thought you might need some help. My wife and I—"

He broke off. The smile had flashed out, but now it was not the appeasing, uneasy smile he remembered. It was ironic, maledictory.

He went on, doggedly, "talked about you"—why was he telling such a lie?—"and I thought, after Jake told me about you, you might not know many people, you might need a job . . ." his voice trailed off. Why couldn't he say an honest word?

"I'm married too," she said, speaking tonelessly so that her statement seemed no more than a token to match his, as though they were about to start a game and each one must assure the other there was a manikin in his corner. The import of what she said hit him suddenly. He looked around the room as though Annie's husband might be there, hidden in the shadows.

"I don't know where he is," she said. "I haven't heard for a long while. Murmansk perhaps."

"Murmansk!"

"He's a seaman."

"The man you were going to meet that day?"

"Yes. That one."

"You look ill."

She looked exhausted as though she'd been kept up all night by some savagery in another room of this miserable little house. Yet her youth was plain to see; the whole balance of her body, slumped over as she was, one hand against her stomach, belied her weariness. She shook her head and bent farther over, then gripped her belly; he watched, panicked, helpless. Then she looked up, her eyes again so wide they appeared, for a moment, to be lidless.

"What is it?" he cried.

"No, no . . ."

She stood up suddenly. "Can I make you some coffee?"

"No, thanks."

"I don't think I have any in any case."

"Why is he in Murmansk?"

"I don't know that he is. But he said he might go the Murmansk run. The bonus is big. The money . . . that was it." She sat down again on the corner of the bed, twisting her feet beneath the covers on the floor. "I'd like to find my shoes and put them on," she said timidly. He understood she didn't want him to observe her in this commonplace act. "Aren't those shoes?" he asked pointing to a pair of huaraches under the sink.

151

She went quickly and took them up and slipped them on, her back to him. She was taller than he'd remembered but he knew she'd not been so ribby, so gaunt.

"Jake said you had a dreadful job."

"Oh, that was then. I've had a lot more since I saw Jake. They've all been pretty much the same. Worm jobs, for the worms."

"Don't think that way."

"How shall I think?"

"It's hard to find work—if you're not trained for anything special. And the Depression isn't really over yet."

"People who've been through that, they seem to think it's a medal they've earned."

"It is."

She looked at him with interest.

"A lot of people didn't survive it," he said, indifferent to what he was talking about, grateful only for her interest.

"Oh, the people who killed themselves . . ."

"No. What you called the worms. They died on their feet, eaten up with indignities they suffered."

"How about three meals a day?"

"Most of the people in the world don't eat three—"

"You sound like Walter. My husband. Three meals a day and people will be good and kind and happy."

"It would help."

"What thing is it in people that it would help?"

He stirred restlessly. "I'm sorry," she said. "I'm ignorant of nearly everything. Not that I don't read. But I can't read books about the way things are, history and economics, all that."

"What do you like?"

"Stories."

"What kind of stories?"

"Tony, my father, sometimes gave me a book. I lost most of them because of moving around. The last one I read was *Passage to India*."

"Did you like that?"

"Oh, yes."

"There was a girl in a class of mine in college. She kept asking all of us, 'What *was* going on in those Marabar caves. What *was* the noise Mrs. Moore heard?'" Annie didn't seem to find that as funny as he did.

"I wonder . . ." she said, seriously.

"What else?"

"James Huneker."

"He didn't write stories."

"He wrote some," she corrected, without emphasis. "And Conrad. And Chesterton. *The Man Who Was Thursday*. And Dickens. *Robin Hood.*"

"Faulkner?"

"I don't like all those idiots. Tony calls him the Mississippi ghoul."

"That's an odd group of people you like."

"Oh, well, there are others. I used to make lists of things I liked to read. I loved to write their names down."

"And what about modern writers? Like Joyce? Or Virginia Woolf? What about the Russians?"

"Lawrence," she said. *"Sons and Lovers.* Do you remember, when Mr. Morel brings home the packages, and she and Paul—"

She clutched her belly again. He stood up, alarmed.

"You *are* sick."

"It'll go," she groaned. And then a look of horror came over her face again. Her mouth stretched oddly. He went to her and took one of her hands.

"Can't I help you?" he begged.

"No. I hate to tell you. I hate to say what it is."

"I'll call a doctor."

"I have a doctor." She slid her hand out of his and said, "Sit down. It was nice to talk about stories. It made me feel better."

He sat, his knees trembling.

"Jake was sick too, wasn't he? Colitis? What happened to Jake?"

"He wants to go in the army."

"Yes. His friend Brody thought that would be a good idea for everybody. The army."

He must make an effort to speak plainly. They were adrift in this cellar; their conversation was out of time. Her thinness, the pain that showed on her face, her exhaustion, the tap that dripped, the disarranged bedcovers, the shadowed dampness, the sense of a day blown by the wind into night just outside one small window made him feel as though he was being dissipated into some other medium. The tight knots of certainty and attitudes, opinions, of

153

daily habit, of responsibility to his wife and his child, his political commitment were unloosened.

"Do you need a job?" he asked abruptly.

She laughed. "I can get a job, like that," she said. "There are nothing but jobs at my level of competence. Ten or fifteen a week. The last job was eighteen, really. That's why I'm sick." She looked faintly sly for a moment. He was surprised, not thinking she would be sly. "I'll tell you about it," she said.

"I didn't mean that kind of job."

"I was a stock girl when I knew Jake Cranford," she began, and he could not tell if she was mocking herself with the faint theatrical flourish of her beginning history, or whether she was making an effort to distract herself from the affliction in her belly.

"I worked in a basement full of rats. One day I could not go down there where the water dripped all day and half the merchandise was growing living mold. I ran out of money on the third day after I was fired. I hocked an engagement ring Walter had given me. I stayed inside for a week, except for going out to buy groceries. I lay in bed and it was a dream in which hours simply went by with no thought, no motion, like a pale sky without clouds or birds, nothing to mark the time. The money was going again. This time there was nothing at the end. Walter wrote me from New York. He said he couldn't tell me exactly where he was going but if I used my head, I'd remember, and not to expect to hear from him for a while. He sent me a money order for twenty dollars. I cried with relief. I would not have to leave the room yet, except for food. And then *that* came to an end. On the day I had one dollar left in my bag, a man who wrote me the same time you did, a friend of Walter's, stopped by. I was sitting in the room on the bed and there was a knock on the door. I couldn't see his face for the stack of books he was carrying. He called me Annie as though he'd heard all about me. He set the books down on a chair and I watched them slip off as he spoke. He didn't pick them up. Neither did I. He was a very small man with a little pointed beard, grayish all over, wearing a smart suit. He said—one of those people who say your name between every word as though reassuring you that they know who you are, leading you to the exact opposite conclusion—that he'd be around to see me soon, give me time to read what he called 'the literature,' and that he'd be happy to hear my impressions of what I'd read then. I was to understand that what he'd brought me was only a sampler, but he'd chosen the

works carefully in view of my background, my age, my experience. But what I was thinking about—you see, he was the man
my husband Walter had spent a whole afternoon with in a cutting
room looking at pictures of a South American dancer who'd forgotten to put on her pants. What *he* was thinking about, I couldn't
guess. I thanked him and he stood at the door a minute, then
touched two fingers to his hat like a movie actor and left."

"He was a film cutter?" Max asked softly, his curiosity stronger
than his wish to not interrupt her.

"Yes."

"Paul Lavan?"

"Yes, yes," she said, nodding, no surprise in her voice. Then
she looked directly at him. "You were going to a Communist convention that day, weren't you?"

Max recalled Fern's precautions and laughed.

"Yes."

"Oh," she cried, and clutched herself.

"Please . . . what is it?"

"Tapeworm," she gasped. "In its death throes."

He sat back in the chair, flinging a hand toward her as though
to ward off a blow.

"The doctor gave me something. Malefern. It takes twenty-four
hours. I haven't eaten anything."

Max stood up and went to the sink and turned the tap into a
tumbler he found there. He drank every bit of the water down. He
felt ill.

"Is there anything—"

"Nothing," she said. "I have to wait it out. I want to die. That's
the truth. How can I live through this? It's *thrashing* around. God
knows how big it is. Do you see? I want to go off a cliff to get
away from it, to drown, to be burnt up. Anything."

He was so astonished that he stood there like a limp doll, his
back against the sink. "I'll stay," he muttered. "I'll stay with you
until it's over."

"Will you? Now that you've come here, I wouldn't want to see
you go. As long as I was alone, my mind seemed to go. I had to
make it go because I can't stand the thing that is happening. But
now, my mind is back. My mind and the worm."

"You haven't slept."

"No, I haven't slept."

"Can you have water?"

155

"No. Not yet."

"Do you have a telephone?"

"Upstairs. The woman who owns the house."

"Does she know? Could she help you?"

"She can't help anyone. She's mad with trouble. She ran away from her husband a year ago and came west. And her lover took a chain to her two weeks ago in front of the little girl. The little girl ran away. I went and found her. Maybe she would let someone use the phone. Who do you want to phone?" Her voice had risen on her last question. It was like a smothered scream. He shuddered, knowing she didn't care whom he had to phone.

"I'm going to stay with you. I have to call my wife."

"Will it be all right?"

"Yes. But I don't need to phone her yet. Talk. Keep talking."

"I will . . . I read one book that day. It was short. *Ten Days That Shook the World*. Then I started another, *Marching! Marching!* by a woman with a strange name, Weathervane?"

"Weatherwax."

"Yes. And the *Communist Manifesto* and something I've already forgotten by Lenin. There, right over there," and she gestured toward a corner where he saw a pile of books against the wall. "I'd better keep on," she said. "I get taken up by fear now and then and see myself running down the street, but how can you get away from such a thing? I got another job. Sorting rivets. Three men ran the place. A long narrow room with a roll-top desk in the front and ten bins in the back. There were eight Mexican girls picking through the rivets and a ninth chair empty in front of a bin. They paid nine dollars a week and said when things really got going, they'd pay us piecework wages and we'd make fifty dollars a week." She lay down.

"Let me just rest a minute. I'll talk again in a while."

He stayed quiet in the chair, watching her, seeing her white face shining with sweat. She had drawn up her knees, the discolored leather of the huaraches among the blanket folds. A faint trail of light crept along the floor, gray light like the trail of a slug; a ray of street lamp filtered through the little window. He would call Eva. What he had to tell her assumed no reasonable shape.

The girl lay quietly. She was waiting for the next thrust of the obscene thing in her vitals, for the dread of that moment. She remembered how the Mexican girls had bought her orange Popsicles, laughing as she licked them, standing outside on the sidewalk

156

during their brief lunchtime. *Huesos* they'd called her, *flaca,* because she grew thinner daily, as though she were being rendered by the California sunlight. She told Max about that, and he leaned toward her as though he were going deaf. Was she whispering? She didn't know.

In the back of the shop, it had been cool and cavelike; the unshaded bulbs hanging over the bins had thrown an orange cast on her hands. They sat sorting rivets, dropping the damaged ones into baskets at their feet. The Mexican girls brought their lunches in tin pails, cold omelets, beans, tacos. Annie bought a hot dog now and then from a wagon at the corner and drank Cokes. She sometimes didn't eat, buying cigarettes instead. On an empty stomach, the smoke made her lightheaded; her chair seemed to rest not on a dirty floor but on a moving tide, and her hands trembled. She felt off balance, on the verge of illness. She discovered she could arouse a reckless hilarity in the girls. She was their clown. Sometimes the three men drove out to Lockheed-Vega aircraft plant to pick up sacks of unsorted rivets and deliver the sorted ones. The Mexican girls often walked during their lunchtime, their arms encircling each other's waists, looking like a flock of plump brown birds.

Bent over her bin all day, Annie labored toward six o'clock while in the front room, on the roll-top desk, the men played craps. They threw the dice back and forth, swearing at each other, the smell of cigar smoke drifting back to the bins. Annie stooped beneath the day's torpor.

"Those Jews!" said Laurita.

"Annie, *chica,* ask them when they're gonna pay us by the sack. They'll listen to you," said Natalie.

She tried.

"That's all right, kid," one of the men said. "Soon as we get straight with the airplane people, get all this worked out, get the contract, you fellows will go on straight piecework. Takes time—you get me? We got practically not two bucks between us. Understand, we're trying to get this thing set up for all of us, but we got to pull in our belts until the good times come. When they start making planes for the war, you'll see. You got to remember, we're not one of your rich outfits with plenty of capital." She went back to her bin and listened to the dice hitting the wood. Suddenly she'd shouted, "When are you going to pay us enough to live on? Don't give me any story about contracts!"

157

The three men came to the door, their heads all held at the same angle of indignation.

"Out," said one to Annie. "You're just out."

She began to laugh. "Crooks," she screamed. Around her the girls were silent. She glanced at them. They had drawn back their chairs. Their eyes glistened. She could hear their accelerated breathing.

"I've been fired," she said gaily, weakly.

Laurita stood up, then the others.

"We'll all go," said the girl. There were distressed murmurs from the others. They needed the money; they couldn't quit.

"I'll go," Annie said, pulling back her chair. "But you don't have to. Thanks anyhow."

She wasn't angry any more. After she left, there would be no sign she'd ever been in that room. There was nothing to take from it except her old black pocketbook. As she walked toward the front where the three men were standing in a line like an ushering service, one of them stuffed a five-dollar bill in her hand, unclenching her fingers and closing them around the money.

"I'm going to the union," Annie said softly.

"Ha! The union," said the one who'd given her the money.

"What does she know," said another. "The stupid!"

Max was standing over her looking down.

"You're all right?"

"I was remembering that place," she said. She sat up slowly, as though afraid she'd empty out.

"This will be over," Max said. She looked up at him. They remained that way for what seemed a long time, simply looking at each other. Then he went back and sat down.

"I went to the union about them," she said. She had hardly known what a union was. John Lewis, the CIO, that was all. She discovered the central office in the phone book.

The CIO headquarters were housed in an old frame building with dusty floors. A man was sweeping up some debris. She was directed to an office where a man wearing a gray fedora sat behind a scored oak desk. There was nothing on it except a telephone and an ashtray. Sunlight knifed through a torn shade and left a scar upon the floor.

"I've just been fired from this place," she had said.

"Hold it. What's your job?"

"I was sorting rivets."

158

"That's not a category."

"The men who own the shop hired nine girls. They collect rivets from the airplane factories, then sort them according to size, and the ones that aren't damaged they sell back."

"What rivets?"

"The ones they use in airplanes. When they're riveting, the rivets fly all around. They lose a good many."

The man laughed. The sound of it echoed in the big empty room. "Americans, they'd sell brimstone in hell," he said. "If there was a place where there was nothing, *nothing,* you understand, and there were two citizens of our country standing there in that *nothing,* one would rent out standing space to the other, and the other would tax him for running a space-renting business."

"They paid us nine dollars a week," said Annie.

"Well, you can't go far on that kind of wage."

"They kept promising us piecework."

"Mexicans? I mean were the other girls mostly Mexican?"

"All except me."

The man looked shrewdly at his desk, then took a cigar from his jacket pocket. He lit it and threw the cellophane wrapper on the floor.

"Reason I ask is because they couldn't get away with it if the girls weren't Mexican. See, anybody else would know better." He grinned at her.

"I'm not Mexican and I took the job because I needed the money."

The man stared at her. She thought she knew what he was thinking—you'd have to be Mexican for nine dollars to make a difference.

"I didn't say you were. Not that it's a disgrace. I'm what they call in Pennsy a hunkie. All right, gimme the address." She wrote it down on a piece of crumpled paper he took from his pocket. "Maybe we can scare them," he said. "Listen, there's lots of good jobs. And there are going to be lots more, once we're in the war."

"War?"

"My Christ! Listen, don't think they're not going to pass that selective training and service act! How old are you?"

"Nineteen," she lied.

"How come you come to us?"

"I didn't know where else to go," she said backing toward the door. "I'd heard about you."

159

"You heard about us, eh?"

The man wanted her to stay. A fly buzzed somewhere.

"Well, in a sense, you got the right idea. You go to the A.F. of L., they won't give you the time of day if you haven't been on a machine for eighty years. You people haven't got no skills, you'd just be up the creek without oars if it wasn't for us."

"What did the union do?" Max was asking her softly.

"I don't really know. But a month later, I went by the place and it was boarded up."

"Then what?"

"Then I got a good job. In a Greek restaurant where I used to eat. With tips, I made about twenty dollars a week. That's why I'm sick now."

She paused, taking up the blanket and wrapping it around herself.

"Are you cold?"

"I can't tell."

"I know a couple who run a little ceramic place," Max said. "They make their own things and sell them to retailers. The pottery is pretty awful, vases with sleeping Mexicans in sombreros painted on them, all that, birds for the lawn, but still, they're always needing people. Have you ever done any drawing—anything like that?"

"I went to the Art Students League for a while," she said. "It wasn't anything, just something to do."

"You wouldn't have to be Leonardo for this. It's mechanical."

"I'm not ungrateful. But the thing is—I have a job waiting for me—in a drive-in at Laguna Beach. As soon as this—this thing is out of me. There's a waitress where I worked who's going down there. The tips are supposed to be good, and it's supposed to be nice there."

Despairing at the thought of her disappearing again, he cast about in his mind for something compelling enough to hold her, here, where he could see her. But what was he thinking of?

"Do you know what time it is?"

"My clock is broken," she said. "But I'd guess it's around six or so." She switched the blanket away from her feet and went to the window. "What a joint this is!" she exclaimed. "I have to put my head out the window into the flowerbed to see what the weather is. But it's so cheap." She pushed aside the cloth and looked out. "How odd! There's actually a cloud in the sky, like real weather."

160

"I must telephone now," he said. "Is there a drugstore around?"

"It's three blocks from here," she said. "Far."

She looked at him quickly, then away, and he realized she was making an effort not to ask him to stay. "I won't be long," he said, "I have to call the neighbor who takes care of my son—"

A curious expression crossed her face. He knew he'd given her an important piece of news, one that disturbed her.

"My wife has a secretarial job and the neighbor will tell her I'll be late."

"How old is he?"

"Not quite three."

"Is he alone a lot?"

"No, no. I'm home a good deal. It's Eva who goes off in the morning. He loves the neighbor." Then he added for no reason, "She's a big dumb woman, easy on a child."

She laughed a little; the laugh broke off as she lowered herself carefully to the bed. "It's moving," she gasped.

She had turned to lie on her stomach; her face was hidden by a pillow. His skin prickled as he gripped one hand with the other. There was nothing he could say to her. The worm was dying. It was as if she were dying.

She was very good to talk the way she did, losing herself in her stories, not clinging to the ghastly process taking place inside her. But he could not really think about what she was telling him. He was listening for that other thing—as though it would have a voice, a subterranean mouthless moan.

He had been with her for hours now, and his memory of her had faded, replaced by a living presence.

That quality he had attributed to her when she'd walked away from Fern's car in San Diego, of stubbornness, of will, was here confirmed. What at first had been so easy for him to grasp, the forlorn *facts* of her life, the room, the damp, the dripping tap, her poverty, her jobs, the marriage that seemed so negligible, had gone feeble, tenuous, as he had begun to feel the force and mystery of her nature.

He reminded himself sharply that everyone was made of class and fortune and circumstance, of food and work, given or withheld. But in the rawness of his openness to her, he kicked all such categories out of his mind like bums, knowing at the same time that he could not utterly abandon the beliefs he had acquired over nearly a decade. Ordinary life had its ordinary powerful truths.

161

God damn all! She needed work, care, knowledge of the world! How long could that will of hers lead her like a Seeing Eye dog through idiot events? Helpless now to help her, afraid of his own thoughts, he was, on this painful occasion, suddenly happy.

An hour later, he left to phone. She had begged him to go and when he hesitated, she had said, "I've got to collect what comes out for the laboratory. The doctor said the head of it must be there, otherwise it will grow again. And—please go now!" She had turned then and stumbled toward a small door near the couch. His bowels trembled as he went down the street. What she must be going through in the bathroom he visualized at once, obliged to attend every second of her travail as much as he was able.

He made his phone call, then bought two egg sandwiches and a Hershey bar from the drugstore luncheonette counter and walked back to Annie's cellar. In the twenty minutes he had been gone she had managed to pull the bed together, and she was sitting up in the large chair, her face ashen but tranquil.

"Is it all right?"

She nodded.

"Did you?"

"Yes. I did. I won't tell you about it. It's done now. I feel very tired."

"I've brought you a sandwich."

She smiled musingly, gently, as though some delicate thought had touched her. She said, "I can't yet. It's that I can't put anything in my stomach. I could eat watercress, but not real food, it's too much like the other . . . I feel as if I never wanted to eat again. I've had a glass of water. It was so good."

"Will you mind if I eat?"

"No. I started to tell you how I got the worm. After I got the job in the restaurant, well, I made more than twenty dollars a week, really, with the tips, although most of the people who come in there aren't rich, just caddies, people like that. And there's a Finnish man, he always gave me a dollar even if he only had a cup of coffee. I've gotten to hate Sibelius though. I didn't eat there except for a sandwich late at night when the Greek closed up. And I developed this craving, oh, it was terrible! For hamburgers. I found a place called Tips. The hamburgers were thirty-five cents but, even now, just thinking about it, I want one. They had about ten different ways of making them. One was with mayonnaise and pickles, and I could have eaten ten. As it was, I used to have two

162

for lunch. The waiters laughed at me, but I was like a hog in a dream, I couldn't ever get enough. I thought about them the moment I woke up and—when I realized I had enough money to really buy them for lunch! Then I began to try other places, drive-ins and drugstores and diners. That's how I must have gotten the worm. I lost weight, and I felt strange, and the girl who works at the Greek's told me I was beginning to look like a nun, that white papery look. I couldn't ever get enough to eat. Sometimes the Greek let me finish the shrimp cocktails and even cook myself a steak on the grill after everyone had left, early in the morning. I ate and ate and ate. I was going crazy with food. But it was the taste for the ground meat—everything else was secondary to that. And finally the girl sent me to a doctor. I took him a specimen and he said I had a tapeworm. Listen . . . when he told me what I had to do, I couldn't make myself do it. I didn't know which was worse, to have the worm or to get rid of it. And then, a few days ago, I fell down carrying a tray to a table, and spilled catsup all over a customer. So I took the pills."

"I think you want to sleep," he said.

"I could sleep, I think."

"I'll stay with you."

She rose somewhat unsteadily and he helped her to the bed where she lay down. He covered her with a blanket and went to the chair. She was asleep almost instantly.

His vigil lasted until late that evening. She awoke all at once, her eyes opening, coming to rest on him. She smiled. "You never believe terrible things will be over," she said.

"I saved a sandwich for you. It's a little stale."

She took it and ate it all.

"Won't you stay here in Hollywood, and let me help? I have a friend, a woman you might like. And that job. Do you really want to go to that drive-in? It's hard work. People won't treat you well."

"I have to. I promised the waitress, Sigrid, I'd go with her. I'll just try it. I can always come back."

He had to leave now. He lit a cigarette, aware he hadn't smoked since he'd been with her—he'd been waiting. She asked him for one and, when he gave it to her, said, "This time, I really don't have any. When you gave me those cigarettes in the car, I had some in my bag. How crooked I've gotten! You know, that woman upstairs, she wants to be listened to. I listen to her because

163

sometimes she makes cocoa for me while I'm sitting at the kitchen table. She says that now that she's up against life, she sees it's a cruel fraud. She likes to talk about that—she seems satisfied to have found it out."

She was too young, he reflected, to know what people were *like* —she only knew what they did to her.

But he was struck by her expression. She was looking up at the ceiling as though she could see the beaten woman and her nervous child. She was smoking; she was thinking. The harrowing hours she'd spent with the worm had left her weak, but her thoughts were already on something else.

"What happened to that woman who drove the car?"

"Fern? Oh, Fern."

"She thought I was foolish to be upset about that dog."

"Fern casts her eyes beyond the bones at her feet."

She looked puzzled.

"She's the kind of person, she—" But he was bored already. Talking about Fern was like eating stale bread. She grinned at him. "She's not so bad," he said, a touch defensive. "She's loyal, she does all the work no one else wants to."

"I suppose that fellow, Lavan, came looking for me at the place I used to be. Walter wanted me to go to meetings. He wanted me to be in the party."

"Why aren't you?"

"What would they want with me?"

"What would you want?"

"I went to a meeting in New York. Bourgeoise, Walter calls me. I had never thought of that, belonging to a class, a class that oppresses others."

"People suffer needlessly," he said, exhausted now.

She flared up. "Everybody suffers. I don't know what you mean —needlessly. You think suffering is a failing?"

"I mean, there are sufferings that can be stopped. There is slavery, corruption, exploitation of many by a few."

"You think you can make it different?"

"Better. Socialism can make it better. Things are awry." He thought for a moment. Class conflict, the English orphans virtual slaves in factories, the mad utopianism of the nineteenth century, inevitable revolution—he'd read so much, Liebknecht and Alcott and Brisbane and Saint-Simon and Fourier and Kautsky, Engels and Marx, and—

164

"How can you do that? With the good will of the capitalists?"

"No."

"Force?"

"The force of the working class."

"And then?"

" 'From each according to his abilities, to each according to his needs.' "

"Who said that?"

"Louis Blanc."

"And when one has no abilities?"

"When true Communism comes, one will receive what he needs, with or without abilities."

"People are too wicked."

"Because of the system."

"It can't be that Communism is the first system that will work. No. Even I know that. Even I know . . ."

"You must read history."

"Walter says bourgeois history is all distortion."

"Listen. You must learn something of the world outside you."

"You stayed with me today. You were so good to do that."

He stood silently by the door, feeling the wrench of leaving her. She walked over to him.

"I'll want to know what happens to you," he said. "Will you write me from Laguna Beach?"

"To your house?"

"Yes, yes. Of course to my house." He found a piece of paper in his wallet, a laundry ticket—he'd never get his shirts back— and wrote down the address and put it in her hand as he visualized himself in mortal combat with the Chinese laundryman.

Suddenly she seized his hand, the pencil still gripped in his fingers, and brought it to her mouth and pressed her lips on it. "Thank you." she said.

He arrived home to find the door ajar and heard voices, one loud, two murmuring. He sighed bitterly.

It was Levi Lewis and his wife, Cleo. Max walked into his living room. Eva was standing in the middle of the room looking rather lumpish, a cigarette hanging from her lips, her eyes fixed on Levi, whose arm clutched Cleo's plump shoulders. As usual, Cleo looked dazed. She was Levi's chief exhibit, perhaps the only one in his life. His Negro bride. His *bona fides* couldn't be questioned.

He asserted himself feverishly on every occasion, talking, talk-

165

ing, talking, as though Cleo's presence—and look how he was gripping her as though she might disappear—gave him limitless license to explore the caverns of his mind. Wretched man! Poor Cleo with her young round soft face, the tendrils of hair that curled around her ears, the neat brown hands pressed against one another on her lap, her whole body pulled into Levi's embrace, his talisman, his object.

He managed to refer to his heroic act in every conversation, at meetings, at caucuses, just as Fern dragged in her family. And some were impressed. Yes, Calvin Schmitter was impressed. Why, Levi had actually married one of *them!*

"Hello, Cleo," Max said warmly. She smiled up at him, trying to inch away from her frantic husband's frantic grip.

"I'm here too," said Lewis. "I realize my wife's *singular* attractions, but you might speak to me, Shore."

Eva nodded at him companionably. That was part of their bargain. If he stayed out, if she stayed out, no questions.

They were both serious people.

"Hello, Levi."

"We were speaking of the repercussions of the Disney strike. Walt and his seven hundred dwarfs. Have you noticed, by the way, that all the mice are white?"

Max snorted. "Not entirely," he said. It was going to be a while before they left. "I'm going to grab a bite," he announced somewhat belligerently, and went to the kitchen.

The Lewises left at one. Eva sank into a couch. Max had been watching her, hardly listening to the conversation. A kind of pity welled up in him. He did not know where it had come from. She looked so tired; she had gained a good deal of weight, he noticed, and her breasts seemed so heavy, and sad somehow. He went over to her and flung his arms about her and buried his face in her neck, smelling her familiar odor, the odor of her thick hair, her neck. He put his leg on her lap and pulled her closer and she said, "Well, what's come over you?" But she was pleased. He knew that.

Sometime during the night, Max awoke in a state of acute alarm. He disengaged his arm from under Eva's shoulders and went to Thomas's crib. For a while, he listened to the child's soft, even breathing. Without touching him, Max leaned over the cribside and examined each small feature of his face by the weak light of a night lamp. Even if Thomas awoke, Max could hardly expect the boy to tell him that everything would be all right.

166

Chapter 12

Sigrid dyed her short stiff hair canary yellow and painted new, swollen lips over her own thin mouth. When Annie drove up to Ivar Street, Sigrid was standing there among packages and a suitcase, looking like a neon sign that had been left on during daylight. They loaded up the car. "Jesus!" said Sigrid from time to time about nothing particular.

Having settled herself at last in the car, she looked calculatingly at Annie. "Well, we'll see what's to happen. You got rid of that worm? My brother's found us an apartment a mile from the drive-in, near the beach. I called that stink of a landlady of yours but she wouldn't go get you. I called three times. The last time I said, 'Jesus! you old bag! why don't you lay off the hootch sometime?' and she hung up. What I wanted to tell you was about the apartment Joe got. Joe's going to stay awhile. There's a room downstairs in the garage with a cot in it. He's got nothing better to do right now. He said he's going to try for a bartender's job. They've got lots of joints down there. You look awful."

Annie told her the worm was gone and that she felt a little weak still but the lab said they'd found the head—

"Jesus! Don't tell me no details!"

—and Sigrid didn't understand about the landlady, who was always being beaten up by her lover and was not drunk but sick.

"I got no charity to spare," Sigrid said. She lit a cigarette and settled back against the cracked leather seat.

Sigrid, who had been to Laguna a few times before, gave directions but was silent most of the time. They stopped once for gas, and later she asked Annie to pull over near a stretch of woods so she could answer a "call of nature." There was no special restraint between them. They didn't ever have much to say to each other. After work in the Greek's with Sigrid, Annie knew that her bursts of conversation always had to do with some immediate or imminent event. The nearest thing that could pass for speculation was that occasional guileful look of the Swedish girl's—as for that, it seemed more mimetic than an indication of thought. But, Annie thought, she was "goodhearted," which was the most one could expect as a rule. One could put up with a lot if people were goodhearted, even their cruelties.

Max Shore, whose visit had only taken place a few days earlier, was more complicated to think about. Shore's presence during that terrible day and evening had been of greater magnitude than mere goodheartedness. Alone, Annie told herself, she might have cut her own throat in order to escape the vermin's emergence. Even as Max had knocked on her door, she had been in a condition of such utter panic, at the furthermost reaches of paralyzed terror, that she had hesitated to open the door for fear that she would fling herself into the street and try, impossibly, to outrun the hours still to be endured.

So he had sat there with her, watchful, tense, his attention, the whole attention of a man she didn't know, given over to her as though he'd handed her himself to use as she might want. They had gone through it together. He had covered her; she had taken the stale sandwich from his hands. Yet she had been unable to take up his offer of help, then anyhow. Her sense of obligation to Sigrid, about whom she cared little, weighed more heavily than the promise of Max Shore's taking a place in her life. Not that she believed there were any jobs for her except drudgery. As for the lady friend he'd mentioned, what did she care about her except to see who it was Max had as a friend.

She had told him her stories out of dread lest her mind be consumed by the worm. But she'd not told him all her stories.

There were the movies. She spent days at the movies; she went to work from the picture houses; she bore on her forearms the imprints of the movie-chair arms because she pressed down so in

168

dread that a man would come and sit beside her and put his hand on her thigh—or worse, as had once happened when, instead of a hand, a man laid across her skirt, like a bound roll of pennies, his naked penis.

It was movie music that hypnotized her—those swollen pulsating chords, the pudding texture of beaten pianos and whipped violins as the lovers kissed, as the mist covered the mansion, as the ship's prow rose and sank upon orderly oceans, as calendar pages fell through apple blossoms and snowflakes to tell of the passing of time, as cowboys took their guns from holsters, as Bogart drove straight toward her down a narrow city street, as girls danced in dreams for themselves. Dimitri Tiomkin! It was a name that made her reel even as she carried four shrimp cocktails along her arm to a table full of sallow-faced caddies munching crackers at a corner table.

That movie music, when she left the theater, lifted her from the sidewalk, obscured the light, whether of afternoon or night or morning. She knew it was awful stuff; she wept, not for the humble Viennese girl who, deserted by the successful composer, threw herself into the Danube, but because of that music, a smothering syrup that drowned her brains, yet released in her a flood of melancholy that through some alchemy became a kind of exaltation.

Gunther Wildener, the white-haired man she'd met at the actor's house where Walter had taken her, managed to track her down. He had the weighty jocularity Annie had come to recognize in middle-aged men who wanted to put their hands on the bodies of young girls. He had advised her what to do with her life from the same chair in which Max Shore had sat; he suggested she make a little extra money posing for pictures. She was driven to someone's estate. She sat naked on a diving board, the rough warp of its rope surface cutting into her buttocks, while several men who did not speak to her took photographs. She moved this way and that according to Wildener's directions. Someone said, "Do something about the nipples."

She dressed. Wildener took her to a restaurant on Sunset Strip. An actor she recognized was sitting in a corner drinking by himself. After a number of drinks, he threw up, without apparent strain, into his handsome gray fedora. Then gave it to a waiter and staggered out. Brocade hung in threatening folds from the corners of the room. She felt she was in a tent that was about to collapse.

169

"There's nothing wrong with it," Wildener assured her. "You have a marvelous body. So we make little color pictures and gentlemen from all over the country can enjoy and admire you. Have the stroganoff." He ran his thick strong hand down her arm. "You need some clothes to set you off," he said. She asked him about his students. He was not distracted for long. They both understood. After he'd gotten up heavily from the bed in his apartment, he headed toward the bathroom and said, "Poor thing," in such a tone she thought he was about to burst into tears. She thought he'd meant himself.

She discovered, or, rather, recognized at last, that men wanted to do this thing to her that they wanted to do to anyone. Her body, the object, was of no value to her. Yet somewhere, like a hidden depravity, she felt love for it, pitied it like the lost animals she sometimes saw slinking into the doorways of closed shops late at night.

The movie music was almost always with her. A man's glance, the million-dollar chords began; he spoke, a violin played a cheap and tender tune; they walked down the night streets of Hollywood, cellos stained the night sky plum; they looked at each other in his or her room, a low muffled roll of drums. Then the male body covered her and the whole orchestra fell into its own pit with a tinny crash of instruments. Yes. Then the whole goddamned bunch picked up their lunch boxes and instruments and put on their old coats and went home.

Paul Lavan had caught up with her too. She'd told him she'd read all the books. She hadn't. He took her to several meetings.

She felt she had no right to be in the bare rooms with the rows of ordinary people, some of whom dropped cigarette butts on the floor and carefully smashed them out, all of whom listened to the speaker with silence and attention. "The inherent contradictions of monopoly capitalism." What a roll of drums that was! They were so *serious!* If Lavan knew, if they knew what her life was like, if they had known about the movie music, the hamburgers, the men, the distraught midnight wanderings.

But Lavan did, apparently, know something. "You're neurotic," he said to her one evening after they'd heard a discussion on "art as a weapon." He was taking her to her streetcar. He had his own car, but said his wife had a new baby and he really couldn't take the time to drive her home.

"Neurotic?" she asked.

170

"Have you ever heard of Freud?"

"Yes," she answered. She tried to recall the jokes she'd heard that somehow involved Freud.

"Listen," he said with sudden uneasiness, "don't mention what I said to anyone. Actually, I shouldn't employ such phrases. It's only that you seem so troubled and I—"

"I won't say anything," she said quickly. What did he care whether she "mentioned" what he'd said? Perhaps he knew she slept with men. Perhaps he felt bad for Walter. She went home that night, brooding about Walter, whose infrequent notes always ended with the admonition to keep her legs crossed. Why didn't she feel something about Walter? About the men she "betrayed" him with?

She knew that people, once married, were not supposed to do what she did; somewhere in the back of her mind hung pale abstractions, motionless as painted clouds, God, orderliness of meals, gravity of mien, classroom papers, one's name neatly written on the upper-right-hand corner, families grouped around the dining table, the elders teaching the young, undying love, music of the spirit, not of the kisses and deaths of movie stars.

She burst out laughing, and Sigrid said, "Jesus! You scared me!" and Annie said, "Only a thought, an old joke."

"Tell me, I wanna laugh too," Sigrid demanded. So Annie told her an old grammar-school series of jokes that had to do with book titles—*The Halt in the Desert*, by Mustapha Pee. . . . And Sigrid shrieked with laughter.

It would be fine to travel on forever like this, safe in the car, carrying in the trunk a rag or two to throw on one's back, plenty of cigarettes in the side pockets. But a large sign announcing the imminence of Laguna Beach dispelled the snugness. A touch of dread, familiar as morning light, made Annie's hands tighten on the wheel.

The village lay still beneath the midday sun. With wary eyes, Annie took in the expensive-looking small shops that lined the ocean side of the road. On the left, up in the hills, the blood-red roof tiles of estates hung like awnings among the brilliant leaves of the trees.

"There's the drive-in," Sigrid announced, pointing to a circular building on the ocean cliff. One car was parked on the asphalt apron, a tray clamped onto the driver's window, a crumpled paper napkin on the tray.

171

Less than a mile farther on, Sigrid shouted, "Here! Turn here!"

They drove up a crushed-shell-covered road to an innocuous little house that might have once been the servants' quarters of a large estate. Flowers climbed along the outer walls, one thick vine followed the rail of the stairs that led to an upper floor. As Annie parked, Sigrid's brother, his white shirt sleeves rolled up, opened the narrow door on the ground floor and stood blinking there in the sunlight, stretching and rubbing his face.

He was a slender boy of about twenty and he looked less like Sigrid's brother than a son she might have thrown off in an earlier, more innocent time when her hair had been the same light-brown color as his. Sigrid leaped upon him, and Annie had a sudden picture of Sigrid love-making, awkward, bumpy, an inept farmer girl, cows thumping in barns, smells of clover and sweat and dung.

They went to work the next day. Ernie Cotts was from Oklahoma and he intended to make his fortune out of the drive-in. His pale, flat-chested wife did the books on a cleared table in the back of the kitchen, sitting there like a weed, her face wrinkled in distaste among the thick smells of fry cookery. A Filipino, erect as a toy soldier, his apron unaccountably clean, bowed to Annie whenever she looked in his direction. The cook, an old navy man, sometimes wore his false teeth. On days when his face was symmetrical, he was sober and occasionally made a sour joke. When his teeth were out and his mouth caved in, he was bound to be full of gin and given to violent rages, smacking the grill with the long-handled spatula as though he would murder it, grabbing off orders from the wheel that hung between kitchen and counter, and cursing at what he read as he seized the French-fry basket to shake out portions.

Ernie slouched around, his ham face nearly expressionless, with lips like two leeches lying one on the other. When Annie passed him, he often reached out a hand and let it fall where it might, on her back, her buttocks, or her belly, keeping a dead eye on his wife. The Filipino called her "Miss Annie" and looked up at her from his five feet of self and spoke to her incoherently, when they weren't too busy, about his thoughts.

Weekends were marathons of exhaustion. Sigrid did the outside car work, and Annie was behind the counter, where there were three rows of customers stacked up, shouting and yelling and laughing, most of them young and rich from Hollywood, movie children, children of *the industry*. They demanded elaborate concoctions that Annie had to make, mixtures of soda and ice cream and walnuts and whipped cream and sauces and pistachio nuts. The girls were brutally rude to her; the boys flirted and looked at her suggestively past the bright clean hair of their girl friends.

She imagined herself as they saw her, a young waitress who did their bidding with an imperturbable face, sweat stains on her uniform from her exertions for them, a working-class girl, poor, out of bounds. One night, she and Sigrid found mouse turds in the whipped-cream containers. Sigrid laughed but Annie, still shuddering at the memory of her own grisly parasite, threw all the cream out. When Ernie found out about it, he took the little skimp of her skirt in his hand, held it tight across her rear end, and hollered that he'd fire her if she ever threw out anything again without his permission. There was spit on his lips.

One afternoon an actor, famous for his gangster roles, came in and ordered ginger ale. The killer sat there in his silk shirt, a little thin man with graying hair. He gave her a dollar tip. She remembered Tony's story of the young girl who'd been taken backstage to meet Sarah Bernhardt and when the girl wept with excitement, the great actress took her hand and kissed it and, Tony said, she wouldn't wash that hand for weeks. The actor's dollar disappeared into her pocketbook, and she spent it along with the other dollars. Sigrid warned her that Ernie's wife was working on him to get rid of her. "That dried-up old tit wants you outa here, honey, 'cause that Okie hick can't keep his hands off you. Stay out of his way."

There were bloody automobile accidents almost every weekend; that same group from Hollywood roaring down in their little convertibles, slamming themselves into eternity with the same dumb insistence with which they ordered their sickening sweets. So on the weekends the police often came around and stood inside the drive-in to "keep a lookout for troublemakers," they said. They were two middle-aged local cops. When the crowd got too obstreperous, the cops would collar the young men and throw them back into their cars, telling them to be sure and kill themselves outside Laguna. Sometimes, they drove Annie home in an old police car that rattled like a half-empty toolbox. One night they took her down to San Diego, then to the Mexican border, right across from Tijuana. They had been kind to her; she felt their protectiveness toward her. But that night they'd talked as if she weren't there; yet she knew the conversation was for her to hear. It was about the

173

parties that went on up in the hills in the beautiful, opulent houses, and a kind of terror seized her as they all sat with the motor idling at the border crossing, the two stocky middle-aged men in their blue uniforms gagging with outraged laughter at the doings of the rich and exempt, and she thought, What if they knew about me? What if they knew I had been to Communist party meetings? What if they discovered I'm married? To a Communist? Ernie had told her not to wear her wedding ring to work. He'd grinned and said, "I suppose I don't have to explain, do I?" She'd heard about Red Squads by then; she'd heard from Paul Lavan about cops in their strongholds, kicking the genitals of men who'd marched for Tom Mooney, or who'd tried to organize unions. She thought for a terrible moment she was simply going to cry with fear; then it would all come out. But nothing happened; they drove her home, quiet all the way, and when she got out of the car, one of them said, "Be a good girl, Annie-Fannie."

On afternoons when she was off work, she went to the beach in her new green bathing suit she'd bought with her pay, and lay in the sun. She grew quickly bored and began to walk along the lovely shore with its fine sand and intricate rock formations, looking up sometimes at the house on the cliff that someone told her belonged to Bette Davis.

One night, all the lights in Laguna Beach went out. She learned for the first time that there was a submarine alarm system set up between Laguna and Catalina Island. Something had triggered it. The waves pounded on the shore; the street was full of people, "What happened? What happened?" giggling, drunk, some of them, the smell of honeysuckle everywhere, and of roses. She left the drive-in and went to the bar a few hundred yards down the road where Sigrid's brother had gotten a job as bartender. Candles had been lit and she saw Joe smiling, his arms on the counter, talking to a pretty girl. He waved when he saw her.

The three of them, Annie, Sigrid, and Joe, had a kind of spiritless family life, eating breakfast together, sharing domestic chores. Annie had lost her passion for hamburgers, and ate so much of Sigrid's colorless, starchy food that she put on weight.

"I can't get over it," Joe said to her. "I mean, maybe there's a real Jap sub out there." The girl he'd been talking to left the bar stool and disappeared into a dark corner where a young man lay sprawled in a wooden captain's chair among the shadows.

Other people drifted in and talked over the possibilities.

Annie never looked at a newspaper, not because Lavan had told her that the press was controlled by the capitalists and all the news was biased, but simply because the very idea of sitting down to actually read a newspaper seemed preposterous.

She really wondered if she'd missed the news that war had been declared between Japan and the United States, knowing at the same time that, of course, it hadn't. People were excited by the momentary death of electricity. Joe made drinks steadily. Bourbon mostly. Annie had two drinks, and found herself talking to a group of people with faintly English accents, which, she judged, were put on. She realized suddenly that these people were the very ones who lived in the houses up in the hills.

Like the people at the party St. Vincent had taken her to, these people, too, developed an intense, if brief, interest in her. They were older than she had thought they would be, the men were perfumed and the women had that lifeless deep tan of middle age, of passive self-indulgence and idleness. They bought her more drinks. She made up a fanciful story for them, thinking they were not the sort to come to a drive-in. She told them she'd been brought up in Paris, that her parents had been killed in a plane accident, their private plane, that she had determined to make her own way in the world—that she intended to become a pianist, that her fiancé had been drowned in the south of France—

The lights came on.

Later, someone said a duck had got itself entangled in the underwater alarm system. It became a village joke. No one ever found out what had really happened.

She and Joe swam together. She observed that their limbs were somewhat alike, blond limbs covered with light-blond down. He told her he hated his sister's dyed hair. He told her stories about Minnesota Indian families he'd known. He longed for cold winters where you could see your breath, where trees were black against the snow. He rolled over closer to her on the sand and said, "I didn't want to come out here, but we were so poor after Mama died and Pa just went to the dogs drinking, so Sigrid and me, we've gotten jobs, you know, and kept ourselves together but I don't know what it's all about, this life, maybe I'll go back someday and get a farm of my own. Boy! I miss those winters."

There was a much-forwarded letter waiting for her from her father.

"My idiot girl," it read, "where the hell are you? I'm supposed, they tell me, to know such things. Did you really marry that gink? Margo and I are going to Massachusetts for the fall and winter. She's writing a book about the history of turquoise jewelry, and is very good and disciplined and puts me to shame. I've done some good work and should be cheered up by a firm gallery offer for November, but am not. The Indians get me down. They all look half starved and yet keep fat horses. I've developed an absolute terror of rattlesnakes. Margo found one, an infant, under a bucket yesterday, and since then I've been trying to devise a method of walking without touching the ground. I long for a more intimate landscape, so off we go, to the Cape or Salem or someplace. But I will write even if you are stubborn and won't. Did you ever look up St. Vincent, my old pal? Love, you little rat."

It was nearly the longest letter she'd ever gotten from him and she carried it around in her hand until it was time to go to work. She'd answer it one of these days. If she could think of something really funny to write about.

That night, late, she took a short walk along the shell road. When she came back, Joe was leaning against the door of his little room next to the garage. He was smoking a cigarette, the light from the ember grazing his narrow mouth. He kissed her, leaning forward to do so, without touching her. She started to go into his room. He put an arm in front of her so that she couldn't pass. She backed away instantly. He seized her hand and crushed the cigarette beneath his shoe. His skin was damp. "You're married," he said almost inaudibly. She pulled her hand away and went toward the steps. Sigrid, a stolid sleeper, suddenly moaned in the bedroom above, and Annie felt a shock as though something made of stone had lamented. "Wait!" Joe caught hold of her skirt.

They undressed in the dark. She lay on his cot. He said, "I've never—before." She was afraid for him, she was afraid for herself. He stood above her, shifting from bare foot to bare foot. "You don't have to," she whispered. "I've got to," he said desperately. "I'm afraid."

"Of what?"

"I don't know," he cried softly and fell down by her side. He didn't touch her. In the end, he lay across her, and by a sad, humiliating, brief motion of his hips, stained her belly. He cried softly, "I don't know what's the matter with me."

"Nothing," she said, and held him tightly.

"Yes, yes. I've heard about it all," he said indistinctly into her

176

neck. "It's been like some terrible thing I've had to do, like being shot, like being taken out into a field and shot. And see, see? I can't, I can't."

"It's the first time."

"No, no, no. I've tried before. My friends have told me, my friends back home from when I was little. I let an older boy—do something to me. I hated that too. But I want—"

"It's all lies," her voice rose. "We all hear those lies."

"Ssh!" he whispered fiercely, rearing up. "I don't want Sigrid to know. I've seen her with men. She doesn't care. She's like a wild-cat in the woods. She'll say things to me. Oh, please, don't tell her."

She hugged him and kissed his soft arms and covered him with a sheet and went upstairs to bed, tears in her eyes, the scent of hon-eysuckle all about, thinking, *Everything* is a lie, and found Sigrid sitting up in bed. Annie could see her face by moonlight; she was grinning.

"I *heard* you," she sang softly. "My little brother couldn't lay nothing."

"You don't know a goddamn thing," Annie said in a voice so hard it seemed to freeze her throat muscles. "You say one thing to me about that and I'll kill you!" She threw her clothes down and went off to the bathroom to wash herself. When she returned, Sig-rid was smoking a cigarette.

"I'm sorry," the girl said humbly. "You're right. I'm sorry. Jesus! None of my business anyhow. I got my own troubles."

Annie stayed wakeful. She'd never spoken to anyone like that before in her life.

A week or so later an army Jeep swerved into the drive-in and a tall young redheaded man got out of it in a lieutenant's uniform. He ignored the other customers—it was active ignoring, as though he'd ridden into a peasant hamlet looking for the local lord. He swung himself down on a counter stool and gave Annie a patron-izing grin. One of his bright blue eyes was slightly askew; his bril-liant coloring, the tense alertness of his movements, his palpable arrogance made him distinctive if not endearing. She found herself looking at him in the way she knew gratified him.

"Something cold," he said in a clear flat voice, instantly looking away from her toward the back of the kitchen, and as though in control of every motion of his life, at the same time pulled out a flat leather case rimmed in gold from which he extracted a cigarette with a gold tip. She could have stopped the whole show right there, she supposed, if she'd asked, "What do you want?" Instead, she filled a glass with ice and poured ginger ale over it. She placed it in front of him, centering it carefully, and instantly turned her back to him. He laughed. She observed that the other customers had begun to examine him with the kind of interest people give to an odd member of their species. He sipped his drink slowly. She went about other tasks. "Come over here," he said. She stood where she was. "Please."

"Will you have dinner tonight?"

"Yes." Her mind said *no*.

Both of them spoke in the same clear flat tone of voice.

"When?"

"Nine, tonight," she said.

At nine on the dot, the Jeep swerved down the ramp, snorted among the half-dozen or so parked cars, and he leaped to the ground with his long legs, then turned to look for her. She'd been waiting around the corner of the counter. She walked toward him, expressionless, got into the Jeep, and he turned on the ignition with a smart turn of the wrist. They roared up the ramp and onto the road.

"We're going to Balboa," he announced.

Having been caught by an impulse, having then decided to outwit him, she was now a prisoner. As they passed the shell road that led to her house, she nearly told him to let her out at once. Then it was too late.

He talked continuously over the sumptuous dinner he bought her. He had enlisted in the army—he'd gone to Reed College. He spoke German and French like a native—an educated native. . . . He'd taken out a reigning beauty queen only last week; she'd just won some kind of national contest. She was vulgar but lively. His cigarette case came from Bond Street but he doubted Annie had ever heard of Bond Street. He was being sent to Alaska shortly although that, in fact, was classified information. He supposed she'd heard about classified information? He was an officer because he was a gentleman. And vice versa. He was staying with friends in the hills above Laguna. Was she aware that one of his eyes was askew? As a child, he'd been teased. It had, he thought, become one of his greatest assets, along with his linguistic ability.

He was, she thought, the most ridiculous fellow she'd ever met.

Later, he drove her up one of the curving drives that led into

178

the hills. The dark lush foliage, the faint glimmer of a street lamp here and there, the glimpse of lighted windows reminded her of Arizona Canyon. They turned into a driveway that led to a vast, circular granite shelf where a huge car was parked. Below them was the village of Laguna, beyond, the great expanse of the Pacific. The house, he explained carefully, was a copy of a part of the Alhambra. In Spain. On one side, there was a large swimming pool. One could swim and at the same time look down on the ocean. Around the pool were delicate columns and sculptures of lions. Starlight turned the lions to tigers.

"A swim?" he asked and, to her surprise, went into a kind of cabana at the end of the pool and came out carrying an armful of women's bathing suits. "Sherry keeps these around," he said. "Take your pick."

She lowered herself into the black water without a splash and extended her arms with as little motion as needed to keep her afloat. She forgot the redheaded fellow; she rolled on her back, the heavens were dark waters; she heard through her wet ears the distant sound of the waves. Enveloped and saved by this darkness, she seemed to hang in a painless void. Then, she caught sight of the man at the other end of the pool, standing in water up to his thighs, an ink drawing of a man, the bright colors of his hair and skin and eyes obscured. She fell, choking, beneath the water, rose and sank again, rose and gasped. Even though her feet came solidly to rest on the tiled bottom of the pool, it was as though there was no bottom anywhere. Clumsily, she ran toward the edge of the pool, moaning a little, indifferent to what strangers she woke in the silent house that loomed above her. He pulled her up and out.

He took her to the dressing rooms in the cabana. He said he was staying until orders sent him north, next week that would be. He made her a drink, taking water from a leather-bound carafe on a table by the side of a wicker couch and adding it to the whiskey. She drank it down at once.

In his bathing trunks, he was like a stork.

"Where are the people? Sherry? The one you spoke of?"

"At a party," he said. "There's a colored maid and a chauffeur, but they're at the other end of the house."

He sounded uneasy.

She simply waited, the wet from her bathing suit spreading into the chintz of the upholstered chair in which she sat.

"It is very important," he said. "Sex is."

179

Important?

"For hygiene. You know what hygiene is? I mean, for tension, the release of tension."

She had heard a tremor in his voice, but as he said the last word, he seemed to gain assurance, and his voice had again the clear flat quality that had attracted and repelled her in the drive-in.

"Well, don't you agree?"

"I'd be glad if you'd take me home."

"You're a cock-teaser," he said in the same tone.

"All right. But—"

"I had a mistress in Paris. I've had women everywhere. It's no trouble for me to have women."

"I'm sorry."

"You're sorry, all right." He smiled at his joke, then as his mouth widened the blue eyes crinkled, and she thought he was going to cry. He pressed his bony knuckles against his teeth.

"Well, old girl, let's go. Get your clothes. We'll be off," he said, and slapping both his knees, rose and took off his trunks and began to dress in his uniform.

She had refused him and his hygiene program, but instead of relief, she felt more than ever his prisoner. Had she let him take her to his bed, she would have won. She did not know what she meant by that. Won her freedom until the next man? For a moment she was tempted to stand naked in front of him, let him do with her what he would. It had been a dreadful evening, as she swung back and forth between opposing impulses. She hated herself with the full consciousness of her self-hatred. How ugly *he* was!

He drove her down the hills to the shell road. She said she would walk the rest of the way.

He stopped the Jeep and let it idle.

"Thanks for dinner," she said, cursing herself for sounding so placating.

"Thank you for your charming company."

She wanted to say something to him, something cataclysmic, something that would melt the gold rim of his damned Bond Street cigarette case. He was staring straight ahead through the windshield. A sudden weakness overcame her.

"I'm really sorry," she said softly. But he did not understand, thinking, she knew, she was apologizing for not making herself available to him, when what she really meant was, sorry about *him,* about everything. He nodded curtly. She walked up the road, listening to the receding sound of the Jeep. The moon had risen and the white shells glimmered like old cleansed bones.

In the weeks that followed her encounter with the soldier, she grew so silent that Sigrid, already worried about Joe for reasons she ultimately revealed, began to hit her lightly whenever she was near her.

"Wake up!" she'd bawl. "Jesus!"

It did not seem to occur to Sigrid to ask what the matter was until one day Annie sat at the breakfast Sigrid had cooked and began to weep. Joe stood up as though he'd been struck, dropped a fork on the floor with egg yolk adhering to its tines, and fled down the stairs.

"Are you knocked up?" Sigrid said, drawing her chair so close to Annie that their legs touched.

"No, no, no." She rubbed the tears off her face.

"It's that damned husband of yours? He hasn't written? Is that it?"

"No. I don't know . . ."

"Ernie? Is it Ernie? Are you scared you're going to get fired? Listen, you been so quiet, that dumb wife of his thinks everything's hotsy-totsy now. Listen. You want a drink? I got a bottle of rum from some guy . . . you want—"

"I feel better," Annie cried. "It was just a fit."

"But you been like this for weeks!"

"I'm tired. Only tired."

"No. You aren't tired."

She was trying to think of an explanation to prevent Sigrid from seeing that she, herself, didn't know what the trouble was. It was that she felt thin and pale and helpless—helpless about what? Incapable of looking at Ernie's face, of speaking civilly to the Filipino, of picking up the stained metal trays that were clamped onto cars, of the wild rages of the cook, of seeing the physical sordidness of that kitchen. Actually, she was tanned, almost plump, and had learned certain habits of hard work—those that bowed you to it, that you did without thinking, bringing about the fatigue, the emptiness of thought that is a mirror image of the work itself.

But Sigrid, her hair in pin curls over her skull, lit a cigarette while another was still smoking in her coffee-cup saucer. Her large face with its thick features looked pasty. She stayed out of the sun, but her arms and neck burned. She was staring at a place just beyond Annie's shoulder. The worry forced her eyes closer together as though she were trying to bear down on it with a lens, take a closeup, see it plainer.

"Joe," she muttered. "You got the weepies. But it's Joe that worries me. Lately, he's been like he used to be. He used to wrap himself up in old blankets and trail off into the snow when he was little and sometimes I would think he'd gone off and froze himself to death. You know he's not said even good morning to me for over ten days now? I see him behind the bar at that place when I walk by at night, going home, and he's making drinks and looking into nothing. Is there something going on between you two I don't know about?"

"Nothing," Annie said. "He hardly speaks to me either." She hadn't even been thinking about Joe. He slipped up the stairs for breakfast every morning around ten, and was there when all their evenings off coincided, which was rare, for one of Sigrid's tasteless, filling dinners; he took out the garbage; he went for groceries; he kept his garage room scrupulously clean. Annie would see him there, a broom in his hands, sweeping invisible dust out to the shell road, a knotted preoccupied look on his face, his shirt sleeves rolled up to his elbows. Annie did the washing for everyone, and hung wet clothes on a small line Joe had strung between two trees. Everyone had their job. What had happened between herself and Joe had sunk into insignificance. He took the car when he wanted it and spoke to her, when he did speak, without any sign of strain, just a certain tonelessness. Only they didn't go to the beach together any more, and when he spent an hour or so in the upstairs apartment, smoking quietly and looking out the window where the vine grew, he was quite silent, Sigrid's tone catching his attention from time to time as she made fun of the customers at the drive-in, or, if Annie laughed suddenly, he would stare at her fixedly, frowning a little as though puzzled.

It was strange how delicate he looked when he was in Sigrid's vicinity. She wasn't actually coarse, but there was that thickness about her, and she'd aged herself with the dead brassy hair, the mascara that stained her eye sockets, the dark-red polish on her fingernails.

The postman called up and said he had some mail for the girls. Sigrid fetched up a letter from Walter with a postmark that couldn't be deciphered, and a note from a cousin of Sigrid's, which she read aloud to Annie, hoping perhaps that Annie would read Walter's letter to her. It was Sigrid's way of seeking distraction from her troubles. She wasn't really curious about Walter.

"My cousin keeps asking me have I got in the movies yet. That's her idea of a big joke."

She shook her head. "Jesus! Sometimes I think, what's going to happen to me? I could go back up to Minnesota. I got so many relatives there. But, oh God!"

Walter wrote that he'd gotten one of Annie's letters and hoped there were a lot more than that waiting for him in New York at the NMU. He'd be back soon, he said. He'd had an extraordinary adventure which he'd tell her about. Was she being good? He hoped she was seeing the right people, and making big tips. The letter was dated a month earlier. She felt a great pang of apprehension, then threw the letter over to Sigrid who read it aloud, mouthing the words like a child learning to read. "He writes good," she said. "He can't be so bad."

Joe came home that night at 3:00 A.M., singing loudly to himself as he came along the road. Awakened by the noise, Annie and Sigrid went out to the steps and watched him stagger in the moonlight, grabbing leaves off the trees and scattering them around himself. "Dead drunk," Sigrid muttered. "Like the old man."

He banged into his door, flung it open, and disappeared. Later, Annie heard him throwing up outside. In the morning, he was out scattering earth over a spot on the grass. He looked shaken, more fragile than ever. He stared up at her in her bathrobe on the steps. They looked deeply at each other for a moment. Then he smiled weakly. "Life's just a bowl of cherries," he said. Reassured, she laughed and went back inside, saying "He's all right," to Sigrid.

"No," said the girl. "That he ain't."

One afternoon that week when the sun was a constant blow of heat, the trees still, the ocean flat, everything gleaming and dead at the same time, Annie went into a bar on Laguna's main street. It was a pleasant place to sit. The bar itself was a long fish tank and while you were drinking, you could look down at the green water and follow the darting movements of the fish. She knew a few of the regulars at the bar. The bartender made her a martini. She'd developed a strong taste for gin. She looked down into the tank. "What did you call this one, Harry?" she asked. "That's a neon tetra," he said. "Lots of those, honey."

Someone was playing a tune on the upright piano in the corner near the window that looked out to the ocean. Annie felt cooled off and light and easy. There was something about being in a bar like this, paying for her own drink, knowing a few people, that was enormously comforting. Her heart seemed to beat more slowly.

"Fish!" said a voice. "They're too remote." She turned her head and saw a man of about thirty-five or so looking at her. He was drinking from a tall glass. Despite the heat, he was wearing a tweed jacket and a hat pushed back on his head. Its soft brim curved around his face.

"They're *only* remote," she replied.

"That's true," he agreed, approvingly. "The adjective, too, is out of place. I meant remote in relation to dogs, I suppose. Fish don't cater to one. They don't know you're there watching them with eyes as big as their bodies."

She turned away, not wanting a conversation.

"Do you live here?"

She nodded.

"You don't want to talk to me?"

He spoke seriously, as though seriously concerned about her answer.

She was annoyed. He was breaking into her quiet afternoon. "I guess not," she said with a polite bow of her head in his direction.

"I wish you would," he said without flirtatiousness.

He heard her sigh, and he looked unhappy. "Oh, well, then."

"It's only that I don't have much time to myself," she said reluctantly.

"What takes up your time?"

She gave up. "I'm a waitress in a drive-in down the road. It's pretty busy. I don't have a lot of private time."

A middle-aged woman in a beach robe was singing "You don't know what love is-is-is-" in off-key accompaniment to the piano player, an elderly sport in a Norfolk jacket.

The man in the hat nodded. "I hardly have any time to myself either. I came down here looking for time but now I seem not to want it."

He waited. She felt his desire to have her question him. But she remained silent.

"From Hollywood," he said.

184

The distinction between Hollywood and Los Angeles was not lost on her. The movies.

"You work in the movies?"

"You see? I can't be plain. I said that so you'd know. I'm sorry."

She didn't understand his apology. Harry asked if anyone wanted a drink, otherwise he was going to eat his turkey sandwich right now. The man bought her another martini. He was drinking plain soda. His eyes were dark, shadowed, and his black hair was thick and curly around his ears. He had small, bony, tanned hands that tapped and moved about above the fish as though accompanying their ceaseless movement.

"I write for the movies," he said. Then he added with deliberation, "I just sold an original screenplay for a lot of money."

"That's good," she said.

"It doesn't make me especially happy," he said.

She looked at him with a certain impatience. "Then you don't need money," she said.

"It's not the answer," he said.

"It's the answer when it's the question."

He laughed and his hands stayed quiet. "Let's have a conversation about money," he said. "I'm really interested in what you think about that."

Made braver than usual because she was in her own bar, she said, "There's no reason for you to be interested in what I think about it."

"There is, there is. . . . You look like a Gibson girl. Isn't that reason enough?"

She moved back, away from the personal comment.

"No. I didn't mean that," he said, "the way you thought."

"I have to leave in a few minutes," she said.

"Could I see you again? I've rented a place down the road for a couple of weeks. To talk. After your work? Could you come here?"

"I don't know."

"Come anyhow. I'll go back and have a nap and dinner and return here—"

He was giving her domestic details, his plan, and she was amused by his seriousness.

"If I'm not too tired, I'll come back around eleven tonight," she said.

"I'm Ben Greenhouse." He extended his hand toward her. "Annie Vogel," she said, touching his hand lightly. "Ann," he said. She felt suddenly breathless and slipped off the bar stool.

"Thank you for the drink."

"My pleasure, Ann."

She put on her uniform in the upright coffin provided by the management. Why had he called her Ann? His tone had been softly insistent; she suspected an intention to make the distinction suggest something about his own specialness.

She spent the next three evenings with him at the bar. He was cross with her the last night because Ernie had kept her late cleaning up. Ernie had begun to play the cruel employer with her recently as though to make up for those earlier days when he'd slid and slipped about her like a suitor.

"I couldn't help it," she protested.

"You could have called here and left a message with Harry," Ben said. He yawned loudly.

"If you're so tired, you could have gone on to your place. I wouldn't have minded."

"I'm well aware of that. That's the trouble with you. You don't mind enough. It's all too soft. You don't know it, perhaps, but what you're expressing is contempt. For men."

She was nervous because of his crankiness, yet faintly pleased. They were arguing tediously, the way she'd heard relatives argue.

The air in the bar had a pleasant bouquet of gin and salt water, tanning lotion and men's cologne.

"We're having a good time, aren't we," she said suddenly. His face broke into smiles. "You are a funny girl," he said. Then he continued where he'd left off the night before. It all added up to a long interview; did he keep notes?

"You said your father never worked when he was drunk. How often *did* he work? How often was he drunk?"

"I don't really know because I haven't lived with him that much. But he told me that. I believe him. Anyhow, he's had an unhappy life."

"Everyone has an unhappy life. That's no distinction."

"Some people *seem* happy."

"Well, they aren't. They're just trying to be superior to the general condition."

"There are people who can't even consider such a question— they suffer from not having enough food or shelter—"

"Stop!"

"I won't. Look at the way you're dressed! How can you speak of unhappiness when you have the choices you have!"

"You don't know anything about my choices, and I'm aware of the suffering of the vast majority of mankind and I don't want to hear about that ideal socialist state full of hairy little domestic groups, running around hacking each other to death in the name of progress. You're looking for a way to explain things to yourself. You've picked the inevitable one at your age. Shaw said that anyone who wasn't a socialist before thirty had no heart and anyone who was a socialist after thirty had no head."

"I'd rather have a heart."

"That's a disgusting line to draw. As if we don't have to live with both! That's the curse of it all!"

"Why are you attacking me so?"

He sighed and patted her hand. "I suppose because you're so young and I'm getting to be so old."

"Why do you want to know all these things about me?"

"Because, because, I like you for one thing. And I have to know everything about what I like—" he laughed. "To the point of wrecking it! Also, I'm consumed with a frightful curiosity. It is destructive, I know that. I'm eaten up with it. When I'm bored, I go into a coma." He looked broodingly at his drink. "I'm like a bear," he said. "I bury myself in silence for half the time, the other half, I'm full of rage and energy. A Jewish bear."

He'd made a number of references to being Jewish. She had some questions of her own but did not know how to put them. She'd known a few Jews. They had happy families. Assured that his interest in her was singular and nonacquisitive, she ventured. "I've seen Jewish families. They're happy."

He shouted unintelligibly, so that everyone in the bar ceased their activities momentarily and stared at him. He shook his head, saying, "Ignorant girl! They live in frozen regions among the Gentiles, huddling together, rending each other in their enforced intimacies, assuring each other of their superiority to the forces that hold them to each other in bonds you can hardly conceive of! Even now—this minute, they're being readied for slaughter— children that look like my children are going to die by the thousands. Happy! It is not the concern of a good Jew! My father was a gross peasant who drove my mother and me mad! A furrier who smelled of animal rot and tanning fluids and went about his life's

187

business like a blind mole, snuffing out passages and hiding places, dragging his food about him in the evenings and grunting as he ate. I ran away . . . I sat on the steps of the telephone company until early morning. I was seventeen. I called my mother and said I would never come back. But I went back and didn't speak one word to him for two years. This! In two rooms no bigger than this bar! He didn't even notice."

She was silent. Jews huddled in warm groups among the frozen Gentiles—the animal-rotted father . . .

"Now," he began, his tone back to its familiar avuncular equableness, "what kind of a painter is he? I mean, is he traditional? Has he been influenced by any special school? Braque? Gris? Picasso? Cubism? Impressionism? What?"

"I don't know," she said. "Have you seen your father since then?"

He cried out again that she was an ignorant girl and brushed aside the question irritably. "I don't want to talk about him."

"Do you always decide what's to be talked at?"

He grimaced. "Yes. Partly as a result of arguing with Communists who drive me wild with their blandness and savagery, their ignorance and insistence. My wife, of course, has the children to talk about. I've read her a number of times. I've read that book so well I know it by heart."

He shook his head and looked in despair. After three evenings with him, each one of which had lasted four or five hours, she was somewhat accustomed to the rapid swings of mood and expression.

"Maybe she knows you like a book."

"Oh, indeed, she does! Did I sound arrogant? Presumptuous? I am. But, poor thing—"

"That's patronizing—"

"I wish I were different."

"Could I have another drink?"

"You drink too much. Yes." He called Harry over and ordered her another drink.

"If I had to work like your father probably had to, I might have been like a mole. He couldn't help smelling the way he did!"

"If you had been like him, then you would have to condemn *yourself!* Do you imagine that objective evil disappears simply because you have a generous imagination? What nonsense! *You* could be that way and so you are all ready to forgive it! How tenderly you hold yourself!"

188

She drank down the gin quickly, angered, frightened by her anger, as though it existed outside her, coming at her from the world. She didn't reply.

"Well, I have gone and offended you now. You are offended, aren't you?" He laughed. "See, I know how you feel. I have a plan. Let's go to the beach in the morning. Let's have a little daylight life! I haven't been on the beach since I got here—knocking about that shack like a prisoner. Don't you think the California beach life astonishing? It's vile. Hundreds of miles of insane maggots stretched out beneath the sun. I hate the Pacific Ocean. I'm really afraid of it. California is the most hostile place I've ever lived! What a perfect setting to turn out sugarplums! Do you know about the San Andreas Fault? We may all of us be spilled out into the water like ants—our little limbs flailing in the beautiful sunlight as we drown."

They stayed a while longer—then he walked her home, leaving her at the beginning of the shell road and going on to his place a half a mile or so farther down. She watched him from behind a tree until he'd disappeared. He wore his hat at all times.

When she saw Sigrid she thought for a terrifying moment that the girl was dead. Her lids were half closed. At first Annie could detect no breathing. Slumped into a chair by the window, a glass nearly escaping from one slack hand, Sigrid's face was like a snuffed-out lantern. Annie thought to run away, to get Joe, to send for people, the police, but to remove herself instantly above all. Then Sigrid belched.

"God! I thought—"

"Wha—"

She was drunk.

She burst into drunken tears, swallowing them as they poured toward her mouth. Her mascara had run; her hair was limp. She was a sad sight.

"It's Joey," she sobbed. "He didn't come home for two nights. Wha's happened to Joey? Oh, Jesus . . ."

Annie had not even noticed. Why hadn't that dumb fool said anything?

"Why didn't you tell me?"

"You! Who could tell you things? With that stuck-up face? Like you're different from everyone else?"

Stricken, Annie fell back against the wall.

"Oh, Jesus!" wailed Sigrid, trying to get up, her legs giving way

189

beneath her, the glass at last released and falling to the floor, where it broke. "Now, look what's happened! We'll have to pay for that glass. You see what's happened?"

"You'd better go to the bar and see if he's turned up," said Annie, thinking, What *stupidity!* Why hadn't she gone to the bar? It was the first reasonable place to look.

"I didn't want to walk in there alone," Sigrid said pitifully.

My God! Is she shy? Looking like a whore the way she does? Timid? Looking, as Walter would say, as if she carried a mattress on her back? Sigrid was staring fixedly, with a drunk's cunning, at Annie.

"You think you're the only one's scared?" the girl asked in an ominous whisper that contained a threat of a scream.

"No."

"Yes you do! Oh, Joey!"

"Let's go to the bar."

"Can't walk."

"I'll go."

"You go."

The bar was closing just as Annie reached it. A last customer, his eyes glittering, gave her a long look as she passed him in the door. "Dear girl . . ." he entreated.

Joey had not been there for two nights. They didn't know where he was but he'd better get his ass over there and explain to them what the hell he thought a job was for!

Sigrid was snoring in the chair. Let it be until morning, Annie decided.

At breakfast, Sigrid was cool although she looked ravaged. She listened calmly to Annie's news of the bar. Then she shrugged. "It's his life and his business," she said, putting on her carhop uniform.

Annie felt as forsaken as though it had been she whom nobody was bothering to look for. "I think you ought to go to the police," she said. The girl gave her a look of pure dislike. "I don't go to the police for nobody," she replied sharply.

Annie met Ben Greenhouse on the beach just below the drive-in. That way, he said, she'd be able to stay until the last minute. She took a path down the cliff to the sand. It was too early for the sun bathers, and the beach was empty except for a boy of about twelve playing a few yards from where Ben was sitting with his hands clasped around his knees.

"Where did you get that blue mark?" he asked pointing at her thigh.

"In school, a long time ago. I was walking back to my desk. A boy stuck out a pen and I walked into it."

"How old were you?"

"Nine. I think it was the fourth grade."

"How did you feel about it?"

"Hurt. I mean, aside from the pain itself."

"Hurt because he'd wanted to hurt you?"

"Yes."

He looked over at the boy. "What a stupid place to sit and talk," he said. His skin was so white and his body hair patchy like indifferently planted shrubbery. "I wonder if children start out by knowing about the world's malevolence and then forget as they join the rest of us? I suspect that people who talk about essential human goodness are the worst ones. It's hardly to be borne, the world's malevolence."

The boy suddenly ran over to them, knelt and said, "Look!" He released a small crab from his closed fist that instantly took off across the sand in a diagonal direction. The boy caught it and put it back where the same action was repeated. He looked up laughing at Ben. "I like that," he said. "The way it moves." He went back to where he'd been playing. "It matches something in his mind," Annie murmured. Ben took hold of her hair. "That's a nice thing to say," he said. "I like that."

Later, they walked, Ben saying, "I can't stand this lying around like a lizard." He talked to her about anti-Semitism. He spoke slowly, as though to a backward student. He mentioned a book, *Moses and Monotheism* by Sigmund Freud. She interrupted him and said, "Someone once said I was neurotic," and he turned and looked at her soberly. "Do you know what it means?"

"In a way," she answered. He seemed to ponder her answer a moment, then went back to the Jews. She was thinking that no one had ever noticed the blue scar in her thigh before. He saw so much; he seemed to live in a hole by himself, going out on forays for information and pulling what he found back in with him, to stare at in the dark with melancholy intensity. In this, she felt herself to be like him. "You are inward, like I am," he said suddenly. "I knew that when I watched you drinking alone at the bar. You had an expression of relief on your face as though you were happy to be alone, happy to not have to respond to anyone. Then I made you respond to me. I want to ask you something very personal."

"That's Bette Davis's house," she said.

"Do you want to be in the movies?"

"No."

"That's untruthful. I would guess that you do. Because everyone does, even if only for an hour now and then. I would say you feel you can't make it, and that you get some profit from saying no. Make yourself different from the peasants."

"Sometimes you make me feel bad . . . you talk about me as if I weren't here, or as if I were my own representative, something like that."

"It's because you're like everyone else. You don't want to *think* about anything. I would guess you already know a good deal but you pay no attention to what you know."

"You just said I wasn't like everyone else, when you talked about my being inward."

"I didn't say you and I were the only two inward people in the world," he said and gave a short laugh. He didn't often laugh. When he did, she had noticed, it sounded more like coughing.

"I'm going to take a swim."

"Wait!" He stood still, looking at her. "Don't. It alarms me. I had, instantly, a vision of you drowning." His face twisted as though he were in pain. "I can't stand watching anyone I know in the water or on the edge of a platform, even getting into a car. My children climb trees. I can't look. The suffering is unspeakable . . ."

"All right, I won't swim then."

"You see how quickly you give in? It's because you understand my feelings too well. I have another question, but let's move on." They walked. She waited with a kind of painful pleasure for what he would ask next. There was something about it that reminded her of modeling. It was as if he could, through her answers, paint a portrait of her. In the same way, when she'd been at the Art Students League, that she had wanted to step off the platform and run to see what the painter had made of her, so now she would like to have asked him how the portrait was coming along. He was silent for a moment, absorbed, apparently, in the placing of his small, white, delicately boned feet in larger footprints which disappeared a few yards ahead into the water.

"You see what I'm doing?" he asked. "It's a kind of humiliation, training perhaps. I don't like to use what other people have used—foot space in this instance. Whose footprints are these? Perhaps it is someone with some horrible fungus disease, or a woman with flabby boneless feet like pork. Now, the question. No. I won't ask it. I know the answer. I think you sleep around a good deal. I would guess you do it because you're afraid to refuse—anything. Now, listen to me. You mustn't do it any more. It's an insult, given and taken. It is a form of terrible silliness . . . there will be consequences later on you can't even imagine. Real morality is fundamentally good psychology—good sense if you like. There's a time for sleeping around and a time for it to stop."

He was monstrous! She wanted to shout denials! She hadn't "slept around" so much, had she? But the truth was there. She would, given a chance, turn down no one. The thought struck her full in the face like a blow. Her heartbeat thickened; her breathing grew rapid. She wished she'd never seen him.

He was looking down at the sand, a grave expression on his face. For all his references to his sensibility, he didn't take into account the way someone might feel being read like a book. She moved rapidly away from him.

"Come back," he said mildly. She stood still. "Don't be ridiculous," he said. "My saying something doesn't make the reality more, or less. I like you. Doesn't that please you? Are you luckier than the rest of us? Do many people really like you—knowing the way you are?"

"I'm not a whore!" she burst out.

"No. I know that. You just enjoy the income from being a victim. Give it up. Try! Look! The boy's in the water. Call him out, can't you? I'm a terrible swimmer. What if something happens? There are sharks in this ocean."

"He's a good swimmer," she said coldly. "And you don't care if he drowns. You just care how you'll feel if he drowns."

"Ann . . . that's right. It's right." He sank down in the sand and she, after a moment's hesitation, sat next to him.

She felt sticky, hot, ashamed. It was all too close. She felt as if she'd been forced into a closet with Ben for hours while outside the door that kept her prisoner the airy world raged with all its promise and freedom.

"Do you have a pencil with you and a piece of paper?"

Determined to do nothing to be agreeable, she glanced nevertheless at her pocketbook a few yards away where she'd left it. "Get it," he said in a kindly voice.

She fetched him back a scrap of paper and a yellow pencil. He began to write, using his knee for a table. "A maniac said this, but it doesn't make it less true. Nietzsche. Funny that I'm quoting him now, at this time in the world. I'm a perverse Jew."

He handed her the paper. "Read it to me."

She read: "The consequences of our actions take hold of us, quite indifferent to our claim that meanwhile we have improved."

He emitted a kind of hag's chuckle as though he'd done her mischief.

"Do you know someone named St. Vincent?" she asked, eager to distract him from the subject of herself.

"Yes. But not to know. He's of an older school, the equivalent of an *ancien régime* out here. He regards us, the Jewish writers from the East, as upstarts. All those people do—the ones who came out in the twenties. His movies are absolutely passé. Old-time romantic plots with mean ironies. Now they've started on the propaganda movies. God knows where that will end."

She wasn't listening. Down the beach, a figure was moving rapidly toward them. It was one of the policemen, Bob, making his way heavily through the sand. He was in uniform. She had the peculiar impression that the man, in his bulky police uniform, restored the beach to its natural state, that it was no longer a playground but only a waste of waters beating against a shore.

"How is it that you know St. Vincent?"

"Why is the policeman on the beach?"

"Tell me . . ."

"He's an old friend of my father's . . . he looks so hot."

"They always look hot. Well then, they were friends earlier, before St. Vincent came out here. How odd to think of the before time, before you came to Hollywood, before I came . . . I had another life too . . . Syracuse, the university, a certain kind of early-winter evening . . ."

She was not listening to him. The policeman waved to her but he was not smiling. Did he want her to go to him? She stood up.

"Where are you going?"

"I think he wants to speak to me," she said, alarmed. She wished Bob had not seen her with Greenhouse on the beach—it might make the policemen treat her differently. She started toward him, intending to keep him away from where they were sitting.

He was panting heavily, sweat poured down his face.

"Where's that Swede girl?"

194

His tone was almost abusive; he was looking at her as if she were pavement.

"She's at work."

"Charlie's gone to your apartment to fetch her. I'll have to— Jesus! I got to take that path!" She thought he was relenting, complaining to her, but he only glared at the steep path leading to the top of the cliff.

"What's the matter?" she asked timidly.

"That brother of hers has done himself in."

"But what's happened?" she asked again, her voice rising; she hadn't understood. What was he saying?

Ben Greenhouse had moved up behind her. "What's the trouble, officer?" he asked irritably.

The policeman didn't bother to look at him as he started on the path, heaving his weight upward and muttering to himself.

Annie remained where she was. Some people had pitched an umbrella down toward the other end of the beach. She saw a picnic basket, a Thermos. A light breeze blew across the surface of the water.

"Ann . . ."

She began to walk in the direction from which the policeman had come. Far ahead, black figures moved clumsily, fragmented through the prism of heat into shards of black cloth.

"Something terrible has happened," she said in a stifled voice.

Greenhouse caught hold of her arm. His hand was damp.

"Let's go back," he said. "Let's go back," he repeated more urgently.

But she went on until she was within sight of a body lying on the sand, a pale mound beneath the black birds moving above. She stopped, paralyzed with dread.

"I don't want to see that," Ben said in her ear. "I will not be made to see that."

One of the figures detached itself from the group and came toward them.

"There's nothing to look at, folks," said the trooper. She saw the tight puttees wound around the man's legs. She moved forward. The trooper held up his hand. "Stay back, please," he said.

"I knew him," she said in a whisper. The trooper shook his head angrily.

Greenhouse dragged her away and they stumbled together in a brief struggle down toward the water and into the surf.

195

She wrenched herself from Ben's grip and turned to see Sigrid running down the cliff in her carhop's uniform, her hands waving as she strove to keep her balance on the steep incline. The brass buttons of the girl's shirt caught the sunlight, and sent off splinters of white light. She hit the beach, fell, got up to her knees, shouted some word, rose and ran on. Just behind her came Bob puffing and waving his arms.

Annie ran. "Sigrid," she called out as the girl flew past her, then stumbled in the sand, sobbing with open mouth, blinking under the brilliant sunlight. The policeman was walking now, looking out at the ocean as though he was merely on a stroll. The three people beneath the umbrella were sipping from small paper cups, watching the scene with mild interest.

"They think they're looking at a movie," Ben said. She'd forgotten he was there. He pulled her down so that they both sat at the edge of the surf, the water circling around their feet then ebbing away.

"Tell me what's it about?"

"She's the girl I live with," Annie said, looking down the beach. Sigrid had become a black figure like the others, as though she'd entered a different dimension. She was being held up by two men.

"Your legs are knocking together," Ben observed.

"I'm scared," she groaned.

"And the—"

"Her brother. The man said he'd killed himself." She was suddenly perplexed. Is that what he'd said? She didn't actually remember hearing the words. "Maybe not."

"In any case, he's dead," said Ben. "Did you like him?"

"No, not especially," she said.

"It's awful anyway, is that it?"

"Yes."

"Let's go and have lunch. I'll buy you a drink although you shouldn't drink so much—there's nothing more absurd than a female drunkard—"

"Don't. Don't *teach* me," she cried in anguished protest, against him, against the body down the beach.

He was silent. "I'd better go," she said, "see if I can help Sigrid."

"No! You don't want to see that!"

She freed herself and got to her feet and started down toward the group. Bob had Sigrid by the elbows. She had covered her face with her hands. As Annie reached them, Bob shook his head warningly. Sigrid dropped her hands and stared at Annie. "Sigrid?"

"Like something'd come off on your hands if you'd touch it," said the girl shrilly.

"He don't feel it," the policeman said, patting her on the shoulder. "Drowning case always looks like that."

"He was always unhappy," she said.

"Maybe he just went for a swim," Annie said helplessly.

"With his clothes on?" the girl asked, and began to laugh, and laughing still, to pound the policeman until he gripped her hands in his. She calmed down at once; almost to a stupor. "You go tell Ernie," she said to Annie and then, still gripped by the policeman, began to move on toward the path.

"I can't have lunch," Annie said. "I'll have to do Sigrid's work and mine too."

Climbing the path, Greenhouse following her silently, she was gripped with terror as though the event which had already taken place was still about to happen.

Joe had been a plain, secretive boy, melancholy it was true. But now he was invested with a powerful mystery. To take one's own life required unimaginable resolution. How long had it been forming in him? Had what happened between him and Annie strengthened the resolve? The sight of her weeping had sent him flying, in terror, from the breakfast table. She did not think, now, that it was because *she* had been weeping that he had fled. He must have lived in unremitting anguish, but it had not been apparent to either Sigrid or herself. How *could* she have known? Oh, Sigrid had been worried in her way, but then had shoved the worry aside brutally. Would she feel responsible now? And should she, Annie, have forced her out of her drunkenness that night to tell her Joe had not been to work?

They had, by then, reached the top of the cliff. Annie saw Ernie's wife carrying a tray of French fries and a malted milk to a waiting car, an expression of loathing on her face. Greenhouse, paler than usual, was staring down at the smooth surface of the macadam with its islands of oil patches where cars had idled.

"The confusion," he said. "I can't bear it. Turgidity, confusion . . ." He looked up at her face. "I came down here to gather up my resources."

197

He was so full of complaint. So elderly.

"It didn't happen to you," she said. "None of us count in your life."

"That's stupid. You don't understand. I've been on the verge of a breakdown. I'm thirty-seven years old. Everything bores me."

People did not grow up—they grew down, to the small patch of earth they'd marked out as their own. He was disgusting!

"Every cliché of Christian sanctimony is written on your mug," he flung at her. "Do you think I can't see what you're thinking? That I should be pitying that dead man? I should be concerned about his troubles? What cant! If you were truthful—"

"I have to go. Ernie's seen me. I have to tell him about Sigrid."

Greenhouse began to walk up toward the road.

Released, she ran to Ernie. He received the news with no comment. After she'd put on her uniform, he came up to her. "Well, how long's Sigrid going to take off? What am I supposed to do meanwhile? My wife can't take this for long. She's ailing. Well . . ." And turned away, shambling toward the table where the accounts were kept.

An hour or so before closing time—Ernie conceded they could close a little earlier since it was a weekday anyhow and they were short-handed, although he had no sympathy for anyone who would take his own life—Ben Greenhouse drove up in a Chrysler touring car. Annie went out to him with order pad in hand.

"You can bring me a ginger ale," Ben said, "so we can talk a minute. I'm going back to Hollywood."

She brought back the drink and hooked the tray onto the rim.

"Don't let it scratch the car," he said nervously.

She was exhausted; her hair untidy, her lipstick chewed away.

"You're disappointed in me," he said.

"No . . . no."

He sighed. "Yes. You couldn't help but be. I wish I could simply *be* awful and not be aware of it."

"The ice is melting."

"You're going to think harshly of me. I wanted to leave you with something—pleasant. I'm sorry about the young man . . . but it's part of my illness, that I'm not more concerned. I'm concerned about you, though. Will you be all right? Do you think so?"

He looked at her with curious eagerness. He was very small in the huge car. For all the romantic swagger of the fedora on the

198

back of his head, he merely seemed forlorn, the dark eyes luster-less.

"I'll be all right," she said, asserting something against his soft sadness, meaning something other than what he'd asked which she understood as a kind of exoneration.

"You're a good girl," he said. "Now take this stuff away. I don't want it. I'm going to write you a letter. I'll try to explain a few things. Good-by, Ann."

She walked home, dragging her feet, aching with fatigue. Sigrid was in Joe's room. From the road, Annie could see her through the open door sorting out clothes. She wished it were a week later, a year later.

On the narrow cot were two or three shirts, some boxer shorts, an old black cardigan with a raveled sleeve. As Annie came in, Sigrid swept some toiletries off a wooden shelf into a paper bag. One book lay on the floor. It was a Boy Scout handbook and there was a ragged marker of newspaper at a chapter on knot-making. When Sigrid moved the pillow, Annie found a length of line with which Joe had apparently been practicing knots.

She pulled one end of the rope and the half-knot gave way— Joe's life went in her hands. An involuntary gasp escaped her. Sigrid looked up from a scuffed suitcase she was emptying. Her face was blank of expression. Perhaps the whole family was like that—snow-faced.

"My family's going down the drain," the girl said. "I called rel-atives all afternoon from the police station. The ones that haven't got phones got the news from the ones who have. They're sending money. I got to get the body up to L.A. and get it on a train. They want him buried out there with the rest of the Swedes. But there's got to be an inquest. Because of the way . . . he's at the undertaker's now being rouged up, I guess. I don't want to know what they're doing. It doesn't count. What's hard is how am I going to get the body to L.A.? It costs too much with the limou-sine. What are you looking so sick about? It's my brother not yours."

"He was learning how to make knots."

"Getting ready to hang himself probably. But it was like Joey to start out with some idea and then drop it. He never could con-centrate on anything for long. You should have heard my Aunt Tilda. She screamed so loud I dropped the phone, then she started right up about California being a sinful place and no wonder he'd

199

killed himself—my Aunt Tilda been living with Indian men all these years, one right after the other. I think she kills them and sticks them in the floor of the icehouse when she's through with them. Then I got this idea." She paused and sat down on Joe's cot. "Maybe it's against the law. Listen. You know that little black-haired bitch drives the school bus? The one's got a husband in the navy and is always fooling around with the Santa Ana soldiers? I thought maybe she'd drive me and Joey up to L.A. in that bus. What do you think?"

Annie had seen the girl at the bar now and then. A greedy nervous girl who stirred up the indolent surface of the bar atmosphere like a water bug, her hands on people, men and women alike, or tending to her long black hair, swinging it back off her face, pulling it down one side, running her long soiled fingernails through it. She had confided in Annie once that she needed a gin fizz, pronto, after a rough night with a couple of boys from the base.

"I'd pay her maybe fifty bucks. A lot less than I'd have to pay the undertaker. What do you think? Jesus! Here I got a body on my hands!"

"Why did he do it?"

"I can't think about that. He was born too sad. Everything that happened made it worse. He should have been a preacher and had God. Then he would have known what he was supposed to do." She was pleating her shirt in her hands, over and over. "I was pretty bad to him," she said in a whisper. "I can't think about it so don't say anything to what I said."

The day following the inquest, which Sigrid attended in what she called her family dress—the one she had in case one of the aunts or uncles should ever come to California—Annie received a package from Ben Greenhouse. It contained, along with a note, a handsome string of large amber beads. She'd never owned anything so substantial. The note read: "Ann, I haven't much to say except that you pleased me, even if not in the traditional way. I hope this string of amber matches something in your mind. I'm tucked back inside my life again, and for a while it won't seem too bad. Be a good girl, not a halfhearted trollop. Your friend . . ."

That day, Joe's body in a pine coffin was loaded onto the school bus, the dark-haired girl in the driver's seat, combing her hair with her fingers, a cigarette end smoking in a bottle cap at her

200

feet. The policeman, Bob, had come along to help. Even with two other men from the undertaking parlor, it was hard to maneuver the box into the bus. They broke the back of one of the seats. "That'll have to be paid for," said the girl driver flatly. Sigrid got in, her white pocketbook clutched in her hands. She was staring at the coffin as the bus started off.

When she returned, after two days, she remarked that every time the bus stopped, a line of cars behind the bus stopped too. It had made them laugh, her and the girl. She'd stopped in at the Greek's, who wanted her and Annie to come back; business was good, a lot of plants going up around L.A. and out in the valley, and he needed some good waitresses. "He said you had class," Sigrid reported snidely to Annie. Then she'd gone on a bat, she said, and drunk up half of Hollywood, and did Annie remember that fat crazy Finn used to come in and play *Finlandia* all the time? Well, she and he, they'd made a night of it, all drinking and sobbing but no funny business. He drank too much for that. It might have eased her mind, Sigrid said, a little roll in the hay, but the liquor was almost as good and she felt better now. "Jesus! I just don't want to think about that gluey way he looked on the sand, and I'm not going to. They say when you kill yourself, your soul haunts the place you did it in. You won't catch me on that beach ever!"

Annie had found the apartment oppressive during Sigrid's absence. All she was doing was biding time. Time for what? She'd had enough of the place. The golden purse of tips Ernie had promised had hardly materialized although she was making more money than she ever had, enough to buy lipsticks from the drugstore, and beach sandals, and things she'd never thought she'd have. She longed to leave the sleepy, sun-washed village with overpreserved, middle-aged rich folk driving their expensive cars through the main street and up into the hills to their fraudulent houses and stale pool water.

She went dutifully to the drive-in but in her mind she was casting about for a place to go, a place to be. She thought, as she frequently did, in little flashes of memory, of Max Shore whose life was continuing elsewhere. Hers wasn't.

The empty room downstairs troubled her, its door open, the blackness within holding accusation against her of wastefulness and desolation. The whole story of Joe was a trouble in her mind.

Although he surely hadn't killed himself for love of her! A picture came and went in her mind, a child dragging cotton blankets out onto a field of snow.

Then everything was solved for her temporarily, two weeks after Joe's suicide. On a Saturday morning at 2:00 A.M., she heard someone stumbling around below on the seashells. She got up and went to the stoop—she'd lost certain night fears recently, as though her irritability with her life had made her brave.

In the moonlight, Walter Vogel's face was turned up toward her, and swept by feelings she didn't pause to think about she raced down the stairs and threw herself in his arms.

Chapter 13

It was to be, Walter said, a vacation, time out before the serious matter of settling down. She had never heard of Yosemite. He had gone camping there as a boy; he wanted her to see it because it was the only place he loved—as places went on this earth. They would stop near Merced to pick up camping equipment from his uncles who were sheep ranchers. They were his father's bachelor brothers, but, like Walter, had no truck with Mr. Vogel, even though they were of the same stripe. When last he'd seen them, he said, they were forming an organization of ranchers to prevent Orientals from buying land.

Walter had not gone to Murmansk but to England, then to South America. It had been in Buenos Aires harbor where Walter, a *Daily Worker* gripped between his teeth, had dived off his ship and swum through the dark water to another American merchant ship to deliver the paper to a "comrade" in the black gang. He spoke of this feat frequently, with a satisfaction that appeared more piratical than political. There had been sharks in that harbor and foul patches of oil and dangerous patrols.

He was histrionically astonished at Annie's ignorance of what had happened that summer in Europe; she welcomed his reproaches; they sheltered her from deeper regrets. Her confession of ignorance was vigorous.

Hadn't she looked at a newspaper once? Hadn't she known about Dunkirk? That the Germans were in Paris? That Italy had declared war on France? He frowned, shook his head, clucked. How had she managed to find such a decadent corner in which to dream away this critical summer? The job, she explained. He pushed that aside. Somewhere in her—he had known from the beginning—was an indolent dilettante. Why was she laughing? Oh, she was happy to see him! Ridiculous girl! The world was going to smash and she was happy to see him! She told him of the young man who had come to the drive-in one evening and wept copiously into his chocolate sundae at the fate of the churches of Europe; all that priceless stained glass that was going to be shattered by bombs, never to be replaced. "Sounds like one of your sort," he commented.

"What are your uncles like?" she asked, trying to imagine herself as the young bride on her way to meet new relatives.

"They're fat."

He hadn't been to the ranch for years and would have to feel his way. They followed a blacktop road for miles, then turned left onto a dirt lane with a high turf ridge which scraped the bottom of the car. A light rain was falling. They both leaned forward squinting through the windshield.

Walter cut the motor. The car's headlights revealed a thick patch of bramble and tall weed. She heard the soft continuous tap of rain.

He led the way to a small shed and pushed open the door without knocking.

"Georgie! Herbie! Get up!" he shouted. They stepped inside, hearing the damp sad groans of sleeping fat men. Walter lit a match. Two large mounds lay on a bed with a metal headboard; a soiled pink blanket left bare large areas of mattress ticking. One thick foot hung over the side of the bed. Walter began a noisy search. After a moment, he appeared next to her with a kerosene lamp which he lit, squatting near the open door where he could make use of the lights of the car.

Besides the bed, the room was furnished with a table upon which sat an empty bottle labeled Muscatel, and a kerosene stove. The only plumbing visible was a water tap which shot straight out of the wall and dripped into a bucket on the floor. Piles of clothes were scattered here and there.

"The sheep get the best rooms," Walter said. The fat men slept on. Walter suddenly jumped directly onto the bed and, hopping up and down, made loud baaing noises.

A forlorn sigh issued from one of the mounds. There was a slight turbulence under the blanket as one of the sleepers rolled out from under it. He was clad in long winter underwear, the drop seat gaping. He knelt for a moment by the side of the bed, then, holding the mattress with huge pawlike hands, rose painfully to his feet and turned to see what was bothering him. Walter leaped to the floor next to him.

"Why, Walter!" he cried in a dinky voice. He yawned and shook his head like a horse bothered by flies. "Why, you've stopped by to see us! Wake up, Herbie. Our only nephew's here. Who's that? You've brought a friend? Just smell that creosote! We've been shearing all day. Wait . . . I'll get a chair for the lady."

He waddled to the door as Herbie rolled off the other side of the bed. He smiled when he saw Walter, staggered to the tap, turned it on full and smacked his face with handfuls of the water. "Must be late," he mumbled. George returned to the shed carrying a stool which he placed just behind Annie. "Sit!" he said.

The smell of creosote was powerful but a hideous odor leaked through it, small, secretive, stinging, vaguely sweet, unmistakably sour.

"I see you're still pleasingly plump," Walter said. George laughed delightedly, his laugh as thin and childish as his voice.

"I live to eat," he said. Herbie mumbled something in the corner where he apparently preferred to remain. He'd draped a piece of tarpaulin over himself. "That's right, Herbie," George said.

"Here's my wife, Annie," Walter said. "We're going to Yosemite for a few days."

"That's nice. A nice little wife. Yosemite's a big place, not much good for anything."

"We need some pots and pans and a knife or two. I thought maybe you could loan us some gear. We'll drop it by on our way back to L.A."

"Fine," George said. "Come over to the tool shed and we'll see what we've got." He picked up the kerosene lamp and Walter and Annie followed him. She looked back and caught sight of Herbie crawling heavily into bed, his eyes already closed.

The tool shed had electricity. George blew out the lamp saying it was no use to waste kerosene. He took a duffel bag from a hook and stretched it out on the floor and began to fill it with saucepans, a coffeepot, a frying pan, knives, cups, and tin dishes. He handed Walter a small ax.

"I used to go camping when I was young and there was nothing else to occupy me. You'll need some blankets. These smell of sheep, but they'll do. The sleeping bags wore out, Walter. I've got some hand lines around here someplace. You like to fish, missus? I hope you got long pants. It's cold this time of year. You got a job, Walter?"

"I will have."

"You get to see your dad?" George looked at him steadily as Walter shook his head.

"You shouldn't be so hard on him. We all get old. You're the only son he's got."

"We didn't choose each other."

George looked sad. "You ought not to treat a silly fellow as if he was wicked."

Walter said, "You don't see him."

"Well, that's different. I don't like him," said George.

Walter seized the duffel bag and made for the car, George and Annie following. The bag was tossed into the back seat. Walter got in as George opened the door for Annie. "Nice little wife," he said soothingly. He peered through the window at Walter.

"You and Herbie doing well with the sheep?" Walter asked. He was twisting the choke button with his left hand, his right still held the small ax. Annie removed it from his grip. He gave her a quick uncertain look.

George's expression of smiling mildness changed. He turned into an egg with painted features. "We make a living," he said shortly.

"Come on, Uncle," Walter said. "I bet you've got a fortune stowed away."

George backed away from the car. "On no account talk of such things!" he cried. "Our business is not yours! Runaway! You have removed yourself from this family! And I have just given you eighty dollars' worth of camping equipment!"

Walter backed violently toward the shed, then shot out onto the road. In the light from the dashboard, his face was pinched and rancorous and, Annie perceived, frightened. How long was it since he had seen those two? What stale cues had set Walter to baiting his uncle, and what accounted for that sudden rage of George's as he flung his heft about in the weeds like a thrashing animal? Driving now at a speed which shook the little car from side to side, Walter bent over the wheel. Emptiness? The father brooding over bathtub rings, the two old sheep ranchers crawling out of their filthy bed morning after morning . . . was that Walter's family? Three old men, two dirty, one clean.

The rain had stopped. A light wind cleared the sky and the moon, looking a bit like Uncle Herbie, fled along the spines of the range of hills at the foot of which they were now traveling. Annie fell into a half-sleep, her head bumping against the window, her legs stiffly drawn up against the seat.

When she woke, it was into utter silence. The rain had begun again. She could hear it tapping on leaves. They were parked on a dirt road in front of a large lodgelike building. Walter was smoking, leaning back, his head against the seat.

"We can stay here tonight. I know a short cut to the valley up this road."

They walked into a gloomy room where two old men stood over a pinball machine next to a long bar. Here stood another old man dressed in a plaid wool shirt. Behind him, on a shelf, were two bottles of whiskey, one half empty.

"How much?" demanded one of the men near the pinball game. "How much you gonna bet?"

"I wouldn't bet with you, you old sheep humper," replied the other.

The bartender said, "Hush! Here's a lady!"

Annie went to the lavatory at the end of the room. Inside, scrawled on the wall above the toilet, a message read: "We aim to please, you aim too, please."

Their bed consisted of planks covered with a piece of straw-filled ticking. From somewhere close by, she heard a voice, fuzzy, quarrelsome, "You gonna bet or I'm gonna tear you up!" There was a mumbled reply. She slept, awoke to hear the drone of that exchange, unvarying, like a ritual, and the dry crackle of the straw as Walter stirred restlessly.

A few miles along the rutted road they followed the next morning, the back wheels of the car sank into the mud. The smell of leaf mold was drugging, cool. Walter piled branches beneath the wheels and just as the car gained traction, the sun broke through and the light grew yellow and bouyant all at once. With a violent jerk, the car emerged from the wet dripping woods onto a paved road.

"Here it is," he said, and shut off the motor.

Annie looked uncomprehendingly at the mild landscape, silent, green, winking where sunlight touched wet leaves. Walter laughed at her expression of disappointment. "Wait!" he said.

He started up the car, rounded a turn and entered a tunnel. As they approached the exit, he slowed, and they crept out into daylight. Below them, gleaming as though an inland sea had only just ebbed away, was a long deep valley. A waterfall, an upended river, fell across the face of a bare rock escarp. A massive sunny silence lay across the valley like a wash of color, yet the naked rock faces, the wooded slopes, the vertical cliffs down which the white skeins of water tumbled all seemed fraught with turbulence.

Farther on, they walked into a silent grove where redwood trees towered. A ranger's cabin, boarded up, its roof fallen in, sat lightly on the forest floor. Nearby, they found a tree with a plaque embedded in its bark. Some of the redwoods, it read, had been growing since before the birth of Jesus Christ. It suggested the visitor might like to press the button just below and play a recording of Nelson Eddy singing Joyce Kilmer's world-famous poem, *Trees.*

They descended to the valley floor, where the Merced River wound among groves of silver pine and oak, past a lodge where a family stood on the rock terrace, posing for a man with a camera. In front of them—they were driving slowly—walked a forest ranger with stately steps, moving aside only when the car was nearly on his heels. In a clearing off the road, a woman hung wash on a line that extended from a small log cabin to a tree.

Walter said the rangers lived in the valley, and when they had vacations, often spent them on camping trips up to the headwaters of the Merced and Tuolumne rivers. "It's another country there," he said.

They bought provisions at a small general store and afterward drove to the upper end of the valley. "Half Dome," Walter said, pointing up at a great gray wafer tonguing out from the cliff which supported it. Annie crouched in the car.

Walter parked close by a meadow in which three deer fed, their mottled backs warming in the sun. Nearby was a small lake surrounded by a delicate single rim of tall grass; it was still, velvet black, like a grape lying on a green leaf.

"This is a good spot." He pointed to three rough cabins raised off the ground on stilts. "There's nobody there. We'll leave our things in them. The bears come to steal food. Here." He handed her a box of dry cereal. "Go feed the deer. I'll set up everything."

He was so calm, so agreeable. He was someone she didn't know.

She walked into the meadow and the deer looked up at once, their neat heads poised. In that quiet greenness, it was strange to hear the roar of the falls. The deer appeared unafraid as Annie moved slowly toward them. She sat down in the grass a few feet away, and held out handfuls of cereal. The largest deer walked to her, nibbled at the cornflakes, and was soon followed by the others. They were so pretty, so delicate, yet for an instant, pressed by their warm flanks, her hands damp from their wet muzzles, she was afraid.

She returned to find that Walter had built a small stone pit near the lake's edge and on one of the stones was an open can of sardines, a loaf of bread, slices of onion on a leaf. He was gathering kindling wood. The expression of concentrated effort made him look young. He'd given himself over to it. He looked at her blankly as he picked up the coffeepot, then smiled out of his absorption, and she caught a glimpse of an earlier Walter, the promise of the years of his life ahead of him, in the swing of his own youth and strength. It was odd that time had merely smoothed out his face. Here, making a tent of twigs, blowing on the smoke, triumphant as the flame caught, his smile was artless.

After they had eaten, they sat with their backs against a tree trunk and threw pebbles into the lake. Warmed by the sun, half-asleep, they hardly spoke. Once Walter took her hand and waved it toward the other side of the lake, where she saw the lumpy brown shape of a small bear as it made its way through the trees. Later, they took a walk and she tried to memorize the names of the plants and birds which Walter pointed out, but her mind refused to record, confounded perhaps by the reckless profusion of wildlife around them and partly by her surprise at Walter's special learning.

They ate an early supper. It had grown cooler. They roasted potatoes in the fire and broke them in half in their jiggling fingers.

209

Night settled in gently, an emanation, a breath from the forest. They warmed their knees at the stone hearth and drank black coffee from Uncle George's chipped enamel cups.

In all the five days they spent in the valley, neither of them spoke of the months that stretched between the time of the bus station where Walter had left her that night and the moment she had stood on the wooden stoop and looked down at him in Laguna Beach. This time they spent was out of time—even the disagreeable parting from Uncle George was forgotten.

In the valley, they lived without memory.

Walks, climbs up the perilous rock steps of the Devil's Cascade, encounters with clumps of bears snuffling at the base of trees like fat spoiled children, the smell of the forest at night, the lake into which they lowered themselves as in baptism, the deer so soon familiar, the sheep-smelling blankets with which they wrapped themselves at night, the making of the fire, the food they ate, the feel of different kinds of tree bark, the afternoon naps in the sun-warmed meadows, the thick, spongy, wet moss beneath the falls, glimpses of other campers far away, seen through their own languor as through a benevolent fog, the love they made that was, for once, at last, as effortless as sleep and, like untroubled sleep, fell naturally without thought into the rhythm of their hours.

The valley held them in thrall—their histories, each so alien to the other, were erased from their consciousness. She thought, once, how odd it was that this release she felt was somehow connected with a surrendering-up of their divergent temperaments, those *personalities* which they seemed to have lost track of in the tunnel above the valley. There was nothing really personal in her observation of how easily he kept his pace on the steep paths, how expertly he made fires. And similarly, she noted how dispassionately his gaze followed her as she walked into the water of the lake, or fed the deer, or folded up the blankets early each morning.

Yet somewhere, stirring at the back of her quietness like that bird over there in the woods among the leaves, was the knowledge that the spell would be shattered soon, would leave hardly a trace of itself when they left the valley.

At the end of the week, they packed up. Walter dismantled the stone fireplace and kicked earth over their cooking ashes. Annie watched him intently through the car window. He put his hands in his pockets and walked slowly toward her. They drove down the valley, up the road to the tunnel, and as they emerged from the other side to the pleasant if undistinguished landscape she had first mistaken for Yosemite itself, he said, "Those goddamned bastards! Now we've got to stop off in Merced to return that junk they loaned us!"

Bad magic. His words thrust her back into the scandalous, miserable time of his absence. She began, timidly, to tell him what the drive-in was like, but he brushed aside her tales of Ernie and the drunken cook. What he wanted to know, he said, was what she'd been reading, what meetings she'd gone to, if they'd given her any assignments, if she had seen anything of Paul Lavan.

She hadn't read much—it was so complicated and so boring.

"Boring! What's that got to do with it?"

Well, she had gone to a few meetings, and she'd tagged along with a woman who was supposed to recruit some Mexicans—

"What do you mean, recruit! The party doesn't send people out with membership applications!"

"The woman was supposed to be investigating jail conditions, but I thought the whole point was to get members . . ."

He looked disgusted.

"I don't like Lavan."

"You don't *have* to like him."

"I did read some books."

He grunted, but didn't ask her what she'd read.

They got to George's and Herbie's sheep ranch around two in the morning. She watched Walter drop the duffel bag among the weeds. As they left, he pressed his finger against the car horn until she grabbed his arm, begging him to stop.

Later, they rested by the side of the road and he told her he'd gotten a job at Lockheed-Vega on the assembly line, and hoping to make some kind of peace between them, she described the rivet-sorting work she'd done and how she'd been responsible for shutting the place down.

"How did *you* shut it down?"

"I went to the CIO."

"The CIO? Whatever did you have in mind!"

"Oh, God!" she cried.

"Annie, you're so tangled, what's to become of you?"

She gave up. He could twist and turn all he liked; he could rebuke and tease and change his tune every two minutes. She'd play dead. Let him heave her around like a sack of grain.

211

By the time they'd moved into a room on Cheremoya Avenue, the time they'd spent in Yosemite was only a dream, as insubstantial as those fancies which effortlessly, as though emanating from a source outside herself, took possession of so many of her waking hours.

She went back to a job at the Greek's, and Walter went on the night shift at Lockheed.

Waiting on tables in the restaurant, she dreamed of concert appearances, of taffeta evening gowns. To customers' demands for shrimp cocktails, she gave a noble, grave inclination of her head, deafened by cries of "Encore! Encore!" She wrote her autograph on her order pad beneath "steak MED/R"; she arrived late at a party in her honor wearing an Irish revolutionary raincoat and a Garbo hat, and all heads turned toward her; in the stunned silence, she lit a Turkish cigarette; lovers circled her at an exact distance of three feet. She measured out the three feet. Even in her daydreams, the men who interested her were those who turned away, their impassive faces hidden by the curve of their hat brims.

In that world of odorless perfume, of soundless applause, where Annie turned herself into a creature of infinite capacities as though bewitched, she knew at the same time that it *was* an act of her will. All at once the memory of a waterlogged body on a beach, the feel of the rough blue stuff of a policeman's uniform against her thigh on a ride that had suddenly turned menacing, the smell of a basement where rats ran along wet floors, an admiring glance that became toxic in her own system, generating an intolerable self-revulsion, would shatter the dreams.

Wrenched from these silent extravaganzas, she considered the worn furnishings of the room in which she and Walter lived, the kitchen of the restaurant where the Greek flung about his great mass, hollering orders in accents made unintelligible by his impatience, the smell of food frying in grease used over and over again, the apprehension which pursued her even into sleep as 1:00 A.M. drew near, at which time Walter, change jangling in his pockets, would unlock the door, undress in the dark, and crawl between the sheets next to her. These sheets were mere rags, even though Walter took them to the laundryman on Saturdays, bringing back last week's load, the frayed scraps clean and neatly folded.

One Friday night, he brought home a group of people from the plant. They went out bowling. Somewhere along the way, they picked up one of the men's wives, a tall, shelf-breasted woman

212

with red hair and a thick wet red mouth. Early in the morning, they returned to the Vogels' room and began to drink bourbon. Annie sat on the floor, her back against the wall. The redheaded woman, Augusta, lay on the bed. Why in God's name was she eternally laughing? Her legs were sprawled out, her mouth open, her hands flattened on the blanket, palms up and opened. Half-finished sentences, shouts of laughter, exclamatory cries whirled around above Annie's head like dishes tossed from shelves. Other workers at the plant, foremen and inspectors, were execrated, ridiculed, damned forever. Laughter strained, won, and overcame words, coughs and gargles and snorts.

Augusta's husband, Junior, a thin small man with stubby pale hands, drank steadily from the bottle. He observed his wife on the bed, his black eyes squinting. There were too many girls in the plant, he told Annie, squatting in front of her. "Women!" he cried, then toppled back at once on his skinny haunches. "Ooops! I may have broke a little wind, yer honor!"

She edged away. Junior plucked at his belt buckle. "They ought not to be so many women there," he said. "Makes trouble." At that moment, Annie saw Walter lean over and plant his mouth in the center of Augusta's fleshy fig lips.

"You were shocked," he said, after they had all left. "I didn't know that about you." Still drunk, he giggled inanely. "Oh, Annie, so pure . . ."

Several months later, Junior appeared in a Los Angeles courtroom on a rape charge. Annie and Walter went to the trial, where Walter was to be a character witness.

"How can you witness something that isn't there?" she had asked him.

"You'd like him whipped down the street."

She recoiled physically from him. She wouldn't want that done to anyone, she cried. But he'd managed, as he always did, to push her back into self-accusation. She would like to have asked him why he never saw his old friends, Paul Lavan, or those other people she'd met out at the big house in the valley. What about the party people he'd wanted her to know? In some sense, he was further away from her now than when he'd shipped out—working overtime almost every night, drinking heavily on weekends, or lurching from bowling alley to honky-tonk bar with Junior and his pack of loutish friends.

The rape charge was dismissed for lack of evidence; on the

courthouse steps, the alleged victim, a squatter version of Augusta, looked at Junior and emitted a shriek of equine laughter. "You still think he ought to be whipped down the street?" Walter asked Annie. "I never said that," she protested hopelessly.

Not long after Junior's courtroom appearance, Annie came home from work and found yellow hairpins in the bed and a torn silk stocking. She sat for a long time with these things in her hands. When Walter arrived, his face and hands dirty with grease, she remained unmoving, the hairpins clutched in her fingers, the torn stocking falling across her lap. He washed at the sink. He sang to himself, "I got the blues—and I can't be satisfied . . ."

He looked down at her. He picked up the stocking. He smiled his old smile. "It was nothing," he said.

She was silent.

"Somebody who said she knew you. How did you meet her? A girl named Karin. She came here this morning, said she'd been trying to reach you for months."

Annie opened her mouth and screamed.

Walter threw himself at her clapping his hand over her mouth. She bit down on the soft flesh of his thumb pad.

He jerked his hand away. She gasped for air.

"Stop it! Stop it!" he cried.

"You're trying to kill me!" Her head fell back against the chair. She wept with open mouth—she was deranged. He stood silently, sucking his thumb, his eyes half shut. She slipped to the floor and lay on her stomach, her face pressed into the dusty carpet. He sat down beside her.

"I won't see her again," he promised.

A week later, on a Saturday afternoon when they were drinking coffee together at the table near the window, a large white envelope was poked beneath the door. She went over to pick it up. Inside was a sidewalk snapshot of Walter. Just behind him, wearing a silver-fox jacket, was the girl Karin. She put it on the table. He looked down at it.

She took the old suitcase from the closet and began to pack. As she bent over, her mind on the sidewalk beyond this room, this life with Walter, a coffee cup hit her on the back of her head. She turned. He was standing there, his hands on his hips. She picked up a chair and ran toward him. He began to laugh. She broke the chair in front of him. They stood there with the jagged pieces of wood between them.

When she got to the door, he called, "Wait!" She turned.

"Why can't we live like normal people?" he cried.

She laughed all the way to the sidewalk, aware that she was attracting attention but, for once, indifferent to it. There were coffee grounds on her shoulders. She found a phone booth.

"Hello?" asked a woman's voice.

"Is this Mrs. Shore?"

"This is Eva."

"Is Mr. Shore—"

His voice came on.

"Max? This is Annie. Can I come there?"

She heard a child's voice in the background.

"I don't know what to do . . ." she muttered to herself. Max heard her.

"Come right away," he said. "But I can drive and get you."

"No. I'll get there."

Chapter 14

Nothing that Annie had seen secured her attention so much as Max Shore, his wife and child, and the way they lived in their three rooms among their books, their cooking pots, their child's battered toys. Sometimes Eva was late for work and left before making their bed. From the studio couch in the living room, Annie, drinking a cup of coffee, watched Max at this task through the open door. When the bed was made, the day began even though Thomas had been up for hours by then, building and kicking over towers of blocks, or rolling canned goods across the narrow kitchen floor.

They were kind to her. Eva tended to lower her voice when she spoke to Annie, as though she were convalescent. So she must have seemed to Eva, she knew. Her sense of her own strangeness grew apace with the efforts the Shores made to include her in their life.

She was observing a marriage; in the midst of it, its essential nature eluded her. She waited for a revelation. It never came. Thomas had his routines, as fixed as rituals. His parents went about their tasks without consulting each other. They took turns cooking, but Max was responsible for disposing of the garbage and shopping for groceries, Eva saw to the laundry. On Saturdays, they cleaned the house together. In the evening, Max played chamber music on their record player. Eva called it chamberpot music. She preferred Paul Robeson or folk singers, Benny Goodman or Fats Waller.

Thomas had violent tantrums during which he rolled on the floor like an infant madman, screaming till he choked. At other times, he was a self-absorbed little boy who amused himself by piling objects on other objects. Sometimes he lay in his father's lap, sucking his thumb, staring dreamily up at the ceiling. Eva fed him his supper, her elbow on the table, a spoon thrust out toward Thomas's open mouth. She drank a whiskey neat while she was feeding him, talking idly to Max about the day's events. When Thomas flung a jar of applesauce into the air, he observed his mother implacably as she exhorted him. Mild arguments occurred about domestic matters—a leaking faucet, a chair leg that needed mending. Except for the child's rages, the climate of life was lenient, forbearing. Yet Annie felt a mystery, some concealed drama of temperaments, an excess of emotion that was not so much dissembled as it was restrained. It was not to be found in the hard-surfaced quality of political talk, and she could only speculate about what went on behind the Shores' closed bedroom door at night. She struggled against such speculation, but it won out, awaiting her every turn of thought.

Once she picked Thomas up from the floor during one of his seizures. He bit her hand so it bled. Eva grabbed the wounded finger. Annie was astonished to feel Eva's hands trembling. Max washed away the blood, his face stony. "I don't know why," Eva said, over and over again, as Max wound a piece of gauze around the finger. They both looked haunted. An hour later, it was as though nothing had happened.

Annie was frequently present during political discussions, sometimes between Max and Eva, sometimes when visitors came. She was not exactly excluded but they talked around her in such a way as to make it clear she could listen but not participate. She didn't, in any case, wish to take part. Phrases became familiar without ever yielding up their meaning. The world was laid out before her in blocks, like Thomas's constructions, capitalists, workers, colonial peoples, the masses, the elite, the intelligentsia. In her mind, Annie, like Thomas, kicked away the blocks. It was a wearisome language despite the energy with which it was spoken.

Whatever went on behind the Shores' closed bedroom door, it

217

went on quietly. Annie, on the couch, grinned uneasily, afraid always she would hear something. She tried to distract herself with the books Max gave her to read. They were not the sort that Eva pored over, making notes on a pad. Eva said to Max, "Why are you giving her all that stuff!"

Annie read several Thomas Hardy novels but balked at *The Return of the Native*. The dialect irritated her. She read *Tender Is the Night* twice. Eva picked it up off the floor next to the couch and turned it over in her hands. "I don't know what Max is thinking of," she said, shaking her head.

When the Shores went out in the evening, Annie took care of Thomas. Along with a small weekly amount she gave Eva for food, it was a way of repaying them. Once he woke, and she and he built towers and stockades in the living room until he lay down and went to sleep beside the blocks. She carried him to his crib, thrilled at the lightness of the small body in her arms, and at the thought of the paralyzing power he exerted during his rages. She covered him and turned on the little night lamp near the crib, then stood dreaming. She would become a nun—in an Italian cloister, vistas of Lombardy poplars, a stone cell, a wooden table, a hard cot, her hours ruled and redeemed by chapel bells.

The Shores did not ask her to go to party meetings, not even those open to nonmembers. She was glad of that. Fern Diedrich, the woman who'd driven her to San Diego, stopped in once for some purpose. "You again!" she said to Annie. Fern looked peculiar. Her glance moved restlessly from table to chair to couch to lamp, never resting on a face. She called Eva "Comrade," and talked feverishly of the murder of Trotsky—an event about which Annie had no knowledge—which had taken place a couple of months earlier. Fern laughed dryly and coughed. "Your fate catches up with you, even in Mexico!" she said. Max looked sardonic. "Fate? Why, Fern! What kind of word is that for a Marxist!"

The night Annie had arrived, coffee grounds in her hair, she had told Max about Walter, talking for hours about Walter's friend, Junior, the coffee cup hitting her on the head, the way Walter spoke to her. "He'll never let me be whatever I am . . . he doesn't like me, you see. He can't *stand* me . . ."

"You mustn't go back," Max had said. Eva had long been asleep. Max made up the couch for Annie.

In the two weeks before she once more found a job—she had

told the Greek she wasn't coming back that next morning—she tried to locate Johnnie Bliss. She went to the boarding house where he'd lived.

"That unholy man has gone to his destiny," the landlady said. "Shame on you for knowing him! He'll be thrown from a car after being shot by gangsters. If I knew where he was, I wouldn't tell you. I'm a Christian woman."

She called St. Vincent. The phone had been disconnected. Perhaps they'd run out of credit, and Andrew was driving a laundry truck now, happy Andrew.

Sometimes Annie recalled sitting in a chair holding a woman's hairpins in her fist, the torn stocking across her lap. She was unable to evoke the anguish she'd felt then. That she'd been married to Walter Vogel, that they had lived together at all was without reality. When she got a job working in a small ceramic plant, she used her maiden name. Eva said, "You'll have to get a divorce someday." The thought of divorce was more substantial than the marriage had ever been.

She stayed with the Shores for two months. With her first paycheck of twenty-five dollars she bought them a bottle of whiskey, a stuffed dog for Thomas and a collection of Hardy's poems. She was very happy coming into the apartment with her packages. Thomas tossed the dog across the room, then crept after it on all fours. Eva said she shouldn't have spent her money on such silly things, but thanks anyhow, and Max took the book and put it on a table next to their bed. Annie saw the book there from time to time as she set the table for supper. She felt sinful and triumphant. She'd gotten into their bedroom.

Eva distressed her more and more. Eva never really looked at her. Eva said, "Everything is all right," all the time. Thomas's tantrums were natural at his age; it was *all right* that Annie had married someone like Walter—at her age. Fern was *all right*—it was hard on unmarried women in a male chauvinist capitalist society—yes, Fern was *all right* because her growing untidiness and eccentric ways were appropriate to what was causing them. Marriage was *all right,* and death was *all right.*

When Eva stood for moments at the kitchen counter, looking down into the sink, what was she thinking about? That it was all right to stare down into a sink? Eva moved clumsily; when she was tired, she looked old and heavy.

How broodingly she watched Max, smiling when she caught his

219

eye. *Nothing* was all right, Annie thought, and took pleasure in the cruelty of her knowledge, wanting to bang Eva on the head, wanting to shout at her that her life was held together only by laundry lists and party slogans. To join the damned would be more bearable than the older woman's insistent and meaningless certitudes. But Max's patience with his wife shamed Annie. It was not necessary to behave as if you were damned, even if you were. And thinking that, she was alarmed; Joe must have felt damned before drowning himself. She tried, resolutely, to admire Eva. How well she ran her household even though she worked! What affection she lavished on Thomas!

Max had not explained to Annie what he did for a living until one day he arrived home late saying he had a job with a ship-building plant in San Pedro. He had been going to a machinists' training school and had finished the program.

That night Eva had to go to a church group to try and raise money for some imprisoned Mexican boys who'd been accused of killing an old drifter in Los Angeles. Max and Annie and Thomas ate together. Max was silent through the dishwashing. He put Thomas to bed. Annie was reading *Winesburg, Ohio*.

"Don't read now. I have to speak to you."

She was instantly frightened. In the second before he began to talk, she saw imperiled the warm safety in which she had been living these months. Something was about to blow the walls down.

"Don't be scared. Try not to be," he urged her.

"Have I done something?"

"Eva and I are having a difficult time together." At her look of surprise, he laughed aloud. "I know you," he said. "You think you see everything, don't you?" She turned away so that he would not see her chagrin.

"It's not a *noisy* bad time," Max said. "I won't tell you much about it. Some of it's to do with the way I'm heading, changing, politically. Eva, she's . . . bewildered. And it's not only that." With unexpected bitterness, he said, "I'm not fit to live with."

Her disbelief amused him. "Annie, you live in this house like a child," he said gently. She thought guiltily of her surreptitious and constant preoccupation with their closed bedroom door.

"I don't mean to insult you. But Eva's afraid—afraid of *you* among other things. Your life, the way you walk into the room, everything about you, frightens her. She's gone from one box to another, you see, from childhood to me—answers have flowed toward her. She's not had time to ask questions . . . she's not needed to. She knows I don't love her. This first question of her life is 'Why not?' You understand, it's not arrogance that makes her ask it. Perhaps I don't love anyone. Although Thomas . . . but that's something else. And she wondered if it was you I cared for. I do care for you, Annie."

He was silent, looking down at his hands, then up at her. "Don't imagine—" he began.

"Oh, please," she interrupted clamorously.

"You *are* imagining! You're afraid I'm going to say something shocking! Listen! This is what I want. I want you to move out from here now. I have a friend I've wanted you to meet for a long time. I'm going to take you there now. She's expecting us."

"You've already *told* her!"

He said nothing. "I'll find a place of my own!" she cried, chilled to her marrow; he was looking at a shelf of books, and that aquiline profile she thought so fastidious looked only finicking. Did her fear give off an ugly aroma? What charade was he playing in this slovenly room? *He* didn't belong in it either!

"You can find a room of your own later," he remarked casually.

"Oh, what have I done?"

"Nothing, nothing . . ."

He had said he cared for her. He had told her to leave. She glanced inadvertently at the bedroom door. He caught it and appeared to shake his head ever so slightly. All along, she had thought there was a tie between them, a secret line, but it had gone slack. She floundered, casting about in her mind for some powerful, outrageous thing that would bring his attention back to her. But the room was not hers; the books, the toys, the indifferent furnishings were tokens of a life she had no claim upon.

He was watching her now, smiling. She couldn't help it; self-betrayed, she smiled back. It was exactly the same smile, that of two people in trouble.

She packed her suitcase. She would like to not have anything. But the suitcase was there, its shabby contents reminding her of how many times it had been packed before. The suitcase was always looking for a place to be set down, emptied, and put away. When you carried a suitcase out of a door it was because you'd been asked to leave. If you walked away with nothing, the house fell to dust behind you.

She snapped the locks. He embraced her as she stood up, the

old pocketbook in her hand. She sighed as though life itself were draining out of her, the terrible life of nerves and embarrassment and repudiation. They stood, swaying slightly, for a time. Then he picked up the suitcase and took it to the door.

"Wait here. I'll go get Mrs. Oliver."

Driving to the place of the woman he called Theda, he grew almost gay. Eva was not mentioned. He told her about the plant where he worked, the Southerners who were flocking west to get those lucrative jobs, wages they'd never dreamed were possible; they came from as far as Mississippi. He thought he could get her a job there too. They had a training program—how would she like to learn to operate a drill press? Besides, the company had not really swung into serious action yet, even though they were hiring people by the hundreds. The main thing was, the United States was bound to get into the war at some point. It was the first time in American history there'd been compulsory military service during a time of peace. Money, money. There was going to be a lot of money made; there always was in a war.

Was Theda a Communist? she asked. "You mustn't ask that about anyone," he said. He suggested again that he try to get her into the plant. She didn't want to go on painting sleeping Mexicans on pitchers. Besides, she ought to make some money herself.

"It doesn't seem possible that I could, ever. I go in the other direction, never a dollar ahead of anything."

"You know what? You sound proud of that. I know how it is. One turns one's subjugation into an act of will, in the head anyhow. . . . But what it really means, it means you're on the handout line and unless you wish to become a rich man's dolly"—he turned to smile at her—"unless you want that, you're going to have to make it another way."

"I'm not proud of it. It makes me sick."

"What makes you sick is pretending you mean to be that way —indifferent to money. Tell the truth."

She didn't deny it.

"If you come to the plant, I can see you. We can eat our lunch together. There's a bench I know of. We'll bring our lunches and sit and talk." This rather domestic detail both attracted and wounded her.

"Can't I come to see you at your place? Oh, I think there's something Eva's said, something you're not telling me!"

"No. I'm clearing the field. I don't want a divorce; I don't want

222

to scatter my life around. And Thomas . . . there has been something wrong all along . . . my expectations . . . and you see, the
political thing is fundamental because, in a way, Eva is part of the
decision I made years ago, about the party. Eva is really good,
you know. She is, really, a religious—oh, not the tormented skep-
tical sort, the simpler kind of nun. The party is the way she under-
stands life. She's running scared now. She loves me, in the way
she knows how to love, all patience and fear. She used to order
me around a good deal. I didn't mind. I think I thought it was
funny because I knew, or thought I knew, that my will was
stronger in the end. But she's stopped that. I remember the day,
almost the hour when she stopped telling me to take out the garbage or see to Thomas's supper or straighten out the lapels of my
jacket. I can hardly stand *that*—the way she bites her tongue. I'm
sick with pity, for myself, for Eva, for you."

"Me?"

"You."

Theda stood in the middle of her room, a cigarette drooping
from her mouth, a gun in one hand.

"Were you expecting someone?" Max asked.

"I just found it in an old suitcase," Theda said. "One of the
Brigade people brought it to me several years ago. Simon got it in
France. I can't get over it."

"Stop pointing it at us. This is Annie."

Theda nodded as she aimed the gun into the fireplace. "It's
not loaded," she said, and pulled the trigger. There was a loud report.

"I will never make that claim again," Theda said. "Simon was
always telling me I thought I knew everything. I've made coffee.
You can take your suitcase in there, Annie. Then come back. Be
sure to come back right away."

He stayed an hour, then left them at the table near the window,
Theda chain smoking, one long brown arm resting on the table,
Annie sitting up straight on the other side, watching Theda with
grave admiring eyes. Max saw the pure intelligence, the observa-
tional force in the girl's face; and something unawakened, entirely
untouched that faintly repelled him—she was, in an essential way,
without self. What does the sentry do? On guard all night, alone in
the dark—the relief never comes—he cannot sleep—relief was
promised, but he has forgotten the password, only the urgency of
the duty, not to sleep.

223

Now, another world. Theda knew movie people, ballet people, bums, painters, Negroes.

She gave parties. People drank Dago red. She made pots of chile. People danced, sang, got drunk, slept on Theda's floor. Often she worked on her reading assignments while her guests moved around her, talking and shouting and occasionally fighting. Theda paid no mind. She seemed to like the noise. Sometimes, when there was no one around, she went to a bar a few blocks away and sat at a table, her notebook open, her pencils sharpened, a gin drink at hand.

Annie continued to work at the ceramic shop until Max called her and told her to come out to the plant and be interviewed for a training job. It was a long way, the streetcar, then a bus. The training shop was in a shed reeking of metal and oil, with machines standing in two threatening rows. People worked at them, several wearing isinglass masks. There were only a few women. She would make more at the school than she was making now. The course lasted six weeks.

"It's a long way," she told Max on the phone later. "It took me hours."

He would manage something, he said, when she was through the training school. If they got on the same shift, he'd drive her to the plant.

She began, on Saturdays, to look for a place of her own. Theda's life was an enchantment, a thrall, but it filled every inch of the apartment. Theda's strange hours, her work habits, her morning lust for the newspaper obituary page, her fits of black melancholy, her wisecracks, her broodings, her demands for conversations in the middle of the night—"Let's have a little conversation," she would say, waking Annie up and dragging her to her feet, feeding her pieces of the cake she'd suddenly decided to make at one in the morning—it was like one drunken spree. For the first time in her life, Annie wanted a room of her own.

Wandering around Hollywood on these Saturdays, she began to know its sun-dried puniness, the depthless quality of the little shoddy houses that lined streets which could have been anywhere, the plaster flamingos, ducks, geese, dwarfs, squirrels, cats, stuck into the grass of the small lawns which each house had, a domestic apron of yellowing green that proclaimed its owner's good fortune.

224

She found a boulevard lined with old frame houses, like swollen invalids with half-shut eyes. It was the place of the fortunetellers, the astrologers, the spook cults whose members she glimpsed limping down the stairs to the sidewalk, old women most of them, maggot-faced old ones in print dresses and ugly small hats nailed to thin skulls. Miles away were the canyons where the movie people lived, the hills where their houses hung above the valley, the dream castles of money, half-baked Moroccan and Spanish delights, houses of eighteen and twenty and fifty rooms.

Even in the shabbiest areas, there were nightclubs with Hawaiian motifs, giant pineapples on their roofs, urine-yellow in the daylight, autographed photographs of huge-breasted girls in the windows, girls who sang and danced, or boys with slicked-down hair, comedians and piano players.

Once she came upon a group of people around a red-cheeked, middle-aged man who held a small American flag in one hand, pamphlets in the other.

"America!" he was crying, "thy purity is besmirched by the Jews! By the mixed breeds, by the coyotes, by the yellow races, by the intolerable mutts and mongrels, the godless and the Reds, the grinning Nigras swarming and filthy. Oh, thy wretchedness! God Bless Us! Friends, take my sermons, read! Learn how you may turn back the deadly tide!" He waved the little flag. There was scattered applause. A man standing on the outside of the group shouted, "Fascist!" then took to his heels. The red-cheeked man, his followers, at what seemed a leisurely pace, went after him. He disappeared around a corner. The street was silent again except for a few cars, the sound of a lawn mower somewhere, a window banged shut.

One evening, Annie came home to Theda's and found a party in the making. Among the people, some of whom she knew now, was a stranger, a light-skinned Negro who stood slightly outside the group around the fireplace (the never-used fireplace, Theda had put a basket of fruit on the hearth). He was elegantly dressed in a dark-blue jacket and light flannel trousers, a narrow knit blue tie, a white shirt. Annie went to wash up. She put on the amber beads which Ben Greenhouse had sent her. Theda was setting out a platter of thick cold pork chops and a huge bowl of apple sauce. The Negro was standing where Annie had seen him last. They looked at each other, she smiled, he nodded. She went over to him.

225

"That's beautiful amber," he said.

"Yes."

"Tree resin. Older than anyone can imagine. Sometimes they've found insects imbedded in pieces of it from hundreds of thousands of years ago. Wars have been fought for amber."

"Can I get you a plate of food?"

"No. Thank you, not yet. My name is Cletus Moore."

"Annie Gianfala," she said. "I'm staying here with Theda until I find a place."

"She told me."

He fetched up a drink from the table beside him.

"Can I get you a drink?"

"Yes," she said.

"I think Theda's got some gin tonight."

"I'll have that."

"It eats out the lining of your stomach."

"One thing less to worry about."

He appeared delighted with that. A smile revealed a gap between his upper teeth. He was the color of fine luggage and his eyes were faintly slanted. He looked like a giant chrysanthemum, a pale-golden one. He brought her a glass of gin and water and ice.

He wanted to know what she did. She was in a training school, she told him, learning how to operate a drill press. He told her he wrote continuity for an afternoon soap opera—"All about the trials of white folk," he said with the faintest irony.

Later, they took their plates and sat down on some cushions and ate together. She had never had a conversation with a Negro, a conversation over dinner and drink. He maintained an even, pleasant demeanor although he drank considerably more than she did. He spoke of himself without constraint, yet she felt it was a prepared script he offered her, something to get done with before you got down to the real game. She offered him her own script in return, radically edited.

"Your life's messed up," he said. "But you're just beginning." He began to laugh. "It gets worse, lady."

"It can't."

"Can, always can. Now this week, they wanted to have a colored maid say 'gwine to hebben,' the story's too dull to go into, but just hold that in your mind. They wanted *me* to have that girl

226

say 'gwine to hebben.' I told them I was gwine to my lawyer and break my contract if they were going in for that jive."

"What did you have the maid say?"

"I quit." Her own laughter was not in response to what he had said, but to something playful in him. He was grinning at her. "That's a beautiful jacket," she said. "Yeah. Blues out my dark soul. Leads young women into thinking I'm a safe bet for a soft talk. Isn't that what you think?"

"I don't know much about jackets."

"That's good." He had a lovely thick laugh; he could talk right through it; his Chinese eyes glinted, the fine wrinkles all around them creasing with merriment.

"Where's your daddy and mama?"

"My father—I'm not sure now, somewhere in New England. She's dead. It's been a long time."

"I'm from here. I'm a Californian. My mother was a white woman and when she died, my father married another white. My stepmother is a bad lady. I had to clear out. My old man has a little chicken farm up in Petaluma, the egg basket of the West. He's a dried-up little thing—he's got a Japanese chicken sexer working for him. You know what that is? Somebody can tell what sex a chick is. He bullies that Japanese something terrible. You know the story about the bongo tree? There's an island with a bongo tree. When there's enough fruit on it, the natives don't bother each other, but when the bongo tree is barren, they eat each other. One of those stories . . . the truth is, the natives eat each other regardless of what the tree is putting out. Theda lays on a good table. Some women can't do it, you know. They just can't put a meal together. I've got to go soon. I have to write this crap eight weeks ahead and the seventh week is sliding up to crush me. I'll have to work all night tonight."

"Is it what you like to do?"

"Ho! Choices! That's another life. What I'd like is to write essays. Hazlitt, Arnold, like those people. I'd like to write about dumbness. If you think about it, you'll see how many subtle variations there are, what nuances stupidity has, what grace and style accompany self-stupefaction."

"Don't go!"

"You like to listen to me? You come over and see me. I'll play you some nice music and I'll talk some more. And if the day isn't too hot, I'll wear my Harris tweed which I bought in London, made to fit my own bones and no one else's."

"I'd like that!"

"You know Countee Cullen? No? James Weldon Johnson? I'll fix that."

She stood. He held out his warm, dry hand and she pulled him to his feet. He jumped up and down in place several times, shot his cuffs, and patted her head. "You mixed up with Theda's congregation? The party?"

She shrugged. "I don't know."

"I don't like groups," he said. "Doesn't matter what's in their mouths. Somewhere there's a lynching in the making. Don't join anything. Do you read Kipling? There's a story, *The Cat That Walked by Himself*. I'll read you something else from him when you come over. Theda's gang says he was a dirty old imperialist. Theda'll tell you where I live. You might like it. It's a big barn over a nightclub. Not far from here. Take care now."

She watched him go to Theda, touch her face, then leave. He was quick, moving out of the way of drunken staggerings, moving fast and neatly.

After everyone had gone, Theda told her a little more about Cletus. He'd been in Carmel in the twenties and had known all the Negro poets who'd formed a little community there. No, he'd never married but he'd been in love with a woman for a long time, so long that people didn't gossip about it any more. She was married to a party functionary—she'd been a cabaret dancer, from the South, Theda thought, and Cletus used to hang around their house, fighting with the functionary about party matters, while Leora served up her perfect little suppers on a white tablecloth. Somebody'd said she was half Mexican. And Cletus wasn't interested in anyone else? Oh, well, he'd had a girl now and then over the ten years Theda had known him. He was nice to them. She supposed he took them to bed. But what he really liked to do was to teach them. Cletus knew a lot. He'd gone to Howard University in Washington. It had caused a fearful ruckus in the family because his stepmother wanted him to go to a white college. But Cletus wouldn't budge. He went where he intended. He was a good friend, said Theda. Party people were really down on him. "I heard Calvin Schmitter almost call him a 'bad nigger' once and then bite on it and swallow it and turn green."

The place was a mess. They cleaned for two hours. Theda discovered a gallon of red wine behind a broom in the closet. "We'll drink this," she said, "and make the time fly."

"How is it people can hang *around* the party? I thought . . . I had some idea it was underground."

"Not here. Not now. In some cases I suppose it is. But since the popular front—it's not like the old days, Palmer raids and all of that. Oh, it's too long! I don't feel like talking about it. I'm out, you know. I've quit it."

"How do you quit?"

"I don't really know," Theda said glumly. "They've never paid much attention to me. I've been lectured to a number of times, but I have this terrible faculty of *depressing* them, I mean a kind of personal depression, the way you'd feel about someone you don't much care for who's dying of an obscure disease. I suppose if I were important . . . well, I've used them as much as they've used me. You know, the serious ones, the ones who really *believe,* they even walk differently from other people. . . . They *know* what's right, all of history fits in their fists. Even in my shrillest days— that once upon a time when I thought there was a side I could take and hold forever—even then, I experienced the most terrible irritability—I think it was construed by some as conviction—and I realized that in *me* the idea that no truth could come from the capitalist press, its literature, its movies, its theaters, took the form of raging paranoia. I was tormented by suspicion of simply everything. When Simon went to Spain to fight in the Spanish Civil War, I listened to the kind of grim praise that was showered on him those last days before he left, political praise. But I knew why Simon was going. Simple Simon. He thought Franco was *bad;* he was troubled in his work; he was *bored.* Oh, Simon! He never had a political thought in his life. When I think of him, I become insane."

The rugs had been straightened, the chairs returned to their places, the glasses and dishes washed. Theda had opened the window and a eucalyptus-perfumed night breeze blew across their heated faces. She got up to pour them both more wine. They sat silently for a bit, smoking, looking out through the leaves to where the lamps illuminated the empty street.

"How did you get in?"

"My brother," Theda said. "He's what's known as a party theoretician. He is not without learning, the *shit!* Implacable monster that he is! He went through college like a general, slaughtering his

229

professors, putting Trotskyites to the sword, burning villages . . .
I mean, of course, with his mouth. He has the most terrible mouth
in the history of mankind. He's in the East now, issuing directives.
He came here once. Simon was sitting just where you're sitting.
He began to *tell* Simon about the true function of art. Simon listened. Then he went into my little kitchen and came back with a
five-pound sack of flour. He cut open the top with my nail scissors. My brother, Carl, continued to address the furniture, the
walls, the paintings. Simon dumped the whole sack of flour on his
head. Then Simon said, 'I'll be back after you've swept up.' "

Theda threw back her head and laughed. "I haven't seen Carl
since. I had always been afraid of him until I saw him whitened.
It was a cruel way to lose my fear, but that's the way it happened."

"You loved Simon?" Annie said with heedless emphasis.

Theda drank. "I was taller than Simon. But that was fortunate
because he liked tall women. He liked all women. We must have
been a strange couple. I desired Simon. I desired to be in the
place where he was all the time. Look! Someone put out a cigarette in my rug!"

She got up and went to the white stub crushed in the rug pile
and bent over. God, she *was* tall. She stood up, holding the butt in
her hand. She caught Annie's glance, its import. Annie flushed;
Theda smiled. "Have another drink," she said. "Love is not a subject any more than death is. I'm not especially vain about it, but I
have yet to run out of men who want to make love to me. Make
what? Love!" and she whirled and tossed the butt into the flower
basket in the fireplace.

They drank a good deal more. Theda spoke as though she
plucked her thoughts from some clear medium. It was not her
judgment that so impressed the younger woman; it was the way
she didn't count the costs of what she said.

In her closet of terrors, Annie picked up words in the dark,
hoping they would not turn out to be serpents. But Theda was *un-
congested*. Annie asked her if she knew Fern Diedrich. Theda said
that Fern was going mad—that it was not the party that had
driven her mad, no, the party didn't do that—in fact, it frequently
kept madness at bay—"like religion," Theda said. "She came here
once with Max and Eva. I had a dog at the time. Jimmie, the dog.
The dog jumped into Fern's lap. She sat in a catatonic trance—
Fern with dog on lap. We were all paralyzed, even Eva. Fern

began to grin, her mouth stretched so, I thought her face would break. The dog licked her chin. She stood straight up, so quickly the dog *fell* on the floor. I never saw a dog do that before."

"Max," said Annie sadly, drunkenly. "Max."

"No, no. Not Max."

They stared across the table at each other.

"I didn't mean anything . . ."

"It wouldn't do any good. I asked him once if he'd murdered old ladies in his youth. Oh, he's hopeless. Taking on burdens that appall him. But he can't refuse anything, anyone. You did too mean something. Listen, I'm years older than you. Going to bed with men is your idea of good manners—offering the executioner a cigarette before he chops off your head."

"I think I'm going to throw up."

"Minnie was a moocher," sang Theda, knocking over her glass. "Swine! Warrior runts! Mammary rooting swine!"

"Knockers!" Annie shouted.

"Pear-shaped, pig-snouted, apple-round, melons, moons, bangles, dangles, udders," howled Theda, rising, staggering, leaping into the middle of the room. "Men, the hog species, the boob lovers!"

"Tits!" shrieked Annie. They danced, they minced, they posed, living statues. "The Susquehanna," whispered Theda.

"Shenandoah," sighed Annie.

"The Missouri."

"Monongahela . . ."

"The Santee . . ."

"Mississippi . . ."

"Allegheny . . ."

"The Nile!" Annie cried.

"The Nile?" questioned Theda, and in the middle of a burst of laughter, sank, spinning in slow motion to the floor, where she lay as if dead. The room spun on, still singing to itself.

Annie lurched to the bathroom, knelt and embraced the throat of the toilet bowl, resting her head on the cold porcelain, then shook like a rattle, and gave up her guts.

At last, weak, grateful for the feel of tile and porcelain, for the clear cold sound of flushing water, for all things cold, inanimate and odorless, she slipped to the floor and slept.

231

Chapter 15

Every noon hour, Max and Annie met at a bench in the central machine shed. All around them, the machines stood idle. The whole plant, the workers, the machines, the foremen, were waiting. There were as many explanations as there were people to account for the absence of materials, the lack of work, and, at the same time, the growing labor force. The air of inanition was at its worst in the late afternoon. Yet there were two shifts, and rumor had it there would soon be a graveyard shift from midnight to 8:00 A.M.

Annie was surprised to find that anyone she spoke to attributed sinister purposes, in this hiatus, either to the government or the shipbuilding plant, or both. But Max said it was characteristic of American working people to distrust government and industry. "It has nothing to do with political awareness," he explained. "It's in the character of the people."

She had found a room in a private house on Oxford Street owned by a divorcee. Mrs. Ives lived with her two children and her mother, Mrs. Gannon, an alligator-skinned, knobby-fingered old woman who had spent most of her life in China. She made Annie's lunch for her every morning, avocado or watercress sandwiches and a little glass jar filled with raw carrots and raisins. The old woman seemed to like her and was much given to slapping her on the back like a little jolly old man.

Her daughter was sour-faced and withdrawn but a very good cook. On weekends, with a certain grudging pride, Mrs. Ives taught Annie some of the essential tasks of cooking. She showed her how to make béchamel sauce, to mince onions, to make white and brown stock. She said, "Everyone wants to get away with everything. You can't be a real cook if you cheat. One thing, I never cheated in the kitchen. My mother used to say, if you have a button missing from a blouse, if you use a safety pin where a catch ought to be, you might as well give up. It's not an easy law to follow." She stood in the middle of the kitchen, one finger raised. Annie had the impression she was describing the movements of the planets.

Mrs. Ives and her mother were, they informed Annie, "progressives." Sometimes in the evening if Annie wandered into their part of the house, she would find the two women brooding over the past, speaking in low voices about the outrages man perpetrated on man—and woman. Especially on woman. "If I had left my husband," Mrs. Ives explained, "he would have gotten the children. I'm reasonably sure of that, even though he ran off with a very disgusting girl who thinks she has a stained-glass window between her legs instead of what we are all required to pretend we don't have. It's all very disgusting."

Her children, a boy and a girl of twelve and fourteen, had a strange glacial quality unlike any Annie had encountered in a child. They frequently reported that dogs were mating on the street. Once the boy told his grandmother that he was convinced his civics teacher was going through menopause. The grandmother told Annie that American children were infantilized—"their youth is prolonged into middle age. After living in China for so many years, my daughter and I do not intend for this to happen to Mai and Pavel." The two women never raised their voices to the children. If Pavel made what the old woman or her daughter deemed a childish request, they said as much in reasonable modulated tones. "That is childish, Pavel. If you would give it a moment's thought, you would see that the results of such an action would make you feel like a fool. The world is full of fools. Make sure you are not numbered among them."

They spoke in the same tone about minorities in the United States. The people who oppressed them were fools; the police were fools, especially the Red Squad; the Depression was a result of the mismanagement of fools.

233

The house breathed a cold mild poison. Yet Annie did not find herself uncomfortable with the two women. She simply talked less than was her natural tendency. All in all, they were kind to her in their peculiar icy way.

She did avoid the children. She felt vaguely menaced by their presence. They regarded her with clear brown eyes that seemed to ask, What are you? *What on earth are you?*

Her part of the house, her "apartment," was the most cheerful place she had ever lived in. A crazy quilt was spread over the large bed. There was a writing desk with many pigeonholes, scatter rugs covered the floor, and the furniture was sturdy and useful. The bathroom had a clean white tub, and the rubber stopper that prevented water from flowing away was brand new. A little cooking area was closed off from the rest of the room by a wooden screen upon which had been painted a peacock and three yellow butterflies. There were white curtains at the windows, and a bookcase made of redwood planks and glass bricks near the bed. One window faced the street, the other looked out on a long narrow neglected garden with a dry cement pool in the center. The two women were not interested in gardening, and the children didn't play there. In any event, whatever the children played at, it was not recognizable as such. They read; they played mental chess; they played two-handed bridge. They did not seek out friends.

Max was highly entertained by Annie's accounts of the household. The father, according to Mrs. Ives, had run off to Bangor with his doxy and never wrote to his children. A check arrived once a month with a regularity that Mrs. Ives said was uncharacteristic. "I think," Max said, "the little girl will murder the other three one moonless night and become a famous movie star."

"They're like a gang," Annie said once, eating a cucumber sandwich which Mrs. Gannon had fixed for her that morning. "That's really what they are, a gang of desperadoes."

Once a week, Annie went to a party meeting. She had completed six weeks in what the party called State School and had read only excerpts from books that she was supposed to have read in their entirety. The school was on the second floor of an old office building in Los Angeles. The windows were covered with steel mesh. There was one classroom and an office. It was there she met Ethel Schaeffer. The older woman occasionally took her to a dairy restaurant where, beneath a slowly turning fan which moved flies languidly across the tin ceiling, she tested kasha and matzoth-ball soup. Ethel's voice was like a bubbling stream; she spoke gently, continually, and her conversation had neither beginning nor end, flowing along effortlessly. Annie had trouble understanding the old woman's heavily accented English, but she was content to be bathed in the exceptional, if somewhat impersonal tenderness that emanated from her. She knew Ethel was regarded as a kind of saint, so she seemed to be, yet Annie's judgment did not remain in total abeyance. Ethel was—she could not banish the treacherous thought—too simple. The whole weight of Ethel's nature burdened her comrades with the demand, made ruthless by her single-mindedness, that they release the good in themselves, the virtues they were hiding only out of timidity and ignorance. Only society was complex, not its members. Exclusiveness was patrician; one *must* love everyone. It was a killing tolerance. It embraced even the stiff-faced party doctrinaires about whom Ethel made mild fun. "When you really know," she said, "you are not so uneasy. Like the state, those poor chaps may wither away."

Once she asked Annie, "And how do you like our Karl Marx?"

"Oh—"

"No, no," Ethel had protested, laughing. "You will say something silly. Don't do that. Leave close reading to the ones for whom such activity is meant. For you, only the vision is necessary. No more."

By then, Annie had met Calvin Schmitter. He had given her a curt nod, addressed her as "Comrade," and congratulated her on working in a shipbuilding plant where she would come into contact with real workers. Annie's glance had come to rest on a Soviet poster which Schmitter had hanging on the wall of his small office. In it, four enormously muscled figures strode forward, one grasping the staff of a banner bearing the hammer and sickle. Behind the leading workers, identical replicas repeated themselves, diminishing in size until they disappeared behind the curve of the earth itself.

Sliding and stumbling through the droning afternoons at the plant, Annie thought grimly of the empty-eyed poster monsters. Real workers! She looked around her at the women, bubble-headed in curlers, at the little groups of men near their lockers, playing cards or passing around pints of bourbon. She listened to the talk, often combative, seeming to consist solely of code words echoing from mouth to mouth, about money and sex, sports and drinking. The men looked witlessly and boldly at her body; the

235

younger men seemed older than their years, the older ones, locked up in themselves, dour, hard-voiced. What she found difficult to explain to Max was their friendliness, even if perverted, even if shallow. It was strange, she thought, that Max, concerned about the rights of labor, should be at an aristocratic remove from his co-workers, while she, muddle-brained, and bored with hardly digested Marxist theory about labor and capitalism, should find the people milling around the great shed so familiar, even sympathetic.

He was somewhat offended when she described him as aristocratic, and reminded her that the Communist party was the vanguard of the working class, and what she thought of as *hauteur* in him was simply that he was more advanced in his understanding of social forces. She must have looked bewildered. He shook her arm. "That isn't what I'm talking about," she said stubbornly. "You *are* different!"

"We're all different!" he exclaimed.

"That's not what I meant."

"You're not being clear."

"You're pretending!" she accused him.

He frowned angrily—she kept looking at him. Then his face cleared. "Oh, well, I have to, I suppose," he said.

She became friendly with one or two of the women. One was Hannah Groops, a turret-lathe operator from Alabama. Her family troubles were somewhat rank. Her father, she said, "got this itch for my daughter, his own grandchild. I got to do a search at night, make sure he isn't crawled into her bed."

"Why don't you lock the door?"

Hannah Groops gave her a scornful look. "What door? You think we live in some kinda palace? We had one room back home. Now we got two. We ain't got to locking doors yet."

She went to a meeting where she discovered Max several rows behind her, sitting by himself on a wooden bench. The occasion was in honor of a visiting union leader from Detroit, a comrade who'd come to report on some factional dispute among the United Automobile Workers. She looked around her at faces that were mostly unfamiliar. There were certainly workers *here,* but not like those in the plant. After, she started over to speak to Max, but he waved quickly and left. Later, she asked him why he'd avoided talking to her. He said he didn't know. It had been an impulse. He had found the idea of speaking to her at the meeting intolerable.

236

Inside the plant, Max was special; inside the party, Max treated *her* as special. She didn't understand it but was vaguely stirred.

One day, Max quoted something to her. "Karl Radek said, 'Apart from sleeping, I have never in my life committed any undeliberate action.' "

He looked at her expectantly. She was uneasy. What did he hope she would say?

"I could hardly make that statement," she said dryly, at last.

"It is the most hateful thing I ever read," Max said. "It never occurred to me until last night how hateful it really was, and I've read the transcripts of the Moscow trials often enough."

"How's Eva?"

"Fine."

Annie never visited their apartment any more. Her life had become a series of compartments; the plant, and Max on the bench; the party meetings, where she listened to reports on money-raising for the party paper, discussions on dialectical materialism, Menshevism, the Mexican community of Los Angeles, the writing of a pamphlet for the ship-scalers' union, the discrimination practiced against women in the International Machinists Union, the recruiting drive for Negro comrades, the possibility, always present, of a wave of repression, the cells which would have to be organized, the imperialist war, the Berlin-Tokyo-Rome Axis, and scrap iron, scrap iron, scrap iron!

Christmas, Annie spent with the Ives who had no tree, although Mrs. Ives made a cake in the shape of a Yule log. "This is the way they do it in France, much more sensible, not the orgy of meretricious gift-giving that goes on in this country," Mrs. Ives boasted, and each of the children received a book. Mrs. Gannon gave Annie a metal lunch box containing a Thermos bottle. She had painted Annie's name on it in yellow letters. After the holidays, Max turned up on the bench with a package in hand for her, a collection of the poetry of William Butler Yeats. She put it on her bookshelf next to Engels, *The Origin of the Family, Private Property and the State,* and *Tess of the D'Urbervilles.*

She saw a good deal of Cletus Moore, and through him met other people, some of whom became her friends.

In his big, echoing loft, Cletus entertained her in a smart new hat pushed over his forehead and an old brown flannel bathrobe tied with a tassel. On Saturdays they listened to Gregorian chants, Brahms and jazz. Cletus read her poetry, Countee Cullen:

So I lie, who never quite
Safely sleep from rain at night—

She burst into tears. Cletus roared with laughter, flung his hat on the floor, jumping on it, swung her up from the partly eviscerated couch into which she had sunk while listening to him, and danced her around the room.

She went to a few parties where she met rich people. They weren't Communists, Max explained, but they supported various organizations such as Spanish refugee aid groups. She wandered through beautiful silent rooms full of real paintings and leather furniture and bowls of fresh flowers. In the living room, Calvin Schmitter might be sitting bolt upright, at his feet the hostess in a long gown, gleaming up at him with factitious interest. "They only play," Max said.

One of Cletus's friends was a trumpeter named Melvin Johnson. His skin was black, his eyes were huge, his teeth were white and even. He was in the navy for a six-year hitch.

"Guess how old I am?" he asked Annie. "Thirty," she said. He hooted with triumph. "Forty-three!"

He carried his trumpet around with him in its purple velvet case. Sometimes he took it out and fitted it together and blew a riff. He had an Italian woman friend whose husband was away in the army, stationed in the Philippines. He showed Annie her photograph. "Beautiful!" said Annie, looking at the somewhat blurred but opulent figure of a handsome middle-aged woman.

"Like me," said Melvin.

He told her stories about the great jazz musicians. He'd been with Basie for a while. He'd played with different bands all over the country, even up north near Canada where your cheeks froze solid and you couldn't hardly blow a note. He was just a little kid when he'd started working back down South in the hotels, bringing the men their whiskey and women. He loved the horses and, when he was in the money, used to spend all he had at the track. By some special magic, he was able to imitate the particular characteristics of famous racers. Gallant Fox was his favorite.

"See, he had those short little legs, up to here, you see?"—measuring on his own long legs—"and just when you thought he was dying on his feet, here he'd come!" And Melvin would gallop along the rail with his arms. "Look," passing the first horse, "now, see!" passing the second, "and here he is!" racing past Annie's shoulder, "winning!"

Melvin brought around a beautiful blonde girl to Cletus's loft. Her name was Miranda Katz, and she was the adopted child of a wealthy Chicago clothing manufacturer. She drove a taxi for a living and had a mania for clothes. Her latest purchase from Bullock's Wilshire was a red wool coat with an enormous fox collar which had cost five hundred dollars. They were garnisheeing her salary because, of course, she couldn't pay for the damn thing all at once! Her other passion was the ballet, which she attended at any opportunity, escorted by several rich homosexuals she knew. They liked to be seen with her, she remarked without emphasis. It was possible to stare unrestrainedly at Miranda; she neither preened nor fidgeted, accepting impassively examination of her features as though she were a garment being tested for the fineness of its seams. Cletus reported that the only way to distress the girl was to mention her family's wealth. She refused to take a cent from them—he didn't know why. Yet she continually indulged in such extravagances as the red coat. "There's a net of money around her wild preserve," Cletus remarked, "and she knows it's always there. She can't help knowing it." Annie gazed longingly at the golden hair. Miranda had never had a permanent wave; she cut her hair herself, bringing it around her neck and lopping it off with heavy shears. Without making the slightest claim on individuality, she was unlike anyone else. "She's not even like herself," said Cletus.

Often, the four of them played poker late into the night, and even though Annie had to get up so early for work and drooped with fatigue, she could hardly bear to leave. Each evening she spent with them ended in uncertainty; she felt a pang of grief as she stood at Cletus's door, her hand raised briefly in farewell, that the four of them might never meet again. It was more than Melvin's magically evoked horses and Miranda's yellow mane, more than the charm of Cletus's knowing ways, that made her tarry at the door.

How had the three of them met? Perhaps in the same way she had come to know certain people in the party, the ones Schmitter called "unstable." Like attracted to like. Her few party friends joked about Calvin, about the local functionaries with their Stalin mustaches, about a slogan someone reported was actually used by the New York party branch: PEASANTS OF BROOKLYN, ARISE!, and a pamphlet entitled: "What Means This Strike in Steel?"

Oh, they laughed! But yet the party was creeping over Annie, making her judgments about Stalin mustaches irrelevant, her laughter the laughter of contingency. No one had to tell her that there was a growing order in her life.

But there were terrible nights when something heavy and dank and lifeless came to lie upon her like the cat that breathed away the infant's life. She lay rigidly, gasping for breath. She got up and turned on the light and paced the room, she took a book and tried to read the incubus away.

At first, she attributed it to fatigue or, more fancifully, told herself it was Joe's poor sea-soaked ghost. Then, sitting on the couch at Cletus's one afternoon, watching him work at his typewriter, it came to her that the night visitation was the weight of her life, that earlier life she had put out of consciousness. The room on Hollywood Boulevard was still there, and Johnnie Bliss still slept on beside her on the bed that pulled down from the wall; Uncle Greg waited in the dark house on the Hudson; Samuel, trailing odors of musk and dust, opened his cigar box again and again, counted out five ten-dollar bills again and again; Walter Vogel was still her husband, and her father caught still another train to a destination unknown to her. She had imagined she'd learned a few things. Delusion, all of it!

In a panic, she left Cletus—"Hey, girl, where are you going?" —and ran down the stairs to the street. In a telephone booth, she rang up Bea. No answer. St. Vincent's phone was permanently disconnected. Hadn't Tony said where he was going the last time she heard from him? Wasn't there a letter from him at home in the box where she kept her papers? She would call Uncle Greg! But when she emptied her pocketbook of change, she saw there wasn't enough. She took a cab for the first time since St. Vincent had sent for her that night so long ago. She went to Theda's.

A kind of white light filled Theda's apartment. How scarred the old table legs were! And Theda was wearing glasses. Had she always worn them? Annie stood in the doorway, looking at the woman sitting at the table, a typewriter near her arm. The woman was looking up at her in astonishment.

"Annie!"

"Can I use your phone?"

"Are you ill?"

"Ill?" Annie's voice rose hectically. "No. Not ill."

"Use it . . ."

"It's long distance. I'll pay the charges."

Theda looked at her mutely.

She thought she'd forgotten the number but it rolled effortlessly off her tongue.

It had been over a year since she'd heard that phone ring, since she'd imagined the stairs, the stained-glass window, the pier glass, the lion and the mouse. The phone rang and rang. She heard Theda saying something about a time difference. "What?"

"It's eight in the evening there."

"Sometimes on Saturday, the church has a social," Annie said and replaced the receiver.

"You look terrible."

"I was trying to call my uncle. Do you know that feeling? That something awful has happened?"

But it was not to her uncle that Annie thought something awful had happened. She looked desperately at Theda as though the woman might evaporate in front of her.

"I hate California. I hate this state."

"It's only another place . . ."

"No. It's absurd and cruel, and it's all made up."

"You ought to divorce Vogel. Have you done anything about it? I have a lawyer friend. It's not so hard out here. You ought to get clear of that."

How like Theda to have picked out one of the threads that bound her now to this senseless fear! Theda wanted her to get rid of something, a lump sticking out in the middle of her new smoothed-out life. She supposed she ought to, she supposed—

"You're too goddamned self-involved," Theda said in a hard unforgiving voice. "Look at you!" She hit the table with the palm of her hand, then looked silently at her fingers. Her expression softened, and her eyes met Annie's with a kind of apology.

"It's true, what I said. But the way I said it wasn't true. It's like telling someone they breathe. People come here and I drink with them and feed them and they imagine they have my attention when all the time I think of nothing but a dead man. I'm sorry. . . . It's all so painful. But about the divorce . . . maybe you could get an annulment. That might be better. After all, you hardly lived with him."

They talked for a while about Theda's lawyer friend, of how

much of a fee he would demand and whether Walter would be willing to pay for it or not. They spoke of the book Theda was reading for the studio, and then Theda said she did have some good news; she had been hired by the story department beginning the first of June, and she would be working steadily there. Perhaps she would write a scenario and make a mountain of money.

"When did you start wearing glasses?"

"I've always worn them," said Theda. "Oh, Annie!" and she broke into laughter.

Annie told her about the young painter who'd been to the party State School with her. One night he asked if he could drive her home to Oxford Street. He took her out on a country road. A few miles along he stopped the car and put his arm around her. "You remind me of the paints in unopened tubes, crimson and alizarin and vermilion." Then he kissed her once, grinned toothily, and drove her home with not another word. Later, at some party meeting, someone had pointed out the painter's wife. One of her legs was drastically shorter than the other so she seemed to topple forward at each step. She was a hairy woman who looked ten years older than her handsome young husband. "I think," Annie said, "that I am full of cruelty. I had to go out to the street to laugh."

"Only admit it," Theda said dreamily. "Perhaps you'll be saved."

"I've told such awful lies."

"Have a drink."

"No. I'm going home. I have to wash out some things."

"How is the job?"

"Dumb. A dumb job. Nothing's happening there. I go through the gates every morning with my badge pinned to my blouse. The place is like some sullen social club where half the members are drunk all the time and the other half wishes it were. Max says things will change once there's plenty of work to go around. Meanwhile, I have some money. I've not had money before. Neither have most of the people there, I guess."

"I saw the Shores the other night."

Annie stood up, ready to leave. She didn't want to hear about the Shores, only about Max. She sighed, felt the tangle of her recently permanented hair and thought of Miranda.

"I'll tell you something," Theda went on. "I think Max is killing Eva. She's like some helpless thing breathing in poisoned gas. She *watches* him all the time. He's so *nice* to her. Something

deadly is happening between them. He's so ruthless in his insistence on being . . . good."

"He's been my best friend, except for you and Cletus," Annie
said. "I thought if I grew up, I could become good too."

"You'll drive me to drink," muttered Theda.

———

Annie's haunt pursued her into daylight. She thought people
looked at her in a different way. One morning she knocked over
the screen with the three yellow butterflies, frightened to see that
behind it was what she had known all along was there, the little
clean cooking place which she hardly ever used. She brooded constantly on that other life of hers that had been nearly blotted out
by the last six months.

In the plant, people were growing fat in anticipation of the
coming meal of a holocaust. Or their diets had changed for the
better. Hannah Groops said, "In Alabama, we only *heard* about
eating the way we do now. Not a single one of us got a worm
now, not even the children." Annie shuddered.

Her own room was growing fat with things: a radio, four pairs
of shoes, dresses, lipsticks, a new leather pocketbook with cash in
the change purse. But the tweed suit still hung in the closet, its
iron-textured nap undiminished.

The workers at the plant to whom she sometimes condescended
by laughing too much at their asinine jokes, or by touching the
women because she found them repellent, began to look different
to her, too. She wondered that she had ever thought she had anything in common with them, in common with anyone. Only Max
seemed unchanged by the painful inconsistencies of her own vision. Still, Theda's words had bothered her, and at their lunch
meetings on the bench, Annie searched his face for the mark of a
murderer.

Party meetings, at which she once sheltered, had begun to afflict
her with the sickness of boredom. She dreaded the dry, mildly
threatening lectures by people sent down from the party headquarters to remonstrate with her branch because they hadn't raised
enough money, because certain comrades were defaulting on their
dues, because some of the comrades, it had been reported, were
not clear in their understanding of the European war. There were
to be seminars and discussions to be led by reliable Marxists. The
comrades were faltering, they were being taken in by propaganda

243

about concentration camps and persecution of Jews. Their thinking was not "correct."

Then Ethel Schaeffer was taken to the hospital for an exploratory operation. A cancerous growth was discovered in her lower intestine.

Annie went to see her. Ethel was shrunken, her silver hair a ghostly breath on the meager hospital pillow. Horribly, a tube led from beneath the sheets to a bottle on the floor. She was heavily drugged. Her eyes opened and then shut as though under the press of unbearable weight.

She took Annie's hand and held it limply.

Annie told her stories about the plant, about some of the people there. Ethel smiled remotely. Then she said, "Dear girl, I have been thinking of what Marx said. He said"—and she stopped and moaned, and the tube echoed with a ghastly rasping sound—"he said that the Jews were a bourgeois group, and therefore a bulwark of the exploiting class. Dear girl—it seems I've forgotten your name, but, oh, I do know who you are—it seems that I am frightened." She opened her eyes very wide and looked straight at Annie. "Not of this," she said. Then she made a joke accompanied by a small smile. "Even Communists don't live forever."

Annie discovered from Paul Lavan, whom she saw now and then at party meetings, that Walter was still living in their old room. She wrote him a stiff little note suggesting that he might like a divorce, there didn't seem any point. . . . A few nights later as she was reading in bed, she heard a car idling outside on the street. She went to the window. It was their old car and Walter was sitting in it, smoking a cigarette. She put on her new bathrobe and went out the door to the car.

They drove around the Hollywood Hills. He was a little drunk. He rambled somewhat. He was going back into the merchant marine. Was Annie serious about a divorce? He thought they'd started off on the wrong foot, the cart before the horse. He could see she'd changed. Yes, that was clear to him. He felt those things instantly. Did she know that when he'd been a boy, he'd gone up into the San Francisco hills and wept? What did she think of that? He'd wept for the beauty of things and the hopelessness of life. That was a nice bathrobe. She looked well in mannish clothes because of her lovely figure. Actually, they'd be fine together now, he thought. They'd both probably got a lot out of their systems. Would she like to go to the beach awhile?

They went and sat on the sand at Santa Monica. The dawn began to break. It was chilly. Thank God for the chilliness, she thought. She'd forgotten what real weather was like. The gray waves beat hugely on the shore. Walter put his arms around her. No, she said. He laughed his ironic laugh, his only possession, she thought, of any consequence. "You'll go up and I'll go down," he said. "It's in the cards."

He drove back to their old place and got out of the car, then flung the key onto Annie's lap. "You ought to get something out of all this," he said. "I'll mail you the registration, all that. Too sad now, Annie . . ." She watched him stumble up the stairs. When he'd disappeared from view, she started up the car and drove back to Oxford Street, singing wildly and tunelessly to herself all the way.

Mrs. Ives was looking out the front window. It was 6:00 A.M.

Annie hastened to explain. Mrs. Ives waved an imperious hand. "Your life is your own. As is mine. I have news. Mr. Ives phoned at midnight from Bangor, Maine. I have been packing all night. Here. Have some coffee. Mr. Ives wishes us to return to him. He said—he wept too—he said he'd made a ghastly fool of himself. Would we forgive him? Didn't I think it better for the children? My mother and I discussed it. He was paying for the call so I merely put the receiver down, and my mother and I considered various aspects of the matter. To make a long story short, we decided it would be best to return to him. My mother is very fond of California because of the sunlight and the salt air. But Mr. Ives seems to have started a little business in Bangor and has already priced a house where the children will have three acres to explore and play in."

Still standing, she took a great draught of coffee. Then, staring down at the kitchen table, she burst into a shriek of laughter. "I'll have his balls for this!" she cried.

Mrs. Gannon, dressed in a kimono, at that instant appeared in the doorway. She looked at her daughter, then at Annie. Her expression was unfathomable. As Annie drank the last of the coffee, she saw one huge tear make its way down across the ridges of Mrs. Gannon's old face. But the old woman said nothing.

Cletus Moore helped her move. She had acquired more than would fit into the old leather suitcase. She'd found a room only a block from Theda's in a huge frame house that reminded her of the place where Jake Cranford had lived. But it was clean inside,

245

the banisters shone with wax, and the landlady, a middle-aged, strong-looking woman, was herself working in a defense plant.

That first night, lying in the strange bed, she listened for the sound of the Ives children talking through the walls, playing their interminable word games, speaking their special language in spite and triumph against the world of all adults.

Chapter 16

When Annie drank too much alone in her room amid the mild evening sounds of the boardinghouse, she was transported into the realm of her most secret, most hidden self where a mythic life, without law or reason, held sway.

As she slowly drank her first gin, she dreamed of Max. His belt buckle gleamed at her eye. Above it was his diaphragm, his rib cage, the swelling of his chest, the straight line of his shoulders, his compact upper arms, his narrow wrists, the articulate hands which never flung themselves about in vague gesture, never threatened or importuned or hung in foolish vacancy. His neck rose out of a closely buttoned collar, supporting the classic, careful face with its unexpected joke of blue eyes beneath dark eyebrows, his dark hair.

She took her second drink more quickly, and turned about the figure of the man, a tight, nervy figure with a distancing refinement, as though his body refused to join the causes of his mind.

By her third, fuller glass of gin, Max evaporated, his place taken by unknown players caught up in a painful scene of reconciliation, forgiveness, weeping. A few tears flowed down Annie's cheeks. How good everyone was to her! Even Hannah Groops, that base Southern weed, rested an incorporeal head on Annie's incorporeal shoulder. In the forest of her fancy, Cletus and Theda and Melvin advanced toward her with open arms.

She ate a piece of bread. But *were* they so good to her? Or did they only tolerate her? Did they laugh at her among themselves? Black Melvin and putty-skinned Hannah danced around her, joined together in scornful joy.

She knocked back a fourth gin; the silent actors returned, in dramas that *felt* more epic as they grew more incomprehensible. Figures writhed among flames, and Annie pulled them out like twigs; great clouded mirrors crashed, people fled crumbling houses. Annie moistened the lips of unknown victims with brandy. After the conflagration, in the smoky dark, Max returned. She felt her arms gripped strongly.

But it was not Max. It was the young Catalan welder, the one whose eyes so often followed her as she walked through the shed. One day, her hands clumsy, she had been trying to insert a drill in the drill press. She had been sweaty, holding the bit in her hand, twisted around her machine, when he'd walked by, come back a few steps, watched her silently, and when she'd scowled at him, ashamed of the shirt clinging to her wet back, he'd placed his hands on her arms and pressed them deeply, then released her almost at once. The touch of his hands stayed with her all that day, and every time she saw him, she felt the force of his hands and looked at them intently, as though the square brown fingers might explain why she had been so helplessly stirred when they'd clasped her arms. And it was the Catalan who followed her patiently into an alcoholic sleep.

Each day, at the plant, she sought him out with her eyes, and having assured herself he was there, kept her back turned to him whenever he came near her.

Then one day he followed her out of the machine shop, a few steps behind her, all the way to where she had left the car. She turned to look at him, the key in her hand. The whole force of his question was concentrated in his large black eyes. He suddenly smiled, very faintly. God! He wasn't much older than she was! She was breathless; the afternoon sun enclosed them in warmth. She left the passenger door open and got into the driver's seat. The Catalan swung himself into the car and dropped his lunch box in the back seat.

In her room, he looked at her books. He picked up a lipstick tube on her bureau and opened it and held it to his nose. Then he said, "Your name is Annie?"

She heard a tremor in his voice. She took a step toward him, almost weeping with the desire for him to take her arms in his hands again, to feel that extraordinary breathless release where, it had seemed, body and spirit had been clasped together, the ragged rift healed. His hands rose as she drew close, then caught her arms. She forgot everything, lost in the apple and salt smell of his skin.

He came home with her every day for two weeks. They learned about each other in the late-afternoon silence of her room; he spoke little English, but enough to tell her he had been born in New Mexico in the mountains above the desert, that he was unhappy among so many people, that he was saving money to go back and buy a farm, that he had five brothers and a sister, that when she had first come to the plant, he had looked at her. "So tall, I thought," he said, leaning on his elbow, looking down at her. "But not so tall, after all."

They did not meet on the weekends. He lived with a married sister in Pasadena. But it was not because of that, his family, that they didn't meet. Everything was clear between them; it was their privacy they guarded.

They hardly spoke in the machine-shop shed. And ashamed of her shame, Annie didn't want Max to even guess that she knew the Catalan. But more important than that concern was the power of their secret—she looked up to see him in the distance, walking to his locker with a patient countryman's walk. On her way to buy an afternoon soft drink, she saw him look up from his welding, lift the heavy protective mask for a minute as she passed.

Then, several weeks after the Ives family had departed for New England, Max failed to appear one noon hour at the bench, and Annie felt a tick of dread. She spent the afternoon in desultory conversation with Hannah Groops, although now and then they had to go and stand at their machines. Things had been stiffening in the shop, and the foremen who passed through had begun to make a show of efficient impatience. "Goddamn lend-lease," Hannah said. "We're gonna be working soon, and here I got used to taking my ease."

That afternoon, she told the Catalan she could not spend the evening with him. His mouth turned down. He scraped the sidewalk with his foot. Then he looked up quickly. "Is that man? The man you eat with?"

"No, no . . . I have some things I must do. No. Not that man. He's my friend."

He shook his head. "Friend?" he said with a slight touch of disbelief. As she drove away, she saw him in the rearview mirror, standing there, his hands in his pockets.

Her room seemed exceptionally silent. There was a sallow yellow light in the sky that evening which persisted in the dark like a flush of illness. Not a leaf moved. She tried to read. She turned on her radio. A sweet tenor voice sang "I'll Remember April." Annie tried to remember April. She flung herself out the door and walked down to Hollywood Boulevard. She walked for miles. Confronted with this special and painful emptiness, she felt uneasy, embarrassed at the thought of phoning Cletus or Theda. Melvin was out of reach of a message and in any case was either with his Italian lady friend or at his naval unit. Miranda Katz was driving her taxi. Perhaps she would call Paul Lavan to ask him about Ethel Schaeffer. She really did want to know how Ethel was. She hadn't been to see her for a week. She drifted into a news store and bought a copy of *Photoplay,* a grimace of self-dislike on her face.

Reluctantly, she made for home. The night was so airless, she felt half suffocated. A throb of pain came and went in the lower regions of her stomach. It was sharp, a physical manifestation of the panic she'd felt at Max's absence from the bench.

She went into a phone booth and looked up Ben Greenhouse's number. He was right there, his name in print; he lived on Beechwood Avenue. She remembered that May Landower also lived there. May! Was there nothing behind her but broken-off conversations? She recognized, then dismissed the combination of mischief and loneliness that had led her to even consider calling Greenhouse, and went directly home. There, she wrote a long letter to Uncle Greg. When she read it over before sealing it into its envelope, it seemed to her that the letter was about someone entirely other than herself. The pain in her belly persisted.

Max was back the next noon. He looked forbidding, abstracted.

"You weren't here yesterday!" she said accusingly.

"I tried to enlist in the army," he said.

He took her hand. "Close your mouth," he said. "You'll catch flies."

"But why!" she cried.

"I'm bound to be drafted unless I get myself into some essential job here. I don't want to do that."

"You're running away."

"If you like. Only I'm not. They won't take me because I'm married."

"Max!"

"It would have been better all around," he said, sighing heavily. "My motive wasn't entirely personal. I do really believe Hitler is the devil himself."

What did he mean, not entirely personal? What was more personal than belief in the devil? Her anger was intensified by her awareness that she had no claim on his confidences, that she was not someone he would take into account when he had decided on a course of action. She spoke with sulphurous resentment, trying, mid-sentence, to modify her tone. But it was too late. Her words snapped out like a whip: "I thought the comrades had decided it was an imperialist war?"

"You are a callow, ignorant girl," he said, "and you have the impertinence to imagine your little political scrapings have something to do with the real world."

She thought she would be able to leave the bench in a minute or two, if only her eyes would stop rolling around like a frightened cow's. She caught sight of the tall metal can provided for trash. Walking in a crouch she took the remains of her lunch and threw them into the already overflowing can. She'd left her cigarettes on the bench, but she didn't go back for them, and Max didn't call her back. She walked the whole length of the shed to where Hannah Groops was talking with some other women and slipped in among them. One thing about the proletariat—they didn't pay much mind to one's comings and goings.

She'd been aware, off and on throughout the day, of the Catalan watching her. Just before her shift was finished, she met him near his locker.

"I can't see you again today. I'm not feeling well."

He took her hand in his. Involuntarily, she looked around to see if Max could see them. The Catalan touched each of her fingers. "I don't understand," he said gravely. "Please," she said gently, holding his steady gaze with her own. Please what? She didn't know herself what she was asking him.

Dreading the long drive back home alone, she offered a ride to one of the men who lived in Los Angeles. He had always spoken pleasantly to her, a tight-limbed, small man who reminded her physically of Walter's friend, Junior.

"This is an old buggy," he said, looking at the panel. He told

251

her that when the war came to the United States, he was going on the graveyard shift, where you could make a lot more money. First thing he was going to buy was an Oldsmobile. He explained why in exhaustive automotive detail. She hardly listened. Then, without any change of tone, he told her how his wife's sister, who'd come out to stay with them in the hope of getting a good job in the plant, had climbed into bed one night with his wife and himself. He described what had followed. Annie looked at her pocketbook and wondered if a stray cigarette might be lying in the bottom. They were driving along Sunset Boulevard. They passed an enormous nightclub, but it wasn't a nightclub; it was a funeral parlor.

She said, "Is that true, what you've been telling me? And if it is, what the hell makes you think I want to hear it? And if it isn't true, why are you making it up? Aren't you embarrassed? What are you trying to do anyhow?" Her voice rose. "You're just scaring me! Why don't you unbutton your fly, you little runt!"

She came to a full stop in front of the Trocadero. The man was trembling, his hands clutching his lunch box, and his breathing whistled as though someone were choking him. Annie trembled along with him. The pain that had bothered her the night before came back with violence as though her shouting had alerted it.

"No!" the man said to her hand as it started to turn the handle of the door. "No! Please! Drive me to Hollywood! I'm sentimental about my wife and her sister's a hag . . . I made up part of it . . . but it could happen. She, the sister, sits around with her legs up on the furniture. I've got a very soft heart. You ask anybody. . . . What's the matter? I didn't mean to make you feel so bad!"

"I've got a terrible pain in my stomach."

She leaned back against the seat, and he got out and waved her to the passenger seat and drove her to the boardinghouse. As she started to open the door, he said, "Is there something I could do? You look bad. I know a doctor in Pasadena. He's a chiropractor but my wife says he's good. You want me—"

"No, no. I'll be okay. I'll lie down for a while."

"I want to say I'm sorry."

"I'm sorry too, that I yelled that way."

He gave her a somewhat sly look, then walked down toward the boulevard.

She got out of the car quickly.

The pain worsened. She vomited up a bitter substance that left

252

her mouth sour. At some point, she dropped the wet washrag she was holding against her face and acknowledged to herself that she had a fever. She called Theda.

At the emergency entrance of the hospital she could barely walk. A nurse pushed her into a wheel chair.

"Where?" the doctor was asking irritably. "Now, wait! Where did it start? Here? Here?"

A blood count was taken. She held Theda's hand and stared up at the white ceiling. "Her appendix is about to blow up," someone said nearby.

"Prep," said the nurse and shaved off her pubic hair. An intern put a needle in her arm. She was wheeled into an elevator. Theda's long worried face was the last thing she saw, until a kidney-shaped white enamel pan tried to eat her. She threw up, gripping her belly, "Oh, Oh!"

"Here," said the nurse. A glass straw protruded from a glass of ginger ale. It was morning. A mustachioed man was looking down at her. His white coat was heavily starched, especially over a breast pocket from which protruded a pen.

"How do you feel?"

"Awful."

"It was pretty rotten. I'm surprised you didn't have warning earlier. It's a good thing your friend brought you when she did. You might have gotten peritonitis."

She tried to smile since the worst hadn't happened.

"Gassy?"

"It hurts."

"It's gas. This little tube will help no end. Or I should say, help your end." He permitted himself a little medical heehaw.

Later, Theda was sitting in a chair near the window. The dark circles around her eyes aged her. In her partly drugged awareness, Annie suddenly saw Theda all alone. How tired, how strained she looked! Theda was staring at a picture on the wall of a vapid Pierrot. Slowly, she turned her head and saw that Annie was awake and looking at her. She got up and came to the bed.

"And what do you intend to do for your next number?"

Annie smiled weakly.

"I've gotten you a private nurse for a couple of days until they take that tube out of you. My new job has started, otherwise I'd stay. Don't look so scared. It's over. Cletus is bringing you books in a couple of days. Max is coming tomorrow. He's taken care of telling the shop foreman you won't be in for a while. I think you'll get some kind of sick pay. Don't worry."

A nurse came in, and Theda left.

At night, Annie waited for the shadow of the nurse to fall across the doorway. That shadow brought oblivion. When she made sure she was alone, she moaned. There was pleasure in moaning. Then she discovered that she was not alone. An elderly nurse was dozing by the window. "Are you there?" whispered Annie.

"I'm here," a voice whispered back.

"I can't stand the tube," Annie groaned.

"Poor tube," murmured the voice.

"Won't it come out soon?"

"After the poison's all gone. I love the tube. And go to sleep."

Max stood in the doorway the next afternoon. He held a bouquet of varicolored daisies. "Which tube?" she asked hopefully. She saw a look of anguish cross his face. It wasn't the nurse.

The nurse took the flowers from him, first burying her nose in them. "Is it you who smells so good or the flowers?" she asked Max.

"You have a nice nurse," Max said stiffly.

"Thank you."

"Oh, I'm so sorry . . ." he said suddenly, and came close to the bed and bent over and kissed her damp forehead.

"I was working out on you," he said.

She slept; the pain had diminished; she felt cradled in a delicious softness and warmth. Someone had forgiven her.

On the third day, the nurse left. The tube came out. The nurse said, "Now that your appendix is gone, be sure and hold on to your table of contents!" A Negro woman, who was mopping the floor beneath the bed, gave the nurse's back a scornful look. "She was nice," Annie said to the woman. "Yeah. They all nice," said the woman and departed with bucket and mop.

Cletus arrived with a small bottle of champagne and a book which he placed on her chest.

"Put your mind on that book and you'll wish you'd never been born," he said cheerfully. A nurse came in to take her temperature, then wrote down the results on the chart which hung on the metal bar at the foot of her bed. She was fully conscious now, and she saw the nurse look at Cletus. Cletus was talking to her about something. She was thinking about the nurse's look. It had been full of—of what? Dislike? Something else. Disgust? Her mind closed painfully around the word as though it were a thorn.

"Don't you skip any part of that book," Cletus said. "You Russian lover! Wait'll you read about these boys." He plucked the book from her chest and held it up. She saw a picture of a church with an onion-shaped dome. *The Brothers Karamazov.*

Cletus sat down. "How are you feeling, girl?"

"Better," she said. "Fine."

"Fine," he said and grinned.

"What's the champagne for?"

"You. They say you can have that. I asked the nurse to put it in the refrigerator." They both looked at the bottle in its silver foil on the chest. The nurse hadn't taken it.

"She didn't take it."

"No," Cletus said. "She expected me to bring watermelon."

She was in the hospital ten days. Max and Eva came together once. Eva had changed. Maybe it was because she was so thin. Eva hardly took her eyes from Max in the hospital room. She had lost some basic confidence of her body; she didn't seem to know how to sit down any more.

The nurses pretty much ignored Annie. It had something to do, of course, with her getting better. It had something to do with Cletus, but especially with the appearance of big Melvin in his sailor suit roaring down the corridor and bursting into her room, shouting, "Hey, baby! What's doing?" After that, nobody said more than was absolutely necessary to her, except the doctor with the mustache who had operated on her.

Although she was prone most of the time, she felt a storm had blown up and furniture and houses were flying around her. Max came alone. As he bent over to kiss her cheek, she felt she must tell him something. He whispered in her ear that Ethel Schaeffer had died, in this same hospital, yesterday. She began to cry. Max said, "Oh, Annie, don't cry."

"She's dead."

"Jesus wept," he said.

"What?"

"A noun and a verb. Life beats stronger in short sentences, 'Exalted, Satan sat.' "

"Oh, Max, don't talk to me about those things."

"What shall I talk to you about?"

"I love you, Max," she said between tremulous sobs.

255

"I hope you do," he said gravely. "I hope somebody does."

Theda had a plan. Annie must get out of that plant. She didn't care if Annie did know how to work a drill press or whatever it was. Theda had found a secretarial training school with night classes. It was only an eight-week course. She'd learn typing and shorthand and then Theda could get her a job at the studio. It was really nice there. The offices were cool and the corridors clean, and they treated you not half bad what with cheap lunches and relaxed supervision, and since all the girls wanted to go into the defense plants, secretaries would be prized. Annie assented without thinking about it.

"You're coming out of this joint tomorrow into a different world," Theda said. "The U.S.S.R. was invaded yesterday and Calvin Schmitter has run off with a seventeen-year-old whore named Ginger Snaps in a stolen Cadillac."

"What!"

"I mean—he's politically disheveled to the point of insanity. I heard that the folk down at the party headquarters are turning out fourteen directives a minute to explain the 'new position.' Well, you can see how it would be! Now it *is* a war against Hitler with our glorious new ally. Monopoly capitalism? Imperialist war? Words, words. Old words. There'll be new words now."

Ethel Schaeffer was dead. Max wanted to run off to the wars. It had been comforting in those bare meeting rooms, people saying "Hello, Comrade." Nothing seemed of any consequence. "I'll go to secretarial school," she said listlessly. "What day is it?"

"June twenty-third," Theda answered. "But the Russians aren't so dumb. They've been building up their armies——"

"The doctor says I have to take it easy for a few weeks because of adhesions. How much is all this going to cost?"

"Cletus and I are loaning you the money. You'll pay us back later."

"I've got some money, saved, in a box in my room."

"You'll need it to live on. I want you to go see that lawyer and get the divorce started."

"All right." There didn't seem any point in swimming, the currents were strong enough to carry her, for a while at least. On her last night in the hospital, Dr. Eagle came to see her.

"You've done well. No mountain climbing for a bit. Is someone coming to get you in the morning?"

"Yes," Annie replied viciously, "a *nigger* friend of mine."

The nurse, who was closing the window, gave her a pitying, disgusted look and left.

"Why did you say that?"

She sat up and swung her legs over the bed. "They've been treating me like a leper, the nurses, ever since two Negro friends showed up here."

"What do you imagine they feel? Have they been bad to you, really? It's something to regret, not to be so self-righteous about."

"I'm not self-righteous."

"Yes, you are. Let's see you walk around."

She paced the room in her hospital gown.

"Like a wounded stork," he said.

She riffled through the pages of the Dostoyevsky.

"Did you read it all?"

"No, parts."

"What are you going to do when you leave here?"

"I'm going to live a proper life," she said noisily.

"You sure sound sore."

She looked at him defiantly. He had soft brown eyes, a rather blank expression, perhaps because of the mustache that hid most of his mouth. He looked plump in his white smock.

"Isn't that possible?"

"Oh, I guess it's possible," he said. "I wanted to go to China years ago, I wanted to be a doctor in China."

"Why didn't you?"

He shrugged. "Circumstances," he said.

"Do you live a proper life?"

"I guess. . . ."

———

Uncle Greg had sometimes talked about the "colored people" moving into Nyack. They had strange ways which Uncle Greg said he didn't much care for. But he didn't much care for Catholics either, and he had the impression that Italians had a criminal streak and all Russians were violent. But live and let live, he would sigh.

Annie had an elusive memory of a maid Bea had hired once during a flush period in Tony's life. In the afternoon, Bea would curse her out for her slovenliness, then as twilight and depression approached apace, insist the woman drink with her. Annie did remember that—the two women crocked at a table, a bottle of whiskey between them.

257

In the way of things, Annie saw a Negro child now and then at the various schools she slipped through. They had been slaves once; they had been freed by Abraham Lincoln but in the South they were hanged from trees and set on fire, and they were not permitted to look at or speak to white people in certain ways lest they give away the odious secret of their emancipation. Cletus had once read her a story, "Bright and Morning Star," by Richard Wright. She had begged him to stop—the torture of the young black boy made her feel faint. Cletus was unrelenting. "Don't interrupt. Don't be craven," he had said and continued.

The people who tormented Negroes were low-class people with long narrow heads and baleful eyes. She had seen photographs of lynchings, gray blurs of men, women and children crowding close to one black body. Were they listening for the last pulsation of its burning heart?

The party had trouble recruiting Negroes. They tended to be elusive, and wary, and besides, as certain party members had remarked, belonged largely to the lumpenproletariat and were therefore less susceptible to political education than industrial workers.

For Annie, who had not joined anything, even in the ordinary sense that children imperceptibly absorb some community of feeling, of outlook and aspiration, Negroes carried an abundant provision, of surprise, of amplitude of being, the rewards of their exclusion. There was a lot of space around them; their triumph, their defeat.

Yet, she thought, and it even made her smile, she *had* involved herself with a kind of community, the party. In ways she only vaguely perceived, she found the party community a very conventional group indeed. She must tell Max that. It would amuse him . . . the party was teaching her to be middle-class.

Theda stopped by most evenings Annie's first week home. But it was Cletus, triumphantly a week ahead of his serial-writing schedule, and Melvin, who got an extraordinary number of passes —"They don't mess with this good-looking hornplayer," he said —who saw to it that she ate and had company.

One evening, Cletus arrived with a small victrola and an armful of records. A few minutes later, Melvin marched into the room carrying a bag of groceries.

"I'm going to make you a hangtown fry," he announced.

The hangtown fry was pork chops with a covering of biscuits. "Look at here," Melvin said. "When the chops get this far done, you drop a little cold water in them. See!" The frying pan emitted a great breath of steam. "That drives the fat up inside them and cooks them through." Then he stirred up the Bisquick and poured the batter over the chops.

Cletus, watching from an easy chair, said, "Melvin, don't feed that girl pork chops after her illness. You're crazy."

"No, no, no," Melvin said. "Good for her."

They drank beer and Cletus played the records. "Listen to this, honey," he said. Louis Armstrong sang, "If I could be with you one hour tonight . . ."

They ate Melvin's pork chops and listened to Louis Armstrong and then Cletus taught them a card game, Hearts.

It was still an effort to walk. Cletus saw her glance toward the hall. "Bathroom?" She nodded. He lifted her up, took her down the hall and placed her on the toilet seat, bowed elaborately, and left. She hobbled back and heard Melvin talking about his girl friend. Cletus said women would be the death of him and Melvin said better women than some other things he knew about.

Annie and Melvin grew bored with the game because Cletus always won. They talked softly into the night. Miranda Katz, Cletus reported, had found out that the Swedish freighters which tied up in San Francisco needed messboys, and she'd gotten some girls and gone to the seamen's union and managed to get seaman's papers from the union officials. She was actually shipping out. Just like Miranda. Annie told them she was thinking of taking a secretarial course. Melvin shook his head and put on his white sailor cap and took it off again. "I like you the way you are."

"She's not going to change just because she learns to type," expostulated Cletus.

"Everything changes a person," Melvin said. "I changed soon as I learned to play the horn."

"For the better," said Cletus.

The feeling of lateness came to them all at the same moment—Melvin yawned enormously, and Cletus nodded dreamily in his chair. But Annie never wanted them to leave. It was a happy evening.

She wondered about the woman Cletus loved. She wished Cletus would love her that way. She wished someone would. That steady longing . . . her father had said that when you get what you want, it turns to ashes. It was all in the anticipation.

And then, as she flung an arm across the pillow, she remembered that only a few weeks ago, the crook of her arm had rested against the neck of the Catalan as he half slept, his breath warming her face. But, like the week she and Walter had spent in Yosemite, the time with the Catalan was sealed away, and though she craved his living presence, if only to see him walk so nakedly across the room to his clothes, she did not think he would come again to her room, her bed.

She would have to go down to the plant to quit and hand in her badge. But she need not go to the shed, although she felt a pang at the thought of Hannah Groops, sloping along past the lockers looking for her. Well, the woman was used to *everything;* she wouldn't think about Annie for long. And she could ask Max to tell her what had happened.

A month later, Annie enrolled in the secretarial school; even though it was the middle of the course, it didn't seem to matter to the instructors. It was like coming into the middle of a movie. You just stayed until it began again.

Paul Lavan came by one Saturday with an excruciating look of self-importance on his face. He felt responsible in some small measure, he said, for bringing her into the party and he owed it to her to tell her that he was dropping out.

"I've started psychoanalysis," he said. "Even though the party asserts that many psychiatrists are stool pigeons for the FBI."

"I don't really understand what you're dropping into," Annie said. Psychiatrists were for maniacs. She didn't think Paul Lavan would know *how* to go crazy. In his gray little face the tiny jawbone flexed with purpose and self-love, the delicate nose pointed at heaven.

"Not many people do," he said grandly. "It is a long exhausting process. I expect my treatment to last at least three years. I have a child to think about. I don't intend to pass my neuroses on to a helpless innocent. Besides, the party is only a political organization. It has arrogated too much to itself. History teaches us that there is more to life than economics and class warfare. There is personality, not to mention inner conflicts, ambivalence. A spectre is haunting the party, if I may paraphrase the *Communist Manifesto*. It is the spectre of individual psychic need. I will be a better person socially if I understand my unconscious and become mature."

"Paul, have you been in the party long?"

He looked faintly nervous. "Actually, I've never really joined in the full sense of the word."

"You mean you don't have a card?"

"Well— Let me put it this way. Paul Lavan is not my real name. I won't burden you with the information of what my real name is. It's better to remain ignorant in the event you're ever questioned."

She permitted herself a comment. "You sound like Dr. Hackenbush," she said.

Lavan looked startled.

"A movie. The Marx brothers, where Groucho—"

He drew himself up to his full height of five feet. "You are not, I'm afraid, a serious person. I think I owe it to you to tell you that you are not regarded as a serious person by people in the party, you are thought of as one of the *dubious* people."

"What about the army?" she asked, suppressing a coarse roar of laughter.

"I had rheumatic fever as a child," he answered coldly, "and my heart's not right."

She detected a note of self-pity. Would his heart stand this new party he was about to join? The psychiatric party?

He put on his pretty little hat. "I hope you won't take this amiss," he said maliciously, "but as I once implied, you are a very driven girl. I would say that if you are ever in a position to afford it—it is an expensive process—you better run, not walk, to the nearest psychiatrist. Frankly, I don't think you have the faintest idea of what motivates you. As a case in point, let me point out that you married a man who is, in fact, tormented by his hidden homosexual drives. It is that that explains his Don Juanism. Well, good-by."

Although Annie's landlady had looked with indifferent eyes at her various visitors, when she brought home a white terrier puppy she had bought, the woman came knocking at her door.

"You cannot keep an animal in my house," she said.

The puppy wagged its tail and sat down at the landlady's feet.

"Animals foul the air. I'm sorry but I can't have it."

"But I'll keep things clean."

"Impossible! I'm quite content with you as a tenant. You're neat, and I appreciate that in a person as young as yourself. I don't even mind your colored friends. One of them, obviously, is of mixed blood and they're often superior types, having the virtues of both races. But a dog is out of the question. Or a cat. Or a bird."

The puppy squatted and urinated.

"Need I say more," intoned the landlady.

Theda said she couldn't take it; the puppy would be alone all day and would go nuts. Cletus said he had all he could do to put up with himself. She found a girl in the secretarial school who was willing. The girl came to get the terrier who gave Annie a lick on the cheek and was carried away.

She took profound pleasure in her shorthand. Once she took down everything Cletus said on a Saturday visit to his loft and read it back to him. "Jesus!" he said. "I don't want you around!" He was only fooling, wasn't he? Cletus came over to the broken couch where she was slumped down holding the notebook and pencil, and lifted her onto his lap. "Now cut that out!" he said.

"I wish you liked me more."

"I love you."

"I don't mean that way."

He stood up and she slipped to the floor. "Listen, you're too nervous for *that way*. I don't want nervous girls hollering and jumping around and suffering in my bed. I don't *want* that suffering."

She saw that his laughter, too, was a kind of nervousness.

She stood up and brushed her skirt. "Okay," she said quietly.

"That's a good girl."

She'd never made a direct and unencouraged offer before. She tried to feel hurt, but when she reflected upon it later, it just seemed comic. Cletus was a deep one. He wasn't just cozy old Cletus with his put-on jive talk and his poetry, his Brahms and Louis Armstrong.

Theda got her an interview with the office manager of the story department. She was given a typing test. She managed thirty-eight words a minute. Then she took down a fast paragraph from a thin impatient writer dragged in by the office manager to dictate to her. She was hired.

———

Had Joe walked out of the bar that night and gone straight to a cliff? Had he jumped? Had he walked into the water from the beach? Had he not thought he was going to die until a spasm of

262

his will made it too late? Had he walked a long while alone, thinking of his yet to be experienced death? Had he pulled the sea
around him as he had once covered himself with a blanket to wander out on a field covered with snow? Cold and wet, in such misery of body and mind and spirit that only oblivion could cure
him? Had he cured himself of life as of a disease? Had he cried?
Once in the water, had he tried to swim? How long had he suffered suffocation?

Why was she thinking about him so much, whose life had
barely touched hers, no more than his body had touched hers? Yet
Joe was taking deeper possession of her imagination. Her thoughts
of him grew ritualized; the unanswered questions a litany she
chanted before sleeping.

In life, he had weighed barely at all, a bland-looking, fair boy
with the face of a sleepwalker, a certain offhand kindness, a
mania, a secretive tight mania for cleanliness. She remembered his
shirt sleeves rolled halfway up his forearms. If he was so light an
object, so insubstantial a being, how could he have felt life so
heavily, so bitterly?

Joe was coming back, his voice whispering to her in the dark,
in a language she strained to understand even as she pretended to
think of other things.

She had shocked him. Her life would have appalled him. But he
had taken his own life. What had he hidden in himself?

Her days were agreeable. She liked the atmosphere in the studio's story department. Somewhere, at the periphery of the small
offices where she accepted uncritically the exaggerated companion-
ability of the people from whom she took dictation, raged a world
of handsome, exotic half-wits—or so they were described by the
writers—and in the evenings she often went to the movies, where
she watched stars on the screen whom she occasionally caught a
glimpse of walking from the commissary to a car, or a lot or an
office, the very real movement of their legs making them smaller
than life.

Since Ethel Schaeffer's death, she had not attended a party
meeting; Theda told her grimly that 110,000 Japanese had been
tossed into concentration camps, whole families going down like
the *Titanic*—people would never change—one had to make a safe
hole for oneself and survive—as long as it was worth it. As for
Annie's going to meetings, it was folly. What did she think *she*
was protesting? "Me, I'm different," Theda asserted. "The Jews

lead a mass life. The Jews are like one body, what happens to any member happens to all. People like you have *personal* beginnings. Why should you be allowed to make believe? Even Max has reasons—he belongs, at least, to a distinct class, but Annie, what are you intending to overthrow?"

Theda was baying at her like a wolf. She took her by the shoulders and shook her. "You see, you're taking what I say in a stupid personal way."

"What other way is there?" Annie protested weakly. "I did not have a personal beginning. I was born and thrown away."

"Poor thing," Theda said sardonically.

"I didn't mean it that way."

"Get off the cross! To be born is the beginning of endless outrage! Your fate is not exclusive."

Theda phoned her at one in the morning. "I'm sorry, I was mean to you. I'm getting so irritable! Everybody seems to me to be lying, lying! The party, some of them, they knew what was happening to the Jews even in 1937. Jews knew about Jews! I don't know what's happening to me! I stopped being a Communist, and this Jewishness—it's been waiting for me all along. I'm in a rage night and day. If Simon were here, alive . . . there was a thing about him that blotted up my acid. Not that he knew what he was doing—do you think he had the faintest idea of why he went to Spain? Simon?" She laughed harshly. "They claim him now as one of the honorable dead in the war against fascism. He couldn't have spelled honorable, or fascism. He had a kind of willfulness. He wasn't against reading, you understand, he only didn't want to read. He never even said people talked too much, but I knew he hated talk. He was, himself, silent. He was so silent!" Theda emitted a little moan. "I wish I could be silent, still in the center, like Simon."

"But why did he go then?"

"Go?"

"To Spain, Theda . . ."

"I don't know, because he was bored, because he felt the motion of it, all those young men leaving. Because he thought he'd get to Paris and find Braque waiting for him, I don't know."

She fell silent. The phone hummed, Annie stirred, pressing the receiver into the pillow.

"Well, I only wanted to say I'm sorry. I'm beginning to feel old.

I should marry a rabbi. It's terrible—not to believe in anything except safety. I don't even like animals." She hung up abruptly.

Annie lay on her back, frightened. Someone seemed to be whispering terrible prophecies. Imperiled and well-fed, mortally afraid, and with money in her pocketbook, she heard her own voice as though it emanated from someone else; "You won't get away with it," it said, pitilessly.

Miranda was given a party by Cletus two days before she was to embark on a Swedish boat from Long Beach. Melvin was there, his great white eyes moving from face to face, laughing, telling his horse stories, his big-band stories. Listening to him were a dozen or so other people, some of whom Annie had met casually. Miranda wore a black velvet dress, her blonde hair falling across her velvet shoulders. "I'll pay for it when I get back," she whispered to Annie's compliment. "My body belongs to Bullock's."

Cletus said to Annie, "Beautiful, isn't she? Nobody's girl." Annie told him what Miranda had said. "Her clothes are her house," he said. "She wants the first fifteen minutes of any love affair. She's got a lot of fifteen minutes in front of her, before the rest of the hour catches up."

Miranda's skin gleamed in the light. She was pale and queenly, and her large blue eyes were empty. Just before Annie left, Miranda asked her to keep her clothes for her. "You can wear the leopard jacket, if you want," she said shyly, almost apologetically. She would bring them round to Annie's room. "He has a car." She pointed to a young man talking to Cletus. "Or so he told me. I'll get him to drive me over to you with everything."

Long after Miranda left, and until she finally returned to claim her clothes, Annie would open the closet and look at the dresses, the coats, the leopard jacket, hanging there like the wardrobe of somebody who was dead. No books, no jewelry, a pair of fawn-colored thin-heeled soiled shoes, no letters or pictures, nothing but clothes.

It was incongruous, unbelievable to think of Miranda, with her unknown antecedents, her capacity to always lay her hands on cash, her careless rich-girl's fearlessness, walking the passageways of a Swedish ship on its way to Australia, those waters across which she voyaged being inexorably possessed by the Japanese as though they were drawing up the ocean like a carpet, rolling within it the Philippines, Malaya, Burma, Indonesia.

265

In February of 1942, men with dependents were permitted to enlist in the army. In March, Max enlisted. He had decided not to offer himself as a candidate for officer candidate school. He expected to be sent away on the day of his enlistment. The night before, Eva prepared a large but spiritless dinner for a few friends, including Theda and Annie. Among the other guests was William Lester, a short man whose skin was the color and the apparent texture of white sole. He gazed up at the ceiling when he spoke, as though addressing a higher authority, and referred frequently to "Uncle Joe." Each time he invoked Uncle's name, Max managed, with unconcealed irritation, to say "Joseph Stalin." William Lester's every action and word contained a strong note of disapproval except for the reverential way he named the almost ineffable name of Uncle. He ate very little. From time to time, he drew his hand across the thin strands of hair on his head as though reassuring himself of the sound condition of his somewhat pulpy-looking skull. Eva treated him with respect but was noticeably cool to Mrs. Lester. Lester evidently disapproved of Max's enlistment in the army, alluding to it as "Max's impulsive action." Eva looked miserable most of the evening.

Theda, meeting Annie in the hall outside the bathroom, informed her that Lester was a minor party functionary, and his wife the beloved of Cletus. After that, Annie paid little attention to anyone else.

Mrs. Lester was a very strange-looking woman; rising from the table, sinking into the couch, curling and uncurling her legs, sliding and coiling and twisting, she was like a mildly unhinged acolyte of modern dance. Annie wondered if Mrs. Lester imagined herself in brown homespun, raising dust with the meaningful slap of a bare foot on a stage. Her tight cap of dark hair with its Psyche knot at the nape of her neck, her small head on the smooth long neck, the opposing rigid angles of her body as she lay back against the couch pillows all added to Annie's conviction that the woman was engaged in a sacred drama of self. She hardly spoke, nodding her head or shaking it with languorous exposure of her neck. There was an Oriental cast to her features. Her skin was the color of a reddish plum. Sometimes she held her fingertips together, exactly meeting, and regarded them with amazement. Her name was Leora. When her husband was speaking, she kept her head bowed.

Theda whispered to Annie, "Mad love!"

But Annie was astonished that Cletus nurtured passion for such an odd creature and wondered what on earth had drawn him to her.

War talk rose around them that evening, an ineluctable flood. For William Lester, it was a chapter that would someday be included in a Marxist history he intended to write about the United States. When Max said there might be no United States if Hirohito and Hitler had their way, Lester predicted, "That matter will be resolved by the international solidarity of the working classes joined together against the moribund forces of international monopoly capitalism of which this Pacific adventure is but an expression." Leora Lester swayed back and forth in her couch nest, communing with her cobras.

Cleopatra, that was it! thought Annie, the old queen of the old Nile.

At the door, Max said, "I'll try to get by tomorrow evening for a few minutes." Eva looked at her blankly. She was clearly on the verge of tears.

After work the next day, Annie bought a small bunch of roses and put them in a glass. She neglected supper to clean her room for Max's visit. He came around nine. His hair and suit were damp from the slow insistent rain which had been falling all that day. Night had come as a deepening of the grayness of the sky. Max bent over and pushed his face into Annie's bouquet.

"Will you go and see Eva while I'm gone?"

"She doesn't like me."

"No, no . . . you've got it wrong. Anyhow, I'm asking you a favor. It's you, you know. You don't like Eva." Wanting to deny it, Annie said nothing, feeling a vague holiness attached to this occasion, one which obliged her not to dissemble. Max might be killed. She experienced his death, her loss, all in a moment, and turned her face away lest he see her mourning him in his living presence. "I'll see her," she said.

"And you'll write to me. Everything. What you do and think, everything, will you do that?"

"I'll write to you."

"I'm being sent to a training camp in Montana. As soon as I have it, I'll send you an address."

"You look happy. I haven't seen you look like that in so long."

"It's true. I shouldn't be, either. You don't know it yet, but it's freedom, to find out what I've found out about myself."

267

She waited.

"No," he said insistently, as though she'd contradicted him. "It's not that I'm sure of what I'm doing. But I have a sense of what I've done, all along."

"You want to get away from them," she murmured, "Eva, the party."

"Yes. It's wrong of me. But I'll come back—to her. You have to bear the consequence . . ."

"You sound so—you *condescend* so! Maybe she's glad you're going! Maybe *you're* the burden!" she cried.

"Oh, I am, I am!" he agreed fervently.

"Oh, God!"

"You're my friend, aren't you?"

"Yes, I guess so."

"You see how ridiculous I am? A scrap, a rag of a person! Thirty-six thousand men have just surrendered on Bataan, and I'm bent on salvation!"

How excited he was! She did not like him this way. She longed for the gravity, the authority of the old Max, on top of his own life, not this man who looked at her so hopefully, as though she, as though anyone, held the power to release him, to forgive him. She laughed angrily, reluctantly, and said, "I forgive you."

"My dear girl," he said, putting his arms around her, "you can't. You only mean you'll put up with your disappointment in me." He drew away. With their faces nearly touching, he said, "You still think there's a world of grown-ups somewhere—a place, a way of being, a message, that will reveal the nature of things. There isn't! There isn't."

"Children, all of us?" she said sarcastically.

"No. Not that either."

He kissed her forcefully, said, "Thanks for the roses," and shut the door. She wept a little as she picked up the glass of flowers and held them to her nose. How like him to realize they were for him.

As she lay down upon her bed, she admitted to herself why she had put fresh sheets on it earlier in the evening, admitted it and felt ashamed, and grateful he'd not had the chance to find her out.

She felt stale for days and went about her secretarial duties lifelessly, skipping lunch half the time. At night, she ate some fruit and crackers, whatever was easy, and turned on the radio and fell asleep with it still on, just as she had back in New York City.

Men in the office, the ones who made seventy-five dollars a week in little cells, working on story "projects" that came to nothing, sometimes asked her out.

She turned them down without emphasis, secretly astonished she could resist the compulsion to say yes. She imparted this triumph of will over weakness to Theda. Theda listened with a smile of derision. What was happening to Theda? The patient listener had become querulous, jittery. Annie was frequently mortified by Theda's responses to her confidences, her reports of office gossip, her efforts to re-establish the old, kindlier relationship. "Oh, so what!" Theda would say wearily, or interrupting Annie midway through a sentence, "What if he is a phony? All that matters to me is whether I like him or not." And Annie would protest that she hadn't meant to criticize whoever it was, only to tell Theda something she had hoped would interest her. It was like being slapped lightly across the mouth. She began to be cautious. During the day, she rarely saw Theda; the older woman worked incessantly in her cubbyhole, crumpled sheets of paper strewn about the floor.

Annie suffered. Theda no longer cared for her. She probably talked to Cletus about her, and Cletus talked to others, even strangers. No special intimacy was possible. No use wanting to hold forever someone's good will. People were carrion crows, bartering fragments of each other among themselves, a vast trading network of crushing judgments. Or perhaps they didn't have anything so durable as real opinions, only opportune ones. It was a disease of reflectiveness, she told herself, thinking of those who didn't reflect, the Catalan, Hannah Groops, Melvin, Johnnie Bliss. If she only knew what *someone* really thought about her, how they saw her! One morning, Theda came to her desk, drinking coffee from a paper cup. She looked down at the girl broodingly.

"I'm tired of apologizing," she said. "I know you must think me a graceless old bitch. I hope you have some charity left for me, though." She dropped the empty carton in a basket and smiled wistfully and returned to her office.

Annie's gratified surprise gave way to confusion. It was worse than she'd imagined! Even *she* was credited with judgments, begged for charity!

Annie became a newspaper reader. Reading the paper was the high point of her day. She followed the war dispatches so closely that she grew sensitive to the ignorance of the people with whom she worked. They hardly knew where anything was except Santa Monica Beach.

Max wrote to her at last. It was an animated letter, peculiarly noisy, even jocular. He described basic training as a vaudeville routine. "Having seen to the exact angle of your tie, they then send you out to be killed." She smelled the paper, brought the writing closer to her eyes, looked at the neat signature, "Max." She phoned Eva and they made a date for dinner the following week. Eva, to Annie's surprise, was genuinely glad to hear from her.

One night she lay in bed reading a Gide novel, *The Counterfeiters,* which Theda had loaned her. A small alarm clock, a new one, ticked softly at her bedside. At the foot of the bed, the day's paper lay, spread out. It was 3:00 A.M. and, bathed and having eaten a good dinner at Theda's, she felt oddly weightless, as though time had stopped, as though everything was in its place and there was nothing more to do. It wasn't even important to sleep. The phone rang.

She hardly recognized Cletus's voice.

"Hospital?" she exclaimed. "You're in—"

"Wait! Listen!" He seemed to be screaming at her from a distance. "Get this address down. It's on Ivar Street, a little apartment house. A girl's there, Lucy Griggs."

"Cletus!"

"Go to that girl! I've been beaten up! She was raped! Just go there, Annie, right now."

"Cletus, where are you!"

"In the emergency—" Other voices broke in, Cletus protested something. "I'll come there to that place when they let me out," his voice came on again, a high screech buried somewhere in it like a shard of glass cutting toward the surface. "Go there." She heard a street number repeated, then the phone was hung up with a clatter.

Her heart thumping with dread, she dressed, kicking her way into her clothes, gulping for air. The house was still and only a small night light burned in the hall as she fled down the stairs and out into the street. The sound of the car motor was shockingly loud.

In the entrance hall of the small apartment house on Ivar Street, she found a mailbox bearing the name *Lucy Griggs* and her apartment number. There were two other names scribbled on the piece of cardboard. It was stale inside; it smelled of marginal decency, soup and garbage. There was no elevator. Annie went up a narrow staircase, the steps of which were covered in gray linoleum. On the third floor, one door was slightly open. She pushed it aside, her hand leaving a damp imprint on the frame. An unmade studio bed stood against the opposite wall and next to it, on a wooden box, a lamp with a colored-glass shade burned with weak pinkness.

"Lucy?" she whispered.

Against another wall ran a counter on which dishes and glasses were carelessly stacked. If the girl wasn't here—relief flooded over her at the thought. It was so silent. She was frightened by the slovenliness of the room, the lamp burning with such a sickly light, the lateness of the hour, the open door. Where were those other two whose names she'd seen on the mailbox? She shuddered. Had they all been butchered? Were their bodies awaiting her discovery? She heard a long sigh. It was as though the entire apartment had exhaled a breath of sorrow at its wretched condition. She was still holding the front door. She pushed it, recognizing consciously what she had felt and not acknowledged a minute earlier. Someone, something, was obstructing the door. She looked behind it. A small girl lay on the floor across the threshold of a room not much larger than a closet. Her head was cradled in her slender arms. The girl's bare feet were shoved against the door, Annie's shove had forced the girl into this accordion position.

The girl's feet were narrow, thin-toed. Her hair was bright red, her child's arms freckled.

"Lucy!" Annie called.

The girl stirred and moaned.

Annie sat down on the floor and put her hand on the girl's shoulder. She shuddered and inched away from Annie's touch. "Cletus sent me."

Slowly, the girl turned, revealing a narrow face with half-closed eyes and a bruised mouth. Her skin was blotched, as though she'd been burned. She began to sob.

Annie wedged her arm beneath the girl's back and, half dragging her, got her over to the bed which took up most of the space in the room. There, the girl curled up again, her knees nearly to her chin. She looked no older than twelve. With a start of fear, Annie closed and locked the front door, then came back and sat on the bed. The thinness of the girl's skin, the reddishness that shone through it, the long radial bones of the arms, the delicate bird neck, exposed now as the girl clutched at her own hair, gave a somewhat repugnant fragility to the whole body, as though the girl had been born without an adequate covering of flesh.

"Lucy. My name is Annie. Cletus called me from the hospital. He's all right now. He told me what happened to you."

The girl's sobs ceased and she sighed again, that terrible long sigh that whistled and whispered until Annie placed her hand around one of the narrow ankles next to her hand.

"Can't talk," she muttered.

"Tell me. It'll be better."

The sobbing began again.

Annie sat straight up. What could she do for this misery lying here? The sobs were so sickly, so weak!

"Talk to me," Annie said loudly.

"Oh!" the girl cried out suddenly. "Oh! Oh!"

"I'm going to make you some tea," said Annie, looking distractedly at the sink. But the girl's arm darted out and the narrow finger bones closed around her wrist. She raised herself up and through swollen lids gazed at Annie's face. "Don't go."

Annie slumped back against the wall, aware she'd felt disgust, horror. The tea had been an excuse to free herself from the clutch of the girl's hand.

A slight smile appeared on the wounded face, a beggar's mollifying smile. It disappeared almost at once.

"They—" the girl began, then stopped. She began to force herself all the way up, to sit like a broken sack of bones. She pushed tendrils of curly hair from her face.

"Tell me . . ." Annie said.

"Cletus and I had gone to a rent party. He was bringing me home. Then we were walking up Cahuenga, and this gang of men —" The smile touched her mouth again; her teeth were small and widely separated. "Boys, maybe. They made a circle around us. And they said *nigger man* and moved closer. A car went by, but it went by. There were maybe four or five of them and one had a cane or a stick. I don't know what he had . . ." Her voice rose and Annie loosened the hand on her wrist and held it in her own.

"Easy . . ."

"Cletus told me to try to run through them where there was a little space, then I saw two older men in a doorway, watching, and I ran past two of those boys to the men and one of them said,

272

Your friend's in trouble, you'd better come with us, and I begged them to help him, and one of them said, No, those boys got knives, that's what he said, the fat man said it. I said, But we'll get the police and the other man said, Yes, there's a drugstore where we can phone just down the street and I was so scared, I didn't think how late it was, that there wouldn't be a drugstore open. And I heard grunts and I saw they were beating up Cletus with that stick and a belt, something shiny I could see in the street light and I started to go back, but the fat man said—he talked very soft and kind—he said they would kill me and Cletus if I went back because that's why they were beating him, because he was a colored man and I was white. And then Cletus fell down, and the boys ran away, up the hill, and I started to go back again but this time both men were holding me by the arms and I said I was going to scream and I did, and they pulled one of my arms behind my back and said they'd kill me right there on the street, they said they'd break my little neck if I let out a peep and I turned just once and saw Cletus getting to his feet and shaking his head. There was a dark streak on his face and I knew it was blood. Then these two men took me for blocks until we came to an old house and they forced me up the stoop and then up the stairs to a room."

She gasped. Her teeth chattered noisily. Annie pulled a blanket from the floor where it had fallen, and carefully covered the girl up to her chin and said, "Let me make you something hot," but the girl shook her head, *no, no*. She was silent for a long time, her eyes glassy, staring out into the larger room where the lamp burned.

"I'll get you a doctor," Annie said, not knowing how she'd get a doctor, not knowing any doctors except the one who'd taken out her appendix and she'd forgotten his name except it was a bird of some kind, but she could call, she'd seen a phone on the floor on the other side of the studio couch, she'd phone the hospital—

"No!" The girl cried out. "No doctor. I'm going home. I'm going to my own doctor back home."

"Tell me the rest of it."

"In that room there was a religious picture of Jesus's mother on the wall, and a bed and a sink. One of the men—relieved himself into the sink while the other held my arms. There was a suitcase on the floor. I asked them if they believed in Jesus and they said sure, sure, they believed, and now I was to lie down on the floor,

273

and I saw there was someone else in the bed, an old man and he was snoring and all the time I was there on the floor, the old man didn't wake up once. I prayed to them, but I forgot everything nearly about praying, but they said—listen to what they said—they said they were *sorry,* but what was going to be done would be done. Then the fat man lay down on me first. The other man was little and smelled mildewed. I cried out—the fat man looked so terrible with his fat hanging over me—but he just took his trousers down and his belly was hanging there. I was afraid to make any noise, I thought if I made noise, the one on the bed would get up and he would have his turn with me too."

The girl drew her legs up again beneath the blanket. Her inflamed eyes were wet but no tears fell.

"The little fellow kept saying he was sorry but the big one, his name was Mario, I heard him called that, just pulled up his pants and said *hurry up* to the other. Then they took me to the street and said don't ever come back here with the police because we'll be long gone and from now on you stay away from coons because that's what you get from hanging around with coons. The little man whispered he was sorry again. I walked home. Nobody I saw asked me anything, even though I was crying and limping. When I got here, Cletus was sitting on the floor in the hall all bloody and half conscious and he started to cry when he saw me, even before I told him. Then I told him, and he said he had to go to the hospital and I must go with him. But I wouldn't go, and Cletus tried to make me and then I got frightened of Cletus, then someone upstairs came out in the hall and we both came in here and were quiet for a while. Then Cletus went to the hospital."

Annie got up from the bed. The girl let her go this time, and she went to the refrigerator where she found a half-bottle of milk. There wasn't anything else on the shelf except a shrunken lemon and a crumpled gardenia lying on a white plate, its petals nearly black.

She found a pan and heated the milk and washed out a cup and brought it back to the girl who drank it down quickly, exclaiming a little at its hotness. They sat there without speaking, Annie holding the empty cup. Through the window over the bed she watched the light change. In the large room, the pink lamp looked feverish as the dawn touched the room.

There were women's clothes strewn about the floor.

"Where are the others who live here?"

274

"They went away to Big Bear Lake for the weekend. Harriet and Jean. They'll be back soon. Jean's parents are coming today from San Francisco. We were going to clean up the place."

"Please let me get a doctor for you."

The girl shook her head. "No. I'm going home. I'm going home today. I'm taking the train home to my town and go to my doctor."

"Where is that?"

"Oregon. I live in Klamath Falls. I came down here—" then she stopped as if struck by the recollection of all that had led her to this place, this hour. She covered her face with her hands and rocked back and forth, but no sound issued forth from behind her locked fingers.

A while later, she appeared to sleep. Annie examined the closed face minutely. The splotches of red had begun to fade; Lucy's eyelids were faintly blue; her hands lay one on the other, narrow, childish, the cuticles ragged and bitten. Her breath came softly, innocently.

Around eight, the apartment house woke up, a toilet flushed, a distant alarm went off. There were loud steps on the floor above, someone ran down the stairs and shortly thereafter, Annie heard two women speaking, their voices growing louder as they neared the door. A key was inserted into a lock, and suddenly there were two young women looking down at her. Lucy Griggs woke—she looked up at them calmly, then at Annie, waiting.

One of the women set down a small overnight bag, the other went to turn off the pink glass lamp.

"What's going on?" asked the woman with the suitcase.

"Harriet?" Lucy asked weakly. "Did you have a good time?"

Annie rose and went into the other room. Harriet, who had not answered Lucy's question, followed her.

"Well?"

Annie looked at her. She was tall, dark-haired, muscular. Her expression held nothing but antagonism and suspicion. A young crone, Annie thought. She told her Lucy's story quickly. There was no pity on Harriet's face. Her narrow lips, her unblinking eyes proclaimed that she already knew what the world was.

"I think she should be taken to a doctor. She says she just wants to go home."

The other girl was making clucking noises near the studio bed. "I knew she'd get into trouble," Harriet said grimly.

275

"Poor soul," said the other softly.

"Poor soul, my eye. There are certain things one simply doesn't do if one wants to avoid certain consequences."

"Oh, Harriet!"

"Oh, nuts! She's alive, isn't she?"

Annie turned away from that rocklike face. Lucy, wrapped in the blanket, was standing just behind her. She thought of Joe—it was only a flash, a shadow moving across her inner vision.

"We'll take care of things," Harriet said, dismissing Annie. She looked at Lucy, but Lucy was watching Harriet.

"I'll go then," she said.

Lucy glanced at her; for a moment she looked as if she was about to collapse. Then her face cleared and she turned back to Harriet.

"I'm going home today."

"Yes," said Harriet.

"I can't stay here now."

"I think you'd best go home."

The other girl said, "I'll help you pack up, Lucy."

Annie walked to the door.

Lucy called out, "Thanks," in a lifeless voice.

Annie ate scrambled eggs in a drugstore, and drank a cup of thin, sour coffee. Then she drove to Cletus's.

Outside his loft, the morning life of the city cried its noises. Inside, it was quiet. Cletus was sitting on the old couch, a large bandage on his head, one finger splinted, his right arm in a sling. He barely glanced up at her.

"I stayed with her until her friends came back," Annie said softly. He nodded.

"Have you eaten? Shall I make you breakfast?"

"No."

"Cletus? Can I put on a record?"

"Get out of here," he said.

"Cletus!"

"Get out!"

276

Chapter 17

August 8, 1945

Dear Annie,

Happy Birthday! Although by the time you receive this, several days will have passed. I was reminded this morning when I saw the red maple I planted the day you were born twenty-two years ago. My mind has been very distracted these last few years which I suppose everybody's has been. I hardly read history now. I think history has died. The town has changed so much you wouldn't know it. There are many colored now, and some of the grand old families I used to garden for have fallen apart, the children gone off, or killed, no servants to keep up the houses, rationing. Well, rationing didn't affect some of us much as we've always lived lightly. Except for the gasoline. I had to keep my jobs pretty close to home; the old truck drinks up the stuff so I've had to let go of some of my people that I've worked for all these years, not that people have been tending much to flowers. I don't know why, but the sight of vegetables growing in a plot where once chrysanthemums bloomed sets my teeth on edge. I'm just foolish, I guess, as I know those "victory gardens" were a good idea.

Gabriel Heatter says on the radio that the war is really over now they've dropped that bomb on Hiroshima. I sit up here on the hill in the old house at dusk, and I think I've lived much too long. For a while, I read all the stories about the camps in Germany, then I had to stop. My mind wandered away. I hardly know what I'm thinking about any more. The last time I felt all right was in May when I was

277

digging a bed for the Belknaps who still keep up their borders despite the death of their youngest boy. Do you remember him? Brewster Belknap who died in far-off New Guinea?

I seem to be talking all the time about myself. I meant to thank you for your Christmas letter. I was glad to hear of your job. Annie, don't think I'm reproaching you, but I wish you had told me about your marriage, and then the divorce. Tony called me and told me about it and I was grieved to hear that you'd gone through all that at so young an age. I guess you know that Tony has a son now (and you a half-brother!). I was surprised to hear from him at all but perhaps he has memories of your dear mother and remembers me now and then. He sounded like the same old Tony on the telephone. I haven't written you before because I've not been well. I seem better now which shows that it isn't necessary to flee to a doctor the moment you get a pain. Sometimes I think you'll come walking up the hill and open the door. Write to me again, Annie, when you can.

Love,
Uncle Greg

"Letter from the heartland," said Dr. Myron Eagle, handing the sheets of paper back to Annie. "So that's what you came out of."

Annie didn't reply. She dropped the letter on the counter and ran a knife along the sides of the duck she was roasting. The fat poured out and splattered threateningly in the bottom of the pan.

"If it isn't the Communists, it's the Congregationalists," said Myron. "Pay some attention to me."

"I am, through the medium of this duck," she said.

How tall she was! The knife was in her right hand, with her left she pushed back the hair from her cheek where the perspiration from her exertions at the oven had glued it. She was wearing a navy-blue skirt and a white blouse. Myron, as he often did, gazed at her flat belly where, beneath the flannel of the skirt and the cotton of her slip, she wore his scar. It moved him oddly to think of that arrow-shaped indentation she would bear all her life, which, three years ago, he had sewn up himself. Now and then, peering at it as they lay in bed together, he would see a shadow of a stitch working its way through the flesh. There were new techniques now, learned from the war, and scars could be made no more than hairlines. The thickness of hers satisfied him though, gave him the kind of medical pleasure that he referred to as his little touch of sadism.

278

He attributed to himself a small "touch" of any sort of psychological quirk—and proud of it, Annie thought, telling him once that he had a *large* touch of belief in the supernatural.

"You don't want to be surprised by yourself, do you?" she'd observed dryly.

"We're all potentially aberrant," he'd replied. "My patients trust me because I don't put distance between myself and them. I can be as sick in body as they are, and as sick in mind."

She held back an ironic retort. She didn't believe that Myron believed he was a peer among his peers as he did his rounds in the hospital wards. Anyone could be sick; anyone could go mad. "Truths" like that weren't about anything. As far as Annie was concerned, the mere avowal of such commonplaces was boasting, an effort to raise oneself above the common lot by dint of superior comprehension. Myron irritated her faintly, mildly, always. Their arguments were low-keyed. He always had the answers, yet she knew she disconcerted him, and although he laughed at her assertions, he couldn't dismiss them. They'd spent the afternoon wrangling about cause and effect. There was nothing without an original cause, he'd said. "But some things spring into being out of nothing!" she'd said.

"That's irrational."

"Myron, you're trying to chain water!"

"I can!" he said triumphantly. "Look at the TVA! Now, give me an example of something springing out of nothing."

"A poem."

"Oh, Jesus!" he cried.

She watched him walk over to her bureau and lift the cover of the leather cosmetic case that always rested on the bureau top.

"The bastard," he muttered as he took out a pink jar and sniffed at it. Tony Gianfala had brought her that luxurious case two years ago when he'd come to Hollywood for a brief visit with news of the birth of his son, Ned. She'd taken Tony to a restaurant, letting Myron know in advance where they were going to be so he could get a look at her father. But she hadn't introduced them. "Don't you know why you didn't want him to see you with a man?" he'd asked portentously. She affected not to notice his emphasis. But it embarrassed her.

"Every time I look in here, it's the same stuff. Don't you ever use it?"

"I smell it," she said. "I love the smell."

"It must have cost over a hundred dollars. Do you want another drink?"

She nodded and began to shell peas. He mixed a martini for himself, and handed her bourbon and water. "When are you going to stop drinking this peasant swill?" he asked. She smiled and said, "I have a touch of the peasant." Then she burst into laughter, and Myron smiled at the sound of it. "Listen! Did I tell you Bea uses a hammer to mash garlic?"

"Swell."

"No. Really. I just remembered that, thinking about the salad I'm going to fix for us. That time I went to see her last spring, she was sloshed to the gills, tripping over her old black lace peignoir and smashing the life out of a little clove of garlic."

"There's nothing funny about it. You were depressed for a month after you saw her."

"Oh Mike, it doesn't matter."

After dinner, they turned out the lamps and sat by the window looking out through the leaves of the eucalyptus tree over the lights of Hollywood. Theda had left her scarred old table for Annie when she'd moved into the San Fernando valley into her own little house. Sometimes, when Annie was alone on a Saturday or a Sunday, when Mike had to be with his wife and children, she sat there just as Theda had, her arm where Theda's had been, a book open in front of her, looking out as though from a lighthouse.

"It was strange of Tony to come out," Annie said softly, "just to tell me about the baby, after not bothering all the other years." They had speculated about her father's visit often enough. Some of their conversations were old conversations. They had a history now, after two and a half years.

"Stalingrad," said Mike, touching her hand. She withdrew it. "Was I vulgar?" he asked, offended yet apologetic. She had been listening that November in 1943 to the radio, and a labor reporter from a San Francisco newspaper had wept over the air waves as he described the battle then taking place in Stalingrad. A few months later, they had both heard the same reporter read letters from the Russian soldiers who'd been imprisoned by the siege in November.

Mike Eagle, out on his night calls, had knocked at her door. "Wanted to know how you're feeling," he'd said, standing there with his black medical case in one hand. She'd been struck by the absence of a pronoun. He hadn't said *I*. He had stood there like two decisions colliding—his presence affirming his wish to see her, the unidentifiable person, *I, he, they,* who? not present.

Myron Eagle was thirty-five. He had a daughter named Brett and a son, Tracy. They were fancy names, Annie had remarked. "For a Jew?" he'd asked. "For anybody."

She rarely inquired about his wife. He found her lack of curiosity unnatural. "She's limited," he'd offered once. "Who isn't?" Annie had replied. "It's beastly," he'd protested, "to answer anyone that way."

She'd laughed at the word, beastly. After that, he used it often. Annie might have confessed to him that she did not feel she was vying for his attention; she was *on the side*. She had, in fact, once touched upon her sense of her transitoriness ever so indirectly. She'd seen how uneasy her words had made him; he'd accused her of false humility, of not even taking his marriage seriously! And she hadn't defended herself. Underlying whatever she might have said would have been her consciousness that she didn't love Myron. She suspected he nurtured an inner vision of himself, torn between two women, and that for all his vaunted rationality, he yearned to be struck down by passion. A lunatic romantic was on the loose somewhere in Myron, waiting for the curtain to rise at last. Crediting him with this secret dream, she felt tenderly toward him, as though he were innocent.

Besides, she was grateful for his presence, for the freshly laundered smell of his shirts, for the domestic aura which clung to him and from which she drew illicit sustenance, for the authority of his medical knowledge, for his humor, quick and sardonic, for his sexual diffidence, which while it sometimes made her laugh to herself—he always covered his nakedness when the lights were on, grabbing up a towel, a blanket, once a sweater she'd left lying in a chair—made her feel less *responsible*. But she was most indebted to him for those very things that—if she'd imagined such an affair, such a long one as this, several years ago—she could not have conceived then would become central to it. He sent her to a good dentist. Outraged yet amused, he tore into her eating habits with grisly explanations of what she was doing to herself with her impulsive and irregular snacks. Because of him, she had begun to cook. He kept her drinking down. He brought her a good reading lamp. He stuffed her with fresh fruits from the Farmers' Market and demanded, with uncharacteristic aggressiveness, that she drink milk and eat vegetables.

He made her vegetable soup. "Do you like it?" "It's good," she admitted. "But it's boring to eat soup." "Boring?" he'd asked. "Like peeing." He laughed. "You eat like a ragamuffin."

He really was concerned about her, one of his more interesting patients, she guessed. For if he wasn't encouraged by her to speak of his home, she implored him to tell her about the people he treated on his night calls. She never tired of their histories—the elderly men living alone in rooms, morphine addicts, pregnant runaways, the demented, the poor, the declassed—those were his patients, his real patients. Despite their arguments, he'd brought a new idea into her mind, psychology. She was struck by the thought that people were ruled by laws of which they had no knowledge. He gave her a book called *Totem and Taboo*. She read a few pages, until she came to this sentence: "The prohibition owes its strength—its compulsive character—to its association with its unknown counterpart, the hidden and unabated pleasure, that is to say, an inner need into which conscious insight is lacking." Her alarm outdistanced her comprehension. She dared not bring it up to Myron for fear he would explain the meaning of the sentence by applying it in some measure to her. Or to himself. She could not grasp the sense of it—yet it frightened her, like a voice speaking about her in an unknown language. Everything she was ignorant of spoke of her—and, she told herself, she was nearly ignorant of everything. Was that a reason to learn? To stop the world's whispering? She noted the sizable library she had been gradually accumulating over the years. But those books, except for the few political tomes, were only stories; they did not turn in unfavorable reports on your own existence.

She told stories about people she'd known and knew, and Myron delighted in them, saying there was more than a passing resemblance between her friends and his patients. She wrote to Max, copying out Freud's sentence, saying that all such information, if that's what it was, filled her with dread as though she'd been suddenly struck blind. Max replied from North Africa. He said she ought to read history, it would give her perspective, she would not feel so persecuted by learning. Had she ever heard of mechanism, of Descartes? And was she still seeing that doctor?

Seeing had been her word to Max. She had mentioned Myron only in passing. Max hadn't forgotten.

Well, a lot was missing between herself and Myron, she knew that. Passion? What was it? She had once entertained dark nebulous thoughts about Bea and her father, thoughts she fled from no sooner than they occurred to her. And the romantic light in which she had once seen Theda had long since begun to fade. She didn't know that she really believed in Theda and Simon any more. Once, so deeply stirred by the idea that this lanky self-ruled woman had been ruled by her silent lover, she wondered now how much Theda had invented, or how much, she, Annie, had invented. Theda was becoming what she had always really been, a cranky, sharp-tongued impatient woman, given to morose asides on the fatuity, the futility, of nearly everything, sclerotic in the affections, guarding her health as though she were in perpetual danger—she managed to suggest there were lepers on the loose everywhere—and she had abandoned any talk of marriage and children. As for Cletus and the functionary's wife, what was that all about except a convenient dodge so that Cletus could pursue his lone path?

She had not seen Cletus now in a year. After the rape of the redheaded girl—poor Lucy Griggs, what had happened to her?— things had changed. He had called to apologize for his behavior that morning, a brittle, unfriendly apology, sounding of recrimination. She had fled back to him at once, her friend. She was so grateful that he had not meant her to "get out!" But she found a guarded, sardonic-faced enigma who had once been darling Cletus, and what was crueler, who made it clear that the old habit of familiarity was broken, and walked to the farthest end of his loft, wearing his old robe, laughing unpleasantly at her struggles to speak plainly. "Cletus, what is it? What is it?" He finally put an end to her fumbling efforts, saying, "I apologized. I thanked you for your help. What do you want me to do now? Be your pet darkie a little bit longer till you give up being the poor little match girl and take up with your proper life? My, my, my!"

Melvin listened to her story and shook his head and opened his trumpet case. Drawing his long black fingers along the shining surface of the instrument, he said, "Look, girl, there's things here you don't know about and you'd best not mess with them. If Cletus had lived more like me, he mightn't be so surprised. He got this

283

little corner for himself, you see, and thought the good world was where he was, and then he found out it was just a mouse hole, and the cats was the same as he'd heard rumors about all his life. He got scratched. He found out he was a nigger just like all the other niggers."

"Oh, Christ! Melvin!"

He grinned. "I knew two things from the beginning," he said. "I knew I was black. I knew I was going to die."

"But I loved him!" she cried.

"Oh, yeah! I know that, baby! But he got the news, see? He's always been a nervous man, Cletus. Now he got the news what he's nervous about. He's not even *thinking* about you, girl! He's thinking about *himself*."

Melvin was glad; she heard the triumph in his voice. The corrupt passion to be *right* was everywhere. Given the chance, she too would not pass up an opportunity to win. She tried Freud again; it whispered severely that her life was a lie.

She continued to see Cletus until he moved to San Francisco. He'd gotten some kind of job with the OWI and after a while, before he'd left, seemed to become his old self—almost. But she too had changed. She was uneasy with him.

"For God's sake, will you stop waiting on me!" he cried out once as she was pouring him a cup of coffee, racing for the sugar bowl, placing an ashtray near his arm. "You got Saint Vitus's dance?"

After Cletus left, she tried to get an overseas job. She'd heard file clerks and office personnel were in great demand at overseas army bases. She wrote to Uncle Greg for her birth certificate. When it arrived, she discovered she had no middle name after all. She was tempted to claim Elizabeth, dark, lissome, velvet Elizabeth, for her middle name anyhow. The passport division turned her application down. For the first time, the less romantic aspect of her involvement with the Communist party revealed itself in the person of a man named Dooley who interviewed her for one hour without raising his eyes from a folder that lay on his desk in front of him.

"Congratulations," Theda said. "You've got a dossier."

But she'd hardly been to a dozen meetings! Theda said, "You can get pregnant from one-night stands."

The party had changed its name to the Communist Political Association. "Why, they're practically Native Sons now," Annie protested. "And I can't leave this country." She panicked. The entire country was no larger than Theda's living room, and she couldn't get out! She wanted to write to Max about it, but Theda warned her not to because of mail censorship. When she told Eva, she suspected she was gratified by the news in the way Melvin had been gratified hearing about Cletus. And Annie, listening this last April to Eva and some people who'd stopped by after supper to discuss the French Communist leader Jacques Duclos and his letter accusing Browder of "revisionism" and "right deviationism," listening to the furious argument, the heated voices as they labored with the thick, unwieldy language of political talk in which the only vivid note was personal acrimony, had felt an exhaustion of all interest and, underneath that, the uneasy sense that she too was receiving "news," although not about Browder and some distant Frenchman crushing the American Communist party with all of Stalin's authority.

Myron Eagle had come to stand behind her and he now placed his hands over her eyes. "Staring like that . . . I can see your eyes, shining like a bear's in a cave . . ."

She took his hands away, and he covered her breasts in the same way and she removed them again.

He grabbed her in the dark, danced a comic lindy with her, swinging her out so she banged into the furniture. "Dancing in the dark," he sang in foolish tenor mimicry.

They talked about the ending of the war, the surrender that was being signed that very day on the battleship *Missouri* between the Americans and the Japanese. She recalled the day Roosevelt had died, how she'd gone to a coffee shop she was in the habit of frequenting and told the man behind the counter of the President's death, and of how he had answered, "How'd he die? Lead poisoning?" and how it had taken her a while to get it, and the shock of it.

She realized then she'd told Mike about that incident because she'd been offended by Mike's reference to Stalingrad. How could he refer to their personal destinies in the same breath in which he was speaking of three hundred thousand dead? How could they jitterbug in the dark after that appalling unimaginable bomb had been dropped on two Japanese cities?

"I'm going to make another try at the State Department," she said. "I want a passport."

"Where the hell are you going to go?"

285

"Out. Away."

"To what?"

"I'll get a job."

"Where?"

"I don't know. England."

"Why?"

"I don't know that either."

"You're brutal sometimes, Annie," he said.

"No!" she cried. He turned on a light. It was the worst charge.

———

Annie had been asked to model some clothes for the wife of a Hungarian screenwriter. They were poor, they were "progressives." One of the writers at the studio had stopped her one day and told her about Heida and her husband, the couple's struggles after they'd managed to get to Portugal from unoccupied France in 1939. Would she do it for free? Heida hoped to become a *couturière,* but they had no capital. She'd agreed, not so much from sympathy for Hungarians as for the pleasure of wearing clothes.

She felt somewhat nervous about it, even though she'd rehearsed the runway walk several times, how to turn and bend and hold her hands, so she was ready an hour early. She drifted restlessly around the room, stopping finally in front of the bureau where she kept her papers in a tin candy box. Inside it was her divorce decree, her Social Security number, the letter from the State Department refusing her a passport "at this time," a large bundle of letters from Max, and two notes from her father, one announcing his arrival in Los Angeles two years ago, the more recent which she'd received earlier this week.

In pity, she'd written him of the death of James St. Vincent, for once not the carefully careless letters she sometimes wrote with an observation she'd worked over, a story she thought might amuse him and bring her the painful pleasure of his appreciation.

She had seen St. Vincent only a few weeks earlier. He'd had a heart attack. Hope, her face blank, her mouth a dead line, was sitting by the bed. St. Vincent's face was as white as the sheet that covered him, which he held to his neck as though the heart itself, faulty and wounded, would be revealed should he relinquish a corner of the cloth. His voice was so weak. Yet he made an effort to talk in the old cadences she remembered. But he faltered, and closed his eyes after smiling a little and asking her how she was, and then Andrew came in, eyes only for his father, looking at Hope for one split second, dread in his face as though he knew only too well what his fate was to be once his father was no longer there, his father, his shelter. Andrew's features had thickened in some indefinable way and Annie recognized that Andrew, indeed, was "different."

It was Andrew who called her to tell her his father had died, and although after having seen St. Vincent she couldn't imagine how he could have continued to live, and although she was shocked and frightened, she was distracted by Andrew's voice, which was so strange. Then she realized he was trying to speak as his father had. It was a grotesque parody. The boy telling her the news with James St. Vincent's beat and jargon, Andrew's voice breaking suddenly into gulping sobs, wailing out, "What will happen to me? To me?"

So she'd written to her father at once, and for once, he'd replied by return mail. "Sad, sad," he'd written, the passing of one's youth, one's era. Oh, the times they'd had, he and Jim, gone, gone. Who the hell was keeping her these days? That plump nice doctor fellow? Her little brother, Ned, was a dummy, but sweet. He had broken Margo's new potter's wheel.

She hated the letter. It was the part about Ned. The rest was Tony's old song. It was the casual executioner's judgment against the child she'd never seen that made her queasy, made her restless and angry.

Max's letters, the correspondence of over two years, were mostly written on the self-sealing stationery that she'd frequently torn in trying to open. At first, the letters had been avuncular, concerned for her well-being, with a few comic asides on his army experiences. But as the months went on—he'd been transferred from Montana to England with a brief furlough during which he'd phoned her—the letters grew into a continuing reverie of his own life. In one, he told her a story of killing a cat. He'd been nine, he and the other boys—the horror remained with him—he'd never told anyone about it; he'd never seen the boys again. Only Eva, his life with Eva was unmentioned. But of an eccentric uncle, of school and college, of poker playing and radicalization, although about the latter he was quite circumspect, a result she imagined of his caution concerning censorship, of girls and boys he'd known, of the house he'd lived in, the pictures on the wall, the books he'd read, the view of the world from the house a few miles outside of

Portland, Oregon, he wrote fully. She had responded in kind. When she wrote him of Joe's suicide, he'd written back that she'd taken on the responsibility of the death, and that she couldn't arrogate such power to herself. Perhaps Max's letters, read at the same time as the war news, increased the sense of unreality of what was happening in Europe. In Los Angeles, there had been so many soldiers coming and going. She'd met a few at Eva's, "comrades," some of them, or "progressives." And Miranda Katz had gone on two voyages, returning from the last one pregnant by a Swedish junior officer who'd subsequently jumped ship to be with her.

Annie had been awakened one morning at three by the doorbell. Mike had fallen out of bed, dressing in panicked haste in the dark while she delayed answering the persistent ring as long as she could. It had been an immigration officer. Did she know of Miranda Katz's whereabouts? No? Well, then, did she know of a certain Jensen, an officer from a Swedish ship? Had she seen this man?

Standing there with a raincoat thrown over herself, she had finally lost the faculty of speech, aware that Mike was buttoning his shirt, in silent terror, in her bedroom. When she'd returned, she'd said, her voice trembling, "The immigration man was after a Swedish seaman . . . a girl I know . . ." But they'd looked at each other straight through rational explanations, and both had felt at once the underlying vulnerability of their arrangement. But her fear, not of informed wives and outraged neighbors, was an old one. His was plainer, more immediate. She'd known then how irrevocably he was a husband.

After that, he never stayed later than midnight.

She picked up the divorce decree. Max had written it was a good thing to have finished with it, and after all that anguish, the time in court had been negligible, the procedures fraudulent, community property none, alimony none. She'd stepped down from the oak witness chair, glanced briefly at the judge and left the courtroom.

She put away her papers, threw a sweater over her shoulders and drove out to Sunset Strip, where in a small empty store, Heida was shouting at a group of young women who were wandering about the back room in various stages of undress. They would have to wear Band-Aids over their nipples, Heida was screeching. Her dresses were not made to be worn over those medieval siege

288

weapons, American brassières! They rehearsed for a bit, then Annie and one of the girls who had an apartment nearby went there to have a sandwich before the show began at eight. The girl, Laura, was someone with whom Annie had a slight acquaintance. She was the girl of a screenwriter who'd been in and out of the party a number of times, and who referred to himself ponderously as a universal gadfly, *épat*aying the comrades as well as the bourgeoisie. He was rich.

Laura was beautiful. Dark-haired, romantic eyes, perfect teeth. When she wrapped a silk scarf around her head, binding in her dark hair, she looked like the heiress of California. Her apartment was full of flowers, a piano stood in one corner, and there were pictures of herself on all the walls, Laura in riding breeches, her eyes sad, her smile gay, Laura on a sailboat, in a jersey, her eyes sad, her smile gay! Clumsily, she prepared them some sandwiches. When she sank into a chair, she was perfect. Doing anything at all, except being looked at, brought out a peculiar awkwardness. Annie watched her, fascinated. The girl's total intelligence was directed toward her own person. In her own milieu, couches, soft chairs, on the makeshift runway in the shop for tonight's show, she attained perfection.

Eating a lettuce and tomato sandwich, she spoke of proletarian revolution; she referred to the "little people."

"Little people!"

She pushed back her glorious hair. "The little people," she murmured, "the oppressed masses."

Little people . . .

"Richard's making a film in Mexico. Everyone's against it. He doesn't care . . . about the peons. I'm going with him . . . his own money."

"Mexican dwarfs?"

Laura looked at her blankly. "Well, I don't know about dwarfs."

A woman got into the elevator with them. She seemed galvanized the moment Annie entered. It was a slow elevator.

"Why are you staring at me?"

"You're so beautiful," said the woman. Annie flushed, looking apologetically at Laura and then down at the Heida-designed black suit she was wearing. It was a beautiful suit, expensive, the kind of cut and fit and cloth that made all the difference.

The show was over at eleven, and Annie emerged into the street, intending to get into her car which was parked on the op-

289

posite side, when someone hailed her. She turned and looked down to another more elaborately lit storefront. A short man, whose face she couldn't make out, was waving to her. She walked over to him. She was quite sure he had called her, Ann.

It was Ben Greenhouse.

"My dear Ann," he said. He was drunk, and he had become stout.

"Hello, Ben."

"Come in here. We're having an art show. The studio's going all out for culture, a spasm that will pass. Come in and look at the freaks."

She hesitated, but he took her arm and as soon as he'd touched her, she remembered the lifeless fastidiousness of his ways.

Inside the room, swarms of people in evening dress moved from group to group in front of the paintings. In the middle of the room, on a velvet-covered couch, sat an elderly actor whom Annie recognized from a dozen movies. Sitting along the back of the couch, drooping over him like week-old gladiolas, were a number of girls. Ben was sarcastic in his introduction of Annie to people who affected to take no notice of his words and who moved out of range of her vision no sooner than they had touched her hand. She wanted to leave. "I must go," she said. "I have to work in the morning."

"Oh, but I want to hear about you."

"You've changed," she said, angered by his grip on her arm.

"So have you. You're all grown up, aren't you?"

"No," she said furiously. "I'm not."

"I never thought you'd remain a child," he said interestedly.

"You haven't thought of me at all!"

"Oh—that poor young man. You remember the day on the beach? His body?"

"Listen, I do have to go."

He released her then. He looked offended. "Well, if you want to . . . I'm simply curious. It's my field you know, curiosity . . ."

She was thinking how often she'd known people she really hadn't liked, had spent hours and days and months with them. Greenhouse was ridiculous. Thin, he'd been nervous and jumpy and interesting. Now, he was merely fat.

"I detest your curiosity," she said suddenly in a loud voice, attracting the languid interest of several people nearby. "It's only greediness."

"You'd *better* go."

She did.

She drove past the Trocadero, past the roads to the canyons where once she'd gazed up at the houses of the movie people, where James St. Vincent had sat, his head covered with a linen table napkin, where an opium-addicted cook played golf on his time off, news of another world, a flat world, all tricks of the eye, there for an instant, then dead, fallen into the reality of death.

The party had not so much taken her in as given her temporary shelter, and when she'd wandered in and out of it, not a "serious" person, after all, they'd paid little enough attention to her.

The "serious" person had died. Ethel Schaeffer with her single-minded vision, her kindness a lambent wash of feeling that blindly blessed the self-deceivers around her, the small tyrants, the secret bullies, or people like Theda and Max, turning and twisting inside definitions they were endlessly questioning, or someone like Lavan, scuttling from one dogma to another, carrying his own betrayer in himself, always secret, always transparent in his secrecy, a kind of underground man of fashion.

What had she understood from all of it? That she belonged to something even as abstract as a class? How primitive she had been, she thought, if only now she had begun to classify that which was not herself. A flash of memory illuminated a picture from years gone by: she was sitting on the stony driveway of the old Nyack house with a large flat stone near her knee, her hand gripping a round stone as a hammer, and cleaving open other stones, discovering how different each was from the other, and she had named them names of her own imagining.

As she parked in front of her apartment, she felt a powerful rush of gratitude, even toward Calvin Schmitter, and realized at that same moment as tears came to her eyes that her emotion was facile. What lay behind it was the knowledge that she was going to leave California as soon as she could.

The war was over; Max, she'd heard from Eva, would be coming home soon, coming home to Eva. She did not think she could slip back into their lives again like the nervous castaway of that earlier time—nor, she knew, could they allow her to.

In all of Max's letters, he had never written of his domestic unhappiness which Annie had seen so clearly, if not understood. As for love between Annie and Max, she did not understand that either. She put it down to a kind of passionate interest which satisfied her sense of its uniqueness without binding her to the frightening uncertainties of loving.

She would have to put aside some money; she had four hundred dollars in an envelope. It had seemed a mighty sum, but with moving on in her mind, it was nothing. She lived for the next few months without movies or purchases or restaurants. She saved another one hundred and fifty. She took the amber beads Ben Greenhouse had given her and showed them to Theda. Theda draped them around her long neck and they slid down over her green sweater. Theda smiled, pleased, peered into a mirror. "I want to sell them," Annie said.

"They suit me," Theda murmured, turning her head this way and that.

"What do you think?"

"They're worth more than I can pay—three hundred dollars probably."

Annie gasped. Greenhouse must have been crazy. Theda observed, "People like that, it excites them to pay a good deal of money for things. It reminds them of how much they have. I'll give you two hundred. What do you need it for?"

She looked out to Theda's lawn where a small white goat was tethered.

"Does the goat know you?"

"I should hope to Jesus it does!"

"I mean—does it recognize you, like a dog?"

"Not so I'm oppressed by it, just enough. Enough for me."

"Theda, I'm going away. I'm going to Europe."

Theda disappeared into the kitchen and returned with sandwiches and coffee.

"Graveyard," she said. "Why do you want to go to a *graveyard?*" She looked despondent; her shoulders drooped forward. "Didn't you try once before? Didn't they turn you down?" And then, as though the words were flying through her mind and she must snatch at them, "How *can* you think of it! The air is still full of the smoke of the crematoriums! I can hear the cries—I can hear the crying of children—I can hear the last breath of the children. Have you seen the pictures? Have you seen them stacked up in layers, and the villagers, have you seen the faces of the villagers who *knew* nothing! Don't you know the moral back of the world is broken forever! How can you step on ground where these things have happened! For your own *entertainment?* Because you're *bored?* Because your mind is *empty*—" She sat down and rubbed her face with violent hands, then sprang up and went to a table and opened a drawer and took out a checkbook. She wrote a check and came back to Annie, who had pushed herself back against the wing chair. She thought Theda was going to strike her, but Theda merely handed her a check for two hundred dollars and said, "Come and eat your sandwiches."

They ate in silence, Annie thinking how often Theda had fed her, had sheltered her, had listened so intently to her. The amber beads swung forward as she ate; her expression was abstracted. How deep the lines had become around her mouth! Annie put her hand on Theda's arm. Farewells hung in the air; partings, changes. Theda put down her cup of coffee and enclosed Annie's hand in her own.

"I'll be sorry," she said.

When Annie got up to leave, Theda said with a certain ferocity, "I want my old table back." "I'll get it back to you," Annie promised. "Will you keep my books for me?" "As if I didn't have enough goddamned books," Theda grumbled.

She walked out with Annie to the car. The goat ran toward them until it came to the end of its restraining chain, one glossy eye fixed on Theda's hand. She scratched its head a moment. "You've always reminded me of Simon," she said to Annie. "Like Simon's little sister. I thought that the first time Max brought you, how much you reminded me of Simon."

The last real time she spent in California was in a log cabin in the Big Bear mountains outside of Los Angeles. Mike Eagle had, he said, been told by his wife that he looked like hell and ought to go away for a few days' rest. It was January in the mountains, almost a true January. There were patches of snow on the ground, the air was blue with cold, the small lake frozen, and Annie glimpsed the white flanks of mule-tailed deer among the pines.

They slept beneath layers of cotton blankets and woke to a cold clear light, their breath making vapour in the small cabin. Mike made a fire in the potbellied stove and they ate bacon and drank coffee looking out across the lake at the black tamaracks on the other side. It was hard to leave the warmth of the bed; there was such timeless, mindless pleasure in that warmth, and in the contrasting pine-scented chill air which would soon be obliterated by the wood smoke of the stove.

Annie kept one of the blankets around herself as they ate. Remembering Joe, she wondered if she'd ever be able to look at such a blanket again without its reminding her. She told Mike about him. He listened with his face prepared to smile, as always when she unfolded her "stories," and she grew resentful at the smugness of his anticipatory amusement. She told him more than she'd intended.

"He had no insight," Mike said. "It's clear he was a homosexual. That fact may explain his sister's promiscuity too, or vice versa."

"Fact, vice versa?"

"Lots of people commit suicide."

"What are you talking about?"

"It looms large for you because you knew him. It's a perfectly commonplace happening, especially among younger people."

"Commonplace!"

"Don't get sore. Here, have a cigar."

She dressed, averting her face from him.

Later, walking through the forest, they came to a narrow valley where the remains of an old movie set looked, from their vantage point on the hill above it, like a small frontier village. They walked down and among the façades where snow had caught along the ridges of the wood. In the silence and the cold, they stood huddled together looking up at the saloon, the houses that were only rough-painted wood drawings against the hillside. She wondered if mountain lions walked down the main street. They had heard something cry out the night before, and Mike had said it must be a mountain lion hunting.

On their last morning, she said she had another commonplace story to tell him. He listened impassively to the tale of Lucy Griggs and Cletus, and the two Gorgon women.

"There's a victim theory," he said. "I believe it, too. That little girl was a natural for a rape attack. Listen, some of my patients live in places dangerous to walk in at ten in the morning. No one's ever bothered *me*. It's partly because I don't expect to be bothered."

"You've got an answer for everything."

"I try to understand these things."

"How can you? After you've already decided what they are?"

"I try to understand you."

She shuddered exaggeratedly. "Crated and mailed," she said. "I don't want to hear about it."

294

He embraced her suddenly. "I try, but I don't," he said humbly. "Don't be so mad at me—you can't wander around through a lifetime leaving everything an open question. Look at you! Don't you think you tried to find a *system* when you were hanging around the Reds?"

"It wasn't that," she muttered, her head resting against his shoulder. "Something else . . ."

"You can't ask people not to have a viewpoint—to simply *look,* the way you do. One of these days, you'll have to come to some conclusions—you'll have to be thickheaded and convinced, just like the rest of us."

She hardly heard him, but she was no longer angry. She thought of Uncle Greg who had no answers for earthly matters, who believed in God's heaven.

"You must make judgments," Mike said. "How can a person live without them?"

They packed and made sure the fire was out. Mike went to pay the couple who ran the little cabin community. On their long descent to the warmer regions, Mike spoke accusingly and restlessly about her leaving California. She was simply being ruled by impulse. Her life wasn't bad out here. Now that the war was over, things would be getting better, more opportunities, she might think of going to school. Had she ever thought of becoming a nurse? Or a laboratory technician? She was very observant—she'd be good at that, lab work. He could help—

"No. I'm going."

"It's because you're so young."

"That must be it."

Melvin helped her with Theda's table and the boxes of books. He had a friend with a pickup truck. Melvin had a year to go on his six-year hitch. What would he do after that?

"Maybe Basie remembers me," he said. "I'll get myself a good spot somewhere. I've saved a little money. My, how the old days have gone! You remember what nice times we had? Playing cards up at Cletus's with old Miranda! Those were the good times, weren't they? I've had a lot of good times and a lot of bad times and I don't know which is coming up now. You're taking off too, and that's what I'd like to be doing but I got to finish out my time. I saw Cletus last week, but he don't have much time for me now. He's got a column he's going to write for some newspaper. He asked me if I'd seen you around, but I'll tell you, Annie,

295

it's not the same old Cletus we knew. Nothing's the same now."

She was getting ready to go. She had the car checked and the garage mechanic said she might get to Texas without trouble, after that, he didn't know. She had thought there would be so much to do, but after all, there wasn't so much. Some of the people she'd known had disappeared; some had died, some had changed.

When she saw Mike Eagle for the last time, he had hardened against her in some odd way. She felt he didn't like her at all. But just before he left, he handed her a roll of bills. "Just some undeclared Jewish profits," he said. "God! What's going to happen to you!" Then he kissed her cheeks, and ran his hand down her arm. "I'm sad," he said heavily, looking plumper than ever, and awkward, as though he couldn't feel the edge of his own body. She kissed his olive cheek, tasting the particular smooth, faintly oily quality of his skin. Never again, she told herself. And then, startling them both, she pressed the money he had given her back into his hand.

"No, no. Take it!"

"Help me," she said. "I don't want to this time."

He looked closely at her face, as though examining it for symptoms of physical distress. Then he put the money back in his pocket. "Annie makes a resolution," he said.

"Don't make fun."

"I won't, not even in memory."

She spent a few hours with Eva. Theda was there and had bought her a pretty blue cardigan sweater—"In case you get to Lapland." Eva had made her a lumpy chocolate cake.

But Thomas wasn't there. "At the sitter's," Eva explained. "He's a little nervous these days when people come. It's the eye trouble."

"What eye trouble?" Annie asked.

"I would have thought Max had written you about it," Eva said with a touch of irony. Annie was startled. Max had told Eva about their correspondence!

"No, he hasn't. I haven't heard from him for a while," she said, abashed.

"Oh? Well, you might get to see him in New York. He'll be stopping there before he comes home."

"What about Thomas's eyes?"

"We don't know yet. He's been examined by several doctors. It's all made him very nervous." Eva looked vaguely around the room as though searching for the little boy. "I'm sure it'll be all right," she said. Theda asked, "What's it called? What he has."

"I can't even pronounce it," Eva replied, and offered them more coffee with a rush of words about the cake, why it was lumpy, the recipe she'd used.

Eva shook her hand formally and wished her good luck. Only when she turned back to the apartment did Annie see the anguish on her face. Driving Theda home, she said, "What was that all about?"

"It was Eva, being evasive," said Theda. "Maybe you'd better not tell Max about it, if you do see him. He's used to getting information indirectly."

"Not from me," Annie said.

"He's not yours," said Theda sternly.

"I never thought I owned anybody."

"Hunh."

She telephoned Cletus early in the morning. She could hear Brahms playing in the background. Her heart sank with dread. She was leaving the only place she'd ever been for any length of time, the only friends she'd ever really had.

"Why didn't you come and see me?" Cletus asked. She was silent, looking at the receiver.

"Yeah," said Cletus, as though she'd answered. "That's how it goes. I'll think of you, Annie."

"I'll think of you."

The following morning at six, two suitcases in the back of the old car, and a full tank of gas, off the ration now, she drove out of Los Angeles. A few miles beyond the city limits, on the side of the road, a Negro soldier stood holding a sign that read HOUSTON. She stopped the car. The man ran to the door and opened it.

"Thanks," he said, getting in. "How far are you going?"

"All the way east," Annie said.

"My name's Mason White," he said.

"You live in Houston?"

"I do now. War's all over. I'm going home."

Chapter 18

They drove night and day, spelling each other. He slept, his head against the window, his overseas cap draped over one knee while Annie took them through the Mohave mountains, dropping ever southward, pushing the car to its highest rattling speed through night-shut villages until Mason White touched her arm and said, "Not too fast along in here. We don't want to be stopped." She had forgotten there *were* towns—she had been driving across a map, unpeopled, a matter of road signs, of dirt roads leading off from the main highway to no place at all.

"When I came to California," she told Mason White, "I gave a ride to an old cook from a CCC camp. His wife was having a baby up in a mountain village in the Rockies. He took the wheel and drove like a fury."

"How long ago was that?"

"Five years," she said, and hearing her words, could not believe them, remembering the cook bent over the wheel like a large red bird with lidless eyes, forgetting for a moment all the faces in between that time and this.

"Nearly as long as I been in the army."

"Do you have a wife and children in Houston?"

"Just my mother and sisters. But I think I will have a wife soon. They say things are going to be better now. The magazines, the newspapers say things going to be better for us. Better jobs. Better life."

She felt the slight emphasis he had put on the word, *us,* as though he'd touched her arm; he hadn't meant her.

"They can't go back on it now," Mason White went on. "People had good jobs in the war plants, they aren't going back to mopping up grease."

"You've always lived in Houston?"

"From the time we moved there from Alabama. My father had a little truck farm up there. One day, he was going to market. A white fellow came out of a side road and smacked into my father's truck. My father came home and said, 'Pack up.' See, when they do you something bad, then they're going to do worse. He hammered out the door of the truck where it'd been bashed in and we put what we could carry in the truck and we left that night and came to Houston because he had a brother there. Then, after we'd been there a year or so, my father moved on. I don't know, none of us know, where he got to. My sisters, they're both learning nursing. Things got a little better while the war was on. They can't push us all the way back now."

While Annie slept, Mason White brought them into Texas.

At Mason's insistence, Annie had gone in alone to roadside stops, bringing them out sandwiches and coffee. "But you're a soldier," she'd protested.

"Don't make no matter what I am."

He stopped for gas only at the smallest junction where there would be a combined store and gas station, a few old men rocking on the porch storefront, picking their teeth. These settlements were so negligible that the planks out of which the tumble-down buildings were constructed looked like the debris left after a hurricane. There were no facilities for travelers, only the same old store with its brooms and hoes, bags of feed and sacks of nails and a few canned goods, a gas tank rooted in the ground as though it had dropped straight down from a hole in the sky. Sometimes, in a diner, Annie found a squalid toilet. But Mason White waited until they were out on the main road, then while she rested against the seat, White searched out a hidden place behind rocks and bushes.

He drove with absolute control, the car his servant. His plain brown face was creased with fatigue. He was a reticent man but the little space of the car in which they worked so steadily, erod-

299

ing the distance before them, held the special intimacy that springs from mutual purpose. He was considerate toward her. He observed her for signs of exhaustion. "You're too tired now. You stop, and I'll take over," he'd say.

They advanced hourly into increasingly dangerous territory. As the gas meter dropped down toward *empty,* she felt his fear and knew it was worse than her own.

"You had nerve, to pick me up and drive me like this," he remarked once.

"I didn't think of it like that."

"I know it," he said. "I'm just telling you. Five years ago, they would've broken my legs for this. I'm not sure what they'd do now if I wasn't wearing these sergeant stripes, this uniform, and if all their young men were back, not just those old bones clacking around."

Because her fear began to intensify, because she wanted to get to the other side of that fear to prove it was unwarranted, she insisted, finally, that they both go into a bar that advertised meatloaf sandwiches and cold beer. A few gray shacks like inflated chicken coops lay in the rough field behind the bar. In one, something like a doorway gave onto a dark interior. A shining black inner tube rested against the gray slats, and near it a yellow chicken stood in an attitude of expectancy. There was no other sign of life.

"Listen, you've seen the way these people stare at us? That man at the last gas station, he looked at you like you were trash."

After three days and two nights of steady driving, despair caught up with her as though it had been traveling on the road behind them all the while, waiting for this moment a hundred miles or so out of Houston. She couldn't believe she was going anywhere, or had come from anyplace. It was vital they go into this place together. She was suddenly enraged, deaf to White's pleas of caution. He followed, reluctantly, a few steps behind her into the cool musty long room where a few old men perched along a narrow bar. The bartender himself was bent over arthritically, his turtle head thrusting forward out of his shoulders.

"Take your hat off, boy!"

Annie whirled and saw Mason White, his overseas cap still on his head, backing toward the door.

"He's a soldier!" she cried. "He's been in the war!"

"We got different ideas about that," squeaked the bartender.

300

The old men stared blankly at her. "If you want something, you can have it. But he gotta take his hat off. And we're outa the meat loaf. I got some ham, that's all."

Mason White shook his head slightly. They went back to the car, hearing behind them the sibilance of ancient broken laughter.

She wept a few tears, noting that the chicken was now scratching futilely at the hard yellow earth near the car. "Look at that damned fool!" she said. Mason White's hands were on the wheel. "All right," she said, wiping her face with her hand. "We'll go."

It was early evening when they arrived in Houston. Throughout the colored section to the city, there seemed to be an extraordinary number of policemen.

"Somebody must have said something too loud," said White. It was his first joke.

The Whites lived in a large ramshackle house, a small wilderness of tall grass around the porch steps. As he cut the motor, three women appeared in the doorway. Mason White bounded up the steps. The women clung to him, one of the younger ones looking over his shoulder at Annie with unconcealed amazement.

"Good-by, Sergeant," she called from the window.

"No, no. You come in and eat with us," Mason White cried. Then, turning to his family, "She drove me all the way."

One of his sisters was touching the stripes on his jacket, and her small head with its marcelled black waves nodded in Annie's direction as though she were in favor of this odd notion. White came back down the steps and took her arm firmly in his hand.

"After what you did for me—please stay. Mama?"

"Oh, yes!" Mrs. White said, smiling at her daughters. "She has to stay."

At the dinner table, Mrs. White's face was turned always toward her son. She passed plates of rice and meat to him, watching his mouth as he spoke, enthralled by the motion of his lips, in a dream of welcoming. The sisters talked about their work, the hospital, their neighbors, breaking into giggles when they looked at their brother. "You all grew up so," he said, and they giggled at that too. They stared furtively at Annie; she tried to say something; they nodded in agreement before she'd finished, hurrying her words out of existence.

Would she stay on for the night? Mrs. White asked.

No, no, she had to push on, she said. Mrs. White began to thank her. There was an almost extravagant emphasis on Annie's

301

bountifulness which she experienced as some unconscious irony on the old woman's part, a kind of pushing her away, back into her own place.

White walked out to the car with her, telling her how to get out of Houston.

"You going to drive all night now?"

"You let me sleep most of today. I think I can make it."

"New York," he said.

"New York," she echoed. "Then, I'm going to Europe."

"Everybody's moving on now. Except me. I've been moving on for years, all my life it seems."

She opened the door. A paper bag in which she'd brought him sandwiches lay on the floor near the brake pedal.

"Let me get that," he said, leaning forward to pluck out the bag.

"We marched through Texas," he said.

They shook hands. She waited a moment to watch Mason White run back up to the porch where his mother and sisters waited, their arms entwined, their brown faces so still against the gray shingle, like a photograph pasted in an album.

She drove most of that night, singing or talking to herself, until the morning sun's first rays struck her across the eyes, and she pulled over to the side of the road and slept till midday. Later, at twilight, she just missed a dead cow, its head rising stiffly from the ditch along the highway, and an hour later, she followed a drunken driver in an old Ford, careening from one side of the road to the other, passing him at last in a desperate burst of speed. That night, utterly spent, she paid two dollars for a bed in a log cabin, too tired to care about the stained mattress ticking, the brutal bed springs, the dripping of a tap in a stained basin hanging from the wall.

She was wearing the sweater Theda had given her, and a raincoat on top of that, on the February morning she drove up the Pulaski skyway and saw, in the distance, the towers of New York City.

302

Chapter 19

Annie saw that winter had already played havoc with the driveway. Bumping up the hill toward the darkened house—could the old man have gone to sleep so early in the evening?—she recalled the ravages of those long-ago winters when ice and snow dislodged, then tumbled stones into the gutters, making the road nearly impassable; a car would lift and fall as the wheels gripped and lost traction, then slide and swing abruptly sideways, its front wheels spinning in mud, its back ones caught precariously on the uneven surfaces of rocks. Uncle Greg must have given up; the road had never been as bad as this. She opened her window the better to see, and poked out her head. For an instant, the air took her breath away, Hudson Valley winter air with its lung-drowning dampness, summer's humidity gone dead and inhuman, and she felt on her forehead and nose stinging particles of hard snow as though the block of the invisible sky was being chipped away.

The frozen fields spread out on either side of the road, black where clumps of evergreens sat in their pools of darkness, faintly luminous with snow beneath the leafless branches of deciduous trees that her grandfather had planted in another century.

The car lifted its snout, wheels spun, the motor coughed, and she gained a level area where the road circled the house. A faint light flickered from an upstairs bedroom. He was not dead!

During her first three days in New York, she had phoned Uncle Greg several times, morning and evening, from the Murray Hill Hotel where she had taken a room.

When, at five this afternoon, there still had been no answer, she determined to do what she knew she must do, to drive up to Nyack, to discover the corpse.

She had listened too long to the ringing of the phone, gazing across the inner court of the hotel to a window facing her own. There, next to a half-emptied bottle of milk, she had seen a pair of long white feet resting on the sill. Was that person dead too? Lying on the floor of his room with his feet so neatly, so madly crossed, next to the remains of his last meal? The hotel was not as her father had once described it to her. The grandeur she had imagined, and which she had decided to enjoy for a few days no matter what the cost—at least if it was within reason—was gone, leaving only whispers of itself in the cavernous rooms, the marble bathrooms, the ragged faded carpeting along its dusty corridors. The lobby was full of old people staggering with age, dismayed by drunks, starting nervously at the clang of elevator doors. Here and there, vaguely criminal-looking men in tight blue or gray suits surreptitiously ground out their cigarettes on the floor.

She drew up before the familiar square porch. As she strode across the old boards, the bare limbs of a lilac bush next to the steps rattled noisily. The door was unlocked. She walked into the entrance hall, then stood in the dank silence for a moment. But there was no need for caution; she remembered where everything was, and moved with sure steps toward the stairs, past the tables, the chairs, the coat rack, her hand brushing the back of the bronze lion as she began to climb upwards, feeling the thick dust on her fingers. A curious and irritating sound suddenly struck her ears, a series of steady *pings*. Then a heavier plunking, then a hollow *thunk*.

In the upstairs hall, she saw, straight ahead, the room from where the flickering light had emanated which she had glimpsed from the car. She walked quickly to it. Covering most of the floor was an assortment of receptacles, pots, pails, bowls, vases, pans of all shapes, and into them, with merciless regularity, dripped water from the ceiling. She stepped into the room. The flame of a candle swerved at the draft she caused, she swung to her left and collided against the mahogany sides of the sleigh bed. In it, asleep or unconscious, lay Uncle Greg, a faded green quilt drawn up over his

304

chest. One hand gripped a corner of the quilt; there were spots of wax on the wrinkled fingers. She tried a light switch. The electricity was off.

She touched his face where the white stubble of beard grew up into his cheek. His eyelids fluttered, closed.

"Uncle Greg?"

Water dripped on her hair. She looked up at the ceiling where dark circles marked the holes in the plaster. The roof had triumphed over him at last.

In his face were the dark circles of his closed eyes. Only the wax-marked fingers of his hand seemed alive, although the hand too was unmoving, yet it had gathered the quilt and was holding it still, an echo of force in the knuckled fist. It was as though all the life in him had been carried away except there. But his eyes opened again—she had started away, to the phone. Someone had to be called, the hospital, the police. She paused, wished his eyes were still shut, not staring up at the ceiling with such puzzlement.

"Uncle Greg?" she whispered.

The head barely turned. The mouth, as though dried shut, opened unevenly, the flesh of his lips sticking here and there. For a moment, he looked at her with the same uncomprehendingness that he had looked at the leaking ceiling. Then his mouth stretched slightly; it was a try at a smile.

"You're sick. I'm going to phone the hospital."

"Yes," he whispered. "I'm sick now."

"There's no heat."

"Everything went," he said, attaining his voice as though he'd climbed a mountain and found it at the top, a thin whistle of a voice.

"I'll be right back."

"No. Wait. I don't know about the phone."

"It's working. I called you from the city."

"Yes. That must be it. I thought I heard it ring. But I thought it was part of a dream. I've been dreaming."

He released the quilt and hid his hand; he was trying to sit up.

"Don't. Don't move," she said.

"Annie?"

Had he only now recognized her?

"Do you remember Helen Sears?"

She thought he was going to tell her of the old times, of the Sears family who had lived a few miles away, of the fire started by old Ephraim Sears fifteen years ago when he threw a kerosene lamp at his wife, a woman who had abjured speech in favor of her hands with which she pummeled her husband, her children, her sisters, her own father while he had been alive. The house had burned to the ground. Annie remembered Uncle Greg's stunned horror as he told her that no one had survived except the old woman and her daughter, Helen, forgetting for once that Annie was only a child and should not hear of such things. Smelling of smoke, his hands covered with soot, he'd spewed out the story in the downstairs hall, then tried, later, to retell it and soften it. But it had been too late. She'd sneaked to the still-smoking ruin the next day, walking there directly from school, wondering if old Ephraim's bones were still somewhere among the charred wet boards. And there had been Helen's young brother, burned alive too.

"Uncle Greg—"

"No, no, no." He was abruptly cranky, scowling. "It's Helen I want you to call. Not the hospital. She's got a nursing home. That's where I'll go. I have this hernia. That's all. It's why I haven't been able to move."

"Have you eaten?"

"Not hungry." He sighed terribly. His eyes closed. She put her hand on his head. His hair was wet.

She made her way back down the stairs. He was so wasted! How long had he gone without food? She lit a match. Out of the dense dark, the bronze lion seemed to shake his bronze mane as he reached a paw toward the waiting mouse. She saw the lines where her fingers had touched the lion through the dust. The phone was there as it had always been.

It was easy. The place was simply called the Sears Nursing Home. Miss Sears herself came directly to the phone. Yes, of course, she remembered Annie.

"Uncle Greg is terribly sick. I think he's not eaten for days. The ceiling is nothing but holes, and the snow is melting right over his bed."

"Can you bring him here?"

"I'm pretty sure he can't walk. He says it's a hernia. But he looks almost dead."

There was a pause. Then Helen said rapidly, "A hernia! These old maids! I told him a year ago he ought to be examined by a doctor. He promised . . . of course he didn't go. Oh, these old

306

men! They won't get undressed, you know, not even in front of a man. That's no hernia. I should have told him then what I thought it was. My fault . . . all my fault. I should have gone to see him. But this place wears me out, just wears me down to the ground. I'll send our ambulance there. It'll be about an hour. The driver is having his dinner. Make him a cup of tea, if he's got any."

"There's no electricity."

"Oh, God! They're all alike! No electricity! Do what you can then. I'll be waiting for you."

Annie sat on the bed and held his scaly old hand. He slept; he woke. Sometimes he spoke. She told him she was hoping to go to England soon. He simply looked at her. She saw it meant nothing to him.

"I have to buy new tools," he said suddenly. "My hedge clippers couldn't cut butter. If things aren't scarce, they cost so much! Oh, I could fly to Jericho! The whole world makes me so riled! You see how the town looks? They spit on the sidewalks and don't care about anything. When I think of how my dear father loved this place!" Abruptly his eyes closed. His breathing was so heavy, as though he were drawing the air up out of his lungs with a bucket, not enough air for one decent breath.

They came at last, and wrapped him in the quilt and lifted him to a stretcher, one holding a flashlight as they went down the stairs. Annie blew out the candle. In the darkness of the room, the water dripped ceaselessly into the pots. By morning, they would surely overflow.

The front door latch was broken. She brought the door to, watching the ambulance attendant cover the old man with a pink blanket. As she went to her car, she tripped over the quilt, already water-soaked where it had been tossed to the ground.

At the nursing home, Helen Sears was waiting. She nodded to Annie and gave directions to a nurse who was looking down at the old man as he lay on a table. A young doctor entered the room and peeled off the blanket. Uncle Greg was dressed in pants and shirt, but his feet were bare. The doctor pulled down the trousers, pushed up the shirt. He felt, he probed, he shook his head.

Later, Helen Sears said, "Well, it's unmistakable and much too late to do anything. He's riddled with cancer. We don't need lab reports for that. Even that ignoramus of a doctor, so-called doctor . . . God knows what they're teaching them in school these days, even he knows that. He won't live long."

307

"Long?"

"A day—a few days. Well, we'll make him comfortable. That's what I'm in business for—to make these old parties comfortable. No use taking him to the hospital. I've got a dozen of them here right now, dying. But they're comfortable. Nobody can say they aren't."

Helen Sears looked broodingly at her large clean square hands. "Geraniums in the rooms," she said.

"I'll be back, then, tomorrow."

But Helen wasn't listening. She was staring at Annie, looking through her. "Would you believe it?" she whispered. "My own mother is in this place! Ninety. Defecating and rubbing her feces in her hair, biting the nurses . . ." Her mouth widened; suddenly she shouted with laughter, then clapped her hand over her mouth. "I'm not mad," she said in a moment. "I suppose you know the story? About my father and brother and the house burning? Well, the old witch can't hit anybody any more. Where are you living? I might have to call you."

"I'm at the Murray Hill Hotel, but I've got to find a room to stay. I'm going to look tomorrow. You can leave a message. I'll come up here anyhow sometime tomorrow, and maybe I'll have a place by then."

The older woman nodded. "Would you like some coffee?" she asked with surprising kindness.

"No, no thanks. I'd best be going."

"Are you working, or anything? I always wondered what happened to you. Of course, I didn't wonder all the time, had too much on my back to think about other people."

"I'm going to England. I've saved a little money."

"Does *he* have any money?"

"There used to be some kind of insurance from his father."
"Your grandfather," Helen interrupted. "Yes. My grandfather. I don't know exactly how it worked, but he got a check four times a year. I remember that because he was always planning to fix that roof, then when the money came he had to spend it on other things."

"He must have made something in the way of income from his gardening work."

"I just don't know. I've been away five years."

"Yes. And these old ones, they won't talk about money, will they? Well, he was good to me, especially after my father tried to cremate us. We'll work it out." She rose to her feet. "England. I've never been anywhere," she said. "Well, what are you going to do there?"

"I don't know yet. Get a job."

"Going to England to get a job . . . couldn't you manage something nearer home?"

Helen's curiosity had shifted perceptibly to reproach.

"I want," Annie began, trying to keep her eyes on the woman's face but abashed, looking away, "well, what I want is a place I've not been, you know." Called to account for herself, she instantly shared the suspicion about her reasons she suspected Helen felt. There had been—some time ago—that sudden strong intention. Had she said it to Theda? To Mike Eagle? "I'm going to Europe." Why had she determined to go anywhere? Helen Sears was smiling faintly.

"I've never been anyplace," she said. "I sometimes think there isn't any other place except here, that Europe or Mexico or the Fiji Islands are only places in the mind. Of course—"

"I want a new start," Annie broke in. "That's what I meant."

Helen looked sternly at her watch. Annie got up to go.

"Does he have any relatives anywhere except you?"

"I remember there was a cousin. It was so long ago. She was married to someone in Providence, Rhode Island. I think they still must live there."

"You'll have to go through his papers and find out what you can. He's going to die, you know. It's a tiresome business, funeral, all that. Do you suppose he made a will? There's the house and the land. It's probably worth something."

"Oh—don't you see? I've been away! I don't know about these things. How would I know?"

"You'll have to know, now. I'll make him as comfortable as I can. But what about the house, his things? You can't walk away. He *was* your uncle."

"He's not dead yet!"

"I've taken care of a murdering old woman for fifteen years! It's her fault my father and brother went up in flames. I went to nursing school, hating it! Hating it! But that's what I was *meant* to do. It was the only way I could see to *her!* She would have been in the madhouse if it weren't for me. Do you imagine you can just go off to your England and forget such an obligation?"

Helen Sears was standing near a glass case on the shelves of which reposed a number of steel instruments, some of them scissors with beaks like shrikes.

"I won't. I'm not. I can't go for a while anyhow," Annie protested. "You don't understand. It's that I don't *know* what to do! And he's breathing, right now. He might not die. How do you know he'll die?"

"I only take people when they're dying," cried Helen Sears, "so he must be dying!"

"I'll be back tomorrow," Annie shouted at her, holding up her hands in front of her chest. The woman might attack her! Fling that case at her! She was mad, as mad as her old mother. Helen was looking at her watch again. What could it tell her?

"All right," she said, her voice calm now. "Sorry to be so emotional. I have to deal with relatives, you see. All the time." She emitted a lifeless little chuckle. "It quite turns one sour, cynical, you might say."

In her room at the Murray Hill Hotel, Annie stared for a long time at the telephone. It would only be nine o'clock in Los Angeles. Theda would be up and about. But what could Theda tell her? Did she want to be told anything? Only to hear Theda's voice, to hear a friend's voice!

She knew what she had to do. She would have the photographs taken in the morning for the passport application she had picked up at Rockefeller Center. She would look for a room in the Village. The passport took two weeks, if she got one. She would have to find out about shipping lines. Then she would drive to Nyack, to the old house, and go through Uncle Greg's desk.

She looked at the application. The photographs were simple! And she'd have an address soon enough. But where could she get someone to be the *identifying witness*? She didn't know *anyone* in this city. She began to fill in the application. *A woman applicant must fill in this portion,* it read. *I was never married. I was last married on*—a large ink blot spread out from the point of the pen where she was pressing down on the line. The room was cold. Theda said they would have a dossier on her.

I intend to visit the following countries for the purposes indicated: England, she wrote.

What purposes? The windows opposite her own were dark. It was raining dismally, weakly in the inner court. I will not be able to go, she thought. I have no identifying witness. Uncle Greg will linger on. I will find a room and it will start all over again. There's always a room somewhere.

She undressed and got into bed. The enormity of what she had wanted to do! She had in her folly imagined it was simply a matter of will, and a little cash. But papers. Photographs. Witness. Plan. Reason. Address. Oath. And a few miles up the Hudson, in that collapsing old house, was a desk with drawers full of papers, Uncle Greg's getaway papers, a will, a deed, documents of death. She had already begun her own trail, marriage certificate and divorce decree, Social Security card, a dossier in Washington, petitions she had signed, employment records, driver's license. Oh! God knows what traps she had long since set for herself, timed to be sprung months, years from now!

What would happen to that house? Would he have left it to her? No, surely not. That would be willing her his own fate. She would not accept the house. She would hand the house over to Helen Sears—let her fill it with dying people to be made "comfortable." Gradually, she grew less rigid. She drowsed. A name mumbled in her mind, struggled, an odd name. Jersey Lighter. She sat up in bed and reached for the telephone. Information gave her the number. He had liked her. He would remember her. Hadn't he given her that paper? Something about an angel, andirons, the fate of the world? He would be her witness.

———

Jersey Lighter was waiting for her in a booth close to the kitchen door of the Chinese restaurant where he had asked her to meet him. He didn't see her at first; he was peering through his glasses at a menu which, as she slipped into the booth, he turned upside down. Then he stood up, bending awkwardly over the table.

"How are you, Annie?" he asked gravely, as though only a few days had passed, not years. She shook his proffered hand. He picked up the menu again and sat down. "Are you interested in ideography? I'm teaching myself Chinese characters. It's a good discipline for the hands." She glanced at it briefly, seeing instead of the dirty menu card the faded sepia handwriting of the papers, postcards, and letters she had gone through that afternoon in the Nyack house. Her hands were still dusty; she hadn't had time to

311

stop off at the hotel and wash up. She pushed her hair back from her face, knowing she looked awful.

"How is your baby?" she asked, trying to remember the name of Jersey Lighter's wife.

"Dandy," he said. "We call her that. Her name is Daniela. Elmira likes foreign names." There had been a slight emphasis on *Elmira* as though he'd known Annie had forgotten.

"I'm sorry to bother you," she said, "but I couldn't think of anyone else. It means going with me to the passport office. I hope you won't mind."

"No. I'm glad to do it. It's a slack time now. The spring windows will be along soon, but right now is fine. How was it? In California?"

She must have looked her hopelessness at answering such a question for he smiled and said, "Never mind. It's been a long time. You look as if you'd managed it. Walter's in New York, you know. I saw him a few days ago. He told me he had written to someone out there to try and find you."

"Walter!" she exclaimed apprehensively.

"He says he has to get the divorce decree from you." He paused as a waiter came to their table. "What would you like?"

"I don't know. Could you order? Not too much of anything. I'm not hungry."

He told the waiter what to bring them without looking at the menu. Annie supposed he ate there often. Then he said, with the same quiet detachment she remembered from the night five years ago, "Walter is marrying again. That's why he needs the decree."

She must have looked very shocked for him to touch her arm with his small neat hand. But he had mistaken her response. It was not the thought of Walter remarrying. It was the thought of Walter himself. She laughed a little.

"It's all right," she said. "Only that for a moment, I couldn't imagine Walter. I mean, that he's real, walking around the city. I'm not—jealous."

How little Jersey had changed! The same mild expression, even the same gold-rimmed glasses. She remembered now how he had been sitting in a corner of that loft, peering down at a figurine of some sort.

"Are you still making those—"

312

"The figures. Yes. We've done well. Not as well as we had thought. The war interrupted it. The army didn't take me. I had rheumatic fever when I was a child. I had to work in a machine shop down at Irving Place days. It was a place where they used industrial diamonds, for cutting and abrading. Nights, we made the figures and sold a few. Department stores go on forever. We managed."

"I worked in a shipbuilding plant for a while. I was supposed to run a drill press, but I left before I got around to it."

He smiled. "Well, a little practical knowledge never hurts. It might come in handy someday."

The waiter brought two small bowls of soup. She ate, grateful for the thin broth. She could not have swallowed much of substance. Jersey hadn't asked her yet what she wanted a passport for, where she was going. She wondered if anything excited him, frightened him? Was it resignation that made him so calm? So undemanding?

"I've had a strange day," she said, thinking, He won't mind hearing about it because it won't touch him. "My uncle is very ill and I had to go to his house—where I lived as a child—and try to find his papers. For some reason, I never have even thought of people having to have *papers*. There were some white crackers in one of the desk drawers. They crumbled when I touched them. And another drawer full of big gray coins. But the postcards—there were dozens of them! From all over Europe. And the handwriting was so thin and spidery and in brown ink. I spent too much time reading them, about all those journeys so long ago. Some of them, my uncle had written to his mother when he was in Germany, that must have been before the First World War. And some were from people I never heard of. But I found one from my mother to Uncle Greg. I kept it."

"What did it say?" he asked.

The waiter removed the bowls and brought them rice and two covered dishes.

"It said, 'We have found a lovely little house near the water. I am happy. Home at last.' "

"Where was the little house?"

"In Rockport, Massachusetts. And my father went back. He's there now."

"Went back?"

"My mother died when I was little. He married twice since then. Now he's gone up there again."

Jersey put two small servings from the dishes on her plate. Steam rose briefly from the food, then subsided.

"I think there must be a profound difference between people who like everything in one bowl and the ones who eat one potato and one chop as widely separated on their plate as possible. My mother put the muzzle of a shotgun in her mouth and blew her head off."

She gasped. He looked at her placidly and began to eat. Then he said, "I'm told it makes a difference to a child, how they die."

"Oh, you can't feel that way! You—"

Something flickered in his face. His eyes opened very wide, his nostrils flared. His face was slowly exploding! Then he bent over his food again and took another forkful. When he looked up, his features had assumed their familiar shape. "But I do," he said. "I know I see things somewhat differently from other people. I have this thought that the shot that killed her shifted my balance. I can't explain it. But then, I had a good father. Very good. As these things go. Tell me about the house, your uncle's house."

"It was cold. The heat is off."

"When are you leaving the country?"

"I have to find a ship. I have to find a room. You must have a place for them to send the passport to. It can't be a hotel. I may not even get one. They turned me down a few years ago."

He looked thoughtful. Then he said, "I have some friends in the merchant marine, aside from Walter, that is, who's really not a friend. I think the United States Lines have some partly converted ships that are going over. They were used as troop ships during the war. Now they're taking some passengers. You might try them. And I know some people who've gotten passports, older than you, and I expect a lot more dangerous in the view of the State Department. You're not *very* dangerous, are you?"

He was teasing her a little, soberly, as was his way, she thought.

"No. I wouldn't think I was. But they did turn me down once."

"It's all chance," he said.

"Could you go with me the day after tomorrow? To witness?"

"In the morning. Where are you going to look for a room?"

"Down here in the Village, I thought," she said.

"There's a place on Morton Street, a little old tenement but very clean. An Italian couple look after it. You could try."

314

He walked with her to her subway. "You've helped so much," she said.

"Just information."

"Thanks for the dinner. I didn't mean for you to pay."

They shook hands. He touched her arm lightly. "I did suffer," he said. "The bewilderment was terrible. But one doesn't suffer forever. How could anyone live then?"

"Do you remember that piece of paper you gave me? What was written on it?" she asked shyly.

For a moment, his face was illuminated by an unguarded smile.

"The Giotto," he murmured. "How nice you remembered."

"Is nine o'clock all right at the passport division?"

"Fine," he nodded.

She spent the following morning walking around the Village. Jersey had neglected to give her the street number of the tenement on Morton, but she found one that might have been it. There were many such old narrow buildings, across their façades the black Z of a fire escape. An Italian woman showed her a room on the first floor. They walked back a long passageway, the floor of damp white tiles smelling of wet mop. The room was on an inner court. A screen of chicken wire covered the only window. "So's the cats won't get in," said the old woman. There was, inexplicably, a circular plastic structure slit by a narrow opening in the middle of the room. "Somebody was going to put a shower there. Crazy," said the woman. "How long you want it for?"

"I'm not sure," said Annie, afraid she wouldn't rent the room if she knew the uncertainty of Annie's plans.

"It's thirty dollars a month. You pay gas meter. See?" She put her hand on the surface of a water tank next to a large sink. "A quarter and you get hot water." She whispered this last as though it were vaguely illicit. "But you got to tell me, how long?"

"I just can't—"

"See, it's a sublet. The fellow's an Indian. Billy, he's going back to the place—what's it called? The reserve? And he's only going for six weeks. So you see, that's the trouble."

"That would be fine."

"You don't have to pay electricity."

"When can I have it?"

"Tonight."

The old woman walked to a sofa bed near the window. "He got dirty sheets, hunh?"

315

"I'll give you a month now."

"The toilet's in there." She pointed to a closed door. "The sink's big enough to wash in. Billy don't wash much."

"Do you want the money?"

"Billy be right back. He went to the store. We wait."

They stood there silently for several minutes. The Italian woman folded her hands over her belly and appeared to doze. Annie calculated. She could make herself meals on the two-burner stove. It had been stupid to stay at the hotel—a waste of money. But if she moved in here tomorrow, if she was terribly careful, she wouldn't have to get a temporary job. Of course, it all depended on the ship, when she could get one, how long before it sailed; it all depended too on the passport division; it all depended on Uncle Greg. Thirty days, she told herself. None of these questions could persist unanswered after thirty days. Did she mean for Uncle Greg to die in time? It wasn't that, it couldn't be. Helen Sears had said he'd only last a few days, at most. When she had gone to the nursing home yesterday, after the miserable hours in the old house, he had been in some curious region between sleep and consciousness, recognizing her one moment, forgetting where he was, who she was, in the next. Only once had his eyes cleared; she had started to hang up the bathrobe she had found in the house and brought him.

"Not that one! Oh, Annie, not that old thing. I have a good robe. In your old closet. I kept it in there . . . I don't know why . . . but I won't wear that ugly thing. Now you go and get the good one." It startled her, that unexpected clarity, his insistence. It had touched her, vanity enduring beyond all else. She had rummaged through his clothes. How neglected, squalid everything had been! How awful to grow old, to be so sick, alone, alone, with the sheets growing grayer, buttons gone from shirts—you get too old to bend and look beneath furniture—underwear in rags, suits holding the shape of an aging body, knees worn through.

"I got another one coming up any day." The Italian woman spoke suddenly. "Upstairs. A better room. He's a hophead. He's going to kill hisself."

"This is fine, fine . . . I really only need a place for a few weeks. I'm going abroad."

"What's that? Where?"

"To England. Then to Europe."

"My God! What are you gonna do that for?"

She was saved from answering by the appearance of Billy, a large fat black-haired young man wearing dungarees and a red flannel shirt beneath his jacket. He ignored the two women, going directly to the stove where he dropped a small paper bag.

"Billy, you got a tenant," said the woman. "She's gonna take your place."

Billy tore off his jacket, enormous shoulders hunching into view as he circled and dropped the garment on the bed.

"Okay. She tell you how much? I get five for the furnishings. But I'll take care of the electric. She tell you about the meter? I got some sheets at the laundry down the street. Clean. You can pick them up. I'll be leaving in an hour."

The furnishings! A studio bed, a folding chair with a missing slat in the seat, an unpainted table of the cheapest sort.

"You mean it's thirty-five dollars?" she asked the old woman.

"No. Like I said. You give me twenty-five, him five."

Billy grabbed up his jacket and felt in the pockets. "Here, I got a key made in case someone took the place. You understand, I'm coming back from the reservation in six weeks?" She nodded and took the key from him. The old woman was suddenly seized by a spasm of dry coughing. This furious and rising crescendo of open-mouthed ragged shouts was curiously like a temper tantrum. Billy's attention was caught and held. With a last long rasp, the woman fell silent, tears running down her cheeks. "Boy!" cried Billy.

Annie left thirty dollars on the table—let them divide it up— and retreated quickly down the long hallway, out to the street. What was worrying her now was a coat. The weather had changed abruptly this morning, the damp chilling rainy air had hardened into bitter cold shot through with small bursts of icy wind like the cold springs in a mountain lake. She was wearing two sweaters and the raincoat. It was a narrow edge she was traveling if a coat could throw the whole plan into question. But she would certainly need one in England, wouldn't she? Perhaps there was something in the old house toward which she was now driving. There had been trunks in the attic she had not touched. An old coat of her mother's?

On this third day of her visit to the house, she felt its spirit had died. Perhaps there were mice in the cellar, squirrels in the attic, but the air smelled of rotted cloth and rotting wood, nothing living any more. In Uncle Greg's bedroom, the sheets lay strewn as the ambulance attendants had left them; the pots on the floor were nearly all full, the smaller ones sitting in pools of damp where the water had overflowed and sunk into the floorboards. Annie looked at the sleigh bed. It was hers.

Yesterday she had found a will, witnessed by an indecipherable name. The house was left to the Hudson Valley Historical Association, its offices in Cornwall. The furnishings, with the exception of the bed, were left to Dr. and Mrs. Vernon Fletcher of Providence, Rhode Island. The small hoard of money in a Nyack savings account would just about cover the costs of a simple funeral, Helen Sears had said. "Very simple," she had warned her. With the words still in her ears, she had gone yesterday to stand by Uncle Greg's bed, watching the lift and fall of his narrow chest beneath the blanket. A geranium bloomed on the window sill of the little room. She remembered, horribly, her childhood nightmare of being buried alive, of waking to find herself in a wooden box, deep in the ground.

Today, she would have to telephone Mrs. Vernon Fletcher, Uncle Greg's only living relative that she knew of, besides herself. But first she went to the attic, clinging hopefully to the idea that a coat would be in one of those trunks. In one, among yellowed laces and boxes of buttons and packets of letters, she discovered a velvet cape, caught at the throat by an elaborate gilded frog. She shook it out, smelling an odor of lavender and dust. Then she placed it around her shoulders and stood for a while in the middle of the attic, looking out a small window at the cemetery, the woods, the smoke of a chimney somewhere down near the river. There were two other trunks, their leather straps rotten, and she walked toward them, the train of the cape whispering across the floor behind her. On one, she saw a faded legend: "The Cadogan, Sloan Square, London." Inside it was a doll with a china face lying on a dark-green shawl. She picked up the doll. One of the eyes opened; the lashes were nearly all gone, the painted blue eye gazed blankly up at her. She dropped it back to its bed, tore off the cape and ran down the stairs to the telephone.

Mrs. Vernon Fletcher answered the phone on the second ring. Annie identified herself quickly; the woman's breath was noisy in her ear.

"Well, he *was* getting on," Mrs. Fletcher said. "Of course, we haven't seen him for years, not being close, don't you know? Only

318

second cousins really. I remember you when you were a little thing, saw you once."

"He's going to die," Annie repeated.

"I expect so. But Vernon can't get away easily, you see. We hardly ever go anyplace. We've got eight sick dogs and two sick cats right now and a woman went off to Oregon, just leaving us a yellow mongrel, and he hasn't been able to find a halfway responsible helper for months. These colored people just come and go. You know how afraid they are of dogs? Funny, that. But we'll come to the funeral all right. I suppose you're seeing to all that, being the closest relative and all and him being so good to you when your daddy abandoned you the way he did?"

"He's not dead yet."

"We all die."

"He's left the furnishings of the house to you, except for his bed."

There was a little gasp at the other end. "Imagine that!" said Mrs. Fletcher. "Why, the dear old fellow! Well, that'll certainly give Vernon a lift. A vetenerian's life is a dog's life." She emitted a little cackle. Annie smiled grimly.

"There're a lot of books," she said.

"Books? Isn't there a piano? It seems to me I recall a piano? And a desk with lots of drawers, and a round dining table? Oh yes, I do remember. After all, that's a big old house, isn't it? Well, bless him!"

"Then, perhaps you might manage to come and see him—while he's still alive?" She heard the sardonic note in her own voice and was instantly ashamed. Was she so worried at the thought of Uncle Greg's dying alone without the remnants of his family around him? Or was it more simply her own vile nature, her fear that Uncle Greg's illness would interfere with her plans? Plans! Getaway! Her thoughts squirmed away—she must think about what she was doing, but *England* flashed in her mind like an electric sign on a marquee, and she could not see or think beyond the word itself.

She went into her old room. The leafless branches of the maple tree struck the windowpane lightly, again and again. There was a bookcase next to the bed. She picked up the first volume of *The Jungle Books,* then *A Child's Garden of Verses.* Uncle Greg must have bought her those, she thought, and opened the Stevenson poems to the flyleaf. "For Ann, on her sixth birthday, with love from Tony," she read, and dropped the book on the old pink blanket that still covered her bed.

In the closet, Uncle Greg's "good" robe hung from a wooden hanger. The lapels were purple moire. She was confounded by the opulence of the rich fabric, the elaborate tailoring. Whatever had he had in mind? The cloth smelled old, yet she could not remember ever having seen it before. Secrets. She thought of Uncle Greg's hands, so rough, so formed by the work he had done for so many years, emerging from those silken cuffs.

"He's rallied a bit," Miss Sears reported. "I think it's the care. A little nourishment, a warm room. It may not seem so to you. But we've got him filled with morphine. The pain is bad. I can't think how he stood it for so long!"

"Does he know what he has?"

"Oh—he pretends not to. They often do. He told me this morning that he's worried sick"—she broke off to laugh a little wildly —"because Mrs. Belknap may call about spring planting. Mrs. Belknap! Another one of the old harpies. They're all dying off, you know. . . . The people I grew up with, rich and poor, all dying out. I once thought they'd go on forever. We all do when we're little."

"I have to have a smallpox inoculation. Would you know a doctor?"

"Would I know a doctor!" Helen Sears cried. "My God! That's all I know! Doctors! You can have it done here. I can't get over your going to Europe."

"There's something else," Annie added with sudden anger. She was sick of Helen's hoots and catcalls, her outbursts, her mindless ironies. "Listen to me, please!"

The nurse took a pack of cigarettes out of her skirt pocket. She looked humble all at once, lighting her cigarette and looking at Annie submissively. Was that all it took? A touch of anger?

"That sleigh bed . . . I don't know what to do with it. I know it's very old. I don't want Mrs. Fletcher to have it. But there's no place for me to keep it."

"Put it in storage."

"I haven't got money for that."

"Well—there's a junk shop downtown. The old man who runs it calls it an antique store, but it's junk. Maybe he'd buy it and take it off your hands. But wait!" She held up one hand. "You

320

can't do anything yet. Maybe get it appraised. It doesn't belong to you yet. Oh, I hate it! The way everybody goes out of life, leaving a trail of muck behind them. Once a year, I throw out everything I own. They're not going to catch me with a lot of useless stuff for people to maul and paw over. Not me!"

Annie went to stand beside Uncle Greg's bed. He was dozing. She held the robe across her arm. A few petals from the geranium had fallen on the window sill. The sky was smudged with snow clouds. He was going to die. Walking out the door of the old house an hour earlier, she had thought, I'll never come here again. The gaunt face on the pillow before her, the sunken eyes and the blanched lips, had come to mask the features of the unalterable adult of her childhood. He had always been there when she returned from school. He had always been in the kitchen so early in the morning on freezing winter days, pouring her a glass of milk in which white shards of ice still floated. Adults were there before you on every occasion. And now he was altered; now he would be absent for the rest of her life. She touched his hand where it lay on the coverlet. She did not even know she was weeping until his eyes flickered, then opened. She held the robe up for his dazed eyes, and to cover her own face. She had, she thought, only been weeping for herself.

"That's the one," he whispered.

There were days during which she did nothing, going out from Billy's dreadful little room to buy a newspaper and some eggs and milk in the morning, and spending the rest of the day reading every item in the New York *Times* or the *Herald Tribune,* falling asleep from the sheer exasperation of her boredom. But there were other days when she had the sensation of running through a thick, nearly impenetrable substance that was the hours of the day, not long enough for all she had to do.

The smallpox inoculation turned red, swelled and "took."

She went to the offices of the shipping company and booked passage on a ship called the *Constellation,* sailing on March fourth, in three weeks' time, for Southampton. "It won't be the Ritz," the man had said. "You'll be in barracks for all practical purposes, oh, with women I assure you."

She stopped by the antique shop in Nyack on her way to the nursing home. The owner scoffed when she described the bed. "Oh, yes, there's a positive run on such items," he had nearly shrieked. And asked her what kind of mahogany. Well, she didn't know. Then how did she know it was mahogany at all? But he agreed to go to the house and look at it and give her a price. But mind you, don't expect much! When she saw him again a few days later, he remarked there were a few other items he'd be interested in too. He must have flown through the house like a vulture. But she was surprised by his offer, a hundred and fifty dollars. It would buy her a coat and gloves and leave some over. Then he told her the will would have to be probated and that would take time, "not to mention the actual demise of your uncle," he added. Probably take a year. She looked her chagrin. He scowled. "Well, for mercy's sake, wait till the body gets cold, will you?" She protested. He grinned unpleasantly. "All right, all right. I'll draw up a little paper, you assign the bed to me. Then I'll pay you. But if he doesn't die, my girl, I'll see to it I get my money back."

Uncle Greg's face grew thinner by the day, even as his body thickened, as his feet grew too swollen to fit into his old slippers. He was barely eating now, and the morphine didn't always work. Some days, when she went to see him, he didn't recognize her at all. "You might as well stop coming," Helen Sears said. "He is moving into that stage where they don't know anybody."

"I'll come," Annie said without further comment.

She had written to Theda, and Theda had written back at once. She read the letter over and over, as she had once read Max's letters, touching the words, the signature. It had been a long time since she had heard from Max. After she had written him that she intended to leave the country, she hadn't heard a word. Theda's letter breathed of her presence. She wrote as she spoke. It dawned on Annie, by the third reading, that Theda missed her. She felt suddenly quiet, sitting on Billy's studio couch, holding the blue sheets of paper in her hands. It was as though she had forgotten what it was to be quiet, to be still, to hear her own even breathing, to feel the eased softness of her limbs. Theda missed her. Even her first excitement at Theda's news that Max was being demobilized soon and was only across the river in Fort Dix, New Jersey, and that Theda had sent him Annie's address on Morton Street, was tempered by the extraordinary sensation induced by the affection and sweetness of the letter. She almost fell asleep there, sitting up, her bare feet on the cold floor.

She had called Jersey Lighter to tell him about the room and Elmira had answered, gurgling at her in some peculiar adult baby talk about their little girl. Annie had the impression that Elmira hadn't the least idea who she was. Presumably as a result of that call, Walter Vogel appeared at her door one evening a day or so later. Standing behind him was a plump dark-haired young girl with a pouting mouth like a gulping fish. They entered the room. The girl stared unblinkingly at Annie; what on earth had Walter told her about her?

He had hardly changed at all, even his clothes looked the same, dungarees, a pea jacket, a watchcap. "This is Lou," he'd said, the little smile on his lips, gesturing toward the girl with his thumb. Lou looked at the floor. He had come for the divorce decree; he and Lou were getting married. Just before he left, he whispered to Annie, "She doesn't know *anything*. I had to teach her what *shit* meant!"

Lou had not spoken a word the half hour they were there. Only watched Annie. And Annie, possessed by monstrous embarrassment, had behaved like someone she'd never heard of or imagined, talking animatedly to Walter about her "plan," shouting at him when he questioned her as to any details, laughing hectically at the slightest suggestion of criticism. He, too, had ended up looking at her fixedly, wonderingly. What had come over her? Mortified, she crawled beneath the blanket, cursing herself and imagining scenes in which she simply handed Walter the decree and shut the door in his face, or warned that idiot of a girl what she was getting into. So Lou didn't know the word *shit,* did she? Oh, God! Oh, God! And how he'd looked at Lou once! He'd never looked at her like that. Had he? Why could she not name the quality of that look? Yet at the same time she knew what it meant.

Then quite clearly, as though it had materialized out of the floor, she heard her father's laughter. She turned on the light, dressed and went out to the street. On Seventh Avenue, she found an all-night drugstore with a phone booth in the back. She had to step over cardboard boxes to get into it. As she dialed the long-distance operator, she saw by the clock over the soda fountain that it was just past midnight. In Massachusetts, the phone rang on and on. And then, as she was about to put away her quarters and dimes and go back to the room, a woman's voice entered her ear intimately, sleepily.

"Yes?"

"Is Mr. Gianfala there?"

"Who is this?"

"His daughter."

323

Silence.

"He's drunk," said the voice. "I'm sorry. Too drunk to talk, I think."

"Could he—I'm leaving for England soon. I'm in New York. I only wanted to say good-by."

"I'm Margo. It's very late, you know. We go to bed early here."

"But if he's up—"

"Barely. Well, I'll try. Wait . . ."

She heard a distant roaring, a noisy worldless protest, then so loud she held the phone away—"Annie!"

"Tony. I called up to say good-by."

"Ah . . . good-by. That's all we ever say, we two. Where is it this time? Oh, where are you going? Where?"

"Abroad. Tony, Uncle Greg is dying."

"Dying . . . poor old Sugared-Tomato . . . poor old devil. I'm dying too. We are all dying. Except for Margo, of course. Margo intends to outlive us all."

She wanted to hear him laugh, not listen to the falling and rising tides of alcohol in his voice, his tone so boorish, so truculent, yet straining fatuously for poetic effect. But she could think of nothing that would elicit his laughter, and thought, I will go back to the room, and perhaps I can remember it from there.

The operator said that three minutes were up, would she deposit another quarter please? She hesitated, her hand over the coin. Why not hang up? He wouldn't even remember she had called. But she dropped the quarter in the slot, holding the phone tightly in her hand as though the force of her grip might reach through his intoxication to reclaim his recognition of her.

"I found a book you'd given me," she said. "It was in the house, *A Child's Garden of Verses* . . ."

He coughed violently, then—" 'I had a little shadow—' "

"Yes, yes," she said eagerly.

"All I remember. Annie, can you come here? Come see us before you go? See your fat little brother?"

"No, I can't. I have to be at the nursing home most of the time. The other relatives won't do much. And my ship is sailing in a week."

"Poor little shadow," he said lugubriously.

"I'm not a poor little shadow," she protested, at once warmed and cheered by her indignation. "I'll write from over there."

"Annie? Annie?"

324

The phone clunked. Through the operator's request, she said, "Good-by."

She swept down Seventh Avenue, past Morton, on and on, hurried forward by a wind of surpassing coldness. All at once, the street was entirely empty. She had passed the places where people lived, and was in an area of warehouses and office buildings and lofts, dark, forbidding, a night cemetery. Miles north, her father would be stumbling about rooms she had not seen, harassing a woman she had never met. In that house where they were enacting some habitual drama, her unknown brother might be wakened by their voices. She retraced her footsteps up to Morton Street. Her only obligation was to Uncle Greg.

The following afternoon, she found Mrs. Vernon Fletcher, hatted and gloved, standing in Helen Sears's small office. Mrs. Fletcher gave her an intensely shrewd look, narrowing of the eyes, judgmental pursing of the lips. Annie thought, that's her world face—she's dumb as a log.

"You do look like your mother," said the woman with a dry little laugh. Or was she clearing her throat?

"He's sinking," Helen Sears said.

"I've been to the house," Mrs. Fletcher reported with a tinge of triumph.

"Is he conscious at all?" Annie asked.

"Only a minute now and then," replied Helen Sears.

"It's a disgrace, the way he's neglected it. Some of those fine old pieces."

"The sleigh bed is mine," Annie said sharply, coldly.

"Well! I'm not one to claim what isn't mine."

"We shouldn't talk this way," Annie said, thinking of her visit to the antique dealer, the haste with which she herself had sought some profit before the old man was dead. Suddenly sickened by Mrs. Fletcher, by herself, by Helen Sears's unlined but aging maiden's face, she said, "Although I shouldn't pretend anything. I went to an antique man in Nyack to see if he'd buy the bed. I'm going to sail for England on March fourth, and I simply didn't know what to do about it." She looked apologetically at Mrs. Fletcher's black felt hat.

"Yes, the bed . . ." Mrs. Fletcher said speculatively. "I *thought* that was a valuable article. What did he offer?"

"He said he'd see. Maybe a hundred and fifty dollars."

"Well, you won't be able to get it until the will is probated, you know, and by then——" She shook suddenly with powdery laughter. "Why, you'll be in fresh green fields!"

Helen Sears picked up a pencil and looked at it closely.

"I'll tell you what," said Mrs. Fletcher, recovering her poise at once. "I'll give you the money. Then you can leave the whole thing in my hands. Won't that be helpful?" She turned to Helen.

"In times like this," she said, "one *must* be helpful."

Helen Sears allowed herself a small venomous smile. She dropped the pencil. "Well, if you ladies have finished your business——"

"Can I see him?" Annie asked.

"Of course you can see him."

Mrs. Fletcher cleared the interior of her pale, thickly powdered throat. "I've seen him. I can't say he saw me. It's a vile disease. I'll wait here for you, Annie. We'll finish up the matter of the bed after you've made your visit. Please try to understand that Vernon and I will be left with all the *details*—you understand? Unpleasant details that younger folk leave to us older folk."

In the corridor, Annie walked silently next to Helen Sears, whose hands were clasped in front of her. "It's always like this," she said. "With the relatives. I'm used to it. You needn't feel bad. It's not disease that's vile. It's families."

"I feel awful about the bed. But——"

"No, no. Don't explain. You're on your way. It's the natural thing. Mrs. Fletcher isn't as bad as she behaves. Everybody is scared of death."

Surprised by such magnanimity, Annie touched Helen's arm and said thanks.

"I still have a human feeling or two," Helen said without emphasis.

Uncle Greg's eyes were closed. Annie stared at him a long time. There was no subtle change here, but, rather, one of coarseness; from the middle of his wasted face rose the barely fleshed ridge of his nose; his lips hung loosely, caked with gray froth. It was as though his face were being punched and beaten by an invisible fist.

He opened his eyes a few times during the hour she spent by his bed. He smiled vaguely at the ceiling, murmured something she couldn't make out, went back into that strange vacuum that looked so much like sleep.

Before she left for the city, Mrs. Fletcher explained that she had called Vernon in Providence to bring the money for the bed and that he would be leaving to join her here as soon as he could manage to get things in proper shape at the animal hospital. The word *hospital* reminded her of something. "Well, when you've seen as many dying and dead animals as I've had to, well, we're all animals in the end, not that I don't believe in a supreme power, you understand, but life ends in a mess, it's all a mess if you ask me, still you're young yet and that's the best time. When you're young."

Vernon arrived several days later and handed Annie an envelope containing a hundred and fifty dollars. He was a short dumpy man with a dead white face that looked as if it were waiting for one permanent expression to be painted on it. He had a tendency to clutch his wife's arm.

Annie went to Macy's and bought herself a heavy beige coat that reminded her vaguely of some other coat she had once had. She had enough left over to buy some wool gloves and underwear and a black wool skirt. She couldn't help it, she didn't want to, but she felt a kind of joy as she watched the wrapping up of her new clothes.

On March first, she spent the afternoon at the nursing home. The Fletchers wandered in and out, Mrs. Fletcher pursing her lips and shaking her head as she stared down at Uncle Greg, Dr. Fletcher as expressionless as flour, an unidentified presence of some sort near the bed.

The old man moved restlessly that day, plucking and picking at the thin hospital cover, and he muttered ceaselessly, his words drowned in phlegm, yet carrying the persistent tone of one who tells a story with desperate insistence lest he be interrupted. Twice, a nurse came to plunge a needle into his withered arm. A glass straw was inserted between his swollen lips but the liquid never rose through it. Ambulatory patients peered in now and then and passed on down the corridor; trays rattled at early supper time; the geranium petals glowed against the window, beyond which the flakes of a snow flurry struck the glass, then melted. It grew dark. Time lost its measures. Annie discovered that the loud breathing she had been listening to for some time was her own. Once he spoke: "I've lost that key again," he said quite clearly, then lapsed back into incoherency. Helen Sears came and tapped her shoulder. "You might as well go," she whispered. "This may go on all night. Just come early tomorrow."

In the morning, she parked the car on the thin, soft layer of snow in the driveway. Helen Sears was waiting for her in the little office. The Fletchers sat on a couch, side by side, silent.

"He's dead," said Helen. "He died at three twenty."

They weren't Jews, Mrs. Fletcher said, so the burial would take place after the proper interval and Annie would either have to cancel her sailing or miss the funeral. The choice was so cruel— she was, momentarily, so affected by the injustice of having to make such a decision—that it overshadowed her uncle's death. Helen Sears was watching her with a kind of detached interest, the way she might have followed the progress of an insect confronted with an obstacle in its path.

Annie, unable to bear the Fletchers' complacency, Helen's death professionalism, drove to the cemetery, parking at the circular entrance and walking up the path on the fresh snow. She had not known until this morning that her mother was buried in a "family plot" and the news, given to her by Vernon Fletcher in his pallid fainting voice, had struck her like a blow. Her mother, she thought, as she walked toward the north hill, had been here all along.

She passed a new marble stone in front of which lay one long red gladiola sprinkled with snow. Just beyond, where the hill rounded from east to north, was a group of three small gravestones. As she stood in front of one, a man in a shabby plaid woodsman's jacket came out of the trees bordering the north side of the cemetery. His hands deep in his pockets, he walked toward her, kicking the ground with the toes of his thick work boots.

"Ground hard," he said. "Too hard. Feel that wind? It's likely to bring more snow. Sometimes, this time of year, we have to stack them up in the crypt over there. Well, we'll see."

"My uncle died," she said.

"You're his niece? Well, I knew him. For a long time. Now I got to dig the hole for him."

She looked down at the legend on the gravestone. *Elizabeth,* she read. Next to her would lie Gregory. Behind were the graves of Elizabeth's and Gregory's mother and father, her grandparents. She shivered as the wind hastened among the bare tree branches and lifted the soft snow into small flurries.

The gravedigger hunched his shoulders and walked back in the direction from which he had come. Annie remembered the damp cold feel of the doll she had found in the trunk in Uncle Greg's attic. Then she hurried away from the cemetery. This would be over. Then her real life would begin.

"I can't stay for the funeral," she told the Fletchers. "If I don't go on that ship, I won't have enough money to ever go."

Dr. Fletcher seemed not to have heard her. Perhaps he only heard barking dogs and hissing cats. But Mrs. Fletcher pursed up her lips and shook her head. "It'll be on your conscience, dear," she said with unconcealed triumph.

Helen Sears walked with Annie to the nursing home entrance. She hardened herself against the sardonic comment she expected. But Helen Sears said, "Lots of people don't come at all. You were good to visit all these days. If I hadn't had that fury given me by God's curse, if I hadn't been cursed with that old murderous bitch, I might have gone on a ship sometime, somewhere."

That night, Annie packed her suitcases. She gazed for a long time at the passport that had arrived the week before and which now bore a British visa. Her passport photo smiled inanely up at her. In the space for *next of kin,* she had written Theda's name and address.

"I'm going to England," she said aloud. Then, just as her father's laughter had issued forth so mysteriously in this bleak room a few nights earlier, she heard her own voice of five years ago, saying, "I'm going to California," and the excitement, the expectation, the sense of having thwarted all the forces arrayed against her setting out on this new journey drained away like the fugitive euphoria of alcohol, thinning into sickness. "Hell!" she cried out. Then she sank to the floor and wept for Uncle Greg.

The morning was bright; the wind had died down. She ate breakfast in a drugstore and in the afternoon went to see a movie about gangsters. She had promised herself a call to Theda that night, and she felt calm and determined and even indifferent to whatever lay ahead. It was as though she had delivered herself over to the impersonal force which would bear her along through this night to the gangplank of the ship which she would certainly cross tomorrow morning.

A few minutes before eight thirty, at which time she had decided to go out to the drugstore and try Theda's number, someone knocked at the door. She could not think who it might be. Surely Walter had gotten all he wanted from her! The knock sounded again. She unlocked the door and opened it. A soldier stood there looking at her, a duffel bag at his feet.

"Annie?"

She stared at Max Shore speechlessly. "Annie," he said. They embraced. His hat fell to the floor. Beneath the coarse fabric, the insistent utility of his uniform around which her arms clung, she felt the substance of his bones, his flesh, his actuality.

At last, he did not so much release her grip as unlock them both from each other. He looked at her face; he examined her features minutely. "The door," she said, barely opening her lips to speak so as not to interfere with his rapt inspection that brought her the weight and pain of her own corporeality.

He turned, dragged the duffel into the room, and shut the door. They went to sit on the studio bed. He put his arm around her.

"What did you do today?" he asked after a moment.

"I went to a movie about tough guys," she said.

"Did you like it?"

"Yes. I often want to *be* that way, calling people 'creeps' and shooting them down like dolls—instead of the way I am, always on the lookout for a little smile, a laugh, a tear, a kiss." She burst into laughter. He laughed with her. "You like your own jokes, don't you?" he said.

"I love them!" she cried.

"Today, I was demobilized," he said. "And I made a reservation to fly to Los Angeles on a constellation."

"I'm sailing tomorrow to England on a ship called *Constellation.*"

"And yesterday?"

"Yesterday. My uncle died. The funeral is the day after tomorrow. I won't be there."

"Do you feel bad about that?"

"Only from the outside. What people will think of me. No. He's dead now. I found him when I came back from California, helpless in his bed, the roof falling in, snow melting on him from the holes in the ceiling. He must have been dying for a long time. I think about how alone he was. No living presence for so long, his life leaking away in that old empty house. He'd been a child there. I was, too."

"Let's go someplace and eat. I came straight here. I'm hungry."

330

She was silent a moment, leaning over, her hand on her chin, her elbow balanced on one knee.

"You're going back then, to Eva."

"I'm going back," he said. "Thomas has a bad illness of the eyes."

"Eva said there was something."

"She wouldn't tell me. I had to call the doctor finally. She couldn't say it. She suffers from an appalling tension . . . it's the tension of hope. It's her only savagery—that insistence that everything turn out all right."

"What does he have?"

"It's called *retinitis pigmentosa*. It means the retina becomes pigmented. Eventually, he'll lose peripheral vision."

"There's no way to stop it?"

"I don't know."

She stood up and put on her new coat. He watched her, noting how much she'd changed and yet how much she was the same, thinking of that quality about her which had first taken his imagination and how, after all these years, it still held him, the ineluctable force of her strangeness. Perhaps she was bound to some atavistic memory of his own, an image of life before speech, the mythic world of early life, before he had become linked to others, before he had accumulated the bonds that tied him to the conscious progression of days and years. He saw a strand of her hair on the pillow near his hand. He reached toward it, then drew his hand back. It was everything, nothing; it was too dangerous. His body feared her even as his mind embraced her.

They went to a delicatessen on Eighth Street. She strained to tell him why she was going away . . . "I've been so ashamed all my life. I had this idea that a different country, even places where I couldn't speak the language, would change everything." He thought, but didn't say, that she was going to places where, now, there was only shame. She suddenly swung off on a new tack and began to tell him about Dr. Vernon Fletcher.

"He was so blank," she said excitedly. "Oh, I didn't think he ought to be grieved at Uncle Greg's death. Only that he seemed like the walking dead! And he had that morbid Irish hair."

He laughed and said, "What?"

"As if the hair cells had given up centuries ago and put out a little fringe of gray shred to hide the secret."

"Do you know anything about Ireland? The Irish?"

She frowned. "Not much." Then she smiled. "But I might deduce something from Dr. Fletcher's hair."

He wanted to tell her about Europe, about the war, about the small camp—not one of the publicized ones—that his unit had discovered in the middle of a village in western Germany, about a wheel of corpses in the center of the compound, the stone-faced villagers watching the American soldiers through the barbed wire. But he said little. She would find another Europe, not his, not theirs.

"Would you go with me to a place?" she asked, over their coffee. "I was there the last night before I left for the West. I'd like to go back now, just for a visit. There's a cafeteria. We could have dessert. Tony says I'm one of those people who are always backtracking on themselves. I guess I am. It's a long ride on the subway."

"Anywhere you want," he said.

They got off at One Hundred and Twenty-fifth Street and walked up the incline from Broadway toward Riverside Drive, then south a few blocks. In the lobby of the hostel, a few languid-looking people sat on couches or stood talking in small groups.

"It used to be almost all foreign. But now everyone looks American. Even the Indians are gone."

He followed her into the reading room. She was moving quickly, eagerly, as though sure of finding something of value. A man was reading a book in a corner chair.

He went with her to the windows.

"It was December," she said. "There was a man out there, almost naked. Someone explained he was suffering from shellshock from the first war. He had a ritual he was following. He must be dead by now."

She looked around the room abstractedly as though whatever she was searching for might still be in it. He took her hand. She led him to the piano.

"There was a young boy who came in to play the piano. He was wearing a suit that was too large for him. He was very shy, I remember thinking, embarrassed. I wonder what happened to him?"

He hardly knew what he was saying, but he held her hand firmly.

"What happened to you?" he asked, looking down at the piano keys.

He felt the tension of her fingers in his. She was staring fixedly at the bench as though the boy were still there in his too large suit.

"I was taken to California," she said. "After a while, I escaped."